Sara Douglass was born in Penola, South Australia, and moved to Adelaide when she was seven. She spent her early working life as a nurse before completing three degrees at the University of Adelaide. After receiving a PhD in early modern English history, Sara worked as a Senior Lecturer in Medieval History at La Trobe University, Bendigo, until 2000.

Sara's first novel, *BattleAxe*, was published in 1995 and she has been writing and publishing ever since. Three of her novels are winners of the Aurealis Award for Best Fantasy.

Sara now lives in Hobart, Tasmania.

Visit Sara's website at:
www.saradouglass.com
http://nonsuchkitchengardens.com/wordpress/

BOOKS BY
SARA DOUGLASS

SARA DOUGLASS

THE DEVIL'S DIADEM

HARPER
Voyager

HarperVoyager
An imprint of HarperCollinsPublishers
77–85 Fulham Palace Road,
Hammersmith, London W6 8JB

www.harpercollins.co.uk

This paperback edition 2011
1

A catalogue record for this book is
available from the British Library

ISBN: 978 0 00 736424 4

This novel is entirely a work of fiction.
The names, characters and incidents portrayed in it are
the work of the author's imagination. Any resemblance to
actual persons, living or dead, events or localities is
entirely coincidental.

Set in 10.5/12.5 Centaur MT by Kirby Jones

Printed and bound in Great Britain by
Clays Ltd, St Ives plc

MIX

FSC is a non-profit international organisation established to promote the
responsible management of the world's forests. Products carrying the FSC
label are independently certified to assure consumers that they come
from forests that are managed to meet the social, economic and
ecological needs of present and future generations.

Find out more about HarperCollins and the environment at
www.harpercollins.co.uk/green

Karen Brooks, you beautiful, amazing, courageous woman, this is for you, with all of my love and all of my thanks.

AUTHOR'S NOTE

The Devil's Diadem is set, not in the early twelfth-century England of our past, but in a fictional version of that world. While there are many similarities between our past and the twelfth-century world of *The Devil's Diadem*, and many characters and points of historical reference remain the same, there are still characters and issues which render this England *not quite* the one you may have learned about in history books.

CONTENTS

Twelfth-Century England & Wales

1 Crickhoel & Pengraic Castle
2 Bergeveny
3 Monemude
4 Hereford
5 Derheste
6 Glowcestre
7 Chiteneham
8 Brimesfelde
9 Cirecestre
10 Etherope
11 Badentone
12 Witenie
13 Godstou
14 Oxeneford
15 Walengefort

16 Rosseley Manor
17 Wodestoch
18 Elesberie
19 Sancti Albani
20 London
21 Westminster
22 St Edmund's Burie
23 Dovre
24 Walsingaham
25 Wincestre
26 Scersberie
27 Chestre
28 Cantuaberie

North

R. Severn
R. Wye
R. Usk
Welsh Marches
Black Mtns
Bearscathe Mtns
R. Thames
The Narrow Seas

Sara Douglass Enterprises © 2011

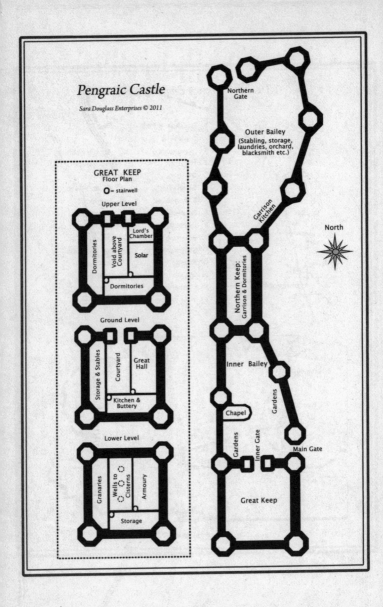

Pengraic Castle

Sara Douglass Enterprises © 2011

GREAT KEEP
Floor Plan

⬡ = stairwell

Upper Level

Dormitories
Void above Courtyard
Lord's Chamber
Solar
Dormitories

Ground Level

Storage & Stables
Courtyard
Great Hall
Kitchen & Buttery

Lower Level

Granaries
Wells to Cisterns
Armoury
Storage

Northern Gate

Outer Bailey
(Stabling, storage, laundries, orchard, blacksmith etc.)

Garrison Kitchen

North

Northern Keep: Garrison & Dormitories

Inner Bailey

Gardens

Chapel

Gardens
Inner Gate
Main Gate

Great Keep

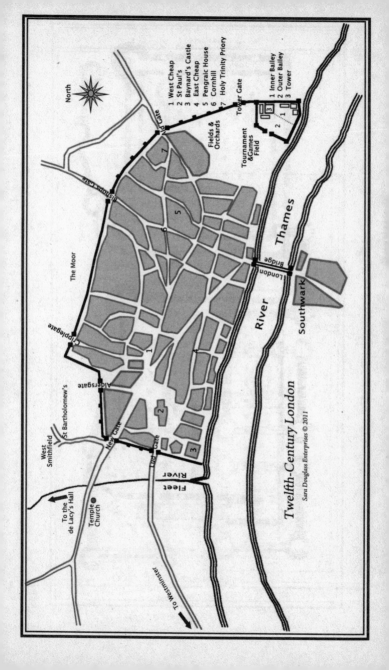

Twelfth-Century London

Sara Douglass Enterprises © 2011

**Top Floor:
the Royal Apartments**

Gallery

North

Royal
Apartments

Great Hall

St John's Chapel

Gallery

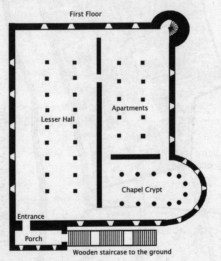

First Floor

Apartments

Lesser Hall

Chapel Crypt

Entrance

Porch

Wooden staircase to the ground

Twelfth–century layout of the top two floors of the Conqueror's Tower.
Wooden stairs led from the ground floor to the entrance on the first floor.

Sara Douglass Enterprises © 2011

PLACE NAMES

Where possible in *The Devil's Diadem* I use contemporary place names. A list of the twelfth-century place names used in this book and their modern-day equivalents follows (an explanation of terms can be found in the Glossary).

Badentone: Bampton

Bearscathe Mountains: the Brecon
    Beacons in Wales

Bergeveny: Abergaveny

Blachburnscire: Blackburnshire

Bochinghamscire:
    Buckinghamshire

Bouland: Bowland

Brimesfelde: Brimpsfield

Cantuaberie: Canterbury

Chestre: Chester

Chinteneham: Cheltenham

Cicestre: Chichester

Cirecestre: Cirencester

Craumares: Crowmarsh Gifford

Crickhoel: Crickhowell

Depdene: Forest of Dean

Derheste: Deerhurst

Donecastre: Doncaster

Dovre: Dover

Elesberie: Aylesbury

Etherope: Hatherop

Eurvicscire: Yorkshire

Exsessa: Essex

Fenechirche: Fenchurch

Glowecestre: Gloucester

Glowecestrescire: Gloucestershire

Godric Castle: Goodrich Castle

Godstou: Godstow

Hamestede: Hampstead

Hanbledene: Hambleden

Herefordscire: Herefordshire

Holbournestrate: Holborn

Lincolescire: Lincolnshire

Lincolie: Lincoln
Meddastone: Maidstone
Monemude: Monmouth
Oxeneford: Oxford
Oxenefordscire: Oxfordshire
Pengraic Castle: this is a fictional castle, but it is situated atop Crug Hywel, or Table Mountain, at the foot of the Black Mountains in Wales.
Pomfret: Pontefract
Ragheian: Raglan
Redmeleie: Redmarley D'Abitot
Richemont: Richmond (in Yorkshire)

Saint Edmund's Burie: Bury Saint Edmund's
Sancti Albani: Saint Albans
Scersberie: Shrewsbury
Sudfulc: Suffolk
Sudrie: Surrey
Summersete: Somerset
Walengefort: Wallingford
Walsingaham: the two conjoined villages of Little and Greater Walsingham in Norfolk.
Wincestre: Winchester
Witenie: Witney
Wodestrate: Wood Street
Wodestoch: Woodstock

Speak not the word, for remember that the wind shall carry your word to all the corners of the earth, as also to the ears of God and of the Devil both.

Traditional folk saying

THE DEVIL'S DIADEM

THE DEVIL'S WHORE

MAEB LANGTOFTE THAT WAS,
HER TESTIMONY

———◆◈◆———

In the name of our Saviour, the heavenly Lord Jesu, and of His beloved mother, the blessed Virgin Mary, greetings. Pray hear this testimony from your humble servant, Maeb Langtofte that was, on the eve of her dying. May sweet Jesu and His Holy Mother forgive my sins, and let me pass in peace, and forgive me the manner of my passing.

My faithful servant and priest Owain of Crickhoel writes down these words and in some places will speak for me when I no longer have the breath. Brother Owain has taken my confession and offered me Godly advice these past thirty years. He has been a good and faithful friend to me and I pray that his reward in the next life will reflect this.

My life has been one of sin, but no sin has been greater than that of my young womanhood. Pray sweet Jesu forgive me, forgive me, forgive me. I did what I thought best and yet I am stained with mortal sin. Pray sweet Jesu do not apportion blame on Brother Owain for what he writes. His pen may wield the words, but it was I who wielded the sin.

Sweet Lord forgive me my lack of trust, and forgive me my lack of learning, for in both I have failed you in this life. I pray that in my next life I can redeem both sins and failures to you. I thank you from my heart for the gift of the Falloway Man, for without him I could have no hope of redemption. Your grace and love of this sinner, this womanly fool, is unending.

But I waste time, Owain, for I do not think I have long left in this mortal life. So we shall begin, and it is fitting I begin with that day I met he without sin, the one, shining, uncomplicated love of my life, Lord Stephen of Pengraic.

PART ONE

ROSSELEY MANOR

CHAPTER ONE

His footsteps tripped down the great stone staircase as if from heaven — their passage rich with joy and authority. Their lightness and pattern told me he was tall, athletic and undoubtedly young; happy, for those footsteps surely danced in their delight of life; confident, and therefore a member of the great nobility who lived in this manor house, for no one else would have dared to so skip through the majesty of the central vestibule.

He would be one of the older sons, a prince in bearing if not quite in rank.

There was a flash of gold and silver as he passed the doorway of the little shadowy alcove in which I sat, waiting. He was tall and golden-haired, bedecked with jewels and vibrant fabrics and with a glint of steel at his hip.

I was dazzled, even by this brief glimpse of a member of the Pengraic family.

Then, unbelievably, he was back at the doorway, and stepping into my alcove.

I rose hastily from the rickety stool on which I had waited and dipped in brief courtesy. I kept my eyes down, and surreptitiously pressed my hands into my skirts so that they may not betray my nervousness.

I prayed my French was gentle enough to sound sweet to his ears. I had spent too much of my childhood practising my English with the village children, and not enough perfecting my courtly French with those of more seemly rank.

'What have I found hiding in the doorkeeper's alcove?' he said, and the warmth in his voice made me dare to raise my eyes.

He was of my age, perhaps nineteen or twenty years, and therefore must be the oldest son, Lord Stephen. His hair was light wheaten gold, his fine beard similar, his eyes a deep cornflower blue. His clothes were of a richness I had never seen before, his tunic all heavy with gold and silver embroidery that his noble mother must have stitched for him.

'Rumour has it that doorkeeper Alaric has only rats in here for company, not beautiful young maidens.'

'My lord, I am Mistress Maeb —'

'Mistress Maeb Langtofte!' he said, and I was amazed that he should know of my name. 'My mother told me she expected a new woman to attend her. But what do you here? In this dark hole? Has no one announced you yet?'

'The man at the door —'

'Alaric.'

'Yes, my lord. Alaric. He asked me to wait here while he sent word to your lady mother.'

'Alaric has always been the fool ... or maybe not, for if *I* had found you suddenly at my door I, too, might have secreted you away in my bedchamber.'

I glanced at the tiny cramped bed nestled into a hollow in the thick stone wall — the alcove had not the floor space for both bed and stool — then met Stephen's eyes.

And then, the Virgin help me, I flushed deeply at the import of his words.

'I only jest, Maeb,' he said gently, and at the care in his voice, combined with my overall awe at his presence and kindness, I felt my heart turn over completely. 'My mother has been resting this afternoon and thus you have been kept waiting, for foolish Alaric must not have wanted to disturb her. Had he told any of us you were here, we would have seen to it you were welcomed far more warmly, and far sooner. Alaric is a fool, indeed.'

Lord Stephen paused to study me, and the gentleness in his eyes and face increased even more, if that were possible.

'You cannot wait here,' he said. 'I shall escort you to my mother myself —'

'Stephen,' said a voice, and we both jumped.

'My lord,' Stephen said, and half bowed as he turned.

A man stood in the alcove doorway — he could not have entered unless he had wanted to completely fill the tiny space of this alcove with the crush of our bodies — an aged and wearied form of the youthful vitality which stood before me.

It could only be Lord Stephen's father, Raife de Mortaigne, the Earl of Pengraic.

Unlike his son's, Lord Pengraic's tone was hard and devoid of compassion, and my eyes once more dropped to the floor while my hands clutched within the poor woollen skirts of my kirtle.

'You have no time to waste in idle chatter,' Lord Pengraic said to his son. 'The bargemen await and we must be away. Have you said your farewells to your lady mother?'

'I have, my lord,' Stephen said.

'Then to the barge,' the earl said.

Stephen inclined his head, managing to shoot me an unreadable look as he did so, then stepped past his father and disappeared from my sight.

The air felt chill and the world an emptier place without him close. I was amazed that so few moments in his company could have made so profound an impression on me.

To my consternation the earl did not turn immediately and follow his son.

'Who are you?' he said.

I dipped again in courtesy, and repeated my name.

'Langtofte …' the earl said. 'Your father was one of the sons of Lord Warren of Langtofte, yes?'

'Yes, my lord. Sir Godfrey Langtofte.' A son left poor, with little land, who left me yet poorer in worldly goods and hope when he gave what he had to the Templars at his death five months ago. My mother, might the Virgin Mary watch over her always, had long been in her grave. My father had left me with the name of minor nobility, but nothing else of any worth, not even brothers and sisters to comfort me.

'And so now you are here,' the earl said, 'waiting upon my wife, which doubtless you think a prettier life than one spent at your devotions in a nunnery, which must have been the only other choice available to you.'

His tone hurt. I kept my eyes downcast, lest he see the humiliation within them.

'Mind your ambitions do not grow too high, Mistress Langtofte. Do not think to cast the net of your aspirations over my son —'

'My lord!' I said, now stung to look at him too directly. 'I did not —'

'He would think you nothing but a dalliance and would ruin your name yet further, and you would grace whatever nunnery I banish you to with a bawling infant of no name whatever, for do not expect *me* to allow it the de Mortaigne —'

'My lord! I —'

'Think not to speak over me!' he said, and I took a step backward, pushing over the stool, so wary was I of the contempt in his face.

Pengraic was one of the greatest nobles in England, not only the most powerful of the Marcher Lords, but also close confidant of the king. He could destroy my life with a word.

'Be careful of your place here, Mistress Langtofte,' he said, now very soft, 'for it rests only on my sufferance.'

With that he turned on his heel and was gone, and a moment later I heard shouting as the earl's party moved down to the great barge I had seen waiting earlier at the pier on the Thames.

I stood there, staring at the empty space which still seemed to me to throb with his anger and contempt. My heart thudded in my chest, and I bit my lip to keep myself from tears.

The earl's unfairness knifed deep, particularly since it contrasted so brutally with the warmth of his son. I eased myself with the notion that Lord Stephen must have received his gentleness and kindness from his lady mother, and that she would keep me under a similarly gentle and most noble wing, and shield me from the unjustified anger of her lord.

Thus began my life in the Pengraic household.

CHAPTER TWO

————◆◆◇◆◆————

I waited in that wretched little alcove for what felt like hours. I felt its cold and dampness seep into my joints, and I wondered how the man Alaric managed to sleep in here at nights.

I hoped the Lady Adelie believed in braziers, or maybe even a fire, in the family's privy chambers.

It was a nerve-wracking wait. Pengraic had struck to the heart when he'd said I had but two choices — enter a nunnery or take the only other offer open to me: serve Lady Adelie, Countess of Pengraic, who was a close cousin of my father's mother. I loved my Lord God and all his saints, but I did not think I would manage well with the isolation and rigidity of a nunnery. Besides, I wanted a home and family of my own one day. After the death of my father I had little choice left in my life. I had stayed some months with a distant cousin, but she and I did not settle well together and she resented the cost to her household of the small degree of food I ate at table. It was a relief to leave her house. I felt keenly the loss of my home on the death of my father; I was well aware that alone, and with no dowry, I was but a hair's breadth away from destitution despite my noble heritage.

How unhappy then, that in this single household prepared to offer me shelter the resident lord appeared determined to despise me.

I sat there and tried to fight back the despondency. I wondered why it took so long for the lady of the house to send for me. Was this a test? Had she forgot me? Should I say something to Alaric who occasionally slid by the door, glancing in as if he, too, wanted me gone?

9

Finally, as an early evening gloom settled over the house, I heard more footsteps on the staircase, and a moment later a woman appeared at the door.

'Mistress Maeb?'

I stood up, a little too hastily.

'Yes.'

The woman stepped closer, holding out her hands to take one of mine. She was older than me, perhaps by ten or twelve years, and even though her face and eyes were weary she offered me a smile and her hands' clasp was warm.

'I am Evelyn Kendal.'

'Mistress Kendal,' I said, and dipped in courtesy.

She patted the back of my hand. 'No need for such formality with me, Maeb, though you should always show Lady Adelie respect. We have kept you waiting long. I am sorry for that. My lady has been feeling unwell and she asked us to sit with her while she slept. But now she is awake and feeling more cheerful, and has remembered you. Is this your bag? So little for all your belongings! Follow me and I shall bring you to my lady.'

I picked up my bag — truly only a heavy cloth wrapped about my few remaining possessions — and thankfully departed Alaric's alcove. A few steps beyond it I heard him scurry inside, a shadowy spider glad to have his home released to him once again.

This was my first good look at the interior of Rosseley manor house. I had been awestruck when I rode up, for the entire house was of stone, a great rarity for its expense and thus only an option for the greatest lords. Inside it was spacious and well appointed — the hangings on the walls were thick and colourful and there were large wooden chests pushed against walls. As we passed the doors that led into the great hall of the house I saw a glimpse of the colourful pennants and banners hanging from the walls and ceiling, and I was much impressed.

But what should I have expected? The Earl of Pengraic was one of the Marcher Lords, almost completely independent of the king, wealthy beyond most of the Norman nobility, and a great man for the influence of his family and of the extent of his lands, lordships and offices.

'This house came to the earl as part of Lady Adelie's dowry,' Evelyn said as we began to climb the staircase. 'We use it during the winter months when the Marches become too damp and cold for my lady to bear. We sometimes spend spring and summer here, also, for the earl often needs to attend court and it is but a day or two's barge ride along the Thames to the king's court at Westminster.'

'Is that where the earl and his son have gone now?' I asked. I had spent a moment envying Lady Adelie for the wealth of her dowry, and then the envy evaporated as I thought on the marriage it had bought her.

Evelyn nodded. 'King Edmond has asked the earl's attendance upon some difficult matter, I believe. Have you travelled far, Maeb?'

'A long way,' I said. 'All the way from Witenie.'

Evelyn stopped on the stairs and laughed in merriment. 'A long way? Oh, my dear! The distance from here to Witenie is but a trifle compared to that which we will cover when eventually we go home to Pengraic Castle in the Marches. *That* is a long journey!'

I flushed, feeling myself a country bumpkin. I had thought the four-day ride along the roads from Witenie — just west of Oxeneford — to Rosseley Manor on the Thames south of Hanbledene, a grand adventure in my life, but when I compared it to the vast distance this household needed to travel from the Welsh Marches to this lovely spot in Bochinghamscire ... I felt the fool.

Evelyn smiled kindly at me. 'It is always an entry to a vaster world, Maeb, when you first join a family such as this. I forget sometimes what it was like for me, eleven years ago.'

I nodded, feeling a little better for Evelyn's compassion, and we resumed our climb up the staircase.

The upper level of the house comprised the family's private quarters. There were a number of smaller chambers, and one large, the solar, and it was to the solar that Evelyn led me.

My first question about the family was answered when Evelyn opened the door, and I felt the warmth of the chamber.

Lady Adelie did like a fire, then, or braziers. At least I should be warm.

We paused just inside the door and I looked about hastily, trying to spot my lady. The chamber was well lit from a window to the east and, indeed, warmed by several charcoal braziers. There was a richly curtained bed at the far end of the chamber, several stools and benches positioned about, a cot

11

or two, and what seemed to me to be a horde of children standing in a group looking at me curiously.

To one side in a beautifully carved chair, alongside the largest of the braziers, sat a woman who, by the richness of her clothes, must be the Lady Adelie, Countess of Pengraic.

I dipped hastily and dropped my eyes.

'Mistress Maeb,' she said, her voice thin with exhaustion, 'come closer that I might speak with you more easily.'

I walked over and took the stool that Lady Adelie patted.

Her hand was bony and pale, and when I finally raised my eyes to her face I saw that it was thin and lined, her eyes shadowed with fatigue.

'I am sorry I kept you so long waiting. The day …' She made a futile gesture with her hand. 'Well, it has escaped me. I should not have so delayed you, for you are family, and welcome here.'

She managed to put some warmth into that last and I smiled in relief.

'Thank you, my lady,' I said. 'You have honoured me by asking for me to be here. I am immensely grateful, and shall do my best to serve you in whatever manner you ask.'

'It will be a thankless task,' Lady Adelie said. 'I shall try, myself, to be of little labour to you, but, oh, the children.'

The children … The words echoed about the chamber, and I glanced at the six children who had lost interest in me and now talked or played among themselves. They all had Stephen's look — fair-haired and blue-eyed — and ranged in age from a crawling infant to perhaps thirteen or fourteen for the eldest girl.

Lady Adelie must have seen my look, for she managed a small smile. 'And this is not all, for there is my eldest son, Stephen.' She sighed, and placed a hand over her belly. 'And yet another to come later in the summer.'

'My lady has been blessed,' said a woman standing behind Lady Adelie's chair, 'that she has lost only two of her children to illness or accident.'

'Blessed indeed,' Lady Adelie said. Then she nodded at the woman behind her. 'This is Mistress Yvette Bailleul. She, Mistress Evelyn and yourself shall bear the burden of my care and that of my younger children still playing about my skirts. But you look cold and tired … have you drunk or eaten? No? Then we must remedy that. Evelyn, perhaps you can take Maeb further into your care and make sure she is fed, then show her to the cot you will share? We will all sup together later, but for now ...'

Lady Adelie's voice drifted off, and I saw discomfort and weariness in her face. No wonder, I thought, having spent her marriage bearing so many and such healthy children to the earl. I hoped he was grateful for his wife, then felt a little resentful on my lady's behalf that he should burden her with yet another pregnancy at an age when most women were thinking to leave the perils of childbirth long behind them.

I rose, curtsied once more, told the countess again how grateful I was for her offer to call me to her service, then Evelyn led me away.

CHAPTER THREE

M y days fell into an easy routine within the Pengraic household. Evelyn — for so she asked me to address her — and I shared a small chamber just off the solar. It was large enough to hold our small bed, a chest for our belongings, and one stool. The room's comfort contented me, especially since I shared it with Evelyn, who I quickly grew to like and respect.

At night we would share the bed, talking into the darkness. I appreciated the chance of such chatter, not only for the friend it brought me, but because I could practise my French with Evelyn. I mentioned this to her one night, thanking her, and she laughed merrily.

'Maeb! Your French is as courtly as any, and with a lovely lilt. Do not fret about it. Your speech does not betray that you spent more time among the village English than among more gracious ranks.'

I relaxed with relief. I had worried that Lady Adelie found it disjointed, or jarring, and had been visited by nightmares of Lord Stephen and the earl laughing about it on the barge journey to Westminster. My father, due to circumstance and his own lack of effort, had been a lowly ranked nobleman and our estate at Witenie had been poor. I'd spent most of my childhood running about with the village English, particularly after my mother died when I was young and when subsequently my father spent years away on pilgrimage in the Holy Lands.

Each day we rose before dawn to join Lady Adelie at private prayers before a small altar in the solar, the family's private living chamber. The ground floor hall was unused when the earl was not in residence, so our

14

days were spent either in the upper level solar or with the children in the gardens and meadows outside.

After prayers, as dawn broke, we would break our fast with a small meal. Lady Adelie and Mistress Yvette, who I quickly learned was my lady's most treasured confidante, then spent the morning and early afternoon at their stitching and embroidery — if my lady felt well — or dozing together on my lady's large bed if she felt fatigued or unwell (which was often). We ate our main meal in the early afternoon, then gathered about the altar again for prayers, and enjoyed the late afternoon spring weather before supping at dusk. After supper, some time was spent listening to a minstrel if the countess was in the mood, more prayers, then bed.

I was surprised at the tranquillity of life within the Pengraic household. The earl was one of the great nobles of England, almost a king in his own right within the Welsh Marches, but Evelyn said that when he was away the countess preferred to keep a quieter routine. All the hustle and bustle of an important noble establishment had departed with the earl and Lord Stephen.

When they returned, Evelyn assured me with a smile, life would quicken.

In the meantime Evelyn and I performed only light duties for Lady Adelie. We brushed out her kirtles and cleaned the non-existent mud from her shoes. We helped Mistress Yvette plait the countess' long fair hair, and twist it with ribbons and false hair and weights and tassels so that her twin braids hung almost to the floor. We mended her hose, pressed her veils and emptied her chamber pot into the communal privy, but she required little else of us apart from our presence at her daily prayers, for my lady was a devout woman, and wished it of us, also.

Thus our days were spent mostly with the children, who quickly became my joy, as they were Evelyn's.

The oldest of them, a fourteen-year-old girl named Alice, was truly not a child at all. She lingered in her parents' house only until a marriage could be contracted for her. Alice was a quiet girl, very grave, but courteous and kind, and helped Evelyn and myself with the care of her younger siblings.

After Alice there was a gap of some three years to her sister Emmette. She, too, was a reserved child, but with a readier smile than Alice. After Emmette came what I thought of as a miracle — twin boys! I had never seen twin children before, nor heard of any who had survived their first

15

year, so they were remarkable to me for that reason alone. Ancel and Robert, eight years old, were also astonishing in that they looked so similar I could not ever tell them apart, which they believed gave them free licence to play trick after trick on me, often before their mother, who regarded them with much loving tolerance. The boys spent the majority of their day with the men of the household — the steward, the guards, the grooms — and disdained learning their letters alongside their sisters. But they were boys, destined for nobleness, and truly did not need the alphabet skills of the clerk. Despite their tricks I adored them, for they always brought a smile to my face. Evelyn told me they were to join another noble household during the summer, as the sons of noblemen were wont to do. I was glad to have at least a little time to spend with them, though, for they never ceased to be a marvel to me.

After the boys there was a gap of four years to the child who quickly became the true joy of my life — Rosamund. She was shy with me at first, but gradually became more confident, blossoming into the most loving child I could imagine. She had her brother Stephen's warmth and charm, coupled with golden hair, the loveliest eyes and the sweetest laugh I ever heard from another person's mouth. I thought her heaven on earth and cuddled her every moment I could, and encouraged her to share Evelyn's and my cot, which imposition Evelyn allowed with much goodwill, for a wriggling child did not always induce a good night's sleep.

Finally came baby John. He was well past his first birthday, and was only just learning to walk. He was chubby and cheerful and rarely cried, and was the only one of the boys that I had much to do with.

Evelyn told me that the earl and the countess had lost two other children, born after Stephen and before Alice. Geoffrey, a son, born a year later than Stephen had died after falling from his horse as a youth, while a daughter, Joanna, had perished only recently in childbed after her marriage to a lord in Yorkshire.

I quickly grew to love all the Pengraic children who still lived. They were courteous, merry, mischievous, all in turn, and I could not believe that any of them had sprung from the loins of one so dour as the earl.

For many days Lady Adelie remained a distant figure to me. She was not well with this child, Evelyn told me, and so rested for many hours of each day, keeping only Mistress Yvette close by her side. On my tenth day in the household, however, Lady Adelie said she felt well enough to sit in the garden, and perhaps have a minstrel amuse her, and so Yvette, Evelyn and myself busied ourselves with her wraps and embroideries and her favoured book of devotion, and carried them out to a group of chairs and benches one of the servants had set up under a flowering apple tree.

Evelyn and I helped settle the countess in a chair, then prepared to withdraw, assuming Lady Adelie would prefer to sit only with Mistress Yvette as usual.

But the countess surprised me by indicating I should sit with her, and sending Evelyn and Mistress Yvette back to the house for some embroidery wools she needed.

I sat on the end of a bench close to the countess' chair, shifting my heavy braids to one side so that they were not in my way, and took up the stitching of a linen shift for Rosamund. I was a little nervous, for I could see the countess' eyes drifting occasionally to my needle, and from there I developed a certainty that Lady Adelie was about to dismiss me from her service for some transgression.

'You are a good needlewoman,' Lady Adelie said eventually, startling me so greatly my fingers fumbled and I dropped my needle, retrieving it hastily from my skirts.

'Who taught you such skill?' she continued. 'Your mother?'

'Yes, my lady. Her embroidery was exquisite. I have never seen the like.' Instantly I regretted the words. What if the countess took offence?

But she only smiled gently, giving a little nod. 'So I have heard. 'Tis a pity she died when you were still so young. But that is the way of life, and of God's will.'

'Aye, my lady.'

We stitched in silence for a little while. I relaxed, thinking myself silly to be so concerned about dismissal.

'Ah,' the countess said, setting her stitching to one side and putting a hand in the small of her back as she stretched. 'My eyes fail me, Maeb. I thought I might see the better in this bright light, but … no. They still strain over this work. Will you fetch my book of prayers, Maeb? It is set there, by that basket.'

I bent over, picking up the leatherbound book, taking a moment to marvel at the bright gilding on the edges of its pages before holding it out for the countess that she might take it.

'No, no,' Lady Adelie said. 'You read to me — you can see the passage I have marked with the silken twist. I do not wish to strain my eyes further with the impossibly small letters of its monkish scribe.'

I froze in horror, the book still extended in my hand.

Lady Adelie looked at the book, then at my face.

'Ah,' she said in a gentle voice, finally taking the book from me. She set it in her lap, unopened. 'You have not learned your letters.'

'No, my lady.' I dropped my eyes, ashamed. It was not unusual for one of my rank within the lower nobility to not know her letters, but sitting before the countess now I felt like an oaf.

'You mother did not teach you?' Lady Adelie said.

I shook my head, hating what I had to say, thinking I sullied my mother's memory after having so recently praised her. 'She did not know herself, my lady.'

'It is a shame,' Lady Adelie said, 'that the comfort of sweet Jesu's words and deeds and those of our beloved saints were denied her in the privacy of her chamber. I could not bear it, if I would always need to wait for the presence of a priest to comfort me.'

I was feeling worse by the moment, and I kept my eyes downcast.

'And I suppose that wastrel, your father, had no learning.'

I shook my head once more, blinking to keep the tears at bay. I knew that the countess had her children tutored in letters and figures, and I was mortified that even the eight-year-old boys, Ancel and Robert, had greater learning than me.

'Do not weep, my dear,' Lady Adelie said, leaning the short distance between us to pat me gently on the hand.

She paused, thinking. 'We shall have you tutored in letters,' she said, then paused again. 'But not with the children, for that should not be seemly. *I* shall teach you, my dear, when I have birthed this child, and am strong again. I have a duty of care to you and I shall not fail.'

'Thank you, my lady.' She did me a great honour by offering to teach me herself, for surely her time could be spent on other duties. I wiped the tears from my eyes, and returned her smile.

18

'And then we shall find you a gentle husband,' Lady Adelie said, 'for your father was remiss in not seeking such for you himself. Did he forget your very existence?'

'He did try, my lady.' Not very hard, I thought. 'But I have little dowry and —'

I stopped, horrified that the countess might think I hoped she would augment that meagre dowry with her own riches. Suddenly I could see the earl standing before me again, his face and tone contemptuous, warning me against harbouring ambitions above my station.

'You are a member of the Pengraic household,' the countess said, her tone firm. 'That alone carries a weight of more import than any wealth of coin or land. An alliance into the Pengraic house is no small matter —'

I wondered what the earl might have to say about this. I doubted *he* would ever think I wielded any measure of influence within his house.

'— and I am sure that some gentle lord shall seek your hand eagerly. You have a lovely face. Such depth in your green eyes — and that black, black hair! As for your figure — that alone is enough to tempt any man into thoughts of bedding. You shall not remain unwedded long.'

I flushed at her words, but was immeasurably grateful to the countess for her support. Where her husband had been contemptuous, his lady wife extended the hand of graciousness and care. I was privileged indeed, and more fortunate than I could have hoped to have been offered this place at Lady Adelie's side.

'You are old not to be wived,' Lady Adelie said. 'How old are you? Eighteen? Nineteen?'

'Nineteen, my lady.'

'Ah! At nineteen I already had three children born.' Lady Adelie sighed, one hand resting on her belly. 'Stephen I bore when I was but fifteen — the earl only a year older. Such young parents. Ah, Maeb, the lot of a wife is a hard one, but you must bear it. The travails of childbirth litter our lives with danger, and we must keep our faith in the Lord, that we may survive them.'

'You have so many beautiful children, my lady. They must bring you great comfort.'

'The earl is a demanding husband,' the countess said, her face twisting in a small grimace. 'Although I fear the dangers of childbed I am grateful each time I find myself breeding, that my husband can no longer make such demands of me.'

I kept my eyes downcast, setting my fingers back to stitching, thinking of the whispered fragments of conversations I had heard over the years from women gossiping about their husbands and lovers (and of what I had seen as a curious child in the village of Witenie). Most of these women had spoken in bawdy tones and words, and I thought the countess must truly be a devout and gracious woman, of exquisite breeding and manners, to find distasteful what other women found delightful.

'The earl is so demanding ...' the countess said again, her voice drifting off, and the look on her face made me think she feared him.

I did not blame her. I feared him, too, and I could not imagine what her life must be like, needing to watch her every word in the company of a man with so uncertain a temper.

'Evelyn has spoken little of Pengraic Castle,' I said, mostly to distract the countess from whatever thoughts troubled her. 'What is it like?'

The countess stilled, and I was instantly sorry for my question.

'It is a dark place,' she said, 'but I must bear it, as must you.'

I opened my mouth, thinking to apologise for my error in asking such a question, but the countess continued.

'It is a *dismal* place, Maeb. Ungodly, and wrapped all about with the mists and sleet of the dark Welsh mountains. The people ... the people of that land care more for their sprites and fairies and tales of the ancient ones than they do for the saints and our sweet, dear Lord Jesu. I swear even the stones of Pengraic Castle are steeped in the ungodliness of those Welsh hills.'

'I am sorry, my lady,' I said. Sorry to have caused her greater distress, sorry that I should need to endure both the Welsh Marches and this castle myself, some day.

'Sorrow's claws have firm grasp on Pengraic Castle, Maeb. But what do we here, speaking of such when the sun burns bright and the apple blossoms? Come, here are Evelyn and Yvette returned, and a servant with cooling cordials, and we shall drink and gossip as women do, and be merry.'

And so we did, our words and smiles chasing away the shadows cast by the final minutes of the conversation between the countess and myself. The sun burned, and it was a good day. Peaceful and gentle, with the scents of spring all about us.

It did not last. The morrow brought with it terrible tidings that meant my days at Rosseley Manor were done.

I would never see it again, in all my days. That was my enduring loss, for Rosseley was a lovely, peaceful place. Even though I spent so little time there, it holds a special place in my heart. Every May Day, when we celebrate the return of life to the land, I think of Rosseley's sweet meadows and orchards, and light a candle in remembrance of a gentle life that almost was.

CHAPTER FOUR

The next day began as had all my previous mornings at Rosseley. Evelyn and I rose early, washed and dressed, then attended Lady Adelie. We made the countess' bed while Mistress Yvette helped the countess with her chemise and kirtle, then we knelt at prayers before breaking our fast with small beer and fruit and cheese with some fresh-baked bread. Evelyn and I then rose, meaning to help the nurse dress the younger children, when Ancel and Robert burst into the chamber.

'Mama! Mama!' they cried.

'Sweet Jesu, children, cease your shrieking!' the countess said. She was out of sorts after a restless night, and Evelyn and I exchanged a glance before turning to the two boys, now at one of the windows, meaning to usher them from the chamber.

'Mama!' one of the twins said. 'Our lord father is home. Look! Look!'

'And at the head of a great cavalcade!' the other added.

I started for the window, but Evelyn grabbed my elbow, pulling me back with a warning look. Then she tipped her head very slightly toward the countess, who had risen and walked sedately toward the window herself.

Of course. I gave a small nod, and berated myself for my stupidity.

It was not my place to be first at the window, but that of the countess.

Lady Adelie stood at the window and peered. Then she took a step back, clearly shocked. 'Mother of heaven!' she said.

'My lady?' Yvette said, going to stand with her.

'Fetch the house steward immediately!' Lady Adelie said to her, then beckoned Evelyn over. 'Ah! Why did I pick such a dull kirtle today? Well, there is no time to change. Evelyn, fetch me a freshly laundered veil and ensure you pick the brightest one. Maeb, make sure the children are dressed and neat, and keep them in their chambers for the time being, even Alice. Ancel, Robert, you can come with me and aid me down the staircase.'

With that she was gone, a twin on either side of her, Evelyn hastening after with a fresh veil for my lady's head.

I looked toward the window, desperately curious, hesitated, then, remembering my lady's tone, hurried to see the children were dressed and awaiting in their chamber.

At least the children's chamber had a window that overlooked the courtyard. Almost as soon as I and the nurse had the children dressed and neat, Alice and Emmette helping, I looked outside.

The courtyard was a flurry of activity. I could see Lady Adelie, Yvette now at her side along with the twins, and the steward, William. Lady Adelie and William were in deep conversation and, as I watched, the steward nodded, then strode away organising some men-at-arms into a presentable line and shouting at two grooms to tidy away some barrels and a laden cart.

Lady Adelie now had her fresh veil, and Mistress Yvette spent a moment fixing it securely to her hair.

Evelyn was nowhere to be seen.

'What is going on?' I said, as I turned to look at the nurse and Alice, who now stood by me. 'Is it always thus when the earl returns?'

Both shook their heads.

'There is always some ceremony,' Alice said. 'My mother likes to greet him in the courtyard together with the steward — but not this fuss. Maybe she is merely surprised by the suddenness of his return. I don't know.'

'It is far more than the suddenness of the earl's return,' said Evelyn, who had just stepped into the chamber.

She joined us at the window, the four of us standing close so we might all have a view.

'Then what —' I began, stopping at the sound of clattering hooves.

Suddenly the courtyard was filled with horses and their riders and a score of hounds. There were men everywhere, horses jostling and snorting, and the newly arrived hounds barking and snapping at the resident dogs.

23

Whatever order Lady Adelie and the steward had managed to arrange was instantly undone by the press of bodies and the raising of voices.

'The horses are lathered and stumbling,' the nurse remarked. 'They have been ridden hard and fast.'

'All the way from the king's court,' Evelyn murmured.

I glanced at her, a dozen questions on my lips, but then Alice nudged me. 'Look,' she said.

Somehow a small circle of calm had emerged in the heart of the chaos. I saw the earl dismounting from his horse, and stepping forth to the countess. They took each other's hands in a light grip, perfunctorily kissed, then the earl and the countess turned to another man, recently dismounted.

He was in dull garb, unlike the earl who shone in azures and vermilions, and I could not understand why the earl and the countess turned to him. Why did Lady Adelie not greet her son, Stephen, now also dismounted and standing close to his parents?

'Who —' I began yet once more, stopping in amazement as I saw Lady Adelie sink in deep courtesy before this other man, the earl having to take her elbow to support her as she almost slipped on the cobbles.

Behind her, the twin boys bowed deep in courtly fashion.

'The king,' Evelyn said. 'Edmond.'

The chaos of the courtyard rapidly spread throughout the entire house. Hounds ran up and down the great staircase, snapping and growling as servants and men-at-arms hurried this way and that. As I stood just inside the door of the children's chamber, watching, I saw William the steward hastening to and fro, barking orders, having bedding rearranged and taken from this chamber to that to accommodate the influx of a score or more men, while stools and benches, trestles and boards, were hurried into the great hall below me.

The earl was home *and* with a king to entertain.

'What should we do?' I said to Evelyn.

'Remain here,' she said. 'Lady Adelie will send when she requires us, and I think we'd do best at keeping the children out from under this hubbub. Poor Rosamund and John would be crushed if they ventured beyond the confines of this chamber!'

At that very moment, John, who had recently learned to toddle, managed to slip between both of our legs and totter toward the dangerous mayhem on the staircase.

'John!' Evelyn and I cried at the same time, bending down to reach for him.

He tried to evade us, gurgling with laughter, and only after a small scramble did we manage to retrieve him and stand upright again, John now safely in my arms.

I felt Evelyn go rigid, and I looked up.

The earl and the king were standing not half a dozen feet away, on the last rise of the staircase before they would step onto the wooden planks of the flooring.

Both were looking right at us.

I managed to register that the earl was furious, and that the king had an expression of some amusement on his face, before I dropped my eyes and sank down into the deepest courtesy I could manage.

My heart was pounding, and I couldn't think. I was terrified, not merely of the earl, but of the fact that *not a few feet away stood the King of England*.

Naturally, in such a state I compounded both my terror and my utter mortification by slipping just as I reached the lowest depths of my courtesy and thumping onto my bottom with an ungracious thud.

I was trying hard not to let John drop (could I manage to deepen my mortification? Yes, I could, if I sent John rolling away toward the king's feet), and from my bottom I slid onto a shoulder with a hard thump, making me cry out in pain.

Out of the corner of one eye I saw Evelyn bending down to snatch John from my hands and, as she raised him up, another hand appeared before my face.

'Take it,' a quiet voice said, and I did, and allowed the king to help me to my feet.

I couldn't look at him. I hung my head in misery, appalled that I could have so embarrassed the earl before the king.

And humiliate myself before the both of them.

Sweet Jesu, perhaps even little John would remember this all the days of his life, and chortle over my misery to his children.

'It is no indignity to save a child from harm,' the king said, and I finally raised my eyes to his face. I did not think it remarkable and was surprised that a king could look so like an ordinary man. He was olive-skinned, with dark wiry hair cropped close to his skull over a strong face. His eyes were brown, and surprisingly warm, and his sensual mouth curved in a soft smile. I supposed he was of an age with the earl, and from my youthful perspective, that seemed very old indeed.

'Your name?' he said.

'Mistress Maeb Langtofte,' the earl said in a flat voice, coming to stand at the king's shoulder. 'Recently joined my house to serve Adelie.'

'Then allow me to apologise for having upset your day, Mistress Maeb,' Edmond said. 'It has been most discourteous of me.'

I thought he must be laughing at me, but there was no malice in his eyes, only that shining, compelling warmth.

I could not speak, still too awed and humiliated. I realised Edmond continued to hold my hand and I tried to pull it away.

He held on to it a moment too long. It would not have been noticeable to anyone else, but both he and I knew it. Something in his eyes changed, just briefly, and then Edmond gave a small nod and he and the earl turned away and walked into the solar.

Evelyn, John still in her arms, and I stepped back into the chamber. Evelyn closed the door and I burst into tears.

I think my tears humiliated me almost as much as my foolishness before the king and earl. I hated to weep and show weakness, but at that moment everything was too overwhelming for me to do anything else.

I would not ever be able to show my face again within the household. The earl would despise me, and Lady Adelie too, and it was her contempt that I feared the most. Maybe life in a nunnery might not be so bad after all … surely I would be better suited to it than a noble household. I could not ever show my face again. I …

Evelyn, having handed John to the nurse, wrapped her arms about me and hugged me close.

'Come, come,' she teased, 'did you really need to throw yourself at the king's feet in such a fashion?'

I began to laugh, even as I was crying, and after a few moments Evelyn dried my tears, and I straightened my back and determined that I would stay out of sight of the king lest my treacherous legs threaten to wobble me to the floor again.

CHAPTER FIVE

—◆◆◆◆—

Naturally, fate and Lady Adelie conspired to make me break my promise within the hour.

Mistress Yvette arrived in the chamber, all bustle and busyness, and said that the countess wished Evelyn and myself to bring the children to greet their father and the king. I sent one frantic look to Evelyn, but she was no help, having turned away to speak with Alice and Emmette, so I swallowed my nerves, settled John on one hip — *Sweet Jesu let me not drop him* — and took Rosamund by the hand.

She was a sweet girl and gave me a happy smile, and I reminded myself that all I needed to do was escort the children into the solar, perhaps hand John to his mother, then step back and wait silently in the shadows.

Ancel and Robert were back with us by this stage, and Evelyn took them in hand, straightening their tunics and hair, and positioning them on either side of her, one hand on each boy's shoulder as if that might actually restrain them.

So, with Mistress Yvette leading the way, we progressed toward the solar.

Two men-at-arms stood either side of the closed door. They were weaponed and wary, and as good an indication, if any were needed, that they protected someone of immeasurable worth beyond the door. I did not know them, nor did their stern faces relieve my nerves. Mistress Yvette looked at them, then nodded back at us. One of the men relaxed enough to stand down from his guard and open the door into the chamber.

We filed in and I kept myself as far as I could in Mistress Yvette's shadow. Evelyn caught my eye, giving a small smile of reassurance.

I was surprised at how uncrowded it was. I had expected the same bustle and chaos in the solar as was in evidence everywhere else, but there was only a group seated in chairs and benches about one of the open windows.

Light spilled in the window and over the group, and I had to blink in order to make them out.

There was Edmond, seated in the imposing chair that was normally the earl's.

Pengraic sat next to him, leaning close as they murmured quietly.

Lady Adelie sat on a chair opposite them. She was packed about with pillows and cushions, and I thought she looked weary.

Beside her sat Stephen, his hair gleaming in the sunshine, leaning in to the service of his mother as the earl did to the king. Two other men — great nobles by their dress — completed the circle; I soon learned they were Walter de Roche, Earl of Summersete, and Gilbert de Montgomerie, Earl of Scersberie, and a Marcher Lord like Pengraic.

Lady Adelie noticed us first, and, as she gave a smile, so Stephen turned.

He noticed me immediately as I hid behind Mistress Yvette, almost as if he'd been looking, and gave an imperceptible nod.

'Ah, my children,' Pengraic said, and then they were all looking at us, and I tried to shuffle even further behind Mistress Yvette.

To no avail. Both the earl and the king looked directly at me, no doubt reliving my earlier humiliation. I glanced at Lady Adelie and saw that her face was sympathetic.

They had told her then, yet she did not condemn me.

The older children, Alice, Emmette and the twins, dipped or bowed before the king, then Pengraic beckoned Alice forward a step.

'Gilbert,' the earl said, 'this is my daughter Alice.'

Alice dimpled prettily at the closer of the two noblemen, and curtsied again. I looked at the gleam of interest in the nobleman's eyes, and wondered if Pengraic was arranging a match between Alice and this man — the Earl of Scersberie. Scersberie was an old man, older even than Pengraic, and I thought it likely Alice was to replace a wife lost to the ravages of childbirth.

I wondered if Alice were to be the first replacement, or a second or third. I had a momentary gladness that I had no estates or dowry, that I, too, might be handed about, offered to old men who lusted after my riches.

Pengraic beckoned Emmette forward, introducing her, then the twins stepped forward at his gesture.

'Ancel, Robert,' Pengraic said, 'you remember my lord of Summersete. It seems you will be going to his household a little sooner than expected.'

The boys dipped their heads and looked suitably restrained. The Earl of Summersete, a much younger man, and darkly handsome, gave them a friendly enough nod.

Sweet Jesu, I thought, was Pengraic about to dispose of all his children at this one gathering?

'And these two are the babies I have left,' the countess said, and gestured me forward.

John was wriggling about on my hip, and I was having trouble holding him, but Rosamund behaved beautifully, walking forward docilely but confidently, and dipping in a little courtesy that put my attempt to shame.

I still could not look at either the earl or the king.

'The little boy I have met previous,' said Edmond. 'On the stairs a short while ago.'

He paused, and I finally looked at him. His eyes were warm, glinting with secret amusement.

Then Edmond saved me by bending forward so he could look Rosamund in the eyes and take all attention away from myself and John.

'And who is this pretty little maid?' Edmond said, his voice soft, and he held out a hand.

I let Rosamund's hand go and she walked over to the king, her arms out, laughing, and the king grinned and swung her up to his lap.

'And this is the daughter *I* shall lay claim to, Raife, should ever I lose my beloved Adelaide.'

All attention was now on the king and the girl in his lap, and I faded backward, keeping a firm grip on the still-wriggling John, who seemed determined to get down.

For a few minutes the group exchanged pleasantries about the children, then Pengraic caught Lady Adelie's eye, who in turn summoned Mistress Yvette over to her side.

Mistress Yvette listened, nodded, then took Rosamund from the king, caught the twins' eyes and jerked her head toward the door.

Alice, ever watchful, smiled and dipped in yet another pretty courtesy, taking leave of the men and her mother. Her sister Emmette followed Alice's example, and both girls walked over to where I stood with Evelyn.

Thank the Lord, I thought, we are to be dismissed.

Mistress Yvette brought Rosamund over, and handed her to Evelyn.

'Take the children, Evelyn, and keep them in their chamber for the day,' she said quietly, keeping our consultations from disturbing the group by the window. 'Their mother does not want them running about the house today. Not the twins, certainly not the girls. I need to find William, and confer with him about tonight's feast.'

Yvette surprised me by taking John from my arms and handing him to Alice. 'Maeb,' she said, 'stay here and serve the men and our lady their wine, and if Lady Adelie should look too exhausted, then run to find me, that I might aid her back to her bed.'

'But —' I started. *But I can't stay here and serve these great nobles their wine! What if I should drop —*

'You will do well enough, Maeb,' Mistress Yvette said in a tone that brooked no dissent, and with that she, Evelyn, and the children turned and left the room.

I briefly closed my eyes, seeking courage. The closest I had ever come to high nobility was standing in a small crowd in Witenie on May Day, three years past, watching silently as a knight wearing a magnificent surcoat over his maille hauberk, and his two squires, rode past in splendid indifference to our awed gaze.

I opened my eyes, automatically seeking out Lady Adelie for reassurance.

She saw me looking and gave a little nod, either to hurry me up or to impart some sense of confidence.

I chose to believe the latter and so, wiping my hands among my skirts to dry away my nerves, I walked over to a small chest on which sat several ewers and a number of silver wine cups.

I poured out six cups of a rich, spiced and unwatered wine, then carried two across to the group, offering one first to the king, and the other to Pengraic.

The king gave me a warm look as he took the cup, the earl a cool and somewhat calculating one. I got the sense from the earl that he could not wait for a chance to berate me again; one did not have to consult all the saints in heaven to know I'd given him reason enough this day.

The next two cups I took to the other two earls, serving the Earl of Summersete first.

Summersete gave me a long look as he took the goblet from my hand. 'Is she to be trusted?' he said to Pengraic. 'I do not see why we cannot this once serve our own wine.'

'She can be trusted,' said Lady Adelie. 'She has no loyalty but to this household, and will not betray it. And she is not here just to serve wine. I am not well with this child I carry, and would prefer that one of my women remain to attend me if needed.'

Over the past weeks I had come to like and respect Lady Adelie. Now she had my complete loyalty for these words of confidence.

Something in my back straightened. 'I will not speak anything I hear in this chamber,' I said. 'I swear it, my lords.'

'For God's sake, Summersete,' said Edmond, 'the next thing you'll be wanting to rack her to see if she will confess to being in the King of Sicily's employ. Leave it be. I am too weary and too heartsick to want to find new shadows among the army that already gather about us!'

A few short weeks ago I had been but the orphaned daughter of a lowly knight, lost in her rustic idyll. Now I was not only serving wine to the King of England and some of his greatest nobles, but this king and these nobles were engaged in an argument about whether I might be a spy in the employ of the King of Sicily.

My mouth twitched. I caught Stephen's eye as I moved about Summersete to serve Scersberie, and, God help me, the amusement in Stephen's face almost undid me.

I retreated hastily to the chest and collected the final two cups for Lady Adelie and Stephen, keeping my eyes downcast as I served them. I then moved to a spot several paces away from the group and sat on a stool, distant enough not to be obtrusive, yet close enough to see if any needed his goblet refilled, or if the Lady Adelie needed my attention.

And close enough to hear the conversation that ensued.

* * *

'My lady,' Edmond said to Lady Adelie, 'I do beg your forgiveness for this unexpected intrusion. I know you prefer to keep a quiet household and my appearance has very evidently shattered the calm. Please, do not trouble yourself to arrange any richness of entertainment or feasting on my behalf. I am content to rest and eat as any member of your household.'

'My dear lord,' Lady Adelie replied, 'you are truly welcome in my house, and whatever feast or entertainment I offer you, be assured it is offered out of love and respect and not out of obligation. My only fear is that your arrival in such hasty manner, and without your usual retinue, foretells some heavy and terrible tidings.'

'I regret to say that it does, madam,' Edmond said. He sighed, fiddling a little with his wine cup before resuming. 'The south-east, from Dovre to Cantuaberie, is struck with plague. We have heard rumours of it in France and further east, but had hoped our realm should be spared. Not to be, I am afraid.'

'We should have closed the ports months ago,' Scersberie said.

'Well enough to say that now,' Pengraic said, 'but then we did not understand how vilely this plague spreads, nor how long it takes to show its evil nature.'

'My lords,' Lady Adelie said, 'please, tell me more. What plague? How dire, that my lord king had to flee Westminster?'

Edmond indicated that Pengraic should respond.

'My lady,' Pengraic said, 'my lord king's council has, for the past several months, received reports of a plague that had spread west from the lands of the Byzantine Empire, through the Hungarian and German duchies and into the French duchies — even the Iberian states of Aragon and Navarre have not been spared. The rumours spoke of terrible suffering —'

'How so?' said Lady Adelie.

Edmond shook his head slightly at Pengraic, and the countess turned to the king.

'My lord,' she said, 'I must know. I carry the responsibility of this household when the earl my husband is not present. I cannot manage it weighted by ignorance.'

Pengraic flicked a glance at me before continuing, and I felt my stomach turn over. Not at the thought that he might be angry at me, or not trust me, but at the words he was now about to speak. Somehow even then I knew the horror that awaited us.

'The sickness begins mildly enough,' said Pengraic. 'A feeling of malaise, then a cough. Then, a yellow phlegm expelled from the lungs.'

'And not any phlegm,' said Scersberie, 'for it is not moist at all, but of a dry, furry nature.'

'From then the sickness spreads rapidly,' Pengraic said. 'Once a man begins to cough the yellow phlegm, his body rapidly succumbs. Eventually, the yellow … fungus … spreads over most of his body.'

He paused. 'And then the final horror, Adelie. This "fungus" seems composed of heat, for all too often it bursts into flame and the sufferer is burned to death in his or her sickbed.'

'Terrible,' said Summersete, shaking his head. 'So many houses burned to the ground. An entire town, so I have heard, in the south of France.'

Sweet Mary, I thought. And what of all the souls burned along with the houses? Have you no thought for them?

Lady Adelie's face was shocked, as I am sure mine was. 'This is of the Devil!' she said. 'What else can explain it?'

I think she expected her husband to respond, but his eyes were downcast to his interlaced fingers in his lap and he did not speak.

'Indeed,' said Edmond. 'Nothing but the Devil could be behind such horror. No one has ever seen the like.'

'God's mercy upon us,' Lady Adelie murmured. 'How is it spread? By touch? By a miasma in the air?'

'We do not know,' said Edmond, 'but physicians believe that a man can be infected many weeks before any symptoms show. We had thought England safe, for there were no cases here, but it was merely that the infection had arrived weeks before any started to cough or grow the evil fungus.'

'Or burn,' said Summersete, and I thought he had a horrid fascination with the flames. Initially I had liked him for his youthful handsome face, but now I realised those pretty features covered a dark nature.

'Dovre and the south-eastern villages and towns are now infected,' said Edmond. 'People are dying, many more are coughing up the furry phlegm. Unrest spreads.'

'I do not doubt it,' Lady Adelie said, making the sign of the cross over her breast. 'Are we safe here? What can we do to protect ourselves?'

'You are not safe,' said Pengraic. 'Not from the plague, not from the unrest. You and the children, and whatever of the household you wish, must depart for Pengraic Castle as shortly as you may. The Welsh Marches are isolated and safe.'

'No!' cried Lady Adelie. 'I cannot! I am troubled enough with this child. I cannot undertake such a long journey back to —'

'You must, madam,' said Stephen, and I jumped a little at his voice, for I had almost forgot his presence. 'You risk all — your life and that of my brothers and sisters — if you stay here.'

'But —' Lady Adelie began.

'You *will* return to Pengraic Castle,' said the earl. 'It is your safe haven. Nothing, not even the plague, can leap its walls.'

'And you?' Lady Adelie said.

'Pengraic will stay with me,' said Edmond. 'I am raising men at Oxeneford — my main party has gone there, while my queen and sons have gone north to Elesberie — and I detoured to Rosseley with your husband only to add my voice to his that you depart for Pengraic Castle.'

'Stephen will stay with you,' said Pengraic. 'Edmond and I will ride with you as far as Oxeneford, and from there Stephen can escort you in a more leisurely manner to Pengraic.'

'And what of the Welsh?' said Lady Adelie. 'If they think England is in disarray may not that renegade Welsh oaf who calls himself prince, Madog ap Gruffydd, lead his army on Pengraic? The castle sits on a direct route from the heart of Welsh darkness into England. Do you save me from plague only to risk me to Madog? Raife, you are sorely needed at Pengraic yourself!'

'Madam,' said Scersberie, 'Madog is currently in the north of Wales. *I* shall need to deal with him, if any.'

'Your words speak your doubt for our son's abilities,' said Pengraic. 'Stephen is well enough the knight and castellan to keep you safe at Pengraic. And he has the garrison commander there to aid him. Ralph d'Avranches comes from a long line of Marcher Lords, both in this land and in our homelands of Normandy. He could hold a castle against the forces of the Devil himself.'

'Where is your courage, Adelie?' Pengraic finished. 'It is not for you to be so fearful.'

'I fear for my children,' Lady Adelie said softly. 'And for this child I carry. But … I shall do as you wish, my lords. Maeb? Will you fetch Yvette? I think I shall need to rest.'

I nodded, rising and starting for the door, my mind whirling with everything I had heard.

'Maeb.'

It was Pengraic, and I turned back to the group.

'Remember your oath that you should not speak of what you have heard in this room. If fear spreads, then you endanger your lady's life.'

'I shall remember, my lord. I will not speak of it.'

With that, I left the solar and sought out Mistress Yvette.

Of what they spoke when I had gone I do not know.

CHAPTER SIX

I found Yvette and she went to Lady Adelie.
I stood for a little time in the courtyard where I had found Yvette in yet another deep conversation with William, and watched the bustle about me. It was clear that Pengraic had not waited for his wife's approval before ordering preparations for departure. Men loaded carts with provisions, as also with chests from the house. I wondered if I were to go with the Lady Adelie, or if I should find myself homeless again.

My question was answered as soon as I returned to the children's chamber. Evelyn was fussing about, packing linens into a deep chest.

'We are to leave!' she said to me as I entered. 'William sent a man to tell us to pack. Ah, to Pengraic at *this* time of year. I am sure my lady is none too pleased. Maeb, what has happened? What did you hear?'

'I may not speak of it, Evelyn. I am sorry.'

'But we *are* to leave for Pengraic?'

'If you have heard it, then, yes, we are.' There was no point denying this.

'But why? My lady is with child, and not well. It is a long and arduous journey and … ah, you may not speak of it. I know.'

Evelyn stopped, and sighed. 'Well, at least we shall dine with the king tonight. A small reward for all this mayhem. Maeb, you have yet to witness such an event, yes? Then you shall enjoy yourself this evening. Whatever else awaits, you may say that at least you dined with the king. Now, come help me with these linens … and do you know where lie Alice's and Emmette's mantles? I cannot find them anywhere.'

England might be gripped by plague, and the Pengraic house might be in turmoil, but even so, it seemed nothing would stop the steward and Lady Adelie entertaining the king as they believed fitting. The great hall on the ground floor had been opened up, benches and trestle tables moved in, the great banners and tapestries rehung from beams and on walls, the fires lit, and I was, indeed, to dine with the king.

Nothing in Lady Adelie's household had prepared me for this. As the evening drew in, Evelyn and I left the two youngest children in the care of their nurse while she and I, together with Alice, Emmette and the twin boys, washed and prepared ourselves for the evening's feast. I had nothing suitable to wear, but Mistress Yvette, in a moment she spared us from her dressing of Lady Adelie, generously offered me one of her kirtles, a lovely spring-green linen garment, adorned with crimson ribbons and embroideries.

'It is so beautiful!' I said as I smoothed it down over my hips.

'And it suits your black hair,' said Evelyn, 'and reflects the green of your eyes.'

Despite everything I had heard this day, and the upheaval of the entire household, I shall admit I was more than a little excited at this evening's entertainments. I had never worn such a rich gown, nor thought I would ever attend a court where a king should be present.

There would not be many women attending — Lady Adelie, Mistress Yvette, and Evelyn only; myself, and the two elder Pengraic girls still at home. There would be no gaggle of painted court beauties, or a bevy of titled ladies. All courtly attention would be on our small group.

I wondered if I would attract any admiring eyes. I fingered one of my heavy braids, shifting it this way and that across my breasts, pleased with the effect of my black hair against the green and scarlet.

Evelyn came over, and I remarked that she had not veiled her head as she was wont to do.

'There will be no veils among the womenfolk tonight, Maeb. It is the new fashion to wear hair unadorned, save for flowers or jewels, at courtly events. Even married women go without their veils.

'And the unmarried ... Maeb, why not wear your hair loose tonight? It will be all wavy from the braiding, and it must surely reach all the way down to your knees. You have such lovely hair ... you do not need to lengthen it with the horsehair that some women require. Tonight you can shine in all your womanly glory, eh? Enough to catch the eye of one of the king's gentle retainers? A youthful knight, or even a baron?'

'Sweet Jesu, Evelyn, you shall have me married before the morn!'

She laughed. 'Ah, come now, Maeb. Here now, it is all loosened. We shall brush it ... and I have just the thing for your brow, this circlet of ribbon and waxen flowers that Lady Adelie once gave to me. There. Done. You shall be beautiful for tonight, and for one evening forget whatever worries you heard earlier. Now, let's see if Alice has managed to dress Emmette's hair, or if we shall have to do it ourselves.'

There was a small looking glass in the chamber, and as Evelyn turned to Alice and Emmette, I stole a glance in its reflection.

I hardly recognised myself. The excitement had put a sparkle in my eyes, and the richness of the verdant green gown, and the unaccustomed sight of my hair unbound and tumbling about my shoulders and back, made me look almost the wood dryad. I bit my lips a little to make them redden and, checking quickly to make sure Evelyn was not watching, pinched my cheeks to colour them, too.

For that moment, the plague and the journey ahead was all lost in my anticipation. I forgot even my humiliation of earlier, and looked forward only to an evening that a few weeks ago I could not ever have imagined myself attending.

My night would be full of earls and kings and feasting. I thought of Stephen, too, and wondered what he would make of me now.

I remembered the jest he made of his bedchamber on that day I had first arrived at Rosseley, and suddenly I had no need of pinching to make my cheeks colour.

I put down the looking glass, and turned to where Evelyn fussed over the girls, and smiled.

Tonight I would enjoy, and tomorrow I would fear.

I had not previously entered the great hall of Rosseley Manor. Its doors were always closed, and there had been no reason for me to go inside. My world had been completely bounded by Lady Adelie and her children — not the larger world of men and court of which I'd only had tantalising glimpses.

So on this night, when I entered, I stopped and just looked.

I had never seen a chamber so huge, not even that of a church! I knew that the hall ran a great distance from seeing its outer walls, but even so, nothing had prepared me for its size once I entered it.

Now I understood why the stairs from the ground floor to the upper level wound up and up for an eternity — they had to somehow surmount the height of the hall's panelled ceiling.

The hall ran back from its entrance doors to an enormous fireplace in its far wall. Before that fireplace — ablaze even on this warm spring night — sat a raised dais with a long table heavy with patterned silken damasks and linens. The light from both the fire and the scores of torches and candles about made the silver and golden plate and cups and pitchers atop the table glint with a rosy light.

I had never seen … I had never *comprehended* such riches!

I knew this all came from the earl's household store, for I'd overheard William on the stairs earlier, handing a key to an armed servant that the plate might be unlocked for the night.

If an earl commanded such wealth, then what might the king's court reveal?

'Maeb.'

Evelyn's voice broke into my awed reverie, and I hastily moved aside at her gentle tug on my hand. We walked to one side of the hall — two long tables ran down the length of the hall, as if they were pillars supporting the cross beam of the high table — and allowed one of the servants to lead us to our places. We were by ourselves now, for we had handed over Alice, Emmette, Ancel and Robert to Mistress Yvette so they could enter with their parents, and the two younger children were with the nurse. Mistress Yvette would stay close to Lady Adelie for the evening, so Evelyn and myself had little to do but enjoy ourselves, with no duties to perform.

The two long tables were already almost full of diners. There were no other women present save for Evelyn and myself — Lady Adelie, Mistress Yvette and the two girls had yet to make their entrance — and we attracted many a glance as we moved closer to the high table.

The glances were admiring and speculative both, and I lowered my eyes that I might not meet any of their interest. I flattered myself that many of those glances were directed at me, but I knew that Evelyn must also garner her share of admiration, for she was still young enough to rouse lust in a man, and looked very fine tonight in her deep red gown and her glistening nut-brown hair heavily braided with blue and silver beads.

Evelyn — usually — wore the veil of the married woman, but was she widowed? Or as yet unwed and only wore the veil as acknowledgement of her rank and age? She had never talked of a husband to me in our nightly chats, and in fact avoided revealing too much personal information at all. I resolved to delve a little this night, if I had the chance.

We arrived at our places, only five or six down from the high table, and Evelyn graciously thanked the servant who bowed and left us to seat ourselves. We were lucky to have a bench of our own, and as we slid into place I was careful not to catch the table linens and tip all the tableware to the ground.

Tonight, I was determined that I should be worthy of my place in this court.

Our tableware, though fine, was not of the beauty of the high table. Pewter bowls held water for us to wash our fingers, and wine cups of similar nature sat before us. There were some pewter spoons on the table, but mostly we would use our fingers or the small personal knives that all carried at belts or girdles. At least my knife would not disgrace me, I thought, fingering it gently as it swung from my girdle, for it was of good craftsmanship — one of the few things I'd had from my childhood that was of any worth.

A servant appeared at our elbows, and filled our cups with a spiced wine.

I took a sip, and marvelled at its headiness. I would need to be careful not to sip too enthusiastically.

'Sweet mistress,' said the man immediately on my left, 'may I ask your name? I have been to the earl's court on many an occasion, but have not seen you previously.'

I turned to look at him, wondering how I should respond. He was a man of younger years, fair of hair and with an open friendly face, well dressed in a heavily embroidered russet tunic with a fine white linen shirt beneath. He wore several gold rings, set with gems, on his fingers, and a small hoop through one ear.

'I am Mistress Maeb Langtofte, and I serve the Lady Adelie. Are you with the king's retinue? Forgive my ignorance, but I do not yet know even all the earl's retinue, let alone the king's.'

'I think any man could find it easy to forgive you anything,' the man said, 'for it is rare to find such beauty without a jealous husband attached to her arm. You must be new arrived at the earl's house, yes? Otherwise I cannot imagine how you yet remain unwed. I swear, within the six month, a score of gallant knights and barons shall beg the earl for your hand.'

I was growing uncomfortable now, for I was not used to such direct conversation nor such admiration. The man also had not yet given me his name, and I did not know if perchance I spoke with one of the king's younger brothers, or one of his lords, or if he was one of the earl's men and sent here to test me. He could just as likely have been attached to either Summersete or Scersberie, and I was at a loss as to how to address him.

The man's blue eyes twinkled, and I knew he sensed my discomfort.

'Forgive me,' he said. 'I am Ranulph Saint-Valery, and I hail from Lincolescire. Edmond amuses himself by keeping me within his court, but for what reason, I do not know, for I cannot think I serve one single useful earthly purpose.'

I smiled, thinking it would not be hard to like this man.

'But for tonight, lovely lady,' Saint-Valery continued, 'I shall be *your* servant, and shall serve you the most delicate morsels from my plate and wipe the lip of your cup with my napkin, that your wine may always taste sweet.'

Now I was blushing, for I had never before encountered such courtliness, nor such attention.

Fortunately Evelyn came to my rescue as I struggled to make some light, witty remark.

'My Lord Saint-Valery, you are making my young companion blush with your pretty words. Maeb, our lord king likes to keep Sir Ranulph at his court for the beauty of his poetry. You have at your side one of England's greatest poets. Is that not so, my lord?'

Ranulph made a deprecating gesture with one hand, then half turned aside as a servant made a fuss in the refilling of his wine cup.

The momentary distraction allowed Evelyn to whisper into my ear. 'Be careful of him, Maeb. A celebrated poet he may be, but he is also one of Edmond's spies at court. He uses his poetry and sweet tongue to coerce even the most well-kept secret from the tightest lips.'

I squeezed her hand, grateful for the warning.

I wondered if my table companion was mere happenchance, or if Edmond had decided I might be a spy in the employ of the King of Sicily after all.

Saint-Valery and I chatted for a while of Witenie, where I was born and raised. He knew of its market, having attended one day, which knowledge surprised me.

'You did not see me?' he said, his mouth curving in a smile. I was a little disturbed to suddenly realise how sensual that mouth was. 'Choosing among the apples?'

'No, my lord,' I said, 'for I should surely have remembered so distinguished a visitor had I seen you. Perhaps you came disguised? A travelling minstrel perhaps. A vagabond. So that none might recognise you and mark your presence.'

The smile widened a little, although the expression on his face was now speculative rather than amused. 'You have courage with your words, Mistress Maeb. You are not afraid to tease.'

'It is the wine,' I murmured. 'It goes to my head.'

'Then I shall press it the more urgently upon you, that I might know you better.'

I was about to reply, but just then the mellow tones of two horns sounded by the door and all conversation stopped as we turned to look.

'The king,' Saint-Valery murmured, and with that all assembled at the long tables rose, and either bowed or dipped in courtesy.

Edmond and the Earl of Pengraic and Lady Adelie had entered the hall. Edmond led the way, Lady Adelie on his arm, with the earl a step behind. All were dressed richly, and I thought that Edmond now looked every part the king in his splendid blue tunic with its gold embroideries, fur-lined mantle, jewelled brooch, and heavily jewelled circlet upon his brow. He wore a sword at his left hip, and its hilt looked to me as if it were fashioned from pure gold inlaid with diamonds.

Lady Adelie looked weary, but otherwise sparkled with jewels in the circlet she wore on her head and wound through her braids which hung almost to the floor. The earl likewise wore rich cloth and many jewels, and a sword as well. He and the king were the only men in the hall, apart from the men-at-arms standing against the walls, who wore their weapons, although all of us carried small eating knives at our belts.

Saint-Valery saw me looking at the swords. 'No one wears their sword in the presence of the king,' he murmured, 'save his host.'

I nodded my thanks.

Behind came Walter de Roche, the Earl of Summersete, and Gilbert de Montgomerie, the Earl of Scersberie.

Lord Stephen walked a few steps behind the two earls, looking splendid in a gold and silver tunic, possibly the one I had seen him in that first day I'd met him, and I am afraid my heart skipped a beat at the sight of him. I wondered if he would see me from where he ate at high table.

After Stephen came Alice and Emmette and the two boys, Ancel and Robert, with Mistress Yvette a step behind. She was dressed in a manner almost as rich as Lady Adelie, which showed as nothing else the favour in which Lady Adelie held her.

Edmond and Lady Adelie drew close to where Evelyn, Saint-Valery and I stood, and while the countess kept her eyes ahead, the king glanced over.

For a moment he met my eyes, then I dropped mine and sank a little deeper in courtesy.

When I looked up again, the entire party had passed me and had arrived at the high table where they were in the process of seating themselves.

Once the high table had sat, Pengraic, who alone had remained standing, raised his wine cup and led the wassail toast in honour of Edmond.

'Drinkhail!' the assemblage responded as we raised our cups and toasted the king. Then we all sat, and the evening's feasting and entertainment began.

Considering the king, the earl and their respective retinues had only arrived this morning, and with no warning, William the house steward had done his earl and his lady proud. A pig and a yearling ox had been slaughtered and roasted: a half score servants brought in the meat piled high on silver platters. As well as the pork and ox, several swans and a score of rabbits had been roasted and served, and there followed several platters of pigeon and fish in various spiced milks and pottages. And yet more men followed, bearing bowls of stews and vegetables, sauces and soups.

A servant appeared at my elbow, placing a trencher of bread before me, as well as a small plate. The high table was served their food first, then the servants came down the long lines of the table, offering us our choice of meats and their accompanying dishes.

Saint-Valery chose for me, selecting cuts of meats and sauces for my plate and trencher, until I thought that perhaps he was intending to feed me for a week. I protested somewhat weakly at the amount of food he thought I might eat and he inclined his head in acquiescence, and thus we began our feast.

Minstrels came to entertain us with harps and pipes and sweet voices.

I was, I confess it, overawed. Nothing in Lady Adelie's household had prepared me for a courtly event like this. I stole glances at the high table, watching the king and the nobles eat and drink, laugh and gesture, and offer each other choice pieces of meat as well as other courtesies. I thought Stephen had been well placed, sitting between the earls of Summersete and Scersberie, and I confess I watched him the most and was both delighted and flustered when he saw me, and raised his wine cup in a greeting to me.

I was even more flustered when it became obvious that Saint-Valery had witnessed the exchange.

'Lord Stephen shines like a young god, does he not,' Saint-Valery said.

I did not know what to say, and hid my confusion with a sip of wine.

'It is said that the earl seeks a foreign princess for his eldest son's wife,' Saint-Valery added.

'And Lord Stephen would be worthy of such,' I murmured, hoping it was the right thing to say.

'But fear not,' Saint-Valery said, 'I am sure that Stephen will not forget you. Most lords take mistresses, and Stephen would treat such a woman well, I think. Perhaps you —'

'I would not want such a thing!' I said, hoping I had injected enough righteous indignation into my voice.

'I was only going to suggest that you might like to attend his wife, as you do now his mother,' Saint-Valery said, his eyes glinting with humour.

I was angry with him. It was not what he had wanted to suggest at all.

'The Lady Adelie says she shall find me a gentle husband,' I said.

'As I am sure she can,' Saint-Valery said. 'A knight such as your father, perhaps … a man of gentle name and rank but with little lands nor any offices to his name. You do not have a large dowry, do you? No, I thought not. Possibly none at all, knowing your father. Virtue is all very well, Mistress Maeb, but not when your "gentle" marriage means you shall need

44

to glean with your peasant womenfolk so you might have bread for your table.'

I could not reply. I was furiously angry with him now, not simply for his ungenerous words and bawdry, but at the fact that he seemed to know my circumstances all too well. He knew of my father and his lack of extensive lordships and coin, but I had not once mentioned it.

Who had been discussing me with Saint-Valery? And why?

'Maeb,' Saint-Valery said, 'I only speak of the ways of the world and of the court. Virtue is all very well, but not when it condemns you to servitude. You are a beautiful woman. You must have seen the eyes that pass your way. And you are spirited, and many a nobleman likes that in a woman. Yet you have no dowry. Not even the care of Lady Adelie could win for you anything but the basest knight. I only wish to open your mind to the possibilities.'

'I can only hope for the basest knight, my lord? Then surely that puts you well within my reach. Speak to Lady Adelie, and I am yours.'

Saint-Valery stared at me, then roared with laughter. Everyone about us paused to look, and from the corner of my eye I saw those at the high table turn to us as well.

I flamed with colour, and wondered if I should stand, and leave.

'Maeb,' Evelyn murmured, 'just dip your head at the high table, and smile graciously, then return to your meal.'

I did so, almost unable to bear to look at them. Stephen was smiling, Lady Adelie looked a little concerned, Pengraic's face was a mask of disdain, and, sweet Jesu, the king actually nodded at me and raised his wine cup slightly.

Mistress Yvette merely looked cross.

All I had wanted was to enjoy the evening, and yet now it was tainted.

'My lord,' Evelyn said to Saint-Valery. 'You speak too boldly to Maeb. She is young, and untutored in courtly ways. You accuse her of teasing, and yet you are unmerciful in it. Be wary, I pray you, for both the earl and the countess take good care of her well-being and happiness.'

I admired Evelyn then as never before. She had spoken gently, and yet even so, she had issued Saint-Valery a stern warning. Well might Saint-Valery have the ear and the regard of the king, yet he could ill afford to make an enemy of the earl.

Saint-Valery inclined his head, accepting the rebuke.

'I beg your forgiveness, Mistress Maeb,' he said, and the apology in his voice seemed genuine. 'I have not spoken well, and that was discourteous of me.'

I gave a small nod, accepting his apology, although the unhappiness must have been obvious on my face. For the next few minutes we ate in silence, then the awkwardness was broken when the Earl of Summersete rose — for what reason I do not know — and in the doing bumped into a servant directly behind his chair. The servant was carrying yet another platter of food, and all went flying, servant and earl both, the food spattering in a gravy-laden arc about them.

My mouth twitched, happy to see that even such a nobleman as the earl could make as much a fool of himself as I might, and I heard muffled chortles all about me.

'I am glad to see you smile again, Maeb,' Saint-Valery said. 'Will you forgive me enough to talk with me again?'

I was happy enough to do so, for in my amusement I had put aside all my anger and embarrassment. Thus, as the meal progressed, we chatted of this and that, Saint-Valery pointing out nobles and retainers at the tables and telling me a little of each.

'Your lord has put on a goodly feast for his king,' Saint-Valery said as the feast drew toward its final dishes. 'He has done himself proud in Edmond's eyes.'

'And his household had little enough time in which to do so,' I said. I did not particularly like the earl, from my brief encounters with him, but I was happy enough to bolster the regard of his household.

'It is all a great flurry,' Saint-Valery said. 'One moment we were happy in court at Edmond's palace at Westminster, the next we are fleeing eastward to Oxeneford, detouring to collect the earl's family. What can be the matter do you think? It must be dire news.'

I had by this stage had a great amount of the spiced wine to drink, and its headiness had fuzzed my mind.

But not enough to endanger my head by babbling the secrets I had heard that day in the solar.

'It is terrible news, I have heard, my lord.'

'Yes?' he said, leaning a little closer.

Beside me, I felt Evelyn stiffen.

'Aye,' I said. 'I have heard ...' I paused, drawing out the moment, '... I have heard that the very dryads from the woods threaten the king! They rustle their leaves, and the king grows anxious!'

Saint-Valery chuckled. 'You have done well, Mistress Maeb. No doubt you know I shall be reporting thus to Edmond. I —'

'Mistress Maeb,' said the Earl of Pengraic's voice, and a heavy hand fell on my shoulder. 'I would speak with you privately if I might.'

My stomach fell away. I looked up at the earl's face. It was impassive, but I thought I saw anger in his eyes.

Sweet Jesu, what had I done so wrong he needed to single me out like this?

I murmured a politeness to Saint-Valery, then rose and walked after the earl out of the hall.

I could feel the eyes following me as I went.

Pengraic led me to a quiet corner by the staircase, then turned to me.

'What did Saint-Valery speak with you about?' he said.

'We chatted of the court, and he pointed out the nobles to me, and —'

'Did he ask about the meeting in the solar?'

'Yes.'

'What did you say?'

'I said that the king had learned the dryads in the forests threatened to shake their leaves at him, and thus he fled Westminster.'

Foolishly, I thought he would laugh at my wit as had Saint-Valery.

'What do *you* know of the dryads in the woods?' the earl snapped.

'I am sorry, my lord,' I stuttered, 'I only thought to deflect Saint-Valery's interest.'

The earl simply stared at me.

'I am sorry, my lord,' I repeated, and hung my head. It was aching now from all the excitement and the wine, and all I wanted was to escape everyone and flee back to my chamber.

'You think too much of yourself, Maeb.'

I bit my lip. I did not know what to say.

He sighed, and I found the courage to look at him again.

The earl's face had lost all its anger and now only looked tired. I realised that he, as the king and everyone who had arrived with them, had been riding for a full day and night and must be exhausted.

'Maeb, my lady wife will need all your love and care on your journey to Pengraic. She is not well with this child.'

'I know, my lord. She shall have it. I care for her greatly.'

He studied me, then gave a small nod. 'I am very much afraid the world shall be a dark place for many months to come.'

I was feeling ever more uncomfortable, mainly because I had not thought to see the earl this vulnerable — he had always been so proud and strong and terrible to me — and that vulnerability frightened me.

'Maeb, remember this, and remember it well. Every word spoken is carried by the wind to each corner of this mortal earth, and to the ears of God and the Devil. Remember it.'

'I will, my lord.'

In my tiredness I could not grasp what he meant, nor could I foretell that my utter failure to remember his words in time to come would make a wreck and a mockery of my entire world.

Just then Evelyn appeared, pausing a few steps away.

The earl nodded to her, then he walked toward the hall.

Before he had gone too far, I called out to him. 'My lord? I have said nothing to Saint-Valery, nor anyone else. Truly.'

He looked at me a long moment. 'I know that,' he said, then he walked off.

I put a hand to my head. 'Evelyn, I think I need to go to bed. Is it seemly that I leave the feast now?'

She smiled and came close, taking my arm. 'Yes. No one will take offence. Come now, I have had enough myself, and I think those at high table are making murmurs about their beds, too. Yvette will look after our lady and we will make sure Alice and her sister and the boys find their beds, and then we will sleep.'

Much later I lay in the bed I shared with Evelyn, unable to sleep even though my head throbbed and my limbs ached with weariness. My mind could not stop, revisiting everything I had seen and heard and done this day.

After a while I felt Evelyn's hand on my arm. 'You did well today, Maeb. I do not know what you heard in the solar, but if all that wine Saint-Valery pressed on you did not loosen your tongue, then little else but torture will … and I do not think you need worry about that in our company.'

I chuckled. 'Not even from the earl?'

Evelyn laughed softly. 'I think he might be too tired, but maybe next week, when he is recovered ...'

'Evelyn ... may I ask something of your life?'

'Of course. I have little to hide.'

'Are you wed? I was wondering this evening, as we walked into the hall ...'

'And you wondered if I could have my pick of all the men?' Evelyn laughed again. 'Maybe so, but I have little interest. Yes, I was wed, but my husband died within a year of our marriage and eventually I took service with my lady. I have a daughter from that marriage, fourteen summers this year.'

'Truly? Where is she now?'

'In service to the household of Sir Roger de Tosny at Redmeleie, north of Glowecestre.'

I considered her words — thinking Evelyn would be a good mother and that she must miss her daughter. 'You do not wish to wed again?'

She took a long time answering, and I wondered if she had fallen asleep or if perchance I had hit on the little she *did* want to hide.

'I will tell you this, Maeb, not only because I like you, but also because you will hear of it soon enough from someone else. I was only surprised Saint-Valery did not speak of it to you — but then I suppose he had his reasons to keep silent. I also tell you of this because of the way Edmond looked at you this morning. When you fell from your courtesy ... by the Blessed Virgin, Maeb, you did not see him almost fall himself in his rush to aid you!'

She paused. 'I did long for another man once, and lived for those hours I spent in his arms, but there was no question of marriage. Maeb, I was the king's lover for one summer. I loved him with every breath I took, but ... his whims burn furious and then fade fast. Many others have replaced me in his bed since that summer and my own passion for him has long since died. It was a summer's fancy only. He looks upon me kindly now, but I swear he has forgot that once he took me to his bed. Now, no, I have little interest in finding myself another husband. I have a secure home with the countess, and after Edmond ...'

I was struck dumb. I had not expected this confession.

'And now he wants you, Maeb. But he will not touch you, not yet. Not while you remain unwed — that is his idea of courtesy.' She gave a brief, soft laugh. 'But if ever you do wed, my sweet, and return to court, beware of his interest. He has marked you well. Saint-Valery was at your side this evening for good reason and it had little to do with whether or not you prattled about what you heard in the solar. Edmond wants to know you better, and the only way he can do that for the moment is through Saint-Valery. Even now Saint-Valery will be at the king's side, whispering quietly in his ear. Be careful, Maeb. Be very, very careful.'

CHAPTER SEVEN

The next day passed in a blur of activity as the household prepared to leave. I think both the earl (indeed, all three of them) and the king were greatly impatient with this necessary delay, but they bore it well, and spent the best part of the day out hunting for venison with many of their entourage, including Stephen and Saint-Valery. I spent my time between the children's chamber and the solar, at one moment helping Evelyn and the nurse pack for the children (and keeping the younger ones from under everyone else's feet), at the next hurrying to Mistress Yvette's impatient call that I aid her and the countess. In other parts of the house, servants packed plate and linens, barrels of wine and salted meats, tapestries and hangings.

I had not realised so much of the earl's house travelled back and forth between Pengraic Castle and Rosseley.

'Normally,' Evelyn remarked to me at one point during the day, 'much of the household would be sent on ahead of the earl and his family, to be waiting for them at the castle. But now ...' She shrugged, and moved back to folding linens and ribbons.

I was glad to be so busy with the packing, and running this way and that.

My mind continued to spin with all that had happened yesterday. I had met a king, and sat in on a privy meeting between him and three of his highest nobles. I had heard of great terror approaching, and yet could speak of it to no one. I had attended a great feast of court and had the king's own man sit next to me.

I had caught a king's eye.

As had, once, Evelyn.

51

I found it difficult to reconcile all of this, and what it might mean for my future. Of everything to be afraid of, it was Edmond's interest which truly unsettled me. His interest would be a passing fancy, little else, and yet it might well ruin my life. I would be discarded as had Evelyn, and as had many others. My only security in life at present was my place within the Pengraic household. There was nothing else. My only future security would be a good marriage to a man with enough estates to ensure I would not lack, through any circumstance. Without that marriage I was truly most vulnerable.

Yet such a marriage rested only on Pengraic's tenuous goodwill, for I had no dowry to attract interest. I could do nothing to threaten that goodwill if I wanted any future security in life. Pengraic had warned me against his son Stephen. What did he think now, knowing of the king's interest? That I had deliberately aimed my ambitions higher than Stephen?

I worried and fretted all through the day. News of the plague slipped into the dim recesses of my mind. It was Edmond's interest that represented my most immediate threat.

Despite what Lady Adelie had said about Pengraic, I could not wait to reach the castle within the Welsh Marches.

The king would be far distant then, and I could relax.

We would be leaving very early the next morning. Lady Adelie had said to me that the first two days would be hard riding, but then, having left behind the king and Pengraic with the greater part of their retinues at Oxeneford, we could travel in more leisurely a fashion to our destination. It was late in the night, and Evelyn and I were readying ourselves for sleep (there had been no feast tonight; merely grabbed food from a platter a servant had brought round), when Evelyn turned abruptly to reach for a shoe she had left to one side of the stool.

Suddenly she cried out in pain, both hands reaching for her back.

'Evelyn! What has happened?'

She was white and biting her lips. 'I have wrenched my back, Maeb. Oh, *such* stupidity! Why could I not have been more careful? And tomorrow we must travel. With *this!*'

I helped her to bed, Evelyn again crying out with pain as she lowered herself down. I wrapped a shawl about my chemise, and went down to the kitchens to get her a warm poultice for her back.

When finally I, too, went to bed, I cuddled up close to Evelyn, desperately tired, but not able to sleep. I wished for those long, calm, bright days of my early days at Rosseley, and wondered if they would ever come again.

We rose early the next day. Well, I rose, but Evelyn managed to get to her feet only with the most heartbreaking cries of pain. Her back was seized and swollen and every movement hurt. After I helped her to dress I left her sitting mournfully in the children's chamber, watching as the nurse and Alice and Emmett managed to dress the children.

I went to aid Mistress Yvette get the countess ready. She was up, already in her linen chemise with Mistress Yvette helping her into her kirtle. The earl was with her, too, and I gave him a brief glance and quick dip of courtesy as I passed.

I could not look at his face.

'Where is Evelyn?' said the countess.

'She wrenched her back badly last night, my lady. Forgive her not attending you this morning. She is in great pain.'

'Oh, poor Evelyn!' Lady Adelie said. 'My lord, she will need to join me in my travelling cart. She cannot ride.'

Pengraic belted his tunic, then reached for his sword belt. 'Your cart is already overladen, madam. The nurse and the two younger children will need space by your side, as will Mistress Yvette, who wobbles off any horse that goes beyond a walk.'

I kept my face downcast, amused by the mental image of Mistress Yvette 'wobbling' off her horse.

'Now we must pack Evelyn in there some place.' The earl paused. 'Mistress Maeb, please tell me you do not require space atop the cart as well. The lighter it keeps, the faster it shall travel.'

'I can ride well enough, my lord,' I said, finally looking at him. He looked tired and irritated, but I think that was so much his normal expression I thought little enough of it.

'By what do you mean "well enough"?' he said.

'I learned to ride on my father's courser,' I said. 'The horse was old, but still of uncertain temper. Few managed him — my father and I alone.'

The earl stared, then gave a nod. 'Well, we shall see. The saints alone know what horses are available. I will need to speak to Ludo. Madam,' he continued, his attention now given back to his wife, 'I will break my fast below. I need to oversee preparations. Be ready soon. It will be a long day's journeying for us, and I cannot wait on your prayers.'

'My lord,' Lady Adelie said, and the earl left the solar.

She sighed, and turned back to Mistress Yvette. 'Fetch me some bread and cheese, Yvette, and a mug of small beer. We can pray well enough when we are lurching along the road, and I do not wish to keep my lord awaiting. Maeb, how do the children?'

By the time I returned to the children's chamber, they had all vanished to the courtyard below, and only the nurse remained, gathering a few last items.

'Evelyn is waiting in the cart below,' she said. 'One of the servants carried her down the stairs. Fetch whatever you need, Maeb, and join us below.'

Suppressing a flare of excitement in my belly, I went to the small chamber Evelyn and I had shared, wrapped my mantle about my shoulders, picked up my bag of possessions and hurried down the stairs.

The courtyard was a mass of movement, cantankerous voices, nervous hooves slipping across cobbles and the excited barking of dogs. The larger part of the entourage that the king and the earls had brought with them was waiting on the road beyond, but the courtyard space was still crowded enough with men and carts and horses.

I stood undecided, not knowing what to do or where to turn, when the earl, who had been speaking to Ludo, his Master of Horse, turned and saw me. He said something to Ludo, and the man hurried over to me.

'Saints save me, girl,' Ludo said, his creased face even more deeply lined than usual on this morning, 'I pray you spoke truth when you said you could manage a horse. Here, man, take this bag and set it into one of the carts — into that of my lady's, if there be any room left.'

A groom appeared beside me, and I relinquished my bag.

'This is the one mount I have available that might be suitable for you,' Ludo continued, 'and I value her too highly to allow her to be wasted on a doltish rider.'

There was a clatter of hooves, and another groom led over a lovely grey mare, all fine boned and dark eyed and flagged of tail. She was a palfrey, and thus an expensive horse — of far more worth than my father's courser had been.

I felt the first needle of worry. What if I allowed her to run away from me and she foundered in a ditch?

'I need to see you ride her first,' said Ludo. 'If I am not satisfied, you will need to walk behind the carts, unless a place is found for you within them. Come, we will go to the orchard. There is space there for me to see you ride Dulcette, yet fence enough to stop the mare should she bolt.'

He led Dulcette to a mounting block. I walked over, trying not to notice that the earl was now standing, arms folded, watching, and mounted with Ludo's help. Once I had settled my skirts and rested my feet in the stirrups, Ludo let me take up the reins, and, my heart in my mouth, I gave Dulcette's flanks a little press with my legs.

She responded immediately. She had spirit and I knew at once that she was unnerved by this new rider upon her and that all she wanted was to dash. I held the reins firmly, and guided her through the mass of people and horses toward the orchard.

The mare's ears kept flicking back toward me, and I could literally feel her trying to decide if she liked me or not — her muscles were bunched tight under the saddle.

I did not care if she liked me. All I asked was for her to respect me enough to obey me.

We reached the orchard and some space and quiet. My heart thudding, I gave Dulcette another press with my legs and clicked my tongue. She tried instantly to run away with me, as I had thought she would, but I pulled her back and spoke disapprovingly to her, warning her with my voice.

She responded, praise the saints, her ears twitching faster than a march fly, and I allowed myself to relax a little. I kept her to a hard walk until we reached the farthest reaches of the orchard, then I turned her back, and gave her a little more rein.

I had thought she might break into a trot or even a canter, but instead Dulcette did something remarkable, something I had never before felt while riding.

She broke into a fast-paced gait that was neither trot nor canter, but which was unbelievably smooth.

She ambled!

I had only ever seen a horse do it once before — the knight who had passed by our village had been riding a horse that ambled, and then I had watched in fascination at its fluid, effortless gait. An ambler was most highly regarded, for in this gait it could cross ground more speedily and with far less effort than could a horse that only progressed at a trot or canter. Amblers could go further and faster than most other horses.

I was riding a prized animal, indeed.

By the time I reached the gate where waited Ludo, I had a huge smile on my face — I simply couldn't help myself.

'She ambles!' I cried, and Ludo's face broke into a grin to match mine.

'You will do well, mistress,' he said. 'My mind is easier now.'

I was still smiling in delight when I raised my head to look to the courtyard.

Instead, I met the eyes of Pengraic, who had been waiting a little further back, leaning nonchalantly against a wall, his arms still folded.

He caught my gaze, gave me an expressionless look, then turned away.

CHAPTER EIGHT

W^e departed Rosseley shortly afterward. The king, Summersete and Scersberie had been with the column forming on the road outside. Once the earl had mounted, he and Stephen led our contingent from the courtyard and the column began to move westward.

I turned on Dulcette's back for a last look at Rosseley. The sun was well up and the manor house gleamed golden in the light, the meadows and orchard green and verdant. I must have intuited somehow that I would never return for the house blurred as tears formed in my eyes, and I turned back to the road ahead, wiping at my eyes as I did so.

I kept Dulcette close to the cart which held Lady Adelie, Mistress Yvette and Evelyn as well as Rosamund and the baby, John. Alice and Emmette rode their horses beside me; the twin boys, Ancel and Robert, also horsed, were far ahead close to their father.

The column held some sixty or seventy knights and men-at-arms. I was somewhat relieved to see that, while they all carried weapons, none wore their maille hauberks, which indicated that the king and earls did not think we were under any immediate threat. I thought the knights and soldiers must be relieved also, for today promised to be warm and the maille hauberks would have been stifling. Most of the knights and soldiers rode at the head of the column, but some fifteen or so brought up the rear behind me.

As well there were two score or so male servants and grooms, and another twelve carts besides that which held Lady Adelie. We travelled fast, even the carts, for we had some fifteen miles of roads and byways to travel to get to our first destination — Walengefort Castle, residence of the Earl of Summersete.

Dulcette was a delight to ride, her amble so smooth and comfortable I could relax completely. She and I had come to some silent agreement: we would respect each other. She no longer tried to run away with me, and I allowed her freedom in choosing her own path and pace. About mid-morning Ludo rode past and asked how I did. I simply smiled in return, and I think he was happy, giving me a nod as he rode on.

The day wore on. We stopped briefly at noon, resting under the shade of a group of beech trees and eating a lunch of fruit and bread and beer. I ate with the countess and her children (save the twin boys who stayed near their father), while the men cloistered themselves into two groups a little way off. Eventually, as servants packed away the lunch and men remounted their horses, Stephen came over to assist his mother and Evelyn back into the cart.

Then he led Dulcette over to a fallen log so that I might mount.

I was a little self-conscious with him this close and with his attention only for me. He and I had exchanged only a handful of words since he'd returned to Rosseley with his father, and the only times I had seen him were with other people attending and little chance for us to speak.

Now Stephen fussed over me as I mounted, making sure my feet were well set in the stirrups and the girth tight.

I prayed that the earl was not watching.

'Maeb,' he said, finally stopping to look up at me, one hand on Dulcette's rein that I might not ride forward.

He paused, and I looked at him, feeling as if my heart turned over at the sight of his warm, handsome face.

He smiled, slowly. 'I look forward to escorting you home to Pengraic,' he said, his smile stretching even wider.

Then he slapped Dulcette's neck and walked back to where his own horse waited.

I sat there a few minutes longer, searching for every layer of meaning to that short statement, and what that look in his eyes conveyed.

Soon enough, I recollected myself to look round. Surely the earl would be sitting his horse, staring at me silently.

But he was far distant, still on the ground, talking animatedly with the Earl of Scersberie, and I had the feeling that he'd not noticed a moment of what had just passed.

I turned Dulcette's head for the road, where Lady Adelie's cart waited for the main column to ride on.

That afternoon Stephen pulled his horse back to ride for a while by his mother's cart, talking to her.

Together with Alice (Emmette rode ahead, before her mother's cart), I rode a little distance behind the cart, which gave me the opportunity to sit and watch Stephen to my heart's content. Of all the nobles and royalty in this travelling band, I thought him the most uncomplicated.

Eventually Stephen reined in his horse so that he fell back to where Alice and I rode.

'Alice,' he said, 'our lady mother wishes to speak with you.'

Alice gave a nod and pushed her horse forward.

Stephen smiled. 'And now I have my chance to dally a little while with the lovely Mistress Maeb.'

'You should not,' I said, 'for your father will be angry with me. He thinks I have unseemly ambitions.'

'For *me?*' Stephen said. 'I am indeed flattered, mistress.'

'My lord, my only security is this household, and —'

'I understand Maeb. I will stay only a moment. After Oxeneford, however ...' He smiled, and I could not help but return it.

After Oxeneford Stephen would lead this column, the earl left far behind and with no chance of seeing how often we talked.

'When you attended us in the solar the day before yesterday,' Stephen said, 'you heard some dark things, yet you have been unable to talk of them since, nor seek any reassurance. When there is a chance, after Oxeneford, I will talk more openly and fully with you of those things. I wish I could do it now ... but ...'

'Is it truly as bad as it sounded, my lord?'

'Yes. I am sorry. There will be dark days ahead, Maeb. I pray we have left Rosseley in good enough time, that ...'

His voice drifted off, but I knew what he meant. *That we have avoided the plague.*

Then the good humour returned to his face. 'You looked so beautiful that night in the great hall,' he said. 'My father ought to be more worried about *my* ambitions. Not yours.'

With that, and a final wicked smile, he booted his horse into a canter and moved forward to rejoin his father.

That evening, as the sun was setting, we rode through Craumares then across the arched stone bridge over the Thames into Summersete's castle of Walengefort. It had been a long day, very tiring, and I was glad enough to hand Dulcette over to a groom and aid my lady (and Evelyn, who was still in great pain) to their beds for the night. When I lay down by Evelyn, we exchanged only a few words before I slipped gratefully into sleep.

We rose early again the next day, mounting our horses and carts just after dawn to ride northward to Oxeneford. We followed the Thames now, riding a wide and well-kept road by the riverside. I kept Dulcette behind my lady's cart, with the two older girls, Alice and Emmette for company. We did not talk much, for the pace was even faster than the previous day, and several times I saw either the countess or Evelyn wince as the cart rattled along.

Both the earl and Stephen stayed out of sight at the head of the column with the king. We had left Summersete in his castle, together with the twins Robert and Ancel (joining his household earlier than expected), but I'd overheard two of the knights saying he might be joining the king at Oxeneford within a few days.

I did, however, have another companion for part of the ride. After our break for the noon meal, and as Stephen had yesterday, Saint-Valery joined myself and the two girls for a while. I was more than cautious of him after what Evelyn had told me, and answered his questions as briefly as I might.

'Have I said anything to offend you, mistress?' he asked eventually, keeping his voice low that Alice and Emmette on the other side of me might not hear.

'I worry only to whom you might repeat what I say,' I said.

'Ah,' he said. 'Mistress Maeb, you are far beyond your rustic childhood now. For better or worse, you have become part of a noble household, and thus will inevitably be drawn into the dealings of the court. Treat everyone with suspicion if you must, but be courtly and gracious in the doing, or else soon your enemies shall outnumber your allies.'

'Forgive me, my lord,' I said, stung by his rebuke. 'It is just that I feel adrift within a dark marshland, where each and every word might sink me to my doom. To me it appears that silence is the greater safety. I fumble. I am sorry for it.'

'Perhaps I also should beg forgiveness, for I have been peppering you with questions and allowed you to ask none. What would you know? This,' he waved a hand at the column containing all its knights and lords, 'must appear so strange to you.'

'Oh, it does, my lord.' I thought for a moment. 'My lord, I am curious as to why the king, together with the Earls of Summersete and Scersberie, came to Rosseley with my Lord Pengraic. I know of the reason why they travel to Oxeneford, as must you —'

'Elegantly put, mistress. For that you have my admiration.'

'— but why did they accompany my Lord Pengraic? Surely they could have ridden straight for Oxeneford? Allowed my Lord Pengraic to collect his household and join them there?'

We continued in silence a brief while, Saint-Valery looking to the road ahead while he thought. Eventually he glanced over to ensure that Alice and Emmette were not close — they were chatting between themselves and had fallen back a little — before he spoke.

'Matters are difficult,' Saint-Valery said, 'as well you know. There is the … sickness … and there is also increasing unrest.' He paused again, picking his words carefully. 'Pengraic is a powerful Marcher Lord, Maeb. He is the most independent and powerful of Edmond's nobles. He controls great wealth and land and thus men-at-arms. He is, in effect, a king in all but name. Edmond, as well Scersberie and Summersete, accompanied him to Rosseley to ensure that Pengraic did, in fact, come to Oxeneford and not make straight for the Welsh Marches where he might collect his mighty garrison and … well … Edmond merely wanted to make sure Pengraic was at his side as an ally and not at his back like … well …'

I was horrified, and more than a little angry on my lord's behalf. I did not like the man, and feared him, yet I felt intensely loyal to him if only for my lady's sake.

'Has not Edmond enough enemies and evils at his door,' I said, not thinking that the words might go straight back to the king, 'that he needs to start inventing new ones?'

Saint-Valery looked at me, then he burst into laughter as he had when I'd snapped at him during the feast. He calmed somewhat. 'You are so much the —' he began.

'Saint-Valery,' snapped a voice behind us, and we both swivelled in our saddles.

Pengraic was directly behind us, his horse's head nodding between the rumps of Saint-Valery's horse and Dulcette.

Sweet Jesu, I thought, how long has he been there?

Saint-Valery evidently thought the same thing, for he had gone white.

'To the front, if you will,' Pengraic said to Saint-Valery, and the man gave a nod and kicked his horse forward.

Pengraic drew his bright bay courser level with Dulcette, graced me momentarily with one of his expressionless looks, then moved forward himself.

I sat Dulcette, shaking as badly as a leaf in a storm. Pengraic had almost certainly overheard what Saint-Valery said, and then my reply. I was not so foolish as to congratulate myself for saying what was, as it happened, precisely the right thing at the right moment. Instead I realised again how close I had come to losing my place in the Pengraic household and embracing penury. I could just as easily have nodded and smiled at Saint-Valery. Even agreed with him, simply to appear gracious to a man who had so recently accused me of ungraciousness.

My shaking grew as I thought that, on the other hand, Saint-Valery might believe that I *had* known Pengraic was there, and had thus structured my outraged response for the earl's benefit — and Saint-Valery's (and through him the king's) discomfort.

And how had Pengraic come to be so close behind us? I had thought him at the head of the column. I did not remember seeing him ride past us to the rear.

I *was* glad I was going to Pengraic Castle. The court and its treacherous eddies were too frightening and dangerous for me. I could not wait to escape them — and Pengraic himself.

Dark and damned the castle might be, but I thought it would prove considerably safer than these sun-drenched lowlands.

CHAPTER NINE

We reached Oxeneford late in the afternoon. The king had a palace outside the city walls, and it was there we would stay for a few days before travelling on to Pengraic in the Welsh Marches.

We skirted the city, turning for the north-western meadows, and suddenly I saw laid out in the fields beyond the palace the encampment of what appeared to me to be a large army. There were scores of tents with pennants flying the colours and heraldic arms of their occupants, long horse lines, cooking fires, men at weapon practice or standing about idling, and maille-smiths sweating over their work. It made the threat of unrest, even outright rebellion, seem very real to me, whereas before it had only been something lurking in the shadows of words and frowns.

Much of the column peeled off into this encampment, but Edmond, his closest retainers (including Saint-Valery), Scersberie and Pengraic and his household continued into the palace. I helped Lady Adelie and Evelyn out of the cart, then took control of John and Rosamund. Evelyn was moving better now, although she was still stiff and sore. We went inside the palace and were shown to our chambers. We were all glad to be allowed to rest, before the evening meal in the king's great hall.

Unlike the meal at Rosseley, Evelyn and myself, and even Mistress Yvette, sat at places far down the hall tables, where we only talked among ourselves during a repast I thought indifferent to that offered at Rosseley. Evelyn was feeling uncomfortable, and no one noticed when I decided to accompany her back to our chamber where I thought I would help her to bed.

I stayed with her for a while, until Mistress Yvette returned and then went with her to help Lady Adelie to her bed. The earl and his countess had a magnificent chamber on the top floor of the main palace building, with a cleverly arched and panelled ceiling, and with its own great fireplace. Their bed, heavily draped in well-worked crimson hangings and festooned with furs, dominated the room and I spent more than a few minutes in some envy at their comforts.

The earl was elsewhere, and once Mistress Yvette and I had disrobed Lady Adelie and helped her into the luxurious bed, Yvette and I carefully folded the countess' robes and lay them in one of the two chests in the chamber.

'Maeb?'

I turned to the countess, sitting in her bed with her ever-present book of devotion in her hands.

'Maeb, Yvette is weary, although she will not speak of it, and is troubled by an ache in her temples. Will you attend me tomorrow morning, at rising? I would allow Yvette a morning to lie abed, for her own rest.'

'Of course, madam.' I was both pleased and a little nervous. I had attended the countess on occasion in the morning, aiding her to rise, but always with Mistress Yvette present.

'In that hour before dawn, if you will,' Lady Adelie said. 'I would rise early for my prayer on the morrow.'

Privately I thought the countess could do with a lie abed herself, for she looked strained, but I merely nodded, dipped in courtesy, made sure that neither the countess nor Mistress Yvette needed me for anything else, and returned to the chamber I shared with Evelyn.

I had thought to find Evelyn asleep, but she was awake, and in some discomfort.

'Evelyn? What is it?'

'Oh, nothing too troublesome, Maeb. Do not fret. It is but this back. It cramps and will not let me sleep.'

'I will fetch a hot poultice for you, Evelyn. It will relax the griping.'

I could see Evelyn struggling with herself. I knew Evelyn well. Part of her would not wish to trouble me, the other part desperately yearned for that poultice.

I laughed. 'Do not fret, Evelyn. I know the way to the kitchens, for I went there earlier for madam's posset. I will fetch the poultice, and then you will rest easy.'

Evelyn's face relaxed in relief. 'Thank you, Maeb.'

I found the kitchen easily enough, and tried to keep out of the cooks' and servants' way as I made a warm barley and herb poultice for Evelyn's back. I wrapped it in some linen, then begged a wooden bowl from one of the cooks that I might carry it more easily.

It was late night now, and many of the torches had burned low. I crossed the small courtyard to the building where our chamber lay, but somehow took the wrong door. I only realised I had mislaid my way when I walked into a store chamber filled with barrels and realised that I had not passed through it on my way to the kitchen. It was very dark, the only light coming from a couple of open windows high in the walls, and I muttered to myself, cross that I had lost my way.

I turned for the door, intending to retrace my steps back into the courtyard where I might find the right door, when I stopped, so terrified that I froze, unable to move or even think.

The door was open, and there must have been a torch in the chamber beyond, for what stood — *crouched* — in the door was clearly silhouetted.

It was an imp — my mind registered that at least. How often had I seen them, crawling in stone across the walls of churches, or grinning down from their gutters high above?

It had a grotesque lumpy body, its limbs thin and stick-like, its hands and feet over-sized and splayed as it rested on all fours, watching me.

A long, skinny tail snaked out behind it, threshing to and fro, like a cat stalking.

Its face was round, with a pig's snout, its teeth small and sharp.

A red forked tongue flicked out as I watched, and its luminous eyes slowly blinked.

Then it hissed and rose on its back legs as if to strike out. Standing, it was taller than a man.

I shrieked, stumbling backward, certain that it would take my life and carry my soul down to hell.

Suddenly something caught me about the waist and I was violently wrenched to one side.

'Get thee back to thy foul master, imp!' a man's voice cried, and I heard the sound of steel being drawn.

I had stumbled against a barrel, and it was only after I had found my balance and could look up that I realised it was Pengraic who stood there, stepping forth to the imp with his sword drawn. He made a lunge toward it and the imp gave a soft sibilant hissing sound, as if thwarted, and abruptly vanished.

A low cry came from my throat, and everything momentarily blurred and darkened about me. I felt the earl grab me about the waist again, and he guided me to sit down on a barrel that lay on its side. He sat holding me until he was sure that I would no longer faint.

'*Saints damn you!* What do you here?'

'I am s... s... sorry, my lord. I came only for a poultice for Evelyn's back.' Amazingly, I realised I still held the thing in my hands. I had been confronted by an imp from hell, but I had not dropped Evelyn's poultice. 'I lost my way ... I am ... I am ... sorry.'

'You are a most foolish woman, mistress!' the earl said as his hands relaxed away from my waist.

I thought to rise, almost as fearful of the earl in his bad temper as I had been of the imp, but he stopped me.

'Wait. We need to talk, then I will escort you back to your chamber.'

'Yes, my lord.'

'You will not say anything, not to anyone, about what you saw here tonight.'

'No, my lord.'

'Not to anyone, Maeb! Swear it!'

'I *swear*, my lord!'

'Not to Evelyn, not to my lady wife, not to Stephen. To *no one*. It would cause panic and dismay, and that we do not need.'

'I will not speak, my lord.'

We were close enough that I could see his face, and I could see that he watched me carefully, his eyes narrowed. Finally he gave a small nod. 'Yes, I will trust you. You will not speak.'

What if he had decided the other way? That I could not be trusted? What would he have done?

I had been trembling, but now I trembled more.

'You are not in danger, Maeb. The imp will not trouble you again … but stray here no more. Stay close to your lady and your chamber.'

I nodded. 'But the imp has seen me, my lord … did it come for me? How do I know it won't return?'

'Maeb, just trust me. It will not return for you. It was not you it wanted.'

'Then who? I —'

'Stop questioning my words, Maeb!'

I cringed at the sharpness of his voice, and he sighed. 'Maeb, now I am sorry for my roughness of speech. And I have yet to express my gratitude for what you said to Saint-Valery this day. That was well said, and I thank you for it.'

I knew he was trying to take my mind away from the imp, but still I appreciated his words. 'Thank you, my lord.'

I wanted to leave. I kept glancing toward the door, but the earl sat as if he still had something to say but could not quite find the words for it. I grew more uncomfortable by the moment, and wished desperately I was back in my chamber, curled up with Evelyn, finding refuge in a deep, unknowing sleep.

The earl turned a little, enough so that he faced me directly. 'Maeb, there is a dark flood coming. You will need to be strong.'

'My lord?'

'The plague. It will be worse than you could ever imagine, worse than you have been told.'

I did not know what to say, for his words struck great fear into me.

'Remember that you promised all your care for my wife.'

'I will be strong, for my lady's sake.'

'Good.' His voice had relaxed now, so I dared also to relax.

A little too soon, as it happened.

'Saint-Valery has asked for your hand in marriage,' he said.

'No!' I said.

'You know full well why he has asked for you, don't you.'

Of course I knew. The king did not want to touch me until I had been wed. It was his idea of courtesy. Saint-Valery would do anything to smooth the path for his master. I was to be used and then discarded in the king's casual game of lust at court. I felt ill, and I think some of what I felt showed on my face.

'Do not worry, Maeb. You will go to Pengraic and there you will be safe. Who knows who or what will be left standing when this flood recedes.'

'Thank you, my lord.' I did not truly know what to say. They were the safest words I could think of.

'Now take that poultice to Evelyn, and forget all you have seen and heard this night — save your vow of silence.'

'I will, my lord,' I said.

I rose, dipped in courtesy, and left the store room. The earl seemed to have forgotten his promise to escort me to my chamber, but I did not mind. I was glad enough to leave him.

I returned safe to my chamber, and applied the poultice to Evelyn's back. She did not appear to notice anything amiss, and I said not a word of what had occurred.

I lay beside her, the poultice warming us both as we curled together, but I did not sleep that night. The hissing imp invaded my thoughts whenever I closed my eyes, and if it was not the imp, it was the earl's words. *There is a dark flood coming. It will be worse than you could ever imagine, worse than you have been told.*

It was all I could think about. The imp and the earl's bleak warning. They pushed away any other thought I may have had, whether of Saint-Valery's offer for my hand, or whatever query I may have raised in my own mind as to what purpose the earl may have had for lurking in that store room.

I was exhausted and gritty-eyed when I crept into the earl and countess' chamber early the next morning. I stoked their fire, adding more wood, set two bowls of water to warm on the hearth, then lit several candles with a taper from the fire.

'My lady?' I bent over her side of the bed, laying my hand gently on her shoulder.

She sighed, then opened her eyes, and thus we began our day.

The countess pushed back the cover and sat on the side of the bed. She took several deep breaths as I pulled a half mantle about her shoulders, and I thought she struggled a little with them. She was very pale, and her distended belly heavily veined, and I wondered yet again how much this child was taking from her.

'My lady?' I murmured, concerned for her.

'I am well enough, Maeb. Fetch the water, and I will wash.'

The earl rose as I carried one of the bowls back to the countess, and as she washed so did he, crouching by the fire and grunting as he splashed water over his face and the back of his neck.

It seemed strange to be working silently with my lady as I helped her to dress, first in her linen chemise and stockings, then in a brightly coloured kirtle that slipped over her head and belted loosely about her swollen body. I combed out and re-braided her hair. Behind us the earl was dressing with the aid of his valet, Charles, and as he and the countess prepared for the day they exchanged quiet words about the countess' continuation of her journey to Wales.

It was almost as if I (and Charles) were invisible to the earl and his wife. They had been naked before me, yet the greater familiarity was allowing me to watch this routine intimacy of one of the most remarkable dynastic marriages in England. There was no passion between them, but there was a strong respect, and they both listened to the other.

It was only when Charles was gone and both the earl and his wife fully dressed, the earl shaking out his mantle in preparation to going outside, that they dragged me into the conversation.

'I saw Maeb last night,' said the earl to the Lady Adelie, and my heart started into my mouth, 'as she was going to bed and I returning to you. I spoke briefly with her about Saint-Valery's offer. She was not pleased.'

Lady Adelie turned to regard me. 'It is a good offer, Maeb. He is a man of wealth, with several lordships and estates and great influence. It is a far better match than I could have hoped for you.'

I stood with my eyes downcast, not knowing how to respond.

'Maeb understands what comes attached to the offer,' Pengraic said.

'Ah,' Lady Adelie said. She took a breath, considering the matter. 'This must seem strange to you, Maeb, and perhaps not welcome, but you have yet to learn the ways of the court. The king is a kindly man and a generous one. He has a warm heart. In many respects, he is the one who will provide the security in your life, not Saint-Valery.'

'I cannot believe that you recommend this path to me, madam,' I said, almost in tears. 'Why not trade me in the cattle yards next market day? You may yet get an even higher offer for me.'

'You have a poor habit of speaking your mind, mistress,' the earl snapped. 'It is not pleasing, nor will it ease your path in life.'

'I have not spoken *all* I could,' I snapped back at him, so angry and hurt that I cared not what I said. 'As well you know, my lord.'

The countess looked at her husband, an eyebrow raised.

'I will not accept Saint-Valery's offer,' I said, still looking at the earl, 'unless you force my hand.'

Lady Adelie sighed, but the earl held my gaze steadily. I was playing a dangerous game here, for he knew that I was threatening to break my silence about last night.

'No wonder your father did not manage to marry you away,' Pengraic said softly, 'for you have the temper and petulance of a harridan. What man could possibly want you for a wife? You would curdle the milk in the dairy as soon as you laid eyes on it.'

'Raife,' Lady Adelie murmured.

'I will tell Saint-Valery that the matter will be settled once the threat of the plague has passed,' Pengraic continued. 'Until then, mistress, you will endeavour to keep your tongue still in that waspish mouth of yours until you are well clear of this court and on your way home to Pengraic. You will *not* refuse Saint-Valery outright; the matter can remain in abeyance for the time being. Madam,' he turned to Lady Adelie, 'you have a long journey to the Marches in which you can instil some manners into this girl. God help us all if she behaves like this at court!'

With that, he was off, slamming the door behind him.

I fell to my knees before Lady Adelie, my tears now spilling over. 'Madam,' I said, 'I am truly sorry for what I said. It was fear that spoke.'

'You must surely loathe the idea of marriage to Saint-Valery,' she said. 'But, girl, do you expect to choose your own husband? It will never be. *I* was not allowed to choose my husband, nor did I have any say in who that husband might be. Saint-Valery is *not* a bad man, and he is of a far better rank and of greater wealth and estates than you could ever have hoped!'

'But it shall be a sham so that the king can —'

'The king's fancy will last but a season,' Lady Adelie said, 'and in the meantime you will have won for yourself a position in society that but a few weeks ago was as far beyond you as are the stars in the firmament. The marriage will be no sham; it will be honoured by Saint-Valery, who will receive the king's favour for it. It is an advantageous marriage to you and to this household.'

Ah, the nub of it. Both the earl and the countess saw this match as a means of placing their own factor in the court and bed of the king, while Saint-Valery was likely anticipating yet more favours from the king for doing his will.

'Maeb,' the countess said, her tone kindly, 'you have come from a simple and uncomplicated world and in a short time have been hurled into such … events. It is overwhelming.'

'You and the earl are asking me to forsake my vows of marriage,' I said, unable to believe the devout countess could overlook this small detail.

'Sometimes,' she said, 'in worldly matters, one has to bend with the wind.'

'Would you have done so, madam?'

Again I risked her anger, but I was still upset and more than a little angry myself.

'For what favour and advantage it would bring to my family,' she said, 'yes, I would. Oh, Maeb. It is but a man. They are simple creatures and so easily sated. You have such a wit and spirit about you …' She paused, sighing softly. 'My dear, such an alliance can purchase you influence; wealth, if that is what you desire, or offices and favours for your children. Marriage among our rank is not merely affection between a man and a woman, but a power-building exercise, a constant accumulation of rank and privilege and estates and offices for ourselves, but more so for our children. It is a game, Maeb, and one you do not wish to lose.

'Now, come with me to chapel, and let us say our prayers. Remember, always in life there is a priest to whom you can confess, and wash away your sins.'

Later that morning, when we had returned to Lady Adelie's chamber, she noticed that the earl had left behind his gloves.

'Oh,' she said, 'he will be cross, but no doubt is too busy to return for them. Maeb, will you take them to him? He will not be far — ask any of the king's servants or men-at-arms and they will tell you.'

It was not a task I felt happy about, but I could surely leave them with a servant somewhere to hand to the earl.

I made for the main quarters of the king, where I knew he met with his advisers and nobles. I would not be allowed in, so I felt sure that I could safely leave the offending gloves with a guard.

But the earl was not there.

'He has just left,' said one of the guards. 'He and his son are heading for the chapel.'

My heart sank, because now I would need to speak to the earl, stand face to face with him, meet his eye, and I did not think I was quite courageous for that yet, not after our morning's confrontation. Already I was regretting pushing him so far, for I did not think now he would treat me kindly in future dealings.

I hurried for the chapel, crossing the main courtyard, and saw the distinctive figure of the earl in the distance, Stephen to one side of him, and another man to his other, to whom I did not pay attention. I wanted only to hand these damned gloves to the earl and then return to my lady, with whom I had much mending of fences to accomplish.

I hurried as fast as I dared over the cobbles, slippery from a recent shower of rain, but even as I drew close the men started to run lightly up the steps toward the open door of the chapel.

The last thing I wanted was to be forced into sidling up to the earl at his devotions.

'My lord!' I cried.

All three stopped, and turned, as one.

A ray of sunshine suddenly broke through the low clouds and illumed the three of them: Stephen, Pengraic … and the king, Edmond.

I couldn't move. I was frozen by the vision on the steps. They all had their gaze on me. Stephen's face was creased in a wide, open grin. Whatever the earl felt was locked away tight behind his impassive façade. The king … Edmond looked at me with a warm regard, and it suddenly struck me that what I feared in the proposed marriage to Saint-Valery was not Edmond, or what he asked, but Saint-Valery and a lifetime of regret at his side.

The sun's ray bathed the three men in a golden, ethereal light, and I knew God had handed me this moment. It caught me in the thrall of premonition, and I realised then, in that instant, that my life would be bounded by the knight, the earl and the king, and no other.

What I did not know then was that this was the last time I would ever see these three men together.

'Mistress Maeb?' said the earl, and somehow I freed myself from my thrall, and walked up the steps toward him.

'Your gloves, my lord,' I said, handing them over, then I dipped in courtesy toward Edmond, nodded at Stephen, and turned my back on them and walked away.

I walked easy, for somehow, in a manner I could yet not discern, my entire life was settled in that one golden moment.

Whatever happened now was in fate's hands, and no manner of struggling would change a thing.

CHAPTER TEN

The next day Evelyn woke me. She'd been up early to go down to the kitchens, returning one of the bowls I had used for a poultice.

'Maeb! Maeb!'

I opened my eyes grudgingly. Mistress Yvette was back tending our lady this morning, and I'd been allowed to sleep until Evelyn and I joined them in chapel for our morning prayers.

'Maeb! I have heard news — of a *plague*. Everyone is talking of it.'

I sat up, wondering what I should say.

'I have heard such terrible things. Sweet Mother Mary, Maeb, is this what you had heard in the solar?'

I nodded. No point in trying to deny it now.

'And why we are fleeing back to Pengraic?'

I nodded again.

Evelyn was white, and she sat down on the bed as I rose, washed my face and dressed.

'Is it as terrible as the rumours say?' she said.

'I don't truly know, Evelyn. I have only heard of it in the vaguest way. I know it is why Edmond has fled here, and why we head for Pengraic.'

'The soldiers ... the encampment. Is there treachery? Unrest?'

'Unrest, I think, but I know little more.'

'Sweet Mother of God,' Evelyn muttered again.

'We shall be safe in Pengraic Castle,' I said, hoping it might be enough to comfort Evelyn.

'Maybe. But I worry for my daughter.'

'I am sure she shall be well, Evelyn. The plague is in the south-eastern counties, far, far away from de Tosny's lands north of Glowecestre.'

Evelyn nodded, but her face was tight, and I knew I had not eased her worry at all.

I spent that day with Lady Adelie and Mistress Yvette in the countess' chamber. The earl was nowhere to be seen. The day was uneventful save that shortly before our noon meal Ranulph Saint-Valery attended upon my lady.

Me, rather.

It was a somewhat awkward meeting. Saint-Valery had come to press his marriage suit and to discover how the land lay so far as I was concerned. I supposed he had not worried over this, as few might have foreseen me refusing such an outstanding offer.

I was wrong. Saint-Valery was actually somewhat nervous.

He entered and bowed to the countess, asking after her health and that of the child she carried.

They exchanged pleasantries, then Saint-Valery greeted Mistress Yvette, then turned to me.

'Mistress Maeb, I beg your forgiveness for this intrusion. I … ah … my lord earl tells me that he has informed you of my, um, offer.'

From the corner of my eye I saw Lady Adelie look at me somewhat sharply.

I inclined my head. 'You do me much honour, my lord. Will you sit?'

I moved a little along the bench on which I sat, to give him room, and he perched somewhat stiffly at the other end of the seat.

There was a small silence.

Saint-Valery gave a nervous smile. 'Mistress Maeb. I doubt you could be more surprised over the suddenness of my offer than I was myself. You made a great impression on me that night at Rosseley. I have not been able to put you from my mind since.'

'My lord, it was but a night — an hour or two, perhaps. Yes, it seems strange to me that on such short acquaintance, and with my complete lack of dowry, that you would make such a generous offer.'

'You seem suspicious, mistress.'

'I am,' I said. Lady Adelie was back to glancing sharply at me. 'I cannot think why you have made the offer, my lord. I have little to recommend me.'

Saint-Valery's eyes widened slightly. 'You have a great deal to recommend you, Maeb. May I speak plainly, for I have little time before I ride out. The offer is genuine, Maeb. You may look for the courtly subterfuge, but there is none.'

My face must clearly have registered my disbelief.

'There is no other voice behind mine,' Saint-Valery said. 'No shadow overlaying mine. Discard whatever rumour you may have heard.'

Both his eyes and voice were steady. I no longer knew what to think. I was still caught in the vision I'd had the day previously of the three men illumed in the shaft of sunlight, and I could not bring myself to believe Saint-Valery would play any significant role in my life. The knight, the earl and the king, yes, but not the poet.

'I must leave court this afternoon to travel to the queen at Elesberie,' he said. 'You leave tomorrow for the Welsh Marches. All of our lives are uncertain now. Perhaps this winter, when all is settled and the plague passed, I may come and press my suit to you, Mistress Maeb. You shall need a good reason to say nay to me then, if you still wish to hesitate. I wish you well, Maeb, in the trials ahead.'

He rose, and bowed toward the countess. 'My lady, I beg your leave.'

She half raised a hand. 'Before you go, Saint-Valery. What news is there? I know that overnight rumours have throbbed about this palace, but as yet I've had no hard report.'

'The news is bad, my lady. Many die, from Dovre to Meddastone, and moving ever further west. This plague is so vicious that fields are left untended and the sick are left to die alone. Towns burn. I know you have heard of how terribly the plague kills.'

Lady Adelie gave a sharp nod.

'People flee,' Saint-Valery said, 'seeking refuge elsewhere. Edmond fears that they will spread the sickness further. He has commanded that soldiers man the roads that lead into the south-east and turn all back who seek to flee. Cantuaberie is a catastrophe. Much of it has burned. There is unrest and brigandry where the plague strikes hardest. I … There are no good tidings, madam, I am sorry. Move west as fast as you can and as soon as you can. I pray God and his saints protect you.'

We three women simply sat and stared at Saint-Valery.

He looked us each in the eye, then he bowed and left us.

I wondered if I would ever see him again.

CHAPTER ELEVEN

W e left very early the next morning. I was glad, for the king's palace and military encampment at Oxeneford had become an unsettling place. I wanted nothing more than to journey westward, all the way into the Welsh Marches, where surely the plague could not follow and life would not be so complicated. Between what I had heard in the solar, the news Saint-Valery had given us (as well as his marriage offer), the imp I had seen, and the earl's warning about the dark flood, I simply wanted to get away. I was growing ever more frightened, and I was not afraid to admit it.

I was not alone in my fright. I slept little on the night before we left, and I know Evelyn did not either. We lay side by side, wide awake, sometimes exchanging a word or two, but mostly lost in our thoughts as we contemplated the terror that had gripped the south-east of the country. When we rose, far earlier than we needed, it was to find that the countess and Mistress Yvette were also awake, dressed and pacing to and fro waiting for the horses to be saddled and harnessed and our escort to be ready.

Evelyn, the nurse and I had the children down in the courtyard well before dawn. Early it might be, but the courtyard was a bustle of activity. Torches burned feverishly in their wall brackets, grooms and servants hurried this way and that. Horses, sensing everyone's underlying unrest, were nervous and difficult to handle. We kept the children well out of the way, and were glad when the groom who drove the cart the Lady Adelie and they were to ride in brought the cart to us and we could pack our belongings and the children inside.

'Mistresses. Good morn.'

It was Stephen. He looked drawn and tired, and sterner than I had ever seen him. He wore a dark mantle about his shoulders against the chill, caught with a jewelled pin, but I was dismayed to see the glint of maille underneath and his coif folded down over the collar of the mantle. He was wearing his hauberk, and a sword and dagger besides. Nothing indicated the seriousness of our situation more than that he was armoured.

'Are you ready to leave?' he said. 'Evelyn, are you riding or journeying in the cart?'

'Riding, my lord,' she said. 'My back is well enough, and it will do me good to ride.'

He nodded, then looked at me, the merest hint of a smile on his face. 'Dulcette is saddled waiting for you, Maeb. I think she has missed you, for she is stamping her feet in impatience to be off.'

I could see something of the man he would become in his face this morning, and it calmed me. 'And I am anxious to see her, my lord, and set her head to the road.'

He looked over my shoulder. 'Ah, my lady mother and lord father.' He walked over to them, helping his mother into the cart, then engaging in a conversation with his father.

A groom came over, leading Dulcette along with Evelyn's horse and he aided us both into the saddle. Dulcette was eager to go, jittery on her feet, skidding this way and that and tossing her head. I hoped we would leave soon, for it was proving difficult to keep her calm in this crowded courtyard. From the corner of my eye I saw Stephen mount up, barking out an order to the column of men already mounted.

I pulled Dulcette to one side, not wanting to get in the way. I was looking to the centre of the courtyard, watching Stephen and the mounted knights and soldiers, and jumped when someone grabbed Dulcette's rein and pulled us closer to the wall.

'Maeb.' It was the earl. He stood close by Dulcette's shoulder, looking up at me. 'You *will* be safe at Pengraic.'

'Yes, my lord. Thank you.'

'Listen to Stephen. Do what he commands. Until you travel beyond Glowecestre you will not truly be safe.'

'Yes, my lord.'

He hesitated, then moved very close and spoke quietly. 'Remember your vow of silence about the imp, Maeb. *Never* speak of it to anyone: not Evelyn, not Stephen, not my wife, not any priest you may feel like confessing to, or impressing.'

'I will not speak, my lord.'

Again he looked at me searchingly.

'I *will* not,' I said. 'I vow it.'

'Very well. Make certain you keep that vow.'

'My lord, what if another imp comes back? I worry —'

'You will be safe enough, Maeb. You will not be troubled by such again.'

'Truly?'

'Truly. The imps are after other prey than you.'

Something in the way he spoke made me relax. I believed him utterly. There would be no more imps. 'Thank you, my lord.'

He patted Dulcette's neck and released her rein. 'Go then, Maeb. May God and His saints travel with you.'

He stepped away and vanished into a shadowy doorway. I looked a long moment, trying to find him again, but Stephen rode his courser near. 'Maeb! Pull over here by the cart. And *stay* close to it. Do not wander to this side or the other. Yes?'

'Yes, my lord.'

He was off, shouting to Evelyn and to his sister Alice to also keep close, then we were moving, the horses skittering and snorting, the carts rumbling, and on the road to Pengraic Castle.

As we left the courtyard I twisted in the saddle, thinking to see the earl again, and perhaps even the king, for some small conceited part of me fancied he would come out to see us (*me*) off, but there was no sign of either man. I sighed, and looked to the front and the journey ahead.

We were a goodly company. In addition to the cart which carried my lady, Mistress Yvette, the nurse, Rosamund and John, there were the twelve other carts carrying various household goods, including gold and silver plate and expensive hangings and cloths that were to return to Pengraic Castle. Myself, Evelyn, Alice and Emmette rode good palfreys; the twin boys, Ancel and Robert were no longer with us, for they had joined Summersete's household at Walengefort.

There were several senior house servants who rode with us, as well as a cleric who would be leaving us at Glowecestre, and two minstrels who wanted to travel westward to Cirecestre and had joined our company for the protection it afforded — their payment for this privilege was to keep us entertained in the evenings. Eight grooms led strings of spare horses and the war destriers that were not currently being ridden.

To protect us came a large company of knights and horsed soldiers. There were two score knights, all heavily weaponed and all wearing their maille, and some fifty of the soldiers.

I thought the entire assemblage almost a small army. While I felt safe, I wondered at the ease with which we would travel. Sweet Jesu, who would put us up? How would we manage on the roads?

As it happened, I need not have worried. Stephen and his father had plotted out a journey that used the lesser travelled holloways and driftways that snaked through the countryside. While they were not the main roads, they were nonetheless well maintained and reasonably wide, for they were used for the droves of cattle and sheep that moved from market to market across the country. The holloways and driftways felt safe, having relatively little traffic on them (the majority of the droving traffic would not truly start until the autumn fairs), and they made for swift and easy travelling. They were exceedingly pleasant, for spring flowers covered their banks and they wound through some of the loveliest country I had yet seen.

We did not travel as fast or as hard as we had on the two day journey from Rosseley to Oxeneford. Instead, we moved at a comfortable, steady pace which covered perhaps half the distance each day, sometimes a little more. It was easier on everyone — as well as the horses — and particularly on Lady Adelie, who found the journey more difficult than others.

We met few people: a handful of pilgrims, some shepherds driving small flocks of sheep, one or two travelling friars, a pedlar or two, a few lines of pack animals and their drivers. There was no trouble on the roads, nor from any of the villages and manors we passed along the way. We did meet with people who asked us for news of what lay behind us, but Stephen was circumspect (as he instructed us to be) and so far as I know did not once mention the plague or the unrest further to the east. I know it was to protect us, but I often wondered what happened to those good folk we met going the other way.

At night we stayed at either religious houses, some of the king's own royal houses and estates along the way (Stephen carried the king's seal, which granted us access whenever we needed it), as well as a few of the earl's outlying manors.

From Oxeneford we travelled to Badentone, and from there to Etherope. We arrived in Cirecestre on the fourth day of our travel, losing the minstrels, and there rested for a day before continuing to Brimesfelde. By this time Stephen had relaxed enough to allow the knights and soldiers to cease wearing their maille, for which I believe all were grateful, for the days grew much warmer as we moved into May and the chain had hung heavy and hot about them. The column grew immediately more cheerful and relaxed once the maille was set into the carts and the men could move more comfortably.

Stephen rode close to the head of the column for the first few days, or back a little further with some of the knights, and I saw little of him during the day. In the evenings he gathered for a while with Lady Adelie, myself, Evelyn, Mistress Yvette and those children not in bed, listening for a while to our chatter, but he did not stay long, for he needed to organise the next day's ride, and I know he spent some time at dicing with some of the knights.

But from the day when he had ordered that the men need not don their hauberks, Stephen became more relaxed and often rode further back in the column. At first he rode next to the cart with his mother, chatting to her, but she grew tired easily, and soon he pulled his horse back to where Evelyn and I rode with Alice and Emmette.

I admit that my heart turned over whenever he did this. The sight of his handsome face, and his easy, charming smile invariably tongue-tied me for long minutes and it was Evelyn who initially responded to his questions and conversation. But I would relax, and join in, and these long hours spent ambling down the back driftways of Glowecestrescire, laughing in easy conversation, were among the happiest of my life.

Sometimes Rosamund, sitting in the cart with her mother, would cry to join us and make such a fuss that Lady Adelie would signal Stephen, who would ride close to the cart and lift the laughing girl into the saddle before him. After a while, she would beg to join me, and so Stephen pulled in close so he could lift Rosamund across to sit before me in the saddle, and

I would warm with pleasure at the bumping of our legs and the graze of his warm hand against mine as he lifted her over.

Rosamund was a sweet child and no bother (and Dulcette, too, was sweet, and did not mind the girl). Usually, after chatting and clapping her hands gleefully for a while, Rosamund would nod off, and I rode along, one arm about her soft, relaxed body leaning in against mine, and Stephen and I would talk as if we had known each other since infancy.

Stephen fooled no one that his interest was chiefly in me. Generally at least one among Evelyn, Alice and Emmette rode with us, but occasionally all three would be riding elsewhere, or called to Lady Adelie's side, or their horses would gradually drop back and they might be caught in a conversation with someone behind us.

Then the conversation between Stephen and myself would veer to more intimate matters, and I found it so easy to talk to him that within a day or two I felt as if I could broach any subject I wanted.

I asked him of the plague, of what he *truly* knew and what he had seen.

'Sweet Jesu, Maeb,' he said, 'it is bad. More terrible than you can imagine. When we left Westminster, the plague had gripped almost all of the south-east in its terror.'

'But London and Westminster were not infected?'

'No. But …' He hesitated. 'You know we think that the plague infects long before it shows its hand. God help us if any of us came into contact with someone carrying the plague and yet who looked perfectly healthy.'

I looked at him, shocked at what he was saying.

'I need to tell you this, Maeb. I am sorry. I do not know if we have brought the plague with us or not. None of us are ill. I ask the knights each evening, I question the soldiers. They are in good health, or so they assure me. Dear God, they all *look* well enough, but …'

'The sickness takes time to manifest itself.'

'Yes. But it has been, what, a fortnight now, and we are all still well. I lie awake at night and worry my stomach into knots with it, but —'

'The king and earl acted as fast as they could, my lord. At least this way, we may yet outrun it.'

We rode a little way in silence, the sunshine a little duller for me now.

Maybe Pengraic Castle was not going to be as impregnable as I had hoped.

'I have heard that the south-east, particularly Dovre and Cantuaberie, are truly terrible, Maeb. Hell has both towns in its grip. People are dying … Jesu! Dying in such agony, the flames melting their flesh, from within and without. At Westminster one knight told me he had heard descriptions of people crouched on the sides of roads like dogs, vomiting forth gouts of sulphurous fungus … choking and retching at the same moment … oh dear saints in heaven, Maeb, why am I telling you this? I am sorry, I just needed …'

To vomit it forth. Yes, I understood. But, oh sweet Mother Mary, what was this thing? My arm tightened about Rosamund, and I started, suddenly horrified that she may have heard her brother speak. I looked down, but she was fast asleep, her face peaceful.

I glanced at Stephen, then nodded at Rosamund.

'Oh, I am sorry, Maeb. I did not think. I will not speak of it again. Not until we are alone.'

Despite my fear at his words, I felt a thrill down my spine at his words. Alone?

'My lord, talk to me of Pengraic Castle. Your lady mother spoke once of it to me, but only in dark words. What is it like?'

To my utter relief, his easy grin was back. 'Pengraic Castle … *dark*? Ah, that is my mother for you. She has never liked it, and so thus our yearly travels to Rosseley. Do you know that I alone of all her babes was born at Pengraic Castle? All the others at Rosseley. Now another babe she will birth at Pengraic and thus maybe he, too, shall love the place. But of the castle … Maeb, I am only happy when I am there.'

He was smiling, looking ahead, introspective.

'But your lady mother, she said …'

'No doubt she said it was inhabited by imps and ghouls,' he said, and I suppressed a jump at the 'imps'.

'But no,' Stephen continued, 'Pengraic is a place of such beauty, such peace … it is a place, Maeb, where you can almost reach into a different world …'

'What world?'

He glanced sideways at me then, as if assessing. Then he shrugged. 'I will show you, when we are there. But know this, Maeb. You have not seen, nor shall you ever see, a place as majestic as Pengraic. It is the greatest castle in England, bar none.'

I would have asked more, but just then Rosamund woke and grizzled, and Stephen rode close and took her from me. Once she was safely in the hands of her nurse, Stephen glanced back at me, then rode forward to talk with several of the knights leading the column.

That evening, as I aided Mistress Yvette to disrobe Lady Adelie for the night, the countess spoke to me.

'My son spends much of the day riding with you, Maeb.'

'Yes, my lady.'

'Nothing can come of this. You know it.'

'I know, my lady. I know it, as does he, and in some strange way ...'

'Yes?'

'In some strange way, it draws us closer. I think he finds me a confidante, and nothing else.'

And yet he had said, *not until we are alone* ...

She considered this. 'Very well, Maeb. But nothing *must* come of this.'

'It will not, my lady. I would not allow anything to threaten my place in this household.'

Lady Adelie nodded at that, apparently satisfied, although I wondered if her weariness made her pass over a subject she might normally have spent more time on.

She appeared exhausted tonight. There were dark shadows under her eyes, her skin was very sallow and her hands trembled slightly when I handed over her nightly posset.

'My lady? Are you unwell?'

'Ah, it is nothing, Maeb. I am always weary when I grow heavy with child, and this is no worse than previous.' She grew waspish. 'Do not fret at me so, for *that* is even more wearisome than the child!'

'I am sorry, my lady.' I withdrew, allowing her words to comfort me. In truth, my mind was so full of Stephen, I did not think to question what she had said.

CHAPTER TWELVE

※◆《◎》◆※

If Lady Adelie had been too tired to pursue me, then Evelyn had plenty of energy. As usual we shared a bed, this night in the female dormitory of a Benedictine lodging house just beyond Brimesfelde. As there were others present, Evelyn had to keep her voice low.

'You need to be careful, Maeb. It is nothing to Lord Stephen. He amuses himself and thinks little of it. You bask in his smile and risk your entire future.'

I sighed. I, too, was weary and wished to sleep.

'By the Virgin, Maeb! Until you are safe wed you live your life at the edge of a precipice. Your place in this household is your only safeguard between you and the roads.'

'Stephen is —'

'Lord Stephen is to be betrothed to an heiress from Normandy. They will formalise the betrothal at Christmastide this year. You are only a pleasing dalliance, Maeb. Nothing else!'

I'd had no idea — all I had heard was the rumour about a princess, and that I had discounted. I felt a wave of black jealousy wash over me and that was the first indication I had that what I felt for Stephen was a little more than simple admiration. I also felt a gut-wrenching fear, an awareness of what such ignorance of my emotions might have meant to my security.

'I should have been careful to ride with you more often,' Evelyn said. 'Maeb, I press this point now because we are close to Glowecestre.'

'Yes?' I was still battling my emotions and to me she made no sense.

'I talked with Lady Adelie today, and she has given me her leave to withdraw from this company there and travel to my daughter's home. I worry about her so. I need to know she is well.'

'Oh no, Evelyn! I shall miss you!' I would, too. Badly. Evelyn had become my closest companion and friend in the Pengraic household. I did not know who I would be able to confide in once she left.

'Maeb, I need you to understand how it is with Stephen. He is promised to a woman of wealth and alliances. He would not in any circumstance forgo that marriage for one to you. Neither would he be allowed to do so. You would only ever be a casual dalliance for Stephen. What might be a summer enjoyment for him would have disastrous consequences for your life. Saint-Valery would withdraw his offer, and you would get none other.'

I remembered that moment in Oxeneford when Stephen, Pengraic and Edmond all stood momentarily bound by that ray of light and I had thought that my life would be bound by all three. But that moment was long past, and my conviction in my intuition had eroded. Evelyn was right. I should not be disdainful of Saint-Valery's offer at all. Lord knows that, had I received it three months past, I would have been delighted beyond measure.

'Be careful where you step,' Evelyn said, 'for our path through life is littered with chasms leading straight to hell.'

We travelled into the town of Glowecestre the next day. Here we were to stay three days at a house owned by the earl, just beyond the town's limits. Here also the cleric would leave us, and Evelyn would travel north to her daughter.

I cried softly when she packed, and carried her small bundle of possessions out to the courtyard where a horse waited. Stephen had detailed three soldiers to accompany her, but there was only I and Mistress Yvette come to say goodbye.

Evelyn kissed me, then hugged me tight. 'I will come to Pengraic once I know my daughter is safe,' she said. 'Until then, you be well, Maeb.'

She turned to Mistress Yvette. 'I will miss my lady, Yvette. I am sorry to have to leave her this abruptly ... but I will be home to Pengraic soon. Before the child is born, I hope.'

They kissed, then one of the soldiers helped Evelyn to mount, and she was gone, clattering out of the courtyard on a raw-boned brown horse.

Glowecestre was the point at which it struck home that Lady Adelie's fatigue might be more serious than she said. We stayed in the earl's town house for three days, days of complete rest, yet my lady's fatigue did not lift at all. For the first time since I'd been in her household Lady Adelie did not rise for early prayers, instead leaving it until mid-morning, when the world was already well on its way, before she rose from her bed. She did not venture far, staying in a chair by the fire until it was time to go back to bed. She ate little and her face remained pale and drawn, the dark circles under her eyes growing stronger. She appeared to have caught a chill, for she coughed occasionally, but said it was nothing.

I did not question her for I knew she would only snap at me, but took as great care of her as I might. I fetched whatever she wanted, sought out a minstrel from the town that she might be entertained, and carried tender morsels from the kitchen to tempt her appetite. Mistress Yvette and I sat with her and kept her company, Mistress Yvette reading from the book of devotion, or the pair of us chattering away in an effort to cheer her.

Stephen came to visit several times each day. I took care to fade away when he came to his mother, avoiding his eye, standing back in the shadow that I might not disturb them … and that I might not catch his regard. I had done much thinking since Evelyn's talk to me, and I realised that I had allowed myself to slip into an affection for Stephen that could lead nowhere but disaster for me. I *did* need to be careful, for my future was not assured. No matter his charm and warmth, Stephen could do little but threaten that future, while Saint-Valery might assure it. I should not disregard Saint-Valery's offer in preference for certain disaster with Stephen.

So I faded into the shadows, and hardened my heart against him.

To be truthful, Stephen did not appear to come to the chamber merely to hope for a glimpse of me. It was clear his mother's fatigue concerned him deeply. He spent some time on our second day in Glowecestre in deep conversation with Mistress Yvette. I did not hear what they said, nor did Mistress Yvette later confide in me, but from the occasional worried glance they threw toward Lady Adelie it was clear what they discussed.

On the third day — the day before we were to depart for the final push to Pengraic — Stephen again came to his mother. This day he voiced his concern openly.

He sat on a stool by her knee, almost like a little boy come to beg his mother's favour, and took her hand between his.

'My lady,' he said, his voice gentle, 'you are not well, and this journey has done you no favours. I grow worried for you and wonder if we should not rest here a little longer that you may regain your strength.'

'We will be safer at Pengraic, Stephen,' Lady Adelie said. 'We will depart tomorrow morn.'

He smiled, and despite myself I felt my heart turn over in my breast. I was chastened by my failure to harden my heart against him completely, and I would have faded further into the shadows if I could, or even quietly left the chamber, but I wanted to know what the outcome of this conversation would be: if we stayed here for the moment, or journeyed on to Pengraic.

'What news of the plague, Stephen?' Lady Adelie said. '*Have* you news?'

Stephen hesitated, then gave a small nod. 'A messenger arrived from my lord father this morning. He has taken a large force and moved south to secure the Cinque Ports, madam, but he is well and sends you his loving greetings.'

'Praise sweet Jesu he continues well,' Lady Adelie said, 'although I fear for him moving toward the Cinque Ports for apparently it is there that the plague rages strongest. I pray sweet Jesu and all saints watch over him and continue to keep him safe.'

She closed her eyes and muttered a small prayer before continuing. 'But the plague, Stephen. How far has it ravaged?'

'It continues to move westward, madam,' he said.

I could see that Stephen squeezed his mother's hand softly. 'But for the moment, you are safe. We can afford a few more days' rest here. You are more important than —'

'No, no,' she said, '*you* are important, Stephen. This plague has not yet passed us by. I can feel it in my bones. Last night ... last night I dreamed ...'

She stopped, and did not continue for a long moment.

'I dreamed such dark things, and thus we will resume our journey on the morrow, Stephen. It is better we reach Pengraic Castle as soon as we may. This child ... I worry about this child. How long, do you think, before we reach Pengraic?'

'Travelling at a comfortable pace? And yes, madam, it will be comfortable, for I will not risk you by hurrying. Maybe five days. Two to Monemude, then a day to Ragheian, yet another to Bergeveny, and then it is but a pleasant morning's ride home.'

Five days. Five days and then we would be at Pengraic Castle.

Stephen rose from his mother, but before he turned to leave the chamber he sought out my eyes.

There was no laughter or warmth there, only soberness and worry.

Once we left Glowecestre we were truly leaving the security of England and moving ever toward the frontier territory of the Welsh Marches. We travelled through winding roads and gentle valleys and forested hills. Sometimes, when we were high enough, I caught a glimpse of mountains to the west. Alice spoke, noticing the direction of my gaze.

'The Black Mountains,' she said. 'Pengraic Castle sits at one of the southern spurs of those mountains, overlooking the Usk Valley.'

I nodded, not moving my eyes from the mountains. As the clouds shifted, so pools of sunlight raced across them. They looked wild and untamed, and a shiver went down my spine.

There lay Pengraic.

We came upon Pengraic on the fifth day, as Stephen had predicted. We'd reached the small town of Bergeveny at mid-afternoon the previous day, the mountains now so close it felt as though I only needed reach out my hand to touch them. I was in a state of part excitement, part dread. Stephen had spoken well of Pengraic, but almost everyone else appeared to have sunk ever further into themselves as we drew close. The past few days I'd barely had more than two words of conversation with anyone. During the day Lady Adelie slipped into a deep reverie as she rocked back and forth in her cart, Mistress Yvette always close by her side; at night she said little as she ate sparingly and then went to her bed.

The girls, Alice and Emmette, hardly talked to me once we'd passed Monemude. It was if, this close to home, they had retreated to a distance befitting nobility, for they no longer rode with me and instead preferred to ride with their brother further ahead in the column.

I was left to trail Lady Adelie's cart on Dulcette by myself, with no company save for the greetings of a passing soldier or knight as he moved up and down the column.

Without Evelyn I felt very alone.

Stephen also no longer came back to talk to me. He did ride back to check on his mother many times during the day, and on these occasions he would nod a greeting to me, but he did not speak.

I wondered if his mother had spoken to him, as well.

Even Rosamund, who had so often enjoyed riding with me, now appeared to disdain the very idea and shrieked if I rode Dulcette to the side of the cart, as if she thought I was about to snatch her from its comforts.

Thus, by the time we left Bergeveny for the morning's journey to Pengraic Castle, I felt quite alone in the world.

That last day we rode swiftly, for no doubt everyone just wanted to be out of the saddle, or the deep discomfort of the tray of a cart. We rode toward a gap in the mountains — the Usk Valley, one of the soldiers told me when I asked. We splashed through many streams and rivulets, across fields and meadows and, close to noon, we entered the valley.

It was wide and fairly flat, a green valley that wound into the distance, bounded on either side by hills and mountains — the Black Mountains to the north, the Bearscathe Mountains to the south. The road followed the path of the River Usk, and was flat and well maintained. The sun shone, the trees on the riverbank dipped and swayed in the breeze, and late spring flowers littered the banks of the road.

It was not what I had expected. All my life I'd heard tales of the Welsh and of their savagery; all children feared them. Yet here we were, deep in the Welsh Marches, and the countryside here was, if anything, prettier than any I had yet seen along the journey. Even the mountains and hills to either side had lost their threatening aspect. Their lower reaches had been cleared for fields, their crowns sometimes bare, sometimes cloaked in thick forest. The Usk was on my left as I rode into the valley, its banks covered by trees whose branches dipped into the water, so that my view of the river was veiled by shifting leaves.

This was not, surely, the dark, damned country of Lady Adelie's description.

We turned a little north, away from the river, and followed a road toward a small village that someone told me was called Crickhoel. I had my gaze set on it, not thinking that we might be very close to the castle, when suddenly Stephen was at my side again.

I jumped, for I had not seen him approach. He nodded to my right, to a spot much higher than the village. 'My home,' he said, and I turned my head, lifted my gaze ...

And gasped.

There it was. Pengraic Castle, sitting far up the side of a mountain, high, high above us.

'There is a spur of land,' Stephen said, pointing with one hand, 'that runs south from the flank of the mountain — the Welsh call it Pen Cerrig-calch. At the end of the spur is a plateau, and it is on that plateau that Pengraic sits.'

I didn't say anything. I couldn't. I had never seen any castle as mighty as this one. We were still some two miles from it, far down in the valley, yet even so it dominated the entire landscape.

Built of weathered grey stone, it rose into the sky — untold battlements and parapets, and sheer walls that rose to merge with the low clouds.

'All you can see of the castle from this spot,' Stephen said, 'is the great keep. But behind that the castle stretches toward the mountain. Through the inner bailey, then into the northern keep and then the outer bailey beyond that. Ah, Maeb, I hope you will love it as much as I.'

I glanced at him then, and I saw such love on his face as he gazed upward that it stunned me.

'It is legend,' Stephen said, very softly, 'that the rock on which Pengraic Castle sits has been sacred since that time when only the Old People roamed these hills.' He dropped his eyes very suddenly to mine. 'Perhaps so,' he said, 'and perhaps they've never left.'

'Old People?'

'The name given to those ancient folk who lived here even before the English or even the Welsh came to live on this island.'

The Old People. I shivered, but forgot them almost immediately as soon afterward we turned our horses and began our climb upward.

* * *

It was hard work, for the way was steep, and the cart horses moved very slowly. I gave Dulcette as loose a rein as I could and let her find her own pace — soon her head was low and bobbing up and down as she picked her way from one side of the roadway to the other, wherever she thought she saw an easier path.

Very gradually we drew closer to the castle. We approached from the south-eastern side, and as we came about I could clearly see that the castle stretched right along the spur of land that descended from the southern flank of Pen Cerrig-calch. I could not comprehend its size; the great keep alone would have awed me, but to see the entire castle stretch back along the spur, its walls and battlements punctuated at regular intervals by towers … in its entirety I thought the castle became a mountain itself, one mountain of grey stone that grew out of another.

The sides of the mountain that led up to the castle were very steep, sloping down on the castle's southern, western and eastern flanks. The only gentle gradient lay behind the castle, as the spur of land rose to join with Pen Cerrig-calch.

I thought the castle must be impregnable.

The roadway doglegged up the steep hillside. We moved northward almost halfway along the long eastern flank of the castle before executing a tight turn — the carts only barely managing to keep to the road — and climbing south back toward the main gate situated in the south wall by the great keep.

When we drew close, within twenty or so paces, the walls of the castle towered over me; they blotted out the sun, casting everyone in deep, cold shadow, and I shivered.

I tried to twist about, to see what I could of the castle, but suddenly Dulcette picked up her pace and entered the gateway and I was surrounded by walls of stone.

And then, as if by magic, Dulcette emerged into bright sunshine and I was inside Pengraic Castle.

PART TWO

———◦◦◦◦———

THE DEATH

CHAPTER ONE

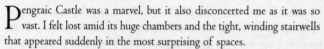

Pengraic Castle was a marvel, but it also disconcerted me as it was so vast. I felt lost amid its huge chambers and the tight, winding stairwells that appeared suddenly in the most surprising of spaces.

My days were mostly spent in the great keep, and those mostly on the upper level … here was the solar and the lord's privy chamber, as well the male and female dormitories for servants and guards. The ground level housed the great hall, the kitchens, and the storage and stabling areas. Because the earl was not in residence and Lady Adelie was not well, I did not eat in the great hall, which was where the majority of the servants, soldiers and knights dined, but rather took my meals with the countess in either the solar or her chamber.

I was awed not only by the size of the castle, and its complexity (which took me weeks to fathom), but also by the richness of its amenities and furnishings. The great hall, the solar, and even the lord's chamber, were well furnished with enormous fireplaces which had chimneys to take away the smoke (the great hall had *two* fireplaces, which would keep it warm on the coldest of nights).

The wooden floors were spread with woven rugs, the walls hung with tapestries of such skilled work that they amazed me, and often, when the countess did not require my presence, I spent much time in tracing the story lines embroidered into their fabric.

The countess kept mainly to the solar during the day, and her privy chamber in the evening and night. She rarely ventured beyond those two chambers. All her meals were taken here. I assisted her morning and night to robe and then disrobe, and attend to her needs at those times, but during the day Mistress Yvette mostly kept her company, and I was left free for other duties.

As at Rosseley, these mostly involved the children. Ancel and Robert, the twins, were no longer with the household so their mischief no longer concerned me. Alice and Emmette, almost grown ladies, tended to keep to themselves, or else sat with their mother learning their stitching and embroideries. That left John, the baby, and Rosamund, and as the nurse tended John for most of the time, it meant that Rosamund and I spent much of our days together.

I did not mind, for she was a delightful child and I loved her dearly. Sometimes she and I played in the solar, but the noise of our merriment oft disturbed the countess, and we sought our amusements elsewhere.

The children, as did the nurse, slept in the female dormitory (itself portioned into different apartments) which ran immediately off the solar (the men's dormitory lay on the western side of the keep). After a few days of running and playing in there, I decided we both needed to venture further than the living quarters on the upper level.

I took Rosamund into the solar, where the countess sat with Mistress Yvette, Alice and Emmette.

'My lady,' I said, 'Rosamund needs to run, and we both need the fresh air. May I take her for a walk in the inner bailey?'

'Be wary of the horses,' said Lady Adelie, 'and do not get in the way of the knights or soldiers.'

'I will be careful, my lady.'

And thus we were free to explore a little. I was thrilled. While I marvelled at the richness and luxury of the lord's chambers, I still longed for the open air and the sun on my face. I took Rosamund by the hand and together we descended the stairwell.

The kitchens and the courtyard of the great keep were alive with activity: servants hurried to and fro, and the courtyard had a half score of horses being groomed. I gathered Rosamund in my arms, not wanting her to be trampled, and together we walked through the gate to the inner bailey.

I'd only had a glimpse of the inner bailey when we'd first arrived, as upon entering the main gate I'd been directed into the great keep's courtyard. I'd had a sense of great space, and I knew I'd seen trees and gardens, which had surprised me.

Now, as I slipped through the keep's gateway to the inner bailey, I could see that the walls enclosed a vast area, two large portions of which were given over to orchards, herb and food gardens. I turned to my left where there was a garden growing in the space bounded by the keep, the outer ring of defence wall and the chapel, a large and gracious building which ran from the outer wall into the centre of the bailey. It was a large garden, sheltered from the constant movement of men and horses through the inner bailey by a waist-height picket fence, and so I was happy to let Rosamund run free once we'd walked through the fence's gateway.

I kept an eye on Rosamund, making sure she disturbed none of the plants, but mostly I let her be as I strolled along the garden paths. The scent from the flowers and the pungent leaves of the herbs, the gentle hum of the bees, the sun on my face ... I breathed in deeply, closing my eyes briefly as I relaxed.

When I opened them again I saw that a man approached from a door in the chapel; the castle priest, from his robes and tonsure.

'You must be Mistress Maeb Langtofte,' he said as he came to a halt before me. He had a pleasant face, well featured, with a strong nose, warm brown eyes and a fringe of dark hair that flopped over his brow. He was only some five or six years older than me.

'You know me?' I said, surprised.

'Who else could you be?' the priest said, then inclined his head. 'I am Brother Owain.' He nodded at the chapel. 'And there my realm. I knew you because I know all of the countess' women ... save for her new attending woman. Thus, you must be she.'

'I am indeed,' I said. I indicated the garden. 'Should I not be here, Brother Owain? I could not resist. Both Rosamund and myself needed the sun on our faces, and the fresh air. I thought ...'

'You are most welcome to the garden,' Owain said. 'Its purpose is to soothe the soul as much as the flesh. But keep Rosamund away from that far corner. It harbours dark plants I use in my herbals, and if she were to eat them, then it would not go well for her.'

I nodded, glancing about to make sure Rosamund was nowhere near the dangerous herbs. She was wandering through the garden close to the chapel, studying various flower heads in childish wonder, and I relaxed.

'How do you find Pengraic, mistress?' Owain said.

For a moment I thought he meant the earl, then realised he talked of the castle.

'I find it very formidable,' I said. 'I feel a little lost.'

'It *is* overwhelming when first you enter it,' Owain said. 'Initially you only see its towering walls, and the great slabs of stone. But after a while …'

'Yes?'

'After a while you begin to see its loveliness, too.'

I looked about, wondering that I should ever find these defences 'lovely'.

I must have been frowning for Owain gave a little laugh. 'You have been here but days, and I wager you have seen little of the castle save the great keep. I have lived here most of my life, and to me this castle is a world all to itself.'

'Most of your life?' I said, curious.

'Aye,' Owain said. 'I was born in Crickhoel — that is the village you passed by to reach the castle — and apart from the years I spent learning my craft in the priory in Glowecestre, I have lived either in the village or this castle all the years of my life.'

'You are Welsh?' I said.

'Indeed, mistress.'

I did not know how to phrase this next question, so I chose vagueness. 'And yet you are happy here?'

'Here? In this castle? In this *Norman* castle?' Owain chuckled. 'Yes, I am. This place … it holds much history among my people. It is a sacred spot. We tell myths that come from the people who were here before the Welsh; we have a strong attachment to the past. It is no wonder that Pengraic's ancestor built his castle here, meaning to impose himself on the Welsh — he had to intimidate both the legends *and* the Welsh. And to answer your next question, for I see it on your face, yes, my loyalty is to the earl, and to Lord Stephen.'

I opened my mouth to ask another question, wondering that Owain mentioned, as had Stephen, the ancient peoples and the sacredness of this spot, but just at that moment we heard footsteps approaching.

It was Stephen — which fact gave me a warm glow — and another knight. I did not know the other man, but he strode with as much authority as Stephen, and carried about him almost as grand an air of nobility.

'Owain!' Stephen said. 'And Mistress Maeb, guarding my youngest sister. Maeb, you have not met Ralph yet, have you? Then may I present Ralph d'Avranches, the garrison commander at Pengraic.'

I remembered his name from the conversation I'd heard in the solar at Rosseley. D'Avranches was from a distinguished and noble Norman family, and was renowned for his military skill.

'My lord,' I said, dipping in courtesy.

'Mistress,' d'Avranches said, with the minimum of politeness. He was singularly uninterested in either myself or Owain, and turned immediately back to Stephen, with whom I imagined he had been deep in conversation before Stephen detoured into the garden. 'If I have your leave, my lord.'

'By all means,' Stephen said, and, with a half bow to Stephen, d'Avranches turned on his heel and was gone, his booted feet crunching along the gravel path.

'I am glad to see you about,' Stephen said to me. 'I am sorry I have not attended my mother as I should, but ...' he shrugged. 'Garrison matters always seem to crowd round me, demanding my attention. How does she keep, Maeb?'

'She is well enough,' I said. 'She has regained some colour, and eats better now she is not constantly travelling. She has a little cough from the dampness of the stone, or perhaps a lingering chill caught while travelling, but otherwise she is much improved.'

'I am relieved I managed to escort her home safe,' Stephen said. 'I worried for her, and the child. There is not yet sign of its birth?'

'My lady thinks a little while yet, my lord,' I said.

Stephen nodded, then grinned at Owain. 'No doubt such tedious household gossip bores you, my friend.'

'Indeed not, my lord,' Owain said. He looked to me. 'I did not know my lady has been unwell. Would you ask her if she would like me to attend on her?'

'Owain is skilled with herbals,' Stephen said, 'and I should have thought to have asked you to visit her before now, Owain. I will attend her this very afternoon, and speak to her of you.'

Owain gave a small bow. 'I was about to show Mistress Maeb the chapel, my lord. Will you accompany us?'

I was not sure I should be seen with Stephen at all, for I still heeded the countess' and Evelyn's warnings. But no one from my lady's chambers could see us here, and the chapel would be private. No harm could come of it, surely.

Stephen made a movement as if he were about to offer me his arm, then thought better of it. 'I would be glad of it,' he said, 'for the chapel always gives me great peace.'

I collected Rosamund, who had by now picked enough flowers to wind into a chain about her head, and together with Stephen and Owain we entered the southern door of the chapel.

The chapel was dim, lit only by a score of candles and the light from the imposing eastern window (which I took a moment to marvel at, for I had never seen the like). My eyes adjusted slowly to the light and by then Rosamund was squirming in my arms, trying to get down.

I looked to Owain for permission.

'Let her run free,' he said. 'I have no objection.'

I set her down with a small sigh of relief and a few words of stern warning not to touch the candles.

She wandered off, happily intrigued by the intricately carved sandalled feet of the nearby stone statue of a saint, and I turned to look more fully about the chapel.

Apart from its size — this was the largest chapel I had ever entered — it was as all chapels in which I had worshipped, save that it was far more richly appointed and that the wall paintings were somehow different. I frowned at them, not immediately able to see *how* they differed from all others I had seen, then ...

'Oh,' I said, and both Owain and Stephen laughed.

'Come,' said Owain, 'walk a little closer. This panel here is among my favourites. What do you make of it?'

All churches and chapels had their walls painted with various scenes from the Bible as well as from the martyrdom of saints and scenes of the last judgment. But here the paintings were markedly different. While they showed scenes from the Bible and of saints' martyrdoms, all these scenes were set within magnificent forests.

The chapel walls were alive with trees. Branches dipped this way and that, and saints, apostles and martyrs danced in and out of clearings and veils of leaves.

Even the figures of the people depicted within were different. All the people were tall and willowy, and had a sense of the otherworldly about them.

'I have never seen anything like it!' I said. 'It is very ... unusual.'

In truth, I found the heavily wooded nature of the walls somewhat unsettling. It made the chapel darker than otherwise it might have been, and, sweet Jesu, I wondered if I looked hard enough would I see any wood dryads or fairies peeking out from the crowns of the trees.

'The chapel was painted many years ago,' Stephen said, walking over and softly laying the fingertips of one hand against a depiction of a gnarled tree trunk. 'I believe my ancestor made good use of the craftsmen in Crickhoel. I saw you looking at the figures, Maeb. They are said to be of the Old People who I mentioned to you, those who were here before the Welsh came. They are long gone now.'

'To the Old People this was a sacred spot,' Owain said. 'On some festivity days the villagers of Crickhoel ask the earl if they can come and worship in this chapel. They like to lay flowers on the heartstone. The earl never refuses.'

I studied the paintings further. 'Why are there wolves running among the people?'

'Again,' Owain said, 'these walls depict ancient myths as well as Christian tales. It is said the wolves are the protectors of this land, and of the ancient peoples, and of those who today still bear their bloodlines.'

'My mother wants these forests and people and wolves painted over,' Stephen said, turning to me and smiling, 'but my father has for the moment resisted her. It would be a shame to lose them, for I enjoy knowing I have a forest so close whenever I need its solace.'

'But these painting are very ... pagan,' I said. 'Do they not worry you, Owain, plastered as they are about a chapel dedicated to our Lord Christ Saviour?'

'No,' Owain said. 'If anything, they give me comfort. I like to think that the Old People are still here, watching over us.'

That was very un-Christian of him, I thought. Perhaps Owain was as much, or more, a man of these mountains and their past than he was Lord Christ's man?

'Maeb,' Stephen said, 'have you seen this? This is the stone of which Owain just spoke.'

He led us toward an immense stone set in the very heart of the nave. It was five or six times the size of the other floor slabs, and irregularly shaped.

It was very smooth, worn smooth over the centuries by the passage of thousands of feet.

'This stone was here before the chapel was built,' Stephen said. 'It was set into the space atop this hill, perhaps by the Old People. We call it the heartstone: heart of the chapel, heart of the castle, heart of the hill, and heart to many of the Welsh who live here.'

'But this is a Christian chapel,' I said, more than a little aghast.

'This was hallowed ground long, long before Jesus Christ set foot here,' said Stephen, 'and I doubt he ever minded much that the place was already warmed and sacred by the time he arrived.'

I am afraid that my mouth hung open a little as I stared at Stephen.

He saw, and laughed softly. 'Come now, Maeb. There are such sacred sites all over the country. Surely you noted the Long Toms we passed on our journey here.'

The Long Toms. The ancient crosses that stood at crossroads and which had been there long before Christianity set its hand on this land. We had indeed passed many on our way here. There had always been one standing outside Witenie, too, and the local villagers laid flowers at its base during the mid-summer festivals.

Yet, still … I wondered that the chapel had been built right over a spot that was so anciently sacred.

'Maeb,' Owain said, 'Lord Christ is a generous and loving lord. He does not mind sharing his home, and he does not mind that sometimes he shares our love. So long as we live our lives with good in our hearts and in our actions, then he asks no more.'

I nodded, feeling a little more at ease. I liked Owain, despite his penchant for the old ways, and in that he was, truly, no different than most village priests.

Owain gave me a small smile. 'I hope you will be happy here. Remember that if ever your soul needs a little comfort, then you can find me in the chapel, or the herb garden. Or in my little dispensary which is on the other side of the chapel. You should explore the castle more, mistress. Perhaps Lord Stephen … in a quiet moment … might like to show you its beauties? More of its surprises?'

Stephen looked a little oddly at Owain at that suggestion, and I was mortified, for I thought him irritated by Owain's presumption.

'I am sure Lord Stephen has many more important things to occupy his day,' I said.

'In a quiet moment, perhaps,' Owain said again.

'A quiet moment it shall be,' Stephen said. 'Maeb, you should look to my sister, for she is halfway up the rood screen.'

I muttered to myself, cross that I had forgot all about Rosamund, and hurried to rescue her, while Stephen murmured a farewell to Owain and left the chapel.

CHAPTER TWO

I slept in the solar, for Mistress Yvette (who slept with the countess) wanted me close if our lady should go into labour.

I now slept alone, unusual for me, as I had shared a bed with either Evelyn or Rosamund since I had joined the Pengraic household.

I had never slept in such a large or grand chamber. Although the chamber was the centre for the family's daily activities, there was a little bed for me tucked away behind a screen in one corner. Once the castle had quietened down for the night I used to like to fold the screen back and go to sleep watching the crackle of the coals in the enormous fireplace. Once I had become used to the isolation of having the entire chamber to myself at night, I luxuriated in its splendour, and sometimes imagined myself as mistress of the castle, sleeping in a grand curtained bed, as did Lady Adelie.

This night began like all others preceding. It was several days since Brother Owain had showed me about his strangely wooded chapel. Owain had visited the countess yesterday, talking with her for most of the afternoon and returning later in the day with some sweet smelling herbal possets he said would aid my lady's cough.

I had seen Stephen only on the two occasions he had visited his mother, once eating his evening meal with her, but had passed no words with him, nor had his eyes sought me out while he was in his mother's company.

On this night I slipped into sleep almost immediately on lying down. I was tired, as the night previous, Mistress Yvette had been worried about our lady and we had sat by her bed as she slept fitfully. I had eventually returned to my own bed, but had lost half the night's sleep.

* * *

I woke deep into the night and to this day I do not know what it was that disturbed my sleep.

Fully awake, I sat up, clutching the bedclothes to my chest. The fire was almost dead and cast only a warm glow about the room, and I had to blink several times to accustom my eyes to the dark.

There was no one else in the chamber and all was as it should be.

Nonetheless, I had the most strange compulsion to rise and go to the stairwell. I tried to ignore it, but the sensation was persistent and only grew stronger.

I sighed and rose, slipping on my linen chemise and drawing a mantle about my shoulders against the night's chill.

I walked a few steps toward the screen that hid the entrance to the stairwell. But I stopped, overcome with the need to have my shoes.

I padded back to the bed and slipped my feet into the shoes.

Then I walked over to the screen, hesitated, and stepped around it.

Stephen stood there, leaning against the wall of the stairwell, arms folded, a small smile on his face.

'The castle is quiet,' he said. 'Would you like to explore it a little?'

I was so dumbfounded I did not know what to say. What was Stephen doing here? It was deep night! I couldn't just walk out and —

'No one will see,' he said. 'All is quiet.'

'I can't —'

'No one will see. All is quiet. Come now.'

He held out his hand, and I stood there like a fool and stared at it.

'Maeb, come now.'

'I cannot go with you. I cannot!'

He reached forward with his hand, taking mine in a gentle grip. He pulled slowly, but still I would not budge.

'My lord, I *cannot*. I am as good as promised to Saint-Valery, and I *will* not! It would shame me to go with you now.'

His smiled broadened fractionally. 'You are not promised to Saint-Valery. I heard that you were digging your heels in over that offer as stubbornly as you dig your heels in now. There is no shame in coming with me, Maeb. No one will know and I shall behave honourably. I just want to show you some of the castle's secrets. It is a quiet moment. Maeb, no one will know. *No one* will wake.'

Still I hesitated, although perhaps he could see the uncertainty in my face, now.

'Maeb, come with me. I will not take long and you will return to your bed long before any wake.'

'There will be guards about. Night cooks in the kitchens. They will see. They will —'

'Not tonight, Mae. Not tonight.'

His use of the diminutive disarmed me.

'I will keep you safe,' he said, and finally I relaxed enough that he could draw me into the stairwell.

We trod softly down. There were torches in the doorways at each level and that was enough to cast light through the well.

'You have not been beyond the inner bailey, have you, Maeb?'

'No.'

'Then we will go to the northern keep — all full of sleeping knights and men *who will not wake* — and I will take you to its rooftop that I can show you the outer bailey. And then, Maeb, then I am going to show you what is so special about this castle. You will remember it all your life, and perhaps you will tell your grandchildren about it and I am sure they will never believe you.'

We were in the courtyard by the end of this long speech. Despite Stephen's reassurances I was certain there would be movement here — horses, grooms, servants fetching to and fro. Even at this late hour there was always life in the castle.

Not tonight.

Stephen still had my hand, and now he pulled me a bit closer. 'I have wanted so much to spend more time with you,' he said, 'but for you it was difficult, I know. I caused you some grief on our journey here with my ill-considered actions. I am sorry for that. But now that we're here, we can —'

'I have heard you are betrothed to a Norman heiress with lands and offices enough to make you a great man in this realm.'

Stephen pulled me to a halt just as we stepped under the keep's gate that led to the inner bailey.

'That pains you,' he said, and to my distress my eyes welled with tears.

'Oh, Mae,' he said, 'there is no straight path for either of us in this world or this life. I fear that neither of us will enjoy considerable happiness. There are such chasms between you and I, but on still nights like this, in such quiet moments as this, perhaps you and I can find a little peace. You and I will both, I think, have to snatch happiness where we can.'

'That is a fine speech, my lord, and one in which I can hear the dread footfalls of my downfall.'

He let go my hand and stepped back. His face had closed down now, save for a glint of anger in his eyes.

'Then go back to your bed if you have no courage within you, Mistress Maeb. Go back to your bed and wake in the morning and tell my lady mother that you will accept Saint-Valery's offer. Your back will be straight and your pride intact, but how shall your soul fare, eh? Will you remember this night and, in your darkest moments, wish you had seen the sacredness of this place?'

It was his appeal to my lack of courage that undid my resolve. I had come this far, I would go further.

'I am sorry,' I said. 'I was just so afraid. I cannot afford to lose my place in this —'

'There are damn more important things in this world and the next than your cursed place in this household!'

He was so angry, and I so upset with myself for causing such anger, that the tears which had for long minutes threatened to fall now spilled over.

'Please do not be angry with me,' I said. 'You do not know what it is like to have such uncertainty as to your place.'

'Oh, sweet God,' he muttered, and he stepped forward, seized my face in his hands, and kissed me.

I froze. I did not know what to do. No man had ever kissed me before. One part of me demanded I should berate him fiercely, perhaps even slap his face for his temerity, but another begged me to submit and to lean in against his body.

Stephen stepped back, giving a short, breathless laugh. 'I do beg your forgiveness for that, Maeb. I should not have done it, for I think that you shall give your heart to another and I do not begrudge it. But I have blackened my name with that kiss. I will not do it again. Please, can we walk on now? This moment will not last forever.'

I nodded, unable to speak, and he took my arm and together we walked through the inner bailey toward the northern keep. Where we might go did not bother me. I no longer cared if any should see us. All I could think about was that moment when he had kissed me, what it had felt like, and the closeness of him now.

Stephen could have demanded anything of me at that point, and I think I would have submitted. But I also knew that he would not, and that for some reason I was safer with him now than I had been when first we walked down that stairwell.

Nonetheless, I wondered ... he thought I would give my heart to another. Saint-Valery? Surely not.

We entered the garrison.

As with the great keep, there was no one about.

Stephen led me to a stairwell and, my hand in his, he led me up, further and further, around a dizzying number of bends, passing several doorways into different levels as we went.

Finally, when I thought I would never breathe easily again, he led me through a doorway and onto the roof.

It was shingled, and very slightly curved from the centre so that rain drained off into gutters and downpipes, but there was a walkway about its rim and he led me along it to the northern part of the parapets.

'Look,' he said, 'the outer bailey. See there, the kitchens for the garrisons. And the buildings all about the foot of the walls are the workshops for the castle: the blacksmiths, the maille-smiths, the arrowsmiths, the bladesmiths ... and there, stables, and yet more buildings too numerous to rattle off.'

I had thought myself over any amazement at this castle, but now it had taken my breath away yet again. The outer bailey was huge, perhaps twice the size of the inner bailey.

'It is the least defensible portion of the castle,' Stephen went on. 'The ground beyond the walls is far less steep than that around the garrison, inner bailey and the great keep. If we were attacked, by a good force of arms, this would be surrendered first and all within taken into the garrison and inner bailey.'

'I cannot imagine *any* force being strong enough to take this castle! My lord, it is impregnable, surely?'

'So we hope.' He tapped his foot on the garrison roof. 'The garrison harbours hundreds of men, and more still in the great keep. There are few armies who would be willing to take us on.'

He glanced up at the moon, now dipping below the western ridges of Pen Cerrig-calch. 'We have not much time,' he said. 'Maeb, do you remember what I said about this castle? That the legends tell that this was a sacred spot for the Old People who lived here in ancient times?'

I nodded.

'Well,' he said, and took a deep breath, 'it is told that once a mighty prince of the Old People held his dancing circle atop this rock. On nights like this you can surely believe it.'

He put a hand on my shoulder. 'Turn around now, and see.'

I turned … and cried out.

The great keep, *all* the castle, had entirely disappeared. Instead the flat top of the plateau where the castle stood was alive with torch-wielding people, their stature tall and willowy.

The Old People?

They danced in several interweaving circles, and in the middle of those circles stood a man atop the heartstone of the hill and on his head was a crown of light.

'Look about,' whispered Stephen, and I did so.

The hill and mountain tops were lined with tens of thousands of people, and all held torches so that the entire valley glimmered with life.

'What is this?' I said.

'A dream,' Stephen said, 'of what once was here. I knew you would see it. I knew it.'

'How …'

Stephen clapped his hands, and suddenly it all vanished, and all I could see was the solidity of the great keep, and the darkness falling over the mountains. 'Some nights, they say, the Old People come back here to celebrate. On those nights, you can hear the wolves howling from the tops of the mountains.

'And thus,' Stephen finished softly, 'the magic of Pengraic. Thus the reason I love it so. This is my home.'

I woke suddenly, jerking up so abruptly the bedclothes fell away from my body.

There was someone by the fire, and it took me a moment to realise it was the servant who habitually stoked the fires in the morning.

I grasped the bedclothes back to my breast. *What had happened last night? Was it but a dream?*

'You'll need to rise swiftly, mistress,' the servant said as he straightened. 'Your lady will be wondering where you are.'

By the time we broke our fast I had convinced myself that my night's adventure *had* been but a dream.

When I rose from my bed I found that my linen chemise, kirtle, mantle and shoes all lay as I had left them when I went to bed.

By the time Lady Adelie had sat down in her favourite chair in the solar and taken up her stitching, Alice and Emmette by her side, I had all but brushed the memory away completely.

Then, as my back was turned, I heard Stephen enter the room and greet his mother.

My heart beating wildly, I turned about.

He did not so much as glance in my direction.

But then his mother spoke to him. 'Stephen, you have such shadows under your eyes. Did you not sleep?'

'Madam, it was a poor night for sleeping. Eventually I took myself to the top of the northern keep, where I could watch the moon rise and fall. Sometimes I imagine I can see such things in the soft, sweet moonlight as though the very mountaintops are afire.'

Then he raised his eyes and looked straight at me, and I knew that what had happened last night was no dream.

CHAPTER THREE

There was no further chance for Stephen to return and walk me away into late-night magic again. The very next day Lady Adelie's midwives arrived in preparation for her lying-in, and they shared the solar with me at night, so that they might be close to my lady.

Their names were Gilda and Jocea and they had travelled from further down the Usk Valley where they serviced the local women during their times of trial. They were both short, squat, taciturn women sharing thick, black eyebrows and narrow dark eyes (much later I discovered they were, in fact, sisters). They spoke hardly at all, not even to my lady, preferring to communicate with those about them in a series of barely audible grunts. The only words I heard them utter for the first few days of their residence were to each other; everyone else required only a grunt.

But Lady Adelie trusted them. Mistress Yvette told me the two midwives had attended the birth of Stephen, which birth had gone smoothly, while the midwives also often attended the womenfolk of Bergeveny, where their names were legend.

Thus Gilda and Jocea became my somewhat reluctant companions and filled my nights with their snortings and snufflings.

Mistress Yvette's and my time was now largely consumed by assisting with the preparations for Lady Adelie's lying-in. The birth of her child was close and Lady Adelie retired almost exclusively to her privy chamber.

This chamber was now readied for the birth. Large heavy drapes were brought in and hung so that we might close off the light and draughts from the windows whenever needed. A birthing stool was placed in a corner, ready for that day when it should be needed.

At Yvette's request, one of the serving men brought to my lady's chamber a large chest, and Yvette and I unpacked it one day as the midwives sat uncommunicative by a window and our lady lay sleeping fitfully on her bed.

The chest contained all the items for my lady's labour. Amulets and girdles, blessed at the shrine devoted to our blessed, most sweet Virgin Mary at Walsingaham, and at shrines devoted to the blessed Saint Margaret of Antioch. I handled these items with awe, for they carried within them the power of the blessed saints, and I marvelled that Lady Adelie had such powerful protectorship.

There were also linens within the chest for my lady and her infant, bowls and straps, vials of oils and unguents, charms and a brownish-bluish rough stone the size of a small chicken's egg.

I raised my eyebrows in query at Yvette as I unpacked this.

'It is an eaglestone,' she said. 'Powerful magic. They come from the nests of eagles ... it is well known that eagles cannot be born without these stones present.'

'Of course,' I said, not wishing Yvette to realise I'd never heard of them. 'I'd just not seen one before.'

'Undoubtedly not,' Yvette said, 'for only the most wealthy and powerful can afford an eaglestone.'

I chose not to believe that was a small jibe at my own lack of rank and wealth. 'Does my lady hold it in her hand as she labours? Does she rub it to invoke its magical aid?'

'It will be tied to my lady's thigh as she labours, thus encouraging the child to escape from her womb.'

I gazed on the stone in wonder, amazed at the charms the wealthy could summon to their aid. No wonder Lady Adelie had so many surviving babies!

I addressed Yvette again, voicing a worry that had gnawed at me for weeks.

'Will my lady be safe, Mistress Yvette? She seems so weak and her colour is poor. At night sometimes I can hear her coughing.'

Lady Adelie's colour was, frankly, appalling. Her skin had a yellowish-grey pallor to it and always seemed to have a sheen of cold sweat. She appeared exhausted by the child, moving only from her bed to a chair by the window in her chamber, then back to her bed again. She rarely spoke, and never smiled, as if even words or emotion were simply too much for her. Lady Adelie had initially appeared to recover from the journey from Rosseley, but over the past few days her health had deteriorated once more.

Yvette paused in her folding of a linen. 'She is well enough, Maeb. Our Lady Adelie's colour has never been good, and her cough is but a mild summer chill, exacerbated by the baby pressing on her lungs. Do not fret. She will do well enough, for she is a courageous woman and strong, despite her apparent frailty.'

I was not sure of Mistress Yvette's explanation and apparent confidence, but then she knew the Lady Adelie far better than I. 'I worry that the child drains her strength,' I said.

'She is not a young woman, but she has birthed many infants. Do not worry, mistress. All be well enough, I am sure.'

Once more I spared a moment's resentment for the earl, as I had that first day I'd come into his household, that he required of his lady so much effort in her later years. Had he not already enough sons?

I clutched the eaglestone and hoped its powerful protective magic would serve to aid my lady.

Two days after this conversation Stephen came to the solar and sought permission from his mother to enter her privy chamber. Now that Lady Adelie had retired to her chamber in preparation for the birth she normally would not have seen any man, not even her son, but apparently Stephen convinced Yvette — who carried word to and fro from Lady Adelie — that it was necessary and important, and so my lady admitted him after a brief whisper with Yvette.

Gilda and Jocea were also in the privy chamber, hunched silent and watchful in a shadowy corner, as were Alice and Emmette. The two girls sat most of the day with their lady mother, sometimes reading to her from her prayer book, or otherwise engaged in stitchery.

Apart from a brief glance as he entered, Stephen paid both the midwives and his sisters no attention. I stood slightly to one side of my lady's bed and Stephen spared me a slightly longer look. I searched for any deeper message in that look, but there was nothing there save distraction and worry — which instantly set me to distraction and worry.

As he greeted his mother and she him, I moved as if to leave my place, but Lady Adelie motioned me to stay, then crooked her finger at Yvette to bring her closer.

'I share my troubles these days, Stephen,' she said, with the ghost of a smile, 'and I see by your face that you carry troublesome news.'

'*And* good news, my lady,' Stephen said, almost managing to raise his own smile. 'I have heard this morning from my lord father.'

Lady Adelie's face brightened as I had not seen it do for many weeks. 'Raife? How is he? What news? *Where* is he? Oh, Stephen, *speak!*'

I had not realised, until this very moment, that my lady loved her husband. I had known there existed respect between them, but not, until now, that so also did love.

'He sent word,' said Stephen, 'that he is now in Elesberie with the king — the plague came to Oxeneford and the king moved his court to his royal manor at Elesberie. He is well, my lady, and sends you his regards and affection.'

Lady Adelie visibly relaxed and actually smiled — my first indication that she had been silently fretting about the earl. I felt shame that I had not known, nor even thought, that she might have been so worried.

'Praise the saints that he is well,' she said. 'And the king. But it is poor news that Oxeneford has been struck with the plague. Poor news indeed.'

'We did well to leave,' Stephen said, 'for even Rosseley has succumbed.'

'Oh,' said Lady Adelie, 'our poor people … I will pray for them, Stephen. Lord Jesu help them all.'

'My father sends prayers for your safe delivery,' Stephen continued, holding his mother's hand between his own, 'and says that he thinks constantly on you, and worries.'

'Then he should not,' said Lady Adelie, 'for both I and my child shall be well. Did he speak of the south-east, Stephen, and what he discovered there?'

Stephen's face darkened. 'Only a little, madam. He said that it was terrible, and that he was truly glad that you were safe here in Pengraic.'

He was lying, I knew it instantly. Not that whatever Pengraic had found was 'terrible', but that he had only spoken so briefly of it. I felt certain that Stephen had received a far more detailed report from his father.

116

'Then what is it that troubles you, Stephen?' Lady Adelie said.

His hands tightened slightly about that of his mother. 'The rider who brought my father's news also brought grim tidings. My lady, the plague draws closer to Pengraic. It travels faster than any thought it might. It —'

'It has reached past Oxeneford?' Lady Adelie said.

'It is far closer than Oxeneford,' Stephen said. 'It appears to have travelled along the drover trails and the pilgrimage tracks, almost as if …'

He stopped, but I knew what he had not said. *Almost as if it were following us.*

'It has devastated Witenie,' he said, glancing at me, 'as it has Cirecestre, and there are reports of people falling sick as close to us as Glowecestre and Monemude.'

Absolute silence greeted his words. Alice and Emmette, who had been listening, clasped each other's hands, their eyes round. I was appalled that Witenie suffered — who among my friends had died terribly? I caught Yvette's eyes — she looked as stricken as I felt — then looked at Lady Adelie.

She had gone white. 'Then we must secure the castle,' she said, and Stephen nodded.

'I have spoken with d'Avranches,' he said. 'The gates are being closed as we speak. No one will leave and no one enter from this hour forth.'

'Pray it is enough!' Lady Adelie whispered, then spoke more strongly. 'Stephen, do we have enough provisions? I had not considered that —'

'Do not fret on this matter,' Stephen said. 'D'Avranches and I had thought this day might come. We have been provisioning, bolstering what we already had.' He attempted a smile, that did not quite work. 'We shall eat and drink and make merry ably enough for many months to come, and for all the mouths that these walls contain. Think only of yourself, my lady, and of your child. The plague shall not enter these walls. It shall not touch us. We are all well and shall remain so.'

My lady and Yvette exchanged a glance, their faces strained.

'Nonetheless,' Lady Adelie said, 'I shall ask Owain to lead prayers to the Saints Roche and Stephen for the entire fortress tonight.'

She sat back, withdrawing her hand from Stephen's clasp. 'I wish I were stronger,' she said, almost to herself, 'that I might the better lead us through the trials ahead.'

My lady's chamber was a subdued world for the rest of that day. I tried to speak of Stephen's news, but Lady Adelie would have none of it.

'We must not worry unnecessarily,' she said, her tone indicating the subject was not to be raised again.

Nonetheless, late that afternoon she summoned Owain, and he led us in prayers well into the evening.

When he was done and taking his leave of my lady, I asked if I might accompany him back to the chapel, and Lady Adelie, tired and strained and white-faced, nodded her permission.

'What have you heard, Owain?' I said as we entered the central courtyard of the great keep.

He gave a small smile. 'Why do you think that I have heard any news that you have not?'

'Because you and Lord Stephen are close, and he trusts you.'

He grunted. 'You are very observant.'

He said nothing else until we were clear of the great keep and into the relatively secluded space of his herb garden near the chapel. Here we stopped and talked.

'Plague is close,' I said.

'Yes,' Owain replied, 'it has devastated Cirecestre and is rapidly tightening its vicious claws on Glowecestre and Monemude.'

'What have you heard?' I asked.

Owain hesitated.

'I was privy to a discussion between the king, the earl and several other nobles about the plague,' I said. 'I *know* how bad it is.'

'They say half of Cirecestre has burned to the ground,' Owain said.

The final horror of the plague: the fungus that was composed of heat and which was inflammable.

'Sweet Jesu, Owain, will all of England burn?'

Owain opened his mouth to say something, but just then one of the guards atop the twin towers that bracketed the gate (now tightly secured) shouted down into the inner bailey.

'My lord! My lord!'

His voice was faint, but the urgency within it was clearly audible.

'My lord!'

I looked about and saw Stephen talking with d'Avranches and two other knights halfway between where Owain and I stood and the closed main gates.

'My lord!'

Stephen looked up at the man, turning a little toward him.

'My lord,' the guard again shouted, 'there is one who pleads entrance.'

'You have your orders,' d'Avranches shouted, no doubt irritated with the man for disturbing Stephen and himself.

'It is the countess' woman,' the man shouted. 'Mistress Evelyn Kendal.'

'Evelyn!' I cried and, skirts in hand, hastened toward the gates.

'She may not enter,' Stephen shouted at the guard. I was almost to him now, and I cried out. 'No! My lord, allow her in, I pray you!'

He turned to look at me, angry, and in that moment I saw his father in him. I stumbled to a halt.

'The castle is secured, Maeb. No one enters. But people can leave. If you wish it, I can arrange your departure.'

I stared at him, horrified not so much by his words but by his almost complete transformation into his father.

Owain had joined us by now. 'Maeb, you must accept Lord —'

'My lord, it is only this past hour you have battened down the castle,' I said to Stephen. 'Just an hour!'

'The gates remain closed,' Stephen said, his voice as hard as the rock of the castle walls.

'I beg you,' I said softly. 'Lady Adelie has a close bond with Mistress Evelyn. Your lady mother would be bereft if she heard you had turned away her favoured servant at the gates, only a short time after the decision to secure them. And she so close to her confinement and fragile.'

I knew I pushed too hard. This was no respectful manner to speak to Stephen before d'Avranches and the knights. I could see Stephen was angry, but I held his eyes and bit my tongue from uttering that one final phrase which I knew would ruin me: *Do this for me.*

He knew I could have said more, I think. Still holding my eyes in a furious glare, he said to one of the guards by the gates, 'Let Mistress Kendal enter, but only her, via the wicket gate.'

There was a smaller but no less solid gate set into the main gates and two of the guards set to drawing the bolts. It swung open, a moment passed, then Evelyn herself came in, atop a small brown horse.

'Evelyn —' I began, taking a step toward where she had pulled up her horse.

'Stay here!' Stephen snapped, walking over to Evelyn's side — although keeping at a safe distance of a pace or two.

They were close enough that I could hear their conversation.

'From whence have you come, Mistress Evelyn?'

Evelyn threw me a glance, but answered Stephen readily enough. 'From the lands of Roger de Tosny, my lord. His manor is near Redmeleie, a day's ride north of Glowecestre. It is where my daughter serves.'

'And your route here to Pengraic?'

'We had heard that the plague raged in Monemude, my lord, so we rode south-west through the Depdene forest along the droveways, avoiding all the towns. My lord, may my escort enter? They are as tired and in need of rest and food as myself.'

Stephen considered her. 'Did you see any sickness as you passed? Tell me true, mistress.'

Again Evelyn flicked a glance at me. 'No, my lord. All was well in the peoples we passed.'

Stephen continued to regard her, thinking. Then he turned to face me. 'Be it on your head, Maeb.' He looked back to Evelyn. 'You may enter, your escort may not. They can find rest and succour enough at Crickhoel. Tell them they may use my name.'

I could not keep the grin off my face. I thanked Stephen as he strode past me, his face impassive. I shifted impatiently from foot to foot as Evelyn spoke to her escort just beyond the gate, then headed her horse toward me.

'Evelyn!' I cried, and she slid from her saddle and held out her arms.

CHAPTER FOUR

We went straight to Lady Adelie. I was thrilled to have Evelyn back and we chatted, our words falling over themselves, as we climbed the stairs to the solar and went into our lady's privy chamber.

Lady Adelie was still abed, asleep now, Yvette by her side and the ever-watchful midwives in their corner. She woke only after we entered, and smiled sweetly as soon as she saw Evelyn, holding out a hand.

Evelyn sank into a courteous dip. I'd had my eyes on Evelyn's face the moment she first saw Lady Adelie, and although she hid it almost instantly, I saw the shock there and it immediately made me worry even more about Lady Adelie.

'My lady!' Evelyn said, sitting on the bed and taking the countess' hand as Stephen had not so long previously. 'How do you? I wanted so to return before your confinement.'

'I am well enough, Evelyn,' Lady Adelie said. 'A little tired — thus you catch me abed when I should be risen. How is it my son allowed you entry?'

'Because Mistress Maeb begged him, my lady. She said you would want me by your side, and it was but an hour since he had commanded the castle closed.'

'And so I do want you by my side. Tell me, how is your daughter?'

'She is truly well, my lady. Grown into a fine young woman and she has a good place in Roger de Tosny's household.'

'He has lands above Glowecestre, yes?'

'Yes, my lady.'

'And the plague has not yet reached there?'

121

'No, my lady, we have kept safe.'

'It has devastated Cirecestre and is now in Monemude,' Yvette said.

'Aye,' said Evelyn. 'I worry about my daughter, my lady, but I worried about you more.'

'And have left your daughter to attend me,' Lady Adelie said. 'You are a good and kind woman, Evelyn, for you must fear for her.'

'My Lord de Tosny is taking his household and riding to more northerly estates, my lady,' Evelyn said. 'My choice was to ride with him or to come here. I chose here.'

'Praise sweet Jesu for you, Evelyn,' Lady Adelie said, patting Evelyn's hand. 'I need all my loyal ladies about me for this birth. I am in so much fear of it. So much fear.'

Her voice trembled on those last words and everyone in the room looked aghast. I had never seen my lady express such anxiety regarding the birth before.

Sweet Mary, she must be dreading this birth, indeed.

Now Lady Adelie appeared discomfited at her display of emotion. She let Evelyn's hand go, brushing away imaginary crumbs from her bed linen, as if bored, or distracted. 'Thank you, Evelyn.'

Evelyn and I did not get a chance for private conversation until later that night, when we went to our bed in the solar. I was very glad to have her back, and despite the warmth of the early summer night we lay close as we whispered. For a while she told me of her daughter and the joy she'd had in visiting her, but soon the topic turned to Lady Adelie.

'By the heavenly saints, Maeb, when did Lady Adelie sicken so badly?'

I had truly not realised how ill Lady Adelie was until I had seen Evelyn's shocked reaction on entering our lady's privy chamber.

'She has been sickening for weeks now, Evelyn. She was weak before we even started to Pengraic, but she has become worse since we arrived here, after an initial rally. She coughs at night, often, although Mistress Yvette tells me it is only a summer chill. I had not truly realised *how* ill she was until I saw your face when you first set eyes on her.'

'Her complexion is dreadful, and her face so gaunt. Has she a fever, Maeb?'

'I thought that perhaps it was the child …'

'No. I have seen her carry and birth five children in my time in this household. Lady Adelie is one of those women who seem to find breeding easy. She has never had any difficulty carrying a child, nor birthing it. Not even the twins.'

'But she is so old now.'

Evelyn chuckled. 'And you are so young!'

I smiled too, and for a moment we lay there in companionable amusement.

'Does she complain of any illness, Maeb?'

'Not to me, although what she says to Mistress Yvette I do not know. I talked to Yvette about Lady Adelie recently, but she evaded my questions. Yvette now cares for my lady almost completely — I no longer even help with her dressing in the mornings.'

'Mistress Yvette and our lady were ever close,' Evelyn said. 'Maeb ...'

'Yes?'

'What other news about this plague? Surely you have heard more.'

'Only what you have already heard,' I said to her. 'That it has reached Glowecestre and Monemude ... and that only this morning, when Lord Stephen brought us the tidings.'

'And what of Lord Stephen?' Evelyn asked.

I smiled. 'I have given myself to him entirely, and he promises to wed me in the autumn.'

'Maeb!'

I laughed. 'I jest only, Evelyn. I have been good, as you asked. I do not wish to lose my place in this household.'

I felt her body relax beside mine. 'Do not tease me on this, Maeb. I was worried for you.'

'There is no need.'

'Is there word on the earl?'

'Only that he is with the king in Elesberie.'

'I wish that he would —'

Evelyn got no further, for suddenly the midwife Gilda loomed over our bed. 'Mistresses, arise. Your lady needs you.'

Lady Adelie's time had come. Evelyn and I hastily donned kirtles over our chemises, Evelyn no doubt wishing with myself that we could have enjoyed a few more cool hours lying naked beneath our sheets. We made sure our hair was neat, then entered our lady's privy chamber.

The air was heavy and uncomfortably warm. The windows were shuttered closed, and heavy drapes pulled across them. Oils and herbs burned in a brazier set to one side and someone had lit the fire as well.

Sweat beaded on my face and I could feel it prickling all over my body under my clothes.

Despite the heat of the chamber, Lady Adelie sat on her wooden chair by the window clad not only in a linen gown laced tightly about her throat, which covered her arms to the wrists and pooled in heavy folds about her feet, but a heavily embroidered woollen, sleeved over-garment as well. I could just see the gleam of one of her precious, blessed girdles underneath it. She was pale, her face unsurprisingly running with sweat, her blue eyes wide with the strain of her labour.

Both hands clutched the arms of the chair. I was not sure what to do. The chamber, although spacious, felt crowded with the two midwives, as well as Mistress Yvette, Evelyn and myself. Gilda and Jocea bustled about: shifting the birthing stool, muttering over a pan of some simmering brew they had set to one side of the coals, moving a pile of linens first to the bed (its sheets and covers stripped back to its foot), now back to the top of a chest.

Mistress Yvette sat on a stool near Lady Adelie, and Evelyn moved to her, asking what we could do to help.

'Evelyn,' Yvette said, 'you may pull up a stool and sit with me, keep our lady company and cheery with our chatter. Maeb, can you descend to the kitchen and fetch for our lady some small beer, as also some crusts of bread in a bowl that the babe can suck on once he is born.'

'The wet nurse is yet to arrive,' Yvette said, almost as an aside. 'She is bedded down in the outer bailey with her husband and children, and no doubt no one yet has been sent to fetch her.'

'I can send someone,' I said. 'There must be a boy awake in the kitchen.'

'Very well,' said Yvette. 'She can be found in the sleep house next to the blacksmithy. Her name is Sewenna.'

'Should I fetch Alice and Emmette as well?' I said.

Yvette thought a moment, then shook her head. 'No. Let them sleep. My lady has enough women to attend her now.'

I nodded, glad of something to do, and of the chance to leave this sweaty chamber for a short while. I was no stranger to births, for from the age of nine I had regularly attended and aided at births in my village of Witenie. But I was unsure how to help my lady for the world of a noble birth was strange to me — what rank attended which duty?

Everything about Lady Adelie's privy chamber, from the draped windows to the fire to the lurking heaviness of the two taciturn midwives to the precious objects I knew would be wielded during this birth made me uneasy and unsure. The world of my experience in birth had been the laughter and raucousness of the village cottage.

The kitchen lay one flight down the spiral stone stairs. At this time of night it was largely deserted, although within an hour or two the serving boys and sleep-soured cooks would be stumbling to set beasts to roast and bread to rise. Yet even though the hour was late (or early, depending on your perspective) there were several servants about, moving slowly through the poorly lit chamber, its huge beamed ceiling lost in the darkness. They were setting out spoons and bowls, flour and salt, ready for the cooks and they affected to ignore me, even though I stood breathless across the table from them, clutching the skirts of my robe and looking, I hoped, importantly impatient.

I cleared my throat.

The three men ignored me.

'My lady's time has come,' I said. 'She needs small beer to sustain her and some bread crusts for her infant to suck.'

One of the men deigned to speak to me, although not once did he raise his eyes in my direction. 'Beer's there,' he moved his head toward a barrel, 'jug's over there,' again the head tilted, 'bread in that basket.'

I didn't thank him, instead hastening to fill a jug with the small beer. It was pleasantly spiced, and I paused long enough to have a draught of it myself. I collected the bread crusts in a bowl, then hesitated.

The men, still moving in their somnolent way about the kitchen, continued to ignore me, yet I needed to send someone for the wet nurse, Sewenna.

I took a deep breath. 'I need a boy to run to the outer bailey for me … to fetch the wet nurse, Sewenna. Do you know where … I could find …'

'There's a boy sleeps by the inner gate,' said one of them. 'In a little alcove. Can't miss him. Wake him and send him off.'

'Thank you,' I said, and hastened out of the kitchen and away from their strange disregard.

I found the boy at the inner gate and had just sent him grumbling on his way when Owain loomed out of the night.

'What is happening?' he asked me.

'My lady's time has come,' I said. 'How did you know?'

He shivered, hugging his robe tightly about him. 'The night has been restless.'

I grunted at his evasiveness. 'I have to get back to the chamber.'

'I will come with you,' he said, 'and wait in the solar.'

In case I should be needed.

'Maeb, has anyone sent for Lord Stephen?'

I had been turning to head back to the stairwell, but now I stopped. 'I don't think so.'

'We should send for him.'

'But shouldn't we wait until … if anything goes awry …'

'I think he needs to know now, Maeb. You go ahead. I will find someone to fetch Stephen, or do it myself.'

I returned to the solar, and thence to the privy chamber beyond. Everything was a-bustle, and Yvette snapped at me for taking so long.

I did not mention meeting with Owain, or that he was fetching Stephen.

I set the small beer and crusts to one side, pouring some of the beer into a small cup should it be needed, then stood aside, waiting for a moment when I could be useful.

Lady Adelie's labour seemed to have progressed apace since I had been gone, and she was now seated on the birthing stool a little distance from the fire. I was surprised to see that she was still clothed in both high-necked and laced linen shift, as well as the outer embroidered woollen robe. She was covered from neck to wrist and toe with several layers of clothing — and surely it could not have been due to any coolness on her part, for her face was bright red and streaming with sweat. Lady Adelie was among women who attended her on a daily basis; we had all seen her naked many times, so this could not be due to unwarranted modesty on her part.

I caught Evelyn's eye and indicated the clothing, and Evelyn gave me a slight shrug of her shoulders as if to indicate it did not matter, but she also looked perplexed ... if this was my first time attending Lady Adelie during childbirth, it surely was not Evelyn's, so this attachment to heavy clothing was something new for our lady.

Still, if this is what my Lady Adelie wanted, then why should I worry?

Yvette noticed me standing about with nothing to do and set me to changing the bed linens with cleaned, herbed sheets, so that our lady would have a fresh bed to return to once the child was born. I proceeded to do so with alacrity, glad to be given another task. The two midwives hovered close about Lady Adelie, Yvette at their backs bending in whichever way she could to see and enquire.

By the time I had finished the bed, our lady was close to delivering her child. From my own experiences, I knew that women who had birthed before had a quicker and easier time of it than first-time mothers. Nonetheless, I murmured a prayer to our sweet mother Saint Mary as Gilda and Jocea bent to their work (I assumed they worked by touch alone beneath Lady Adelie's voluminous and heavy robes), hoping that our lady would deliver with ease. I was glad the child was about to be born, for it had sapped our lady's strength, and I would be glad to see her recover once the child no longer ate of her flesh.

Gilda snapped at Yvette to be ready with linens in her arms, and, from my vantage point on the other side of the bed, I took a half-step closer in anticipation. I looked at Lady Adelie's face — it was bright red and running freely with sweat, her mouth and eyes wide and agonised — and I felt a momentary pang of fear for my own inevitable days in childbed. Could men ever truly understand what they required of us?

Then Lady Adelie gave a yelp of sheer pain, and Gilda and Jocea tugged, and suddenly there was a rush of liquid and I caught a glimpse of a bundle of new, wet skin in the midwives' hands. Jocea tied the cord, biting it free with her teeth, and Gilda scooped up the newborn infant and delivered it into Yvette's waiting linen-draped arms.

I was torn between attending Lady Adelie or rushing to where Yvette and Evelyn now huddled over the infant, dabbing at it with a washcloth and some dry linen. My mind was made up for me by Gilda, who snapped at me to help them move Lady Adelie to the bed.

Lady Adelie was quite faint from pain and effort, and Gilda, Jocea and myself had to carry her to the bed. In the doing, the two midwives also stripped off the outer woollen robe, now soiled with sweat and birth fluids, and bundled it to one side.

'She will need a wash down,' Jocea said, and I nodded, fetching a basin of tepid water that had been put aside a while since. I carried it to the bed, along with linens and towels. Gilda was clearing away the birthing stool and the mess around it, and Jocea said she would help me wash Lady Adelie down.

'The afterbirth has yet to come,' Jocea said. 'When it does, mind you do not break it, for it shall need to be buried whole.' I nodded again, already familiar with the knowledge that it was truly bad luck for the infant if its afterbirth was broken.

Jocea and I leaned the still fainting and limp Lady Adelie forward so we might strip off her soiled linen shift.

God's bones, I thought, *she will be glad enough to be rid of this foul garment!*

Just then I heard Yvette call my name and I looked up. Yvette was staring frantically at me, although Evelyn was looking down at the baby, frowning, a washcloth frozen in her hand in its journey from washbowl to the baby.

'No!' cried Yvette to me, and I wondered, in this last moment of sanity for the coming weeks, what she wanted.

No ... what?

Jocea was pulling hard at our lady's shift and I automatically tugged with her, the shift finally pulling over our lady's head as I stared in puzzlement at Yvette.

'No,' Yvette whispered, but my attention on her was broken by Jocea's low hiss of horror.

I looked down at our lady, naked now in the flickering light, and for one long moment could not comprehend what I saw.

First I wondered why she had yet *another* garment on beneath her linen shift.

Then my mind turned to wondering if a wild beast had crawled into the bed.

Then my eyes blinked and I realised what they saw.

Lady Adelie's shoulders, upper arms, breasts and back were covered by a thick furry layer of yellow fungus, lined and ridged with her sweat.

There were patches of fungus lower down, too, on her still distended belly and her upper thighs.

I blinked again, my eyes seeing, but my brain refusing to comprehend what I saw.

Lady Adelie regained some of her senses and she raised her face to mine.

She moaned, softly, then coughed — that dry hacking cough I had heard so often during the night when I lay in the solar.

A whiff of smoke came from her mouth.

Looking back now, from so many years, I still don't know what I thought at that moment. I think I was in such shock, my brain was refusing to comprehend, because comprehension would have been too much.

Lady Adelie coughed again.

Yvette was at my side tugging the sheets about my lady's strange body, and something in my mind registered that somehow she had known about this … and I thought of all those mornings in the past few weeks when I had gone into my lady's chamber to find her already up and clothed …

Lady Adelie pushed away Yvette's hands, and fell into a spasm of coughing.

And then, sweet Jesu save me from all the horrors of this tainted earth, I saw a faint wisp of smoke curling up from the fungus on my lady's back.

I looked, blinked, looked again, and in that instant a flame spurted. Before I or anyone else could cry out, or act, our beautiful Lady Adelie was engulfed in flames.

I find it difficult to speak now of the dreadfulness that ensued over the next few minutes, but I must, because from it followed all the horrors of the subsequent weeks.

Jocea, Yvette and I were closest to our lady, but all three of us were frozen with terror. Then, suddenly, I found myself able to act, and I seized a heavy coverlet from the foot of the bed and tried to smother our lady's flames with it. I heard screaming and realised that the sound issued from my own mouth, among others, but I kept trying to smother the flames, even though they beat at my own skin.

Poor, piteous Lady Adelie. Through it all her eyes never left my face and I could see her lips moving through the fire. I don't know what she tried to say, but I hoped then, as I do now, that it was a prayer for her soul.

I heard the sudden bang of the outer door being thrust open, and then Stephen was at my side, and Owain, and I felt myself shoved to one side as both men covered our lady in blankets and coverlets, shouting all the while for water.

I stumbled away, seeking one of the many bowls of water which littered the chamber. I found one, finally, and carried it back to the bed in shaking hands, to have it snatched by Owain and its contents dumped over Lady Adelie.

She was blackened all over, her mouth a gaping rictus of agony, her eyes still staring, now from lidless cradles.

Others carried water hence — Evelyn, Yvette, Gilda — until all that was in the chamber had been poured over our lady's form.

I saw her manage to raise one crisped arm for Owain to grasp the blackened claw that had once been her hand.

I don't know how he managed to touch it, let alone hold it as firmly as he did, for I know that I could not have done so.

Owain was chanting prayers, his voice harsh with horror.

I backed away, using as my excuse the number of people crowded about our lady's bed, until I felt the sharp edge of a chest in the back of my legs. I half turned, grateful to have something else to look at and saw Lady Adelie's child lying in his linens on the top of the chest.

A tiny boy, left half unwashed and unattended as his minders had fled to his mother's bed.

I took a deep breath and cried out, for even the infant's thin, half-starved body was covered with the vile yellow fungus.

He tried to cry and a wisp of smoke appeared, and my hand rushed down to his mouth, hoping that I could stop the nightmare before it became any worse.

But I was too late.

The child, too, was engulfed in flames.

Again I grabbed some heavy cloth close to hand and tried to smother the flames — there was no more water in the chamber, and it was an impossibility to run down flights of stairs to fetch more. I was more successful this time with this tinier body, and I thought I had succeeded in smothering the flames. I lifted a corner of the cloth carefully, to look, and a sheet of flame almost roared out at me.

I stumbled back reflexively, then felt hands grab my shoulders and pull me away.

Stephen.

He seized the bundle of cloth and flesh that was his younger brother, even though flames lapped at his hands, and half carried, half threw him onto the stone slab that sat before the fireplace, it's own fire now burning low.

Then Stephen stepped back.

He saw my face. 'We cannot save him,' he said. 'Let him burn. Owain can tend his soul later.'

At the time I thought them terrible words, but now, looking back, I know Stephen was as shocked and numbed as I. The baby meant little to him, his mother everything.

I turned back to the bed.

Everything smoked. The bedclothes and sheets, the hangings about the bed, even a small rug at the foot of the bed, but there were no more flames.

I forced myself to look to the thing that lay still and blackened on the bed. *Sweet Mary, let her be dead!*

I think she was, then, for everyone about the bed — the two midwives, Evelyn, Yvette, Owain, and Stephen — were still and staring.

The only sound was the harsh strain of Owain's voice, and the only movement that of his hand as he blessed and prayed for the soul of our sweet Lady Adelie, Countess of Pengraic.

Suddenly, horribly, I remembered how the earl had asked me to take care of his lady, over and over again, so fearful was he of her safety and I was swamped by guilt.

And fear.

A shadow flickered in a corner of the chamber and for one terrifying moment I thought it the imp I had seen in Oxeneford, come to steal my soul for my sins.

CHAPTER FIVE

∽◈∽

Stephen asked me to go to the kitchen to order food and small beer to be carried to the solar, as well as pitchers of water, and bowls we could use to wash in.

I nodded numbly, deeply relieved to be allowed to again leave the chamber that now stank of burned flesh and death.

'Then return here,' he said.

I nodded.

'You feel able to do this?' he asked, and I blinked away sudden tears at his kindness.

'I can do it,' I said.

'Do not speak to *anyone* of what has happened here.'

I shook my head. Gossiping about what I had just witnessed was not something I could have done in any case. I left the privy chamber, pausing in the solar for a long minute as I heaved in great breaths of fresh air to quell the queasiness of my stomach, before descending the stairs.

There were far more people in the kitchen this time — cooks, servants, butchers — and many of them paused to look at me curiously.

I realised I must be an intriguing sight, covered with damp patches, no doubt some soot, and my eyes half wild and braids hanging in disarray.

'Is the child born yet?' asked one of the cooks.

I remembered Stephen's admonition, but what could I do? 'Yes,' I said.

'And ...?' said another cook.

'A boy,' I said.

There were smiles and a murmur of conversation.

'Are mother and child well?'

Oh, sweet Jesu, what could I say? *Not truly. Both are blackened carcasses, gone either to heaven or hell, as the state of their souls dictate.*

'Both are well,' I said. 'Please send the food and water as soon as you may.'

Then I left, not able to bear any more questioning.

The solar was empty when I returned, and so I clenched my jaw and walked to the closed door of the privy chamber. I tried to open it, but was stopped by the bulk of Owain the moment it had opened a crack.

'It's Maeb,' he said over his shoulder, then he admitted me.

In the short time I had been gone, Stephen had managed to rouse everyone within to effect a remarkable change (I had no doubt it was Stephen, for no one else could have managed this). The bed had been stripped and all its clothes and hangings neatly folded, and placed in piles in the most shadowy corner of the room.

In front of the piles of textiles lay two shrouded bodies, one tiny. They were not immediately apparent, and I noticed them only because I looked for them.

'When the food and drink has arrived,' Stephen said, 'and the water with which to clean ourselves, we shall adjourn to the solar.'

I looked at him, then at the others. They all, as no doubt I, looked haggard and unkempt, everyone's clothes dampened and blackened here and there, hair straggled, eyes wide and shocked and staring at the horror they had lived through. One alone was bad enough, but I realised that if anyone saw this group as a whole they would know immediately that all sat badly with our lady and her child.

Oh, sweet Mother Mary, our lady. I looked again at the shrouded body, and my eyes filmed over with tears. I had loved Lady Adelie for her gentleness and kindness to me, and for her uncomplaining duty as wife and mother. I hoped I could be as virtuous a wife and mother as she.

I didn't think, not until later, that my own life now lay in mortal danger, and if I should live to be a wife and mother then that would be only by the grace of one of Lord Jesu's miracles.

* * *

The food, beer and water came, and the servants departed, and only then did Stephen allow us to move from the chamber of death into the solar. He called a guard to the stairwell, giving the order that we remain undisturbed; asking him also to tell the nurse who looked after Rosamund and John to keep Alice and Emmette in their chamber until Stephen came to talk to them. We all washed, taking our turns at the three bowls, and Evelyn, Yvette and I took advantage of the screen which hid Evelyn's and my bed to change our chemises and kirtles, glad to rid ourselves of our filthy clothes.

Once we were done we sat in a close group about the fireplace which someone, I know not who, had lit. We had all served ourselves some food — ladled meaty broth into bread trenchers, or taken some of the cold meats and cheese — but few among us had great appetite, still lost in the horror of Lady Adelie's and her child's deaths.

Jocea and Gilda shared a look, then put down their food.

'Great lord,' Gilda said to Stephen, and I looked at her, surprised both for the over-grandness of the title and the strange (for her) clarity of her voice. 'Great lord, my sister and I beg your leave to depart for Crickhoel.'

'No,' said Stephen. 'You may not leave this castle. I —'

He studied them for a moment, then rose and summoned yet another guard. This man Stephen talked to quietly for a few minutes, then asked Gilda and Jocea to accompany him.

'He will take you to the dormitories of the outer bailey,' Stephen said, 'for you shall be comfortable there, but you may not leave this castle.'

I felt my stomach turn over as I realised why Stephen said this, and I put my bread trencher down blindly by my feet, spilling a little of the gravy to the floor as I did so.

'My lord?' said Gilda, completely puzzled, unable to work through the implications of what had happened this day.

'Do you not realise what you would carry to the village?' Stephen said, his voice hard-edged. 'Do you not understand that all of us who had close association with our lady, now likely carry what killed her?'

I could not look at him, and there was utter silence after Stephen's words. I wondered who would break it, if any would be stupid enough to say something merry to relieve the tension, and jumped a little when a guard who'd been standing in the stairwell now stepped into the solar.

'My lord, the wet nurse Sewenna is here. Should I admit her?'

I had two thoughts at once: I could not believe she had taken so long to rouse herself to attend her lady — had the child lived it would have been half-starved by now — and I felt some anger that she *had* indeed arrived to intrude on the strange peace of our little group.

'No,' Stephen said, 'tell her to return to her husband and children. We shall not need her.'

I wondered what Sewenna would think of that.

When that man had gone, Stephen sent the two midwives off with their guard and sat down again.

'They are going to no dormitory,' he said, 'but into close confinement. It is necessary, I am afraid. For the moment I want no word of what happened to my lady mother and her child to spread about the castle. Maeb, what did you say when you went to the kitchens?'

'My lord, the cooks pressed me on what was happening, for word had spread that your lady mother was in her labour. I said only that the child had been born, a boy. One of the cooks asked if they were well, and I said aye. I am sorry ... I did not know what else to say.'

'That was good enough,' Stephen said. 'Thank you.'

His face was haggard, and I felt desperately sorry for him.

'You must rue your entrance here yesterday,' Stephen said to Evelyn, and I felt a sudden, terrible stab of guilt. Sweet Jesu, if only I hadn't insisted, Evelyn would now be safe in Crickhoel, planning her journey back to join her daughter and the de Tosny family as they moved to safety.

Evelyn, sitting close to me, reached out a hand and touched my arm. 'Is it the plague, my lord?'

I suppose someone had to ask. To confirm.

Stephen shifted his eyes to mine. 'Aye,' he said, softly.

'What can we do?' Evelyn said, her voice strained but still so very calm.

'Pengraic Castle is closed,' Stephen said. 'Yesterday we were keeping people out. Today ...' He gave a slight shrug of his shoulders, and managed a wry smile. 'Today we keep people in. My lady mother, may God and all his saints hold her and bless her, carried it hence, and now ... It sits so long unnoticed, spreading silently. We have all been near to my mother and will have carried it further afield within the castle.'

He paused. 'Did no one notice? That my mother ...?'

I could not look at Yvette. 'She had been coughing at night, this past week or so,' I said. 'I thought it only that the child … I did not even think … how could she have caught it, my lord? Where?'

Again Stephen shrugged. 'A travelling minstrel, a servant. Perhaps at Rosseley, perhaps on the journey here. Who knows? God, *God*.' Again he paused. 'Did *none* of you notice anything? That fungus was well spread … how could my lady mother have concealed it?'

Now I looked full at Yvette, challenging her.

She shifted uncomfortably, and finally spoke, her voice soft and apologetic. 'The fungus came three days ago, my lord. My lady … my lady begged me not to tell anyone. We kept it well hid.'

Stephen stared at her. 'You did not think for a moment to tell *me*? You did not think that I carry full responsibility for all at Pengraic and should by rights have known? Sweet Jesu, woman, if *I* had known, if *Owain* had known, mayhap we could have prevented my mother's terrible death! She did not even have time to confess! *Why the silence?*'

Yvette raised her head, and her voice was stronger. 'Your lady mother was terrified,' she said. 'As was I. We feared what might happen if we —'

'You think something *worse* could have happened than what actually did?' Stephen all but shouted.

Yvette dropped her eyes to her lap.

Stephen sighed. 'I will speak with d'Avranches,' he said, 'within the hour. He needs to know. Together we shall organise castle and garrison against the panic and sickness that will come. I will also send word to my father. I will need to risk a messenger, someone recently arrived who may not yet have had any contact with the plague in the castle. My father needs to know that the plague is here, and that his lady wife …'

Stephen had to stop and collect himself. 'We cannot let word of what truly transpired here spread about the castle. There would be panic. Thus we will tell people that while my lady mother gave birth to an infant son, both died within an hour. I don't know … there must be some reason we can give?'

'Your lady mother died of bleeding,' Yvette said. 'We could not staunch it. And the child? He was weakly and took a few bare breaths before expiring. If Mistress Maeb told people that all was well, then,' Yvette shrugged, 'she had left the chamber before these tragedies occurred.'

Stephen nodded. 'Good enough.' He rubbed at his eyes, tired and emotional. 'Sweet Jesu. I will need to tell Alice and Emmette their beloved mother is dead, although I will tell them Yvette's tale, not the true tragedy. Owain, what can we do to prepare for the sickness spreading?'

'I will sort through my herbs,' Owain said. 'Some may possibly be helpful. And I will organise men to clean out the chapel for the sick.'

Stephen gave him a slightly puzzled look.

'The sick need to go somewhere,' Owain said, 'and the chapel has a stone floor, walls and vaulting. It will be safe.'

I felt sick. Lady Adelie's torturous death could easily have set the castle ablaze with its wooden floors and panelling. It had only been by the fastest and most concerted effort that the fire had not spread from her bed (I remembered Stephen moving the poor child to the stone hearth to die in flames there).

Suddenly I imagined a score of people burning at the same time.

Suddenly I imagined flames crawling down my own skin.

For the first time, I realised that I would likely die in the coming weeks.

I bit my lip to stop the sob that almost escaped. Sweet Mother Mary, I did not want to die!

I lifted my eyes, and met Stephen's gaze. I saw in his face such sorrow, such care, that tears finally escaped, and the sob from my lips, and I bent my head and cried, given over to the grief of my lady's death and my own impending doom.

CHAPTER SIX

Numbed by all that had happened, I nonetheless managed to get through the day, glad to be busy. Stephen announced the death of his lady mother in childbed, and the baby with her. She was to be laid to rest that very same day (for anyone asking about the rush, Stephen said that his grief and the summer heat did not allow further delay).

It was given to Yvette, Evelyn and myself to prepare Lady Adelie and her child for burial. The castle carpenters were building a casket for her, and we needed to shroud our lady in garments and wrappings suitable for one of her rank.

Normally we would have washed her body, dressed her hair, and garbed our lady in her finest robes for burial.

But none of us could face her blackened, terrible corpse. We had loved Lady Adelie and owed her full respect, but we simply could not touch her terrible corpse in its full, horrific nakedness. To this day it is a guilt I still carry. I wondered how it would be for me upon my own death.

We first re-clothed the bed in fresh hangings and bedclothes and removed any trace of soot from the walls, floor and furniture. Then, gritting our teeth, we took Lady Adelie's hastily-wrapped corpse from its shadowy corner, unwrapped as much as we could bear, then carried her to the bed. There she lay, wrapped in several layers of linen; we could not face unwinding her any more.

We stood, and stared.

'What shall we do?' I whispered, feeling anew the terror of the manner of Lady Adelie's death.

Her corpse was twisted and contracted by the fire that had consumed it. Within the hour we needed to have her prepared for the casket the carpenters would be carrying into this chamber, and poor Lady Adelie needed to be laying flat, her arms crossed over her breast, in peaceful repose. If she were all crooked and twisted, then the tale that she had died in childbed was immediately going to be exposed for the lie it was.

'We will need to fix things,' Yvette said, full of practicality, and, her mouth fixed in a grim, tight line, she grasped Lady Adelie's left arm, which poked upward beneath the wrappings. Try as she might, however, she could not move it.

'We will need to break it,' Evelyn said, and my mouth dropped open in horror as I stared at her.

'When I was young,' Evelyn continued, 'my uncle died in a fire. His corpse looked much the same as the Lady Adelie's. In order to fit him into his casket, we had to break his limbs.'

'What can we use?' Yvette said, and at that moment all I wanted was to flee the room. The thought of being here when Yvette and Evelyn …

'Last year,' Evelyn said, moving over to the fireplace, 'there was a loose brick here in the hearth. If it has not been remortared … no, it is still loose.'

Oh sweet Jesu.

Evelyn came back to the bed, carrying the brick. 'I am so sorry, my lady,' she said, and she lifted the brick high.

I turned away; I could not watch. But I stood there, my face in my hands, for the next while as a sickening series of thuds and snaps came from behind me.

After a while, blessedly, it ceased and I felt a soft hand on my shoulder. 'I am sorry, Maeb,' Evelyn said, 'but it needed to be done.'

I wiped the tears from my face. 'We should pray for her.'

'Later,' said Yvette, 'when she is safely in her casket. We must continue now, for who knows when the casket shall arrive.'

So we continued, the work not quite so vile. Lady Adelie was still wrapped in the linens — somehow Evelyn and Yvette had done their work without the need to unwrap her — and so we merely straightened her as best we could, avoiding looking at the loathsome stains where bodily fluids from her broken corpse seeped through the linens. We collected the form of the infant, also wrapped, and placed it across Lady Adelie's feet, binding it tightly in place. Then we wrapped both corpses in many layers of some fresh unmarked linens, then in a thickly embroidered woollen wrap. These masked the destruction beneath, as well as the smell of burned flesh, and provided a suitable richness for Lady Adelie's, and her child's, rank.

I suppose the other two women, as I did, wondered occasionally about the plague the corpses must carry, but then, like me, they had already been so heavily exposed to Lady Adelie that I think we feared her wrapped corpse less than her living body.

We knelt by the bed, our hands clasped, our heads bent, and we prayed for our lady and her child. We begged Lady Adelie's forgiveness for the vile things we had done to her corpse, and entreated the saints to take care of her in heaven, where she surely was.

Then, when the carpenters arrived, we rose from our knees and allowed them entry.

Lady Adelie and her child were interred late that afternoon in the chapel. It was a sombre affair for most attending — those of Lady Adelie's children present within the castle, the senior commanders and soldiers of the garrison, the castle servants. But for Stephen, Yvette, Evelyn and myself it had an added overtone of dreadfulness. How soon before there were myriad services? How soon before a chorus of grieving carried on through each day and night? How soon before death grew so abundant that services were dispensed with and the dead buried unceremoniously in a pit beyond the castle walls and no one the strength left to grieve?

Several of the wives of the castle servants stood to one side and wailed and sobbed, rending their hair. It was to be expected at a funeral for someone of the rank of Lady Adelie, and no one paid them much mind. Owain conducted the service with swiftness, spending only a little time on the sermon, speaking to us of Lady Adelie's life spent serving her lord, her children and those within her household. He spoke also of the nature of grief and of comfort, and how we should hold dear Lady Adelie's memory.

I listened to little of it as I held dear Rosamund in my arms. I had not spent much time with her in the past weeks, for my service to her mother had taken up so much of my days. But now I cuddled her tight, stroking her forehead now and then and murmuring comfort to her. Poor girl, she did not understand what was happening, and was upset more by others' grief and the wailing of the women than from her own comprehension of the loss of her mother.

I held her tight, and wondered what would become of her.

Looking about the chapel, I could see some of the subtle changes Owain had wrought to turn the chapel's use from worship to care of the dying. Right at the back were stacks of trestle beds, from what I could glimpse beneath the cloth coverings. There were a pile of bowls and some cloths discretely stacked in another corner. The chapel had little furniture in the nave, but I did notice that some of the side screens had been moved against the walls. It would take little time for the sick to be accommodated.

I bent my head and wept, now unable to keep my sorrow from Rosamund, my sobs joining in chorus with those of the other women. I had shed so many tears today, but it seemed that there was supply enough left to shed many more.

That night, late, Stephen came to the solar. All three of us — Evelyn, Yvette and myself — shared this space, but now Stephen did not care overmuch for convention, or what Evelyn and Yvette thought.

More than anything, that drove home how dire he regarded our situation.

'Mistress Maeb,' he said, shaking me awake by my shoulder. 'Rise if you will, robe yourself, and join me. I will be waiting in the stairwell.'

Then he was gone.

'Maeb?' Evelyn, wakening.

I struggled to sit on the side of the bed, not certain if I had dreamed Stephen's presence.

'Was that Lord Stephen?' Evelyn said.

'Aye,' I said, 'he wants me to join him.'

I could almost hear Evelyn thinking this through in her mind, but eventually all she did as I pulled on my robe and laced it tight was to sigh and tell me to be careful.

Yvette, on a trestle bed a short distance away, said nothing, but I could see the glint of her eyes in the gloom.

I kissed Evelyn on the cheek and said I would not be long. Then, straightening out my braids as I went, I joined Stephen in the stairwell.

* * *

He led me upward to the roof of the great keep. It was a vast space, a roof of slate that gently sloped to the outer walls.

In marked contrast to our earlier night excursion, Stephen was in a sombre mood.

'Dear God,' he said as we halted near the southern parapet of the roof, 'this is going to be bad, Maeb. I am sorry you have been caught up in it.'

'I would have been caught up in it wherever I was, my lord. Even had I stayed in Witenie.'

'I sent a messenger to my father earlier. This will take him hard. He believed we'd be safe here. The loss of my mother …'

'He loved her.'

'She was a good wife to him. He held her in high esteem.'

I nodded.

'Look at the river from up here on high. See how it gleams silver in the moonlight?'

I looked. From our vantage point we could look right down the Usk Valley and the winding silver ribbon of the river. The night was so peaceful, I could almost let myself believe that all was right with our world.

'I cannot tell what will happen here, Maeb, but I do not think it good.'

'If the plague has struck all along our route, then any of us who travelled from Rosseley might already be harbouring the death. We cannot assume your lady mother will be the only death.'

He looked at me sombrely, and nodded. 'She was the first, perhaps, because she was already weakened by the child.'

Again, I felt cold, and ill. There was not just the family and Lady Adelie's attending women, but also the servants and the large escort who had come with us. Perhaps even now I was sickening and did not yet realise it. Perhaps even now a soldier in the northern keep was coughing gently during the night and thinking little of it.

'What is going to happen, my lord?'

'People within this castle are going to fall ill. There is nothing we can do to prevent that. We must manage this horror as best we can, but eventually panic will consume this castle, and then, well, then it will become unsafe. I have talked long and hard with d'Avranches. I think we can maintain discipline for as long as the sickness here remains confined to a few. But once … if … it spreads throughout the castle, then panic will be impossible to avoid.'

He sighed, leaning over the parapet, looking at the view. 'Maeb, I brought you here for a reason.'

He stopped then, falling into a silence.

'My lord?' I said as the silence stretched out between us.

'Maeb,' he said, straightening, 'I cannot bear the thought that I might die as my mother has done. The horror … Maeb, I asked you here to ask you a question. If I fall ill … if the fungus consumes me … would you suffocate me? The thought that I might burn …'

His voice broke, and maybe I should have comforted him, but my mind was in turmoil.

'What you ask is a mortal sin, my lord! I cannot murder you!'

'I *beg* you, Maeb!'

'No! My lord, I cannot. Why ask *me*?'

'Because I think only you have the mercy to do it.'

I could not reply. His request had so horrified me that I was now lost for anything to say. It was not just that Stephen was asking me to murder him, a sin that would condemn me to hell unless I could receive absolution, but the idea that he might himself fall ill from this terrible disease was almost too much to bear.

'I would do the same for you,' he said, very gently. 'Maeb, there is no hope from this plague. No one survives it. If I fall sick, if the fungus appears on my skin, please, do as I ask … as I beg.'

I could not believe we were standing here discussing such things.

'No,' I whispered, taking a step back. I took another step, and he came forward, taking one of my hands in his.

'Maeb, I am so sorry. I shall not ask it of you again.'

'I cannot.'

'I know. I am sorry.'

'Cannot.' I found myself unable to stop repeating it.

'Maeb —'

'Surely your father can help.' It was stupid, and I knew it instantly, but I could not bear Stephen to speak so of his death and of murder.

Stephen dropped my hand and sighed yet again. 'The situation in England is worse than I said to my lady mother. Far worse. The plague has

143

spread wide and deep. Many, many thousands have died. Horribly. Some towns have burned to the ground. What has happened in the more isolated villages, I cannot tell. I have heard even that some ships, having sailed from our shores, have sunk aflame within days of leaving port. It is truly a terrible death, Maeb.'

I felt that last was unnecessary, and used solely to advance his own cause.

'All is in disarray,' Stephen continued. 'Edmond has forces spread over much of southern England, trying to keep or restore order, but, of course, even they are being decimated. Now, I think, Edmond has moved to a policy of only entering an area *after* the plague has spent itself. As for the harvest this year, well, God and his saints shall have to get it in, for I fear common man shall be unable to do so. Whoever survives this, Maeb, may face starvation next winter.

'As for my father. What can he do? Maybe he also harbours the death. Maybe he is already dead and my messenger shall have no one to tell of our loss. We are on our own for this, sweet Mae. On our own.'

I felt a rush of sympathy for Stephen. He was of an age with me, and yet had to shoulder the responsibilities and cares for this entire castle.

All I could do was shake in fear.

'What do we do?' I asked him. 'What now?'

'We wait,' he said. 'And watch.'

He reached out and pulled me into a gentle embrace. I didn't resist. More than anything I needed comfort, and to be held.

I rested my head against his chest clad in only a thin linen shirt on this warm summer's night.

Stephen held me close, stroking my hair, and I slowly relaxed. He drew in a deep breath ... and I froze in terror as I heard, very faintly, a crackling deep within his lungs.

CHAPTER SEVEN

W ithout Lady Adelie, Yvette, Evelyn and myself were purposeless. Having cleaned and scrubbed the privy chamber, we spent our time in the solar, indifferently sewing or stitching sundry fabrics that were the worse for our attention. Alice and Emmette sat with us, subdued and grieving the death of their mother. Rosamund and baby John spent several hours with us each day, and they were our only cheerfulness, for neither understood what had happened to their mother and only wanted to play and chortle.

We were waiting for death to strike, all of us save Alice and Emmette who knew not the true nature of their mother's death.

My mind was almost fully on Stephen. I wondered if I had imagined that crackle in his lungs, if my overall fright had constructed it. I could not bear the thought that he might fall victim to the plague, partly because of my own affection for him and partly because I did not wish to be faced with his request that I should smother his breath.

No. No. I could not do that. It was a sin, a dreadful sin, and would condemn me to hell. How could he ask that of me?

So we sat, mostly in silence, our hands jabbing uselessly in and out of fabric, waiting for death.

On the third day after Lady Adelie's funeral it arrived.

Evelyn and I were woken in the early hours of the morning by a terrible hacking cough coming from Yvette's bed. We stumbled up, grabbing at our mantles, terrified at what it might be, and knowing to our very bones that we were right to be so terror-struck.

I lit a candle from the coals in the fireplace and brought it to Yvette's bedside.

She was still coughing as she retched up gouts of yellow fungus.

It was everywhere; spattering her pillow and covers, staining her mouth and chin and breast.

Amid it all, her frightened eyes, staring at us.

'Fetch Owain,' Evelyn murmured. I handed her the candle and fled.

Owain insisted we shift Yvette into the chapel. Evelyn and I said we could nurse Yvette for a few days, surely, in the solar. Owain prevailed.

Yvette could still walk, so Evelyn and myself helped her down the stairwell, across the courtyard of the great keep and through the inner bailey to the chapel. I know Stephen had wanted to keep the fact that the plague had struck inside the castle secret, but it was no longer possible.

Men stopped and stared as Yvette coughed her way across the inner bailey, a yellow-stained cloth gripped to her mouth. When we stepped inside the chapel, it was to see two of the beds already occupied.

'Men-at-arms,' Owain said. 'They came in last night.'

'Were they from our escort?' I said, and Owain gave a tight nod.

I felt my stomach, already twisted with fear, clench even tighter.

'Over here,' Owain said, leading us to an area partitioned with church screens. Owain left us, and Evelyn and I helped Yvette out of her kirtle and put her to bed in her chemise. No one spoke. There were six trestle beds in this area and I had the feeling six would not be enough.

Evelyn caught my eye. 'We can take it in turns sitting with Yvette,' she said, and I nodded dumbly. 'Return after midday,' she continued. 'Have some rest now.'

Again I nodded, leaving the chapel. I did not quite know what to do, so eventually I trod up the stairwell and into the female dormitory where the nurse and the children had their cubicles.

The children and their nurse were gathered in a large space they used as their day room. Alice and Emmette were sitting by a window, looking completely blank.

As I entered, the nurse turned about, John in her arms, and said worriedly, 'He has such a fever!'

I stood there, then burst into tears.

The next week was hell on earth, for it seemed as though hell itself had crawled into the sunlight and infested the castle. The day after Yvette started to hack up the yellow fungus a further twenty people fell ill.

The day after that, with John already ailing, Alice and Emmette both succumbed to the plague. Coughing up the fungus in the morning, by the evening it had covered their bodies, and Owain made the grim decision to lay them directly on mats on the stone floor of the chapel.

'Best to save the beds,' he said.

Yvette was dead. She had died just before the two girls were carried into the chapel, self-immolating in a terrible, shrieking fireball that drove both Evelyn and myself out of the chapel, unable to watch.

The chapel stunk, not only of sickness, but of burned flesh, and smoke seemed to hang continually about its vaulted roof.

Owain worked tirelessly, silently.

Stephen, who had come to see his sisters, was equally grimly silent.

I managed to speak to him outside as he left.

'What can we do?' I said.

'Nothing but endure,' Stephen answered. 'Do you still feel well?'

I nodded, but I lied. My body ached and pained all over, but I didn't know if this was the plague manifesting itself, or just muscle aches caused by sleepless nights and the constant trudging between chapel and keep, the nursing of Yvette and, now, the two girls.

'God save us,' I whispered, looking at Stephen. His face was sunken and grey, his skin waxy, and I could see the fever in his eyes.

I did not have to ask him how he fared.

'I am going to stay with my sisters,' he said to me. 'Do for them what needs to be done.' He paused. 'Do you understand?'

I nodded, hopeless.

'And do you remember what I asked of you?' he said, very softly.

I nodded, too exhausted, too distraught, too heart-sick to be horrified.

'I —' Stephen began, then we both jumped, startled by the sound of Alice screaming.

We rushed inside the chapel and behind the screens of the women's section.

There Alice tossed on her mat locked in some delirium so terrifying she had kicked off all her covers and fought against Evelyn who was trying to restrain her.

'No!' Alice screamed, and, sweet Jesu, there was such *terror* in her voice. 'No! I do not have it! I do not have it!'

'Alice!' Stephen cried, at her bedside. 'Alice, wake, wake!'

But no matter how he shook her, Alice did not rouse from her delirium. 'No! No! Stay away. Begone. I do not have it! Not!'

Suddenly she arched her back completely off the bed, her cries now so piteous they tore at my heart. Stephen grabbed at her, thinking to hold her tight, but Alice was, in her extremity, too strong even for him. She fought him off as if he were the Devil, then shrieked, a sound that I shall not forget to my dying day, and collapsed back to the bed, utterly limp.

We all stared, then Owain bent down and placed his hand near her mouth.

'She is gone,' he said. He straightened, looking at Stephen. 'Three have died this way, shrieking as if the Devil himself were after them, and crying that they do not have "it", whatever "it" might be, nor do they know where "it" is. They have died of sheer dread, I think.'

Owain sighed, then knelt by Alice's bed, murmuring a prayer.

I took a step backward and, as I did so, Stephen put his hand to his mouth and stifled a cough.

Owain's head shot up, his face white.

All order within the castle vanished. People fled, not caring if they took the plague with them. Guards no longer manned the gates and, eventually, they stood halfway open with no one bothered to close them.

No one wanted to enter.

Stephen and d'Avranches had tried to keep order, initially, but had ceased their efforts after it became obvious to everyone that the castle harboured plague.

The kitchen was deserted, save those who, like me, came to rummage about for something to eat. Evelyn spent all her time helping in the chapel, now thick with bodies that coughed fungus which spattered even over the strange paintings on the wall. I tried to bring her some food, but she said she felt ill and no longer wanted to eat.

I had the two children, John and Rosamund, in my care. Their nurse had fled one night, leaving her charges alone. When I checked them late one morning I found both children huddled together in Rosamund's bed, their faces and bottoms wet, their eyes pools of distress.

I was furious with the nurse. Incandescent with rage, but I think, looking back now, much of that rage was frustration and fear finding outlet in anger. I scooped up the two children and cleaned them, and clothed them in fresh dresses and stockings, and hugged them tight.

John had a small patch of fungus on his right shoulder, even though he was not coughing. He had fought this longer than I thought possible, but now it appeared the plague tightened its grip on him.

I had come to expect that fungus now, on almost anyone I met, so it did not set me to tears and terrors as once it had. I merely determined to do as much for the children as I could. I owed that much to their mother, and put them to bed in a cot in their parents' privy chamber.

I thought it would be a good place for them to die.

No one lived through this. Not a single person. Everyone died who went into the chapel, as did those who fell ill elsewhere in the castle and were left where they lay. Two buildings in the outer bailey had burned down. A floor had burned through in the northern keep. D'Avranches, I heard, had ordered any among the knights or soldiers struck down to be dragged — by their heels if necessary — through the keep and into either of the baileys, or to the chapel if they could be got that far. And for those left … I heard d'Avranches wandered the garrison at night, his dagger drawn.

It didn't shock me. Everyone feared the fire, and I am certain those who met their end other than by the flames were grateful for it.

I began to re-think what Stephen had asked of me.

Anything was better than the terrible death the plague dealt.

The day after I brought Rosamund and John to the privy chamber, Stephen met me as I was climbing up the stairwell from the kitchen, a bowl of pottage in my hands. I don't know who was going to eat it; both Rosamund and John were very ill, and I had no appetite.

'Stephen,' I said, my voice cracking, glad beyond measure to see him.

He looked terrible, his cheeks sunken, his skin grey, his eyes red-rimmed and swollen. I tried to persuade myself it was exhaustion from all the care he carried on his shoulders, but in my heart I knew it was the sickness.

'Maeb,' he said, and caught me briefly to him, taking the pottage in one of his hands, the other sliding about my shoulders.

I cried a little as he held me, my heart broken over this waste of life, and that Stephen, too, looked certain to die. He was a good man, kind as well as noble, and he should have lived to become one of the greatest aristocrats of his age.

But no, it seemed that his life was to be forfeit, and all for no reason that I could determine.

'Where are God and His saints?' I said. 'Why are we left to die like this, like dogs?'

He said nothing, just held me tighter, his face pressed into my hair.

After a while he spoke. 'I have come to see John and Rosamund.' Now his voice trembled. 'I don't know if ... if ...'

'They are still alive,' I said, 'although both sicken. Come, I have them in their mother's room.'

'Emmette is dead,' he said. 'The fungus covered her face. I ... I made certain she didn't suffer.'

'Sweet Jesu,' I muttered, 'how is it come to this?'

'Through God's grace,' Stephen said, and his voice was rich with bitterness.

We climbed the stairwell and walked through the solar — empty, its contents scattered as if someone had rifled through them (could it have been me, in some delirium? I couldn't remember) — and into the privy chamber.

John and Rosamund were in their cot, both quiet.

The cot was set on the stone hearth of the fireplace.

We walked up quietly and stood together, touching slightly, looking down.

Both children were sleeping peacefully, God knows why, because both of their faces were covered with the vile yellow fungus and they struggled to breathe through its furry grip.

Tears rolled down my cheeks. Why these children? What sin had they committed to be so punished? They were good children, both of them sunny and happy and a joy to all who spent time in their company. They had been born to a life of nobility and power, and yet what good had it done them? What point their lives?

Stephen caught my eye and gave me a long hard look.

I nodded.

'Wait outside,' he said.

'No,' I said, 'I will do them the honour of standing with them.'

He gave a nod, then took a pillow from the bed. It was large and would cover both their faces at once.

Somehow I was glad.

I took Rosamund's hand and her little fingers gripped mine even in her sleep.

'Do it now,' I said, and I used my other hand to help push the pillow down onto the children's faces.

CHAPTER EIGHT

W e lay together on the bed, side by side, our bodies touching in a dozen different places. The privy chamber was very quiet now that the two children no longer breathed, but occasionally muffled shouts or wails came in through the window from the outer bailey. There was no movement or sound from within the great keep at all, and I wondered if it held nothing but corpses. How we had not yet burned down I did not know.

'I have the sickness,' Stephen said quietly.

'I know,' I said.

'And you?'

I was quiet a while before I spoke. 'I woke coughing this morning,' I said. 'My lungs rattled when I did so. I cannot bear to change my soiled linens and kirtle, lest I see the fungus.'

His hand fumbled to catch mine in its grip. 'I loved you that first day I saw you, did you know that?'

I smiled a little. 'No. I was too worried you might see the love shining from my own face. Your father was not happy.'

He gave a soft laugh, ending it in a bout of coughing. He wiped his mouth with the back of his free hand. 'Before we left Oxeneford he talked to me most plain, said I was not to embark upon any ruinous affair of the heart with you.'

'And yet here we share a bed, and my lord's bed at that.'

Stephen chuckled again. 'Oh, sweetheart, how I wish that …' He stopped and gave a small sob.

I rolled over and buried my face in his shoulder. His arm held me close. We lay like that for a long time, each of us thinking wishes that, when we were well, we dared not consummate. And of which we now felt no need.

'Even that day I first met you,' he said, very softly, 'I knew that you and I could never be.'

'Why say that, Stephen? I love you truly, as I could love no other.'

He kissed the top of my forehead. 'Oh,' he said, 'perhaps you will live, somehow, and wed a great man and love him dear.'

I thought delirium had taken hold of Stephen's mind.

'Have you sent any more messages to your father?' I asked, trying to deflect his mind from me.

'Aye. One. For all the good it will do — even if the messenger lives to deliver it. I know my father. I know he will dash here, if he lives and has the strength. But for what? To find his family dead and gone.'

'And my corpse in his bed,' I said, managing a smile. Then it died. 'Oh, Stephen, I promised him most faithfully I would look after Lady Adelie. He was so worried for her. And now, the worst has happened.'

'It is not your fault, Maeb. He shall not blame you.'

'He does not like me,' I said, 'and I am sure he can find the capacity to lay the blame at my feet. Sweet Virgin Mary, Stephen, I helped push that pillow down into the faces of his children! What shall happen to me, and to my soul?'

In the end it was not the earl's anger I needed to worry about, but God's judgment.

'Who could judge you, Maeb, for what you did? But if you fear, then confess to Owain, and do penance, and all will be well.'

I hoped he was right, for I had been thinking on my immortal soul a great deal over the past days.

'Have you thought on my request of you, Maeb?' Stephen said.

'Oh, Stephen ... yes, I will do it, but that will leave me alone in the world and I shall die alone, and terribly, and I do not think I have the strength.'

He pulled me even tighter. 'I will think of something for you, Mae. Sweetheart, after I die ... will you ask Owain to conduct services for me? Please? Do not forget it. You *must* tell Owain that I have died.'

'He will know that I ... that I ...'

'He will not think less of you for it. He will not berate you. But my soul *must* be given into Owain's hands. Promise me.'

And what if I should die before all this could be accomplished? Stephen seemed to think too highly of my own capacity to survive his death.

But I nodded, wanting to comfort him.

'Thank you,' he whispered.

I woke much later. It was full night and I was cold, but it was not the chill which had woken me.

Stephen was tossing in his sleep. He began murmuring, even as he tossed, and then shouting. 'No! No! I do not have it! Saint Mary save me! Christ save me! Saint —'

I shook him as hard as I could, but even so it took me some effort to shake him awake.

'Stephen! Stephen! It was but a dream. You are awake, now.'

He lay there, his face white and shining with sweat in the night, his breath rattling harsh through his throat. 'It was the Devil, Maeb. Come for me. Sweet Jesu, it was the Devil, not some mere dream. He had me by the throat!'

'Shush, it *was* but a dream. The Devil shall not have your soul.'

'He is after us, Maeb. He is walking this land. This plague is Devil-sent, I know it. Sweet merciful Jesu save us, save us, save us.'

I opened my mouth to try and reassure Stephen, but just then I looked down and, in the faint light, I could see the bruises of finger marks about his throat.

We lay awake until dawn, close side by side, hands clasped, talking. Stephen talked of his childhood, and his youth spent in the household of Edmond, King of England.

'It was such an honour, Maeb, to be taught my skills as a knight within Edmond's household.'

I remembered my conversation with Saint-Valery, and how the king mistrusted Pengraic because of his vast power. 'Perhaps Edmond merely wanted to keep an eye on you.'

Stephen chuckled, although his mirth ended with a wracking cough. 'Perhaps. But I was honoured nonetheless, and I enjoyed my time in his household. Edmond is a strong and cunning man. Too often, all that people see is the mild mannered, overly courteous king, content to spend his time allowing his eye to rove over the beauteous women of court. But that is merely a façade. Edmond's barons may think they wield much of the power in the realm, but Edmond always gets his way. Even my father has oft been frustrated in his dealings with Edmond. Never underestimate him.'

I thought Edmond had done well to accept the young Stephen into his household, for he had won the heart of the young Pengraic who would one day be earl.

I immediately caught myself, my eyes welling with tears. Edmond's efforts had been in vain, for the young, noble Pengraic would be unlikely to survive the next day.

And who knew if Edmond still survived? I wondered how England itself would survive, if so many died, and among them those nobles we relied on to defend us.

But it would not affect me. I would die soon of the plague, too, whatever Stephen seemed to think. My exhaustion had grown worse, and with it the pain in my chest. Breathing was becoming ever more difficult, and I had found myself panting when doing things that normally cost me little effort.

During the night, I had coughed out sputum with a vile, yellow stain.

My clothes were filthy, and I should change them, but I could not for fear of seeing the fungus on my body.

Once Stephen died, I did not know what I would do. I wondered if d'Avranches was still alive, and if he had his dagger to hand. That would be preferable to burning alive. I could not face that.

Or I could climb to the heights of the great keep and throw myself from its parapets, but I did not know if I had the courage for such, and I also feared that I might linger, broken and in agony, on the rocks below until the flames claimed me.

Sweet Virgin Mary, everyone within the castle now understood how the plague claimed its victims. How many others were planning, or had accomplished, their own death? How many more souls were willing to risk hell, if only to escape the most terrible of deaths?

At dawn Stephen fell into a fitful slumber. I did not like to leave him, but there was no water left in the chamber and I wanted to go down to the kitchen and see if the water barrels had anything left within them. I thought Stephen would like to be washed of his sweat, and I could do my face and hands even if I could not bear to strip away my clothes from my tainted body.

To my surprise Evelyn and Owain were seated at one of the tables, sharing a jug of small beer.

They both looked exhausted ... but exhausted only. Neither showed any signs of the plague.

'Maeb!' Evelyn rose, her movements slow and obviously stiff, and hugged me. Then she put her hands on my shoulders and looked at me carefully.

'Oh Maeb,' she said, her eyes filling with tears, 'I wish ...'

I wished too, but wishes no longer counted for anything.

'Where have you been?' she said. 'I have worried about you, but until now neither Owain nor I had any time to come search for you.' She gave a small wry smile. 'We came as far as the kitchen, saw the jug of beer set here, and thought we'd revive ourselves a little before continuing.'

'It does not matter,' I said. I sat down on the bench next to Owain. 'What is happening beyond the keep?'

He sighed, rubbing his eyes and face with a hand. His tonsure was unkempt, and his face lightly beaded. 'The chapel is full of the dying,' he said. 'It stinks of death. D'Avranches tells me that most of the soldiers and knights have either sickened and died, or will shortly do so. Of those who have not sickened, some have fled, but some have stayed to help nurse the infected through to their deaths.'

'D'Avranches is still well?' I asked, thinking of his dagger.

'Aye, if exhausted and heartsick,' Owain said. 'Maeb, have you seen Stephen?'

'He lies dying in the lord's privy chamber,' I said. 'I came down here to fetch some water to wash him of his sweat.'

'Oh, heavenly saints!' Owain said. 'Stephen is to die?'

'He asked that you —'

'Yes, yes. Maeb, he must not burn.'

'Do any of us wish that?' I said, stifling a cough with only the greatest of difficulty. My patience had vanished long ago: my lungs and face were burning, and my head throbbed with a terrible ache. I thought the fever might consume me before I had a chance to return to Stephen.

Owain and Evelyn shared a glance, and I thought, somewhat uncharitably, that it was unfair of them to judge my manners now.

'Maeb,' Evelyn said, 'in the chapel … we …'

'Only a few have died by the flames in the chapel,' Owain said. 'Those we did not catch in time.'

I frowned at them, puzzled, so distracted now by my headache I wondered if I had missed something.

'We have made sure, as best we could,' Owain said, his voice now immeasurably gentle, 'that the sick have died before the flames consumed them.'

You do not worry for your immortal soul? I was going to ask, but there was only one word that slipped my lips. 'How?'

'I have been giving them an infusion of hemlock,' Owain said.

'But we are almost at an end of the herb,' said Evelyn. 'Owain has sent a man, who yet shows no sign of illness, further down the valley for more — there is an apothecary there who will have it.'

'Stephen needs that,' I said, suddenly seeing a way out for Stephen that might be kinder than what he proposed.

And a way out for me, too.

'It is not a pleasant death,' Owain said, 'but better than burning. Maeb, there is very little left. When I have more, I will send Evelyn.'

'Thank you,' I said, my voice thick with relief.

CHAPTER NINE

I found some water, enough to wash Stephen down, and went back to the privy chamber. Stephen had fallen into a fitful sleep, and he did not rouse when I stripped him of his clothes, the effort making me breathe hard and cough several times.

I did not look in the cloth when I coughed, but folded it quickly as I took it away from my mouth. Now, suffering myself, I could understand Lady Adelie's denial. It was easier, this way.

Stephen had several patches of fungus on his body: in his left armpit, over his left knee, and on his right thigh. I washed him down as well as I could, but I was not strong enough to roll him over to wash his back, and Stephen, in his sleep, did not wish to cooperate with me.

I tried to wash away the fungus, but it would not budge.

As I washed, I kept thinking what a waste this was. Stephen was a fine man with a strong body. Why did God inflict this on him? No one would miss me, but England would miss Stephen most terribly. He would have matured into a strong lord. Why take him? What grievous sin had he committed that he needed to suffer in this manner? What grievous sin all those who suffered in this castle?

I wondered about Rosamund and John. Why had God wanted them to die as they did? Neither had sinned ... by all the saints in heaven, what mortal sin could a toddling child commit, save that he had been born?

My thoughts and mood darkened as I washed and wondered. Perhaps Stephen and I deserved it. We had committed grievous sin with the murder of Rosamund and John, true. But Lady Adelie? She had died in a manner most horrid, her death the most agonising possible, a death usually reserved for the most appalling of sinners.

But unless there was some dark, terrible secret in Lady Adelie's life (which I could not believe), there was no reason for the manner of her death.

I grew angry with God for inflicting this plague upon his peoples. Perhaps some deserved it, but I am sure most did not.

When I had done I covered Stephen with linens and a thin woollen coverlet, then lay down beside him. The effort of washing him had exhausted me, and I fell into a doze.

The Devil came for me. I dreamed I was trapped in some dark, confined space. Suddenly something loomed behind me, and I turned, my heart racing.

It was a beast of indescribable horror. It radiated power that crushed me. I could do nothing against it. I could not flee, I could not fight. I was defenceless before it. It opened its mouth, and in that great yawning maw I could see leaping flames and hear from within the screams of the damned.

I thought I would die of terror. I choked on the stench of the monster (*the Devil! The Devil! Somehow I knew it but I refused to acknowledge it, because that admission would have killed me*) and his breath.

Where is it? the monster demanded of me. *Where did you hide it?*

I twisted this way and that, but I was unable to loose myself from his terrible power.

Where is it?

I didn't know what it wanted. I had hid nothing. I could not answer, although I was desperate to tell it what it wanted, so that I could be freed.

I can smell its stink on you! Where is it?

'I don't know!' I screamed.

And then suddenly I was awake, Stephen's concerned face close to mine.

'You dreamed, too,' he said, and I nodded, crying.

He pulled me closer and held me, and we lay there in silence all that morning and into the afternoon.

* * *

159

I dozed off again, although thankfully this time I did not dream. When I woke it was full night and Stephen was struggling for his life beside me.

I lurched upright, cursing myself for falling asleep. Every one of my bones ached and hot pain seared up and down my spine.

I cried out, the momentary agony forcing me to hold my breath until it had passed.

Only then did I manage to turn to Stephen.

He was gasping, unable to breathe properly, almost as if he had something stuck in his throat. One of his hands was, indeed, clasped about his throat.

The other, on the side farthest from me, waved weakly in the air.

'Stephen? Stephen?' I blinked, trying to clear my vision. Earlier I had lit a candle and placed it in a wall sconce, and by its weak, guttering light, I saw that fungus spilled out of Stephen's mouth and down his chin to his neck.

Oh, sweet Virgin Mary! It must be choking him!

His eyes caught mine, pleading, and at that moment — unfairly — I hated both Evelyn and Owain with every particle of my being for not providing the hemlock in time.

The appalling horror of Stephen's suffering made me panic. I knew what he wanted — his eyes were locked into mine, begging, begging, begging — but I could not do it, the horror of it, I could not —

His hand grabbed mine, clutching tightly, and his eyes brimmed with tears.

Do it, they said. *Please. Please.*

I was sobbing at his suffering. I could not bear it. Yet, at the same moment, I could not bear to end his life. Not Stephen, not Stephen …

Please, Maeb. Please.

Consumed with grief and anger and fear, I grabbed one of the heavy pillows. I hesitated a moment, then, wishing beyond anything that it was already over, I slammed the pillow down over Stephen's face, shuffling forward on my knees so I could put my full weight upon it.

I was sobbing so hard my chest felt as if it would crack in two.

Not Stephen, not Stephen, no, no …

Both his hands grabbed my wrists, forcing them to bear down even harder.

His body was convulsing, and all I wanted was for him to die, to let go life, to stop this horror so that I could somehow escape and forget that this had happened, just forget, forget everything.

His grip on my wrists loosened. I think I was shrieking now, or as much of a shriek as I could force out of my painful, hoarsened throat.

Why didn't he die? Why didn't he die? Why —

Stephen went limp under me. Yet still I pushed down on that pillow with all my might.

I don't know how long I knelt there on that bed, Stephen dead beneath me, pushing down on the pillow and shrieking, but I know it was a long time. My own body was screaming in agony, every joint, every muscle afire with fever, but still I knelt … still I knelt …

Eventually I reeled back, almost falling off the bed.

Stephen did not move.

The pillow half slipped from his face, and I saw his eyes, bulging, staring sightlessly into God's judgment.

I slid to my knees on the floor, my hands clutching at the coverlets, partly pulling them from the mattress.

There I crouched, sobbing, so bereft I thought (*hoped*) it would kill me, unable to think, or to rise and walk away.

I became aware of another presence, and I looked to the door.

Evelyn stood there, staring at me, horror on her face.

In her hand she held a small vial.

The hemlock.

Evelyn raised me to my feet, and led me from the chamber. 'I will tend to him,' she said.

'Owain, he wanted Owain —'

'I know. I will fetch Owain. Hush now, I will look after everything.'

She helped me into the solar, and thence to the bed we had shared in those times when the world was sane.

I lay, shivering with fever, every joint aching. My spine felt as if it was on fire, my lungs felt thick, every breath a struggle. I could *taste* the fungus in my mouth.

I wanted to ask Evelyn for the hemlock. I wanted to die, there was nothing to live for any more, but Evelyn was already halfway to the stairwell. Thus I lay there, weeping in pain and fear and loss until I fell into slumber.

I did not dream. When I woke it was because I was finding breathing almost impossible. I put a hand to my face, and felt there the fur of the fungus. I struggled, trying to call out, but I was voiceless.

If I was voiceless, then I was also terrified. I was sure that the fire was not far away, and I was sure that Evelyn had abandoned me.

I was helpless, and hopeless.

And then, suddenly, Evelyn was there.

Please, I mouthed at her, and she understood. She gave me a last smile, nodded, then gently raised my head and put the flask to my lips.

Of what happened next, I cannot speak, for the poison took effect and I was senseless.

Owain shall speak on my behalf.

CHAPTER TEN

OWAIN'S TESTIMONY

This time was that of the Devil, I am certain. Days ran like blood into yet more days, until I knew not where I was within the week and if I had missed the Sabbath or not. All prayers were forgotten, all the hours of the days unmarked. There was nothing but death, near death, longed for death and terrible death. The chapel stank of it: of the fungus, of terror, of hopelessness, of death, *always* of death. Sometimes we did not get to a sufferer in time, and he was consumed by flames, screeching and twisting amid his own terrifying inferno.

We would have to drag those near him away, themselves screaming, frantic to escape the flames.

And then, as if my life had been cast from a cart drawn by bolting horses and dashed against the rocks, everything came to a halt.

My Lord Stephen died. The most precious heir in this land. Dead.

I knew he'd harboured the plague but (perhaps foolishly) I'd hoped that he would somehow overcome it. If anyone could, I reasoned with myself as I struggled through the morass of hopelessness within the chapel, then Stephen could.

He was stronger than most.

If he could not, then he deserved the kindest passage through, as I'd given others.

It was the only reason I'd agreed to send hemlock to Maeb. She was of the old blood, too, even if she did not then recognise it. I knew Maeb loved him, and I knew that she would hesitate until the last moment before she gave Stephen the poison. She would not destroy him unless she absolutely had to, because neither her blood nor her heart would allow it.

In the end, it had been too late. My messenger took longer than I'd hoped, and by the time he arrived, and I'd sent Evelyn with the hemlock to Maeb, Stephen was dead.

Evelyn returned to tell me almost as soon as she'd discovered the fact. I came, with two strong men who'd been helping me in the chapel (they were fatalistic souls, and believed that if God had meant for them to die, they would have caught the plague well before now), and brought Stephen's body back to the chapel where we wrapped it and laid it in the single private place remaining — the space behind the altar. Here Stephen would need to rest until I could do what was needed.

Maeb was dying, too.

I hoped Evelyn would give her the hemlock. I liked Maeb, not merely because of the old blood she carried, but because she radiated warmth and interest. I can confess this here, because I know my lady can never read it, but during my life as a priest there have been very few women who have roused me enough to consider breaking my vows of chastity.

Mistress Maeb Langtofte was one of them. She was so lovely as a young woman. So lovely.

But for now such thoughts were far beyond me. My life was the chapel and the dying. I had not slept in days, and I was wearied beyond exhaustion. I sorrowed for Maeb, but she had Evelyn with her, and that would need to be enough.

It was the day after Stephen had died. I was, as I had been for days, weeks (a lifetime?), doing what I could in the chapel. Administering herbs to alleviate suffering where I could, hemlock to alleviate suffering permanently as I dared, and I ignored d'Avranches, who occasionally appeared in the chapel administering his own form of ease. When he wasn't in the chapel, he was prowling the rest of the castle.

D'Avranches was a man driven, I think, not only by the need to reduce suffering, but also the need to preserve his liege lord's property.

Nothing more would burn if he could help it.

He was also the man who organised the removal of corpses from the chapel, never asking why so many of them were unburned. D'Avranches had managed to bring together enough able men to dig a trench beyond the walls of the castle for the dead. Every so often they would appear within the chapel and remove what needed removing.

I could not have done without him.

I was standing by the door of the chapel, pausing from my ministrations, taking a few deep breaths of fresh air and wiping the cold sweat from my face, when suddenly there was a clatter of horses' hooves. I did not immediately take much note of it — loose horses had been clattering about the inner bailey for days now — but after a moment I realised there was a group of horses and their hooves made sound as if they were being purposefully ridden.

I stepped beyond the door, and for a moment could not believe what my eyes showed me.

It was the Earl of Pengraic, a score of horsemen behind him.

He rode into the inner bailey, his head moving about as he looked, the shock at what he saw registering on his face.

I stumbled forward and, as I came to within fifteen paces of him, the earl saw me, kicking his horse forward.

'By God, Owain,' he said, 'what has happened here?'

'The plague, my lord. I am sorry.'

'Stephen sent me a message ... I could not believe it ... I rode as hard as I might, by heavenly Jesu I killed three horses to get here ... Where is Stephen, Owain? *Where is my son?*'

Sweet merciful saints. 'My lord, I am sorry. My Lord Stephen died last night. I have him laid out behind the —'

'Dead? *Stephen is dead?* It can't be!' The earl swung down from his horse and grabbed the front of my robe. 'Tell me this is not truth, priest!'

I could not reply. Emotion swelled my throat and made words impossible.

He saw from my face. He knew. His hand slowly released his grip and he took a step back. 'They were supposed to be *safe*, Owain. Safe! *He promised me Pengraic would be safe!*'

I did not understand his words, and supposed only that the earl was maddened with grief and shock and did not know what he said.

'Stephen is dead?' he said again, although this time he did not require an answer. I could hear the beginnings of understanding in his voice. 'Stephen is dead … and the rest of my family? My wife? My children? What of them, Owain?'

Stephen's message must have contained news of Lady Adelie's death, but maybe the earl had not believed that, either.

'They are all gone, my lord. We could do nothing to save them.'

'All?' The word was forced through his lips. 'All?'

I nodded. 'I am so sorry, my lord. We did the best we could. We —'

'He did this deliberately!' the earl said, almost shouting. 'Deliberately!'

'My lord?'

'Damn him! Damn him! *Damn him!*'

And then the earl gave an almost hysterical laugh. 'What am I saying? He is already damned, more than I could ever wish on him. Oh God, oh God, what am I to do? Adelie? She is truly gone?'

I nodded again, hoping that no one ever told him the terrible manner of his wife's death.

'And the children,' he said, much softer now, 'the children. *Stephen.* What did they ever do to deserve such a manner of death? They were innocents, especially the babies. Gone, Owain, truly?'

I nodded. 'I have left Stephen's body in the chapel, my lord earl. I thought you would want …'

'Yes. Thank you. Thank you.' The earl rested a heavy hand on my shoulder. 'Who is left of my household, Owain? Who?'

'Of the ladies, only Mistress Evelyn is well. Mistress Yvette is dead. Mistress Maeb is dying, or dead.'

'Maeb has the plague?'

'Badly, my lord.' And then I added, without thinking: 'She has taken hemlock, to die more peacefully than the plague would allow her.'

'*Hemlock?* And where would she get *that*, priest?'

That hand had tightened into a claw on my shoulder now, and I quailed. The earl did not wait for an answer. 'Where is she?'

'In the solar, my lord. I am sorry —' That damned word kept burbling to the surface, and it was the most useless word contained within a priest's — or any man's — vocabulary. I thought of muttering something about peace, and God's will, and thought better of it immediately.

I need not have worried. The earl was already gone, running to the inner gate and the great keep.

He did not come back until that evening.

I saw him enter the chapel, pausing as he stared at the crammed beds, his nostrils twitching at the stink, his face aghast at the moans and wails of the dying.

I hurried over. 'My lord?'

'Maeb is somewhere I cannot reach her now,' he said. He looked me in the eye. 'Running with the wolves.'

I went cold. I knew what he meant.

'I have done all I can for her,' the earl continued. 'Either she will live or she won't. Where is Stephen?'

'Behind the altar, my lord. Do you … do you require my aid?'

Pengraic studied me. His face was weary, so weary, and his skin ashen, as if he suffered himself. 'Do you have the time?' he said, indicating the chaos of the chapel.

'I will always have the time for Lord Stephen,' I said.

'Then thank you,' the earl said. 'Yes, assist me if you will. And after … cause Stephen's name and rank to be carved into the central heartstone of the chapel that his soul may rest in the very heart of this sacred place.'

I nodded, and together we moved toward the altar, and poor Stephen's body.

PART THREE

—••◦◆◦••—

THE COUNTESS

CHAPTER ONE

I drank the hemlock, and was grateful and at peace. I was certain I would go straight to hell for my sins, but at least I need not suffer needlessly in the doing. I lay back and Evelyn, weeping, sat with me, holding my hand and stroking my forehead.

A time passed, and I felt my limbs grow cold. I tried to move my hands and feet and found I could not.

More time passed, and my vision blurred, the high roof of the solar vanishing into myriad patches of indistinct greys and browns.

I could not see Evelyn at my side, which I much regretted for I would have liked to depart this life with my last sight being of her kind and loved face.

After yet more time as my limbs grew heavy, and so cold I wanted to shiver, but could not, my consciousness dimmed and I knew only blackness.

I died. It was utterly wonderful. I did not need to fight any more. It was peaceful. There was, finally, no pain. I had escaped any hemlock and plague both. No demons from hell came to seize me. I had no guilt any more. My world became one of complete serenity.

There was just … nothing, and I could drift uncaring and at peace.

I dreamed as I faded from life. I dreamed I heard an angry man shouting and Evelyn's fearful voice replying. I dreamed of being rocked back and forth, and of being shaken about in my cold, hard bed.

Then my dream grew most strange, and I thought to myself that the hemlock was working fully to drive my senses from my body.

I dreamed I walked down a path in a dark, dark forest, peopled with the trees from the walls of the castle chapel. There was no light. Nothing.

In the forest wolves howled and something monstrous grunted and roared.

I grew frightened. I hastened ever faster down the path, knowing that down here, somewhere, lay safety and peace.

Then something huge blocked my path.

I cried out in fear and fell back, but the massive thing pursued me. I felt hot breath wash over me.

Go back, someone said.

A wolf snapped at my heels and I shrieked.

Again something massive pushed at me, and somewhere in the depths of my mind I think I recognised it as the shoulder of a mighty horse.

Someone, the rider on the mighty horse, was using the animal to push me back.

Go back.

I turned, and fled, the wolves and the horse and rider pursuing me.

I dreamed. I dreamed I wandered the mountain tops, carrying a torch. I was looking down into the valley, and there was the table-topped mountain that now held Pengraic Castle, save that in my dream I again saw the circling dancers and the man standing in their centre, with light about his head.

I wanted to get to that flat-topped mountain, to those dancers, to the man crowned with light, but every time I started down the thing came at me again (*the horse*) and it pushed me back, back, back.

The wolves howled.

I fled along the forest path. Behind me came the thunder of hooves, and the snap and snarl of the wolf pack.

I was terrified, witless with fear, my heart pounding so fast I thought it would burst.

I ran.

Eventually, I collapsed with fear and exhaustion, and the horse and the wolf pack were upon me.

Then, somewhere far distant, I heard the shout of an angry and vengeful man. I trembled within my non-existent state. Was it the Devil, reaching for me?

The man, shouting again, closer now.

Now the voice of a woman. I could sense — hear — her cringing within her reply to the man, hear her fear, and her guilt also.

What was it, this guilt, that it had spread throughout the entire world?

I wished them gone, for they had both destroyed the peace of my death. I tried to ignore them, tried to push myself back into the void of death, but the voices were insistent, and they dragged me closer, closer, closer.

Pain shattered my peace. I found myself within a body again and it was wracked with pain. I gasped, spending a fraction of existence wondering that finally my throat had opened enough to admit air, then gasped again, choking, drawing in painful breath after painful breath, feeling my ribs crack with the force of my coughing.

The pain was terrible but, worse, was the realisation that I was still alive and that, somehow, someone had denied me death.

The hemlock had failed me and now I would burn.

I hated whoever it was had denied me death, and I wept, not wanting to open my eyes in case that action finally sealed my re-entry into life.

'Maeb? Maeb?'

It was Evelyn.

'*Maeb?*'

I wept anew, and finally opened my eyes. I had been seen, it was too late.

'I hurt, Evelyn. I am in agony. Kill me, please, please ...'

'Like you did my son?'

I turned my eyes, and there stood the Earl of Pengraic, and I knew the Devil *had* come to fetch me.

CHAPTER TWO

It took me years to understand why I did not die, and to understand the significance of the horse and rider and the wolves.

But then, in that year after I woke up from death, I had no idea. I could not understand why I had not died. I *knew* I was dying from both plague and hemlock, and yet neither killed me. Strange. Moreover, I was certain that I did die, so how was it I found myself alive? Breathing? In agony?

Neither Owain, nor Evelyn, nor even the earl, would speak of it to me. Owain and Evelyn because, I think, they simply did not know how my health was accomplished, and the earl would not speak of it because that was his prerogative (and he probably did not know, either). I had fragmentary dreams of wolves and horses, but I thought them the hallucinations of the hemlock, not of any true vision.

I found myself in the world, and somehow I needed to find the strength to live once more.

I spent many days, probably weeks, in my bed in the solar. Evelyn nursed me constantly, feeding me broths, washing me, turning me from side to side so I did not develop sores on my body, murmuring to me as to a child, perhaps like she had once murmured to her daughter, who she must have been frantic about … But still she nursed me.

Owain visited many times, bringing both company and his skills as a herbalist. I asked him about Stephen and the children, and he said that the earl had commanded that Stephen be buried under the heartstone of the chapel, and the other children in the aisle with their mother.

When he initially told me this I accepted it, thinking that beneath the heartstone was a fitting place for Stephen to lie. But over the next few nights I had unsettling dreams where I saw Stephen's corpse falling through space until it caught in tangled, mossy tree branches, or being eaten by the wolves I had hallucinated about during my death.

When Owain returned, I asked him if Stephen was truly buried under the heartstone.

'Full six feet,' he said. 'We dug deep into the clay and shale beneath the chapel.'

I shifted uncomfortably on my bed. 'You managed to unearth the heartstone?'

'Yes, why do you ask?'

'I don't know, Owain. I just thought …' It troubled me somehow, that the sacred stone had been disturbed and dug about.

'He is safe now, Maeb. Don't worry about him.'

They were an unusual choice of words, but at the time I did not push Owain, or think too much on what he had said. I was tired and ill, and in much pain. Owain left a strong analgesic draught with Evelyn, patted me on the shoulder, and left.

The earl came and went. He slept in the privy chamber (I prayed to God that Owain had taken the babies' bodies when he had taken Stephen's) and he passed through the solar as he came and went from the privy chamber, barely sparing me a glance. Mostly, he was busy within the wider community (such as was left of it) of the castle, repairing the damage the plague had wrought.

The castle had needed its earl, very badly. Evelyn told me that from the day he arrived, the plague abated. Of those sick in the chapel, most recovered. Those few who died had been in their final extremity anyway. The survivors, either those who rose from their sick beds or those who had escaped the plague entirely, somehow found meaning and purpose again. Loose horses were caught and restabled. The gates and parapets were once more manned. The fire was struck in the smithy, and the kitchens in the great keep and the outer bailey once more provided food.

We were to live again, it appeared.

I spent much of my time wracked with pain. My joints ached abominably, my muscles refused to work, my abdomen was a mass of tenderness, my brain as loose and unthinking as a bowl of cold gruel. I lay in that bed, doing whatever Evelyn required of me, taking Owain's draughts as instructed, and spending the rest of my time staring at the ceiling, grieving for Lady Adelie, and Stephen, and Rosamund and John, and Alice and Emmette, and wondering what would become of me.

I tried not to think of the earl's words: *Like you did my son?*

Aye. I had murdered his beloved son, and somehow he knew.

He had not spoken to me since that night, but I knew that he would. He waited only on my strength returning, that he might assault me with the full force of his rage.

He had hated me from the first moment he had set eyes on me, and I had justified all that hate in full measure.

I wished all the more that I was dead, *that I had remained dead*, for I had nothing left to live for.

Time passed. One morning, Evelyn, despite my weak protests, sat me on the side of the bed, washed my body and my hair, then dressed me in a linen shift and my best rust-red kirtle, finally plaiting my damp hair into two braids.

The kirtle hung loose on me, as I had lost a great deal of weight.

'We will sit you by the fire for the morning,' she announced. I winced and pleaded to stay in bed, to no avail.

Somehow, with Evelyn's aid, I stumbled to a chair by the fire and she settled me into it with cushions and wraps. It was midsummer, and a bright day outside, but I was cold and glad enough of the fire and the wraps.

'I won't be able to stay long here,' I said to Evelyn. 'My joints pain me terribly, and —'

'You *will* stay here for the morning,' Evelyn said. 'Your bed is tired of you.'

And with that she left me.

I looked longingly toward the bed.

It was out of my reach. I would need to wait for someone to help me back to it.

There were footsteps in the stairwell, and I looked hopefully toward its opening. It was likely one of the servants, bringing more wood, or a fresh pitcher of small beer for my lord's —

It was the earl.

He stopped instantly. I was easily ignored when I lay in the corner in my bed, but to see me sit by the fire… he would need to pass right by me as he went to his privy chamber, and that would mean some form of acknowledgement.

I do not think, ever before in my life or ever again, I was quite so thoroughly terrified as I was at that moment. We would need to say something each to the other, and, knowing he knew I had murdered Stephen, what on earth could we say if not to parry recrimination and guilt?

A servant suddenly loomed behind the earl, carrying a pitcher of small beer. I closed my eyes momentarily, wondering at my fate that the servant had not arrived earlier and could have helped me to my bed, and the earl could then have ignored me as usual when he strode through to his privy chamber.

The earl turned, took the pitcher from the servant, thanking him, then walked toward me.

I looked down, trembling in my fear.

I heard the rattle as the earl took two pewter cups down from the hearth mantle, then the gurgle of the beer.

I had to look up. He was standing before me, his expression as unreadable as ever, holding out a cup. I took it from him, thanking him in a soft voice.

He sat in a chair a little apart from mine.

'Tell me about Rosamund and John,' he said.

I licked my lips, not knowing what I could say, what words I could use.

'Tell me!'

'They were suffering, my lord. The fungus had grown over their faces. They could hardly breathe. Stephen —'

'Ah, so it was just "Stephen" then, eh?'

'My Lord Stephen did not want them to suffer. He suggested that —'

'*He* suggested?'

What did he want to hear?

'If you want me to take the blame for this, my lord, then I am willing. I do not care. If you would like me to fabricate a tale for you in which I bear all the sin for what happened in this castle, then let me know. Otherwise I will tell you merely what happened.'

'Then just tell me, mistress, but save me your outrage.'

I told him, in bare, stark words, how Stephen and I had held the pillow over John's and Rosamund's faces. 'It was such a time of horror, my lord. What any of us did, it was only done under the most extreme of circumstances. We will all carry the guilt for the rest of our lives.'

I waited, unsure and fearful of the earl's reaction.

He looked at me a long moment, then gave a simple nod. 'Owain told me that he took the life of Emmette so that she did not suffer in fire, and I am glad of it. If Stephen suggested the same for Rosamund and John, then I am glad of that, too. If you assisted, then I thank you for it.'

I could barely believe the words. I had expected angry recrimination, not thanks.

'And Stephen?' said the earl. 'Will you tell me what happened?'

I did, again in as few words as possible. Not to save the earl his grief, but to save mine.

'At least he did not burn,' the earl said softly when I was done. 'My God, if only I had arrived sooner. If only ...'

'What could you have done, my lord?'

'I could have done *something*!' the earl snapped, and I looked down at the cup in my hands, avoiding the anger in his eyes.

'Did you know that I have received word Ancel and Robert also succumbed?' the earl continued. 'Summersete told me they died not three weeks after joining his household.'

The twin boys were dead, too? Sweet Mother Virgin! He had lost his entire family. I raised my eyes, and thought he looked so old and haggard slumped in his chair that I felt more sorry for him than I had ever thought possible.

He drank the last of his beer and poured himself another, offering me more which I refused.

'Why did you survive, Maeb?'

More guilt knifed through me. All his family had died.

I had not.

'I don't know, my lord. Owain says that maybe the plague had lost its force, or —'

'Owain is a fool if he says that. You took hemlock as well. Both Evelyn and Owain told me this. You were in the final stages of the plague, choking on the fungus, and you took a dose of hemlock that was three times what would kill a strong man. So why did you live?'

'I don't know, my lord.' I fought not to add *I am sorry* because I was suddenly sick of saying that.

'Did you dream?'

That question surprised me. 'I had many hallucinations, my lord. I thought I *had* died, but then …'

'But then?'

'But I dreamed that I was pushed back, by a massive horse … and wolves snapped at my heels.'

The earl looked at me, one end of his mouth twisting in what could have been either amusement or scorn. 'The hemlock, indeed,' he said.

There was an uncomfortable silence.

'How does the king fare?' I said stupidly, grasping at something to say.

He looked at me quizzically, one eyebrow raised. 'Edmond? How does he fare? Full of care, as am I, but his wife and sons live, whereas mine … ah, but I must talk of *Edmond*, for he is the focus of your concern. He is well enough, Maeb. Still well enough to lust after a pretty face. As is Saint-Valery, your betrothed.'

Saint-Valery? How many weeks, months, had it been since I had thought of him?

'Ah,' said the earl, 'see your surprise.'

'Saint-Valery and I were not betrothed,' I said. 'The marriage was mooted, only. I had not yet agreed to his proposal.'

'Good, thank you for reminding me of the fact. This suits my purpose admirably. Saint-Valery might have raised objection due to pre-contract.'

'My lord?'

'To our marriage, Maeb. I need a new wife and a new family and you can provide me both.'

I could only stare, not believing I had heard his words a-right.

'Think of it as a way to assuage your guilt, Maeb. Achieve absolution, if that is what you need. Three of my children died by your hand, including my beloved son. However noble and merciful your motives, still my children are dead. You owe me a family, and you shall deliver me a new one. Now, drink your beer. You need to regain your strength, for I do not have the heart to take a cripple to my marriage bed.'

With that, he put down his cup and left the solar.

CHAPTER THREE

Evelyn came to help me back to bed, happily prattling about some gossip she had heard in the kitchens. She did not notice my silence.

Once I was settled in bed, she sat down beside me. Her face, alive with amusement not a moment ago, now sobered.

'Maeb,' she said, 'now that you are getting better, we will need to think on our future.'

I said nothing. I was still in shock at what the earl had said, and was starting to think I had misheard him.

'The earl will take a new wife, soon enough,' Evelyn said. 'He has lost all his children. He needs heirs.' She sighed. 'There must be heiresses and wealthy noble widows a-plenty to choose from. Apart from Edmond's sons, and maybe even more than them, the earl is the most marriageable man in England. He has such wealth and power. He will choose an illustrious wife, to be sure.'

I just looked at her numbly.

'Maeb,' Evelyn said, in a tone that suggested she needed to explain as if to a small child — and maybe she did — 'such a woman will already have her ladies attending upon her. She will not need us. Indeed, if it were not for your illness, we should already have been required to leave Pengraic.'

'Evelyn …'

'I think I can obtain a position for myself within de Tosny's household. My daughter shall speak for me. But, Maeb, what will you do? Perhaps the earl can find you a household.'

'Evelyn …'

'What is it?'

I did not know what to say. What the earl had said was so preposterous that it now seemed unspeakable.

'The earl …'

'Yes?' Evelyn was growing impatient with me.

'Evelyn … I may have misheard it. Surely, I could not have heard a-right. The earl …'

'*Yes?*'

'The earl has said, this morning, while I sat out by the fire … the earl said that we should marry.'

Evelyn clearly did not know what to make of my words. 'You and me?' she said, incredulous.

'No! The *earl* and myself.'

Evelyn's mouth dropped open, and then I saw in her eyes a flash of pity. Poor, delusional Maeb. The sickness must have scarred her mind.

'Maeb,' she said, gentle as a mother, 'that could not be.'

'I do not think so, either. But … he seemed so insistent.'

'Maeb, the earl will choose a woman of great rank, wealth and alliances. He must.'

I knew what she was thinking. I had set my heart on Stephen, and now that he was dead I entertained childish dreams of the earl.

I began to resent the earl for putting me in this position. 'I know that, Evelyn. I do not know what … he must have been making a cruel jest, I think.'

'Perhaps you misunderstood,' said Evelyn. 'He spoke of his new bride and perhaps said you might have a place in her household? If so, then you have good luck, for your future is assured.'

That wasn't what the earl had said. Was it? Now I could not believe any of my memories. Nothing made sense. Nothing.

Maybe I was still delusional from the hemlock.

I frowned, wondering if I had misheard the earl's entire conversation. 'Perhaps,' I began, then stopped as the earl, d'Avranches, Ivo Taillebois — the new castle steward — as well as two knights, entered the solar. They walked to the grouping of benches and chairs about the fire, although they did not sit down, and engaged in animated discussion about the reorganisation of castle defences with the limited numbers of soldiers and knights currently in residence.

Evelyn and I fell silent as we always did when the earl conducted his daily business within the solar. And, as always, the earl and his men ignored us completely ... until the moment Taillebois turned to leave the grouping. He had walked some three or four paces away when the earl called him to a halt.

'Taillebois,' the earl said, lifting a ring of keys from his tunic pocket and thumbing through them. 'There is a large chest in the lower storage chambers, to the left of the door, pushed hard up against the wall.'

He handed the key to Taillebois. 'Take Mistress Evelyn down with you and let her sort through it. Mistress Evelyn, the chest is full of fabrics that I had imported for my Lady Adelie's pleasure. She never used them, but now ...'

He paused, sent me a glance, then looked at the group of men. 'Now they may be used for Mistress Maeb's pleasure. We are to be betrothed, when she is well enough to stand before witnesses and speak the vows, and I have had the necessary binding contracts drawn up. I have a family to replace, as soon as I might.'

Everyone, including myself, stared at him.

'Maeb will need more gentle kirtles and gowns than she has now, Evelyn,' the earl continued, apparently unbothered by the stunned regard of his listeners. 'Select some fabrics that suit. Take whatever is useful ... the chest has ribbons and baubles enough besides fabric. Make sure you have at least one bright kirtle stitched by the end of this week. I do not wish to delay this betrothal. Taillebois, what women are there in the castle or village, left alive and well, who might be trusted with the stitching?'

'I shall find out, my lord,' Taillebois said, and with a half bow to the earl and a look of enquiry to Evelyn, who somehow managed to rise and follow him, left the chamber.

D'Avranches and the two knights stared at me with undisguised speculation.

I could only imagine the rumours racing about the castle by the end of this day.

The earl dismissed the three men, thankfully bringing to an end their speculative attention, then strolled over to my bed.

'I need to move apace, Maeb. God alone knows when the king will demand I return to court. I would like to have the formalities of the betrothal concluded soon. When might you be well enough to attend dinner in the great hall?'

'Perhaps a week, my lord.'

'A week. Good. Now, we need to discuss the terms —'

'My lord,' I said, prompted by the conversation I'd had earlier with Evelyn. 'Surely you cannot want me to wife. You have the flower of English and Norman nobility, and beyond, to choose for your wife. You cannot want *me!*'

He regarded me a moment, then sat down on the end of the bed. 'I do not have the time to conduct lengthy negotiations, Maeb. I cannot be bothered. I am too tired, and there is much else I need to be doing. All I need is a woman to wive.'

'But you despise me,' I said, remembering that conversation we'd had on the day we'd first met.

'I distrusted you,' he said. 'You would have made Stephen a bad wife, but you will do well enough for me. For sweet Christ's sake, Maeb, the world is turned upside down, and what mattered once now weighs little. I have no patience for your protests. Do as I ask, or face the uncertain cold holloways and byways beyond the gates of this castle.'

I was silent. The earl always had such a way with words.

The earl grunted, as if he had known I would raise no more objection. 'I will settle three or four manors on you, Maeb, as jointure enough should I die before you, as surely I will. It is protection and price enough to silence your doubts.'

He stood. 'You have just made a noble marriage, Maeb. Wasn't that what you'd always wanted from your place in my household?'

CHAPTER FOUR

I lay awake for much of the night. I felt lost, adrift. Everything about me felt false. The plague should have killed me. I should have died. I had wanted to die.

But I had not died. Instead I had reawakened into, as the earl had put it, a world turned upside down.

Nothing was as it should be. All was false.

So false.

In the morning, I woke with Evelyn, and demanded she help me dress.

She did as I asked, as she had since last night. Everything I asked, she did without question.

Everything felt false with her, now, too.

'I want to go to the chapel,' I said, as soon as I was dressed.

I did not stand, for fear I would wobble alarmingly. My head swayed with lack of sleep and weakness, but more than anything I wanted, needed, to go to the chapel.

I wanted to see where the earl had interred Stephen. Maybe there I might find some truth.

'But you are so weak,' Evelyn said. She hesitated at the end of that sentence, as if she had wanted to add either 'Maeb', or 'my lady'. But neither suited. Both of us were lost in some halfway land of indecision. 'You cannot walk.'

Now even our friendship was blighted.

'Then find me a strong man, if any should remain within the castle, and he can carry me there.'

Evelyn hesitated, then gave a nod and left. Within a short while she had returned with Taillebois.

I suppose she felt that a common soldier would not suffice, now.

I did not know Taillebois well, for he had come to the castle after the plague, at the earl's request, to replace Walter Giffard, who had died in the first onslaught of the sickness. But he seemed a gentle enough man and there was no hesitation in his manner with me, as there was from Evelyn. He knew little of me, save that I was to be his lady, so I had never been to him the least of Lady Adelie's women, now to be elevated to a pinnacle unimaginable to those about her.

'My lady,' he said, without any indecision in either word or manner, and swung me into his arms.

We moved toward the stairwell, Evelyn hurrying behind with a warm wrap for me.

The chapel was cold and dim. Outside was summer, all sun and blowsy warm air.

Inside the chapel I could still sense the death, if not smell its stink or forced to endure its shrieks.

Owain emerged as if he had been waiting, carrying a chair, his eyebrow raised as he asked wordlessly where I wanted it.

'At Stephen's grave,' I said, and he placed it by the heartstone in the centre of the nave.

Taillebois set me into it gently, then stood back a pace, waiting to be dismissed.

I felt comfortable with him, whereas with everyone else ...

'Thank you,' I said to Taillebois, and he inclined his head and was gone.

I took the wrap from Evelyn, thanking her as well.

After a hesitation she, too, left.

'Would you like to be left alone, Maeb?' Owain said, and I nodded, already choking with emotion as I looked at the stone that marked Stephen's grave.

It did look as though it had been moved recently. The earth was a little crumbly about its edges, and I fancied it had a slight incline to the north as it settled.

Settled over Stephen's corpse.

There was now script on the stone, too, freshly chiselled. I could not read it, but I supposed that it gave Stephen's name and some prayer for his soul.

I sat there by Stephen's grave and wept. I wept for him and for me. I wept for everything lost, life and death both. I wish I had died with him. Mostly, I wept for Stephen.

Sobs wracked my frame, and I clutched the arms of the chair that I would not fall from its embrace. I felt the unfairness of life and of God's will, that Stephen should have died.

What was this world without him in it? He was such a tragic loss, not merely to me, or the earl, but to the realm.

Everything was wrong with my world, nothing right. The greatest injustice was the fact that I had survived when it should have been Stephen, it should have been Stephen ... people needed Stephen, not me. He'd had such a bright, golden future.

I sobbed until I had nothing left to give. I do not know how long I sat there, but I know it was a long, long time. Eventually, I leaned back in the chair, drying my tears with the back of one shaking hand, still hiccupping a little with grief.

'Owain?'

He was by my side instantly, and I wondered if he had been hovering in the shadows all this time.

'Drink this, Maeb.' He held out a pewter cup.

I took it, and sniffed a little suspiciously.

'It is but honeyed wine,' Owain said, 'mixed with some spices. It will warm you, and give you comfort.'

Comfort. I clung to the word as I drank the wine, soon enough handing the empty cup back to Owain.

'My world has vanished, Owain.'

'I know.'

'The earl has demanded I become his wife.'

'I have heard of that.'

'Why, Owain? I cannot possibly understand why he would want to do this. Does he want to punish me? He knows of Stephen's death, and those of Rosamund and John, and my part in them. He asked me to tell him of them, but he knew beforehand.'

I waited for the *I know*, but all I received was silence.

'*How* did he know, Owain?'

'He asked me how they died, Maeb. I told him.'

I was so angry I hit the chair with my closed fist. 'How could you have done that! How —'

'He needed the comfort, Maeb. He needed to know they had died well. Better than they might have done.'

'But Stephen …'

'Stephen was going to die anyway. It was better that he died by your hand, than the flames of the plague. The earl is angry, but not with you.'

'I committed great sin,' I said.

'Not in the earl's eyes.'

The earl would not be my judge after my death, I thought.

'Owain, I survived. Stephen might have, too. What I did … he might have survived if I had not … if I had not …'

'Maeb, do not torture yourself. From what I know of the plague, then yes, he likely would have died horribly if you had not acted. You did what you thought was right and what he begged of you. You were sick nigh unto death yourself. What happened, happened.'

What happened, happened. What a damning thing to say of my actions. Stephen may have survived if I had not killed him.

'*I* survived!'

'You were strong, Maeb. Please, do not resent the fact that you survived and Stephen did not. Do not bear guilt about it. He would not want it.'

I stared at him, then sighed. 'I feel so alone, Owain. Stephen is gone. Lady Adelie. The children. My entire purpose for life has gone. But yet now the earl thinks we should wed. Owain, why should the earl wish to marry *me*?'

Owain smiled. 'He needs a wife, and you are young. You will be healthy again and you are lovely of feature. If I were to be honest, then I would say that I am not at all surprised the earl wants to wed you.'

'And yet I have no title nor rank nor alliance nor estates. The earl, as any nobleman, values these far more than a pretty face.'

Owain gave a tilt of his head, which might have meant anything.

'Everything feels false, Owain.'

'That feeling will pass.'

'I cannot be a countess. I do not know how. I cannot be Lady Adelie.'

'If the earl had wanted Lady Adelie he would have disinterred her corpse and set it in her chair at high table.'

'Do not jest, Owain!' For a moment I had a vision of that blackened horror seated in a chair at the high table, and it sickened me.

'I am sorry, my lady.'

Why 'my lady' now when a moment ago I had been but 'Maeb'?

'What am I to do, Owain?'

'Accept what lies before you. The earl means you no harm. He is an angry man, but none of that is your fault. He sees his world destroyed, and rails against the injustice. He would not suggest you stand by his side if he did not think you were worthy.'

'How can I be worthy, Owain?'

'You have strength and spirit. You survived what killed most others. Take what he offers, Maeb, and have the courage to see where it leads.'

I will fail, I thought. I cannot be a countess.

'You will be a great countess,' Owain said. 'Stephen saw it in you. I see it in you. The earl sees it in you.'

'Evelyn thinks the world has gone mad and I elevated beyond comprehension.'

Owain gave a soft chuckle. 'Evelyn is a good woman, but she cannot see beyond yesterday.'

I looked at Stephen's grave, remembering that he had said that I would survive the plague, and wed a great man, and love him dear. And so it would come to pass, although I could not imagine loving the earl dear. But remembering those words made me feel as though Stephen had blessed this marriage, and that he would have wanted me to accept it and move on with my life.

He had also said that I should confess to Owain, and do penance. If I did that, then maybe I could clear my conscience.

Stephen was dead and gone. The plague and all that had happened was in my past. I would move forward.

I sighed. 'Will you take my confession, Owain? I cannot step into tomorrow without unburdening myself of my sins to God. Absolve me of my sins, I beg you. And then lend me your arm, for I think my legs might now, with some help, carry me back to the solar.'

'Good,' he said.

CHAPTER FIVE

The visit to the chapel to Stephen's grave, and my talk with Owain, marked a turning point in my life. Before I had been a girl, uncertain, always ready to take a step backward. Now I was a woman and I would step forward into the future with some degree of acceptance, if not confidence.

Once Owain had escorted me to the solar, I instructed Evelyn to ask two of the servants to move our bed from the corner of the solar, where it had rested ever since my first arrival at Pengraic, to the chamber in the women's dormitory that had formerly been that of the nurse and younger children. I was tired from the visit to the chapel and the painfully slow trip back to the solar, but I needed to do this. A low-ranked attending woman might cringe in a bed in the corner of the solar, a soon-to-be-countess did not.

I was also determined to regain my full strength quickly. If I was in the solar, then I would take my place by the fire, not hide away in a corner. If I needed rest, then I would retire to my chamber.

This day also marked a change in my relationship with Evelyn. We were still friends, but the balance of power had changed between us. Formerly it was Evelyn who led, now it was me, and there was distance between us, too, where once there had been none. I would shortly become countess, a rank far beyond Evelyn's, and that difference in rank would always leave its shadow on our friendship.

This was all very ironic, considering all the advice and warnings Evelyn had once given me regarding Stephen.

But I could not dwell on that, or leave room for regrets. This was tomorrow, not yesterday.

Once our new chamber had been scrubbed out, our bed installed, and all the clothes and toys and fuss of the children tucked away in a large chest and sent down to the underground storage chambers, Evelyn and I went through the fabrics she'd had brought up from below.

They took my breath away. There were fine linens meant for chemises (and the very finest for veils), bleached so white they almost gleamed in my hands, many of them already embroidered in intricate designs using white or cream wools. There were bolts of woollen cloths, some fine weave for summer and some heavy for winter. Some of these, too, were heavily embroidered. But what truly amazed me were the silks; rare, costly bolts of fabrics which must have come from far, far away ... I could almost smell the spiced air of their homelands on them. Some of the silks were vividly coloured — saffrons, vermilions, azure — others were of delicate pastels. I touched them in wonder and dared to imagine myself clothed in their glory.

As well as the bolts of textiles there were girdles, ribbons, beads, threads of every hue including heavy, gilded gold, and small delicate flowers, leaves and fruits made of wax.

'There is so much,' I said.

'My lord earl had many daughters he needed dowry and marriage clothes for,' Evelyn remarked.

'Well,' I said, 'now *I* shall take them as my marriage clothes as it is my lord's wish. But I cannot believe Lady Adelie did not make more use of these treasures.'

'She was of simple taste,' Evelyn said.

Indeed, she had been, but for a moment I wondered if Evelyn's words contained any criticism, then I discarded the idea. There was too much else to worry about, and to do, than to dwell on what Evelyn thought.

In the end, what she thought did not matter.

I decided we needed to stitch two fine linen chemises, one good day kirtle, and one more opulent kirtle for feasts in the great hall ... and betrothals. For the day kirtle I selected a light woollen scarlet fabric that we could embroider with flowered designs, and for the richer kirtle an emerald silk fabric that, together with a geometric design in the golden thread, would make a suitable kirtle for formal occasions.

Later that day, two women arrived to help with the stitching — the erstwhile wet nurse Sewenna who, together with her entire family, had survived the plague (why *her* family, and not that of the earl's?), and a woman named Tilla from the village of Crickhoel below the castle.

In truth, I felt a little guilty that these women had left their families at a time when every able-bodied pair of hands was needed to help with harvest. But at the same time I refused to stand before the earl and witnesses for my betrothal in my old, worn kirtle that stank of death and disaster and subservience.

By the late afternoon the four of us had cut out the fabric for both chemises and kirtles to suit my newer, thinner frame and had begun the stitching. We worked through to evening, our work interrupted only by the occasional visit of Sewenna's older son bringing his mother her baby to suckle and by a light supper sent to us on Taillebois' instruction.

I rested comfortably that night, and in the morning dressed, prayed, broke my fast, then told Evelyn that I would take my stitching to the solar for the day.

When I entered the solar the earl was seated under a window with d'Avranches and a knight I did not recognise — he must have recently ridden in. The three of them were poring over large parchments; maps, I thought, by those lines I could see.

I greeted them, dipping in courtesy, and then took a chair by the fireplace — which was alight even on this summer's day to take the chill from the large, stone-walled chamber — where the light from a second window fell over my shoulder. I had my stitching with me, but it was not for either chemise or kirtle. If I was to be betrothed shortly, then I would need a gift for my contracted husband. It was not strictly necessary, and under the circumstances, because of the recent plague disaster at the castle, its lack would surely be overlooked, but the earl had said he would settle some manors on me for my jointure and I wanted, very much, to be able to gift him something. It could be nothing of the value of manors, but it *would* be a gift, and its symbolic value greater, I hoped, than its fiscal value. It would enable me to hold my head high on my betrothal day.

I trusted he would like it, and not be disappointed.

The men resumed their conversation once I was settled, the recently arrived knight talking the most, and occasionally pointing to the map. I was desperately curious — what were they discussing? Army movements?

Brigands? What was being planned? Snatches of conversation reached me, names of towns and manors, and at times the earl asked a sharp question of the knight, who invariably responded by pointing at the map.

I kept my eyes on my stitching, but bit by bit tilted my body toward the group of men, my curiosity insatiable.

'Maeb.'

I looked up. The earl was gazing at me.

'If you are so curious, then come see.'

I thought about protesting that my stitching was more important. In the event, I merely rose, laid the stitching to one side, and walked over.

'This is Gilbert Ghent,' the earl said, 'recently arrived from the south-east. He is one of the senior knights of my household.'

I inclined my head and smiled at him in greeting, as he did likewise. He was a good-looking man, aristocratic, but with a face I liked and trusted immediately.

'Sir Gilbert, does the south-east still burn? The last I heard the plague raged there with such ferocity that all life lay in its grip.'

'My lady,' Ghent said, and I wondered that the honorific now felt almost familiar to me, 'the plague has loosened its grip on the south-east of England. Perhaps there is little flesh left to feed it, or mayhap, now that the summer draws on, the plague begins to lose its strength as do most plagues.'

'We hope it will die down completely over winter,' the earl said, 'and give us some time to recover and plan for its probable resurgence next spring. We were discussing what parts of England still lie in the plague's grip, and which are free.'

I leaned over d'Avranches' shoulder, looking at the map. 'This represents England?' I had never seen a map before.

'Aye,' said d'Avranches. 'See, here the coastline, and see here these little triangles … they represent the mountains of this realm; these wobbly lines are the rivers, and here named the towns and cities.'

'Where are we now?' I said. 'Where is Pengraic Castle?'

'Here,' d'Avranches said, one finger stabbing down onto the map. He pointed out London, and Glowecestre, and Oxeneford, and I slowly grasped how the map depicted in representative form the whole of the realm of England.

'It is amazing,' I said, somewhat awed, 'and useful.'

'Aye,' said the earl. 'I shall have to keep it hid from you, Maeb, lest you use it to plot your conquest of Edmond's realm.'

I glanced at him, worried that he was angry, but to my surprise I saw amusement in his eyes. That amusement deepened as he recognised my startlement.

'I think my lady need only appear at Edmond's court,' Ghent said gallantly, 'to conquer his realm.'

Suddenly the amusement faded from the earl's face, replaced with a flash of irritation.

'How far has the plague stretched?' I asked, anxious to deflect the earl's anger.

Ghent had subsided after looking at the earl's glowering face and it was left to d'Avranches to answer. 'Apart from a few minor deviations,' the garrison commander said, 'the plague has spread in a line from Dovre westward through to Wales. It entered Wales through the Usk Valley here,' now his finger pointed to the valley which Pengraic Castle overlooked, 'and then deeper into Wales once it had struck here.'

'How deep into Wales has it gone?' I asked.

'I am not sure,' the earl answered. He had relaxed again, and I dared another look at him. 'We know it struck Pengraic and Crickhoel, and there have been reports of a few cases further west along the valley at Tretower and Penpont, but beyond that … those are lands controlled by Madog ap Gruffydd, and as yet we have not heard any rumour, let alone fact, of what has happened in his dark valleys.'

I had to think for a moment. Madog ap Gruffydd? Then I remembered the privy meeting I'd attended with the king and his earls. Madog was the Welsh prince against whom the Marcher Lords stood.

'Praise sweet Jesu,' I said without thinking, 'that Madog chose not to attack while this castle lay helpless!'

All three men looked at me, d'Avranches swivelling about to cast his narrowed eyes in my direction.

My face flamed, and I felt the fool.

'Maeb makes a good point,' the earl said, slowly, consideringly. 'The last I heard, in late spring, was that Madog had moved from the northern to the southern regions of his territories. If he had been able, he might not have resisted a tilt at this castle. Mayhap the Welsh have, indeed, been struck as hard as we.'

He continued to regard me, eyes lost in thought, and I breathed a little easier, grateful that I had not made such a fool of myself at all.

'I wonder how far into Wales the plague spread,' the earl muttered. 'How far it looked ...'

I returned to my stitching, Evelyn checking on me every now and then to make sure I had not overly tired myself, and the men continued their discussion a while longer. Eventually Ghent and d'Avranches bowed to the earl, and left.

The earl rose and came to my side, looking down at my stitching.

I folded my hands, the work concealed within.

'You went to the chapel yesterday,' the earl said.

'I did.'

'Owain tells me you walked back to the solar.'

'With Owain's aid. I needed to lean on him heavily.'

'Then, Maeb, lean on my arm and climb with me to the roof. Fresh air will brighten your cheeks.'

I put my stitching to one side and took his arm. I had resolved to be more woman than girl, and to walk forward with more confidence, but this closeness with the earl was disconcerting for I did not know what he wanted.

Also, I was afraid that if I returned to the roof all I would think of was Stephen, and I might not be able to control my tears.

I did not need to worry about the memories of Stephen. The roof of the great keep was bright with sun, and redolent with the scent of cut meadow hay wafting up from the river. We walked slowly in silence about the northern wall, stopping midway to lean against the parapet and look over the inner bailey and the garrison to the north.

Everything was ordered and settled once more. There was not the bustle I recalled from the days before the plague, when many hundreds had lived within the castle, but the chaos and dismay that followed when the plague had gripped the castle had now disappeared. Horse lines — thick with horse once again — were securely tied, and the horses settled with hay and water to hand. A group of knights practised their swordplay at the northern end of the bailey, their shouts and occasional guffaws of laughter reaching us even at the top of the great keep. Owain pottered about his herb garden, which once more bloomed and buzzed with bees. Two men picked cabbages and leeks in the garden against the eastern wall of the castle. A messenger, dressed in the earl's livery, trotted his horse to the main gates, spoke briefly with the guards, then vanished through the wicket gate.

'How strange,' I said softly, 'that normality resumes so easily.'

'Normality is always an illusion,' the earl said, 'and one relatively easily maintained, for all wish to believe in it.'

'How many have returned, or been replaced?' I said. 'When the plague was at its height, so many died, and more fled.'

'If any of those who fled,' the earl said, 'dare to return then they know I will have their balls sawn off with a blunt blade and fed to the dogs. But as to your question, the garrison is now a little more than a third manned, and more men arriving from lands to the north of England every day.'

'You have lands in the north of England?'

'I shall have a map drawn, as you delight in them so much, with all my lands marked in scarlet that you may wonder at your wealth.'

There was a marked edge to his voice, and I spoke no more of his lands. 'It is so strange,' I said, 'to wake each day and remember that I am alive. I should have died.'

He did not respond, and I stole a glance at his face. The earl was looking northward, far beyond the castle, to the peak of Pen Cerrig-calch. There was a look almost of yearning on his face, and I wondered at it.

Here in the strong sun, his face seemed more lined than ever, but paradoxically less old. There was a vitality there, I realised, that I had not appreciated before. I wondered how old he was, and quickly deduced from what I knew of the earl's age when Stephen was born, and how old Stephen was, that the earl was some thirty-five or thirty-six years of age. Well past youth, but not yet the old man I had always thought him.

'Did Stephen bring you up here?' the earl asked, and I realised with a start he was looking at me.

'Yes,' I said, 'and once to the roof of the northern keep at night.'

'And why did he do that?'

'He wanted to show me the castle at night,' I said. 'He told me of the old legends about this hill, of the ancients who believed it sacred. He wanted to show me …'

'He wanted to show you what?' the earl said softly.

'Sometimes, he said, in the illusory moonlight one might see dancers where now stands a castle.'

'And did the illusory moonlight perform for you its tricks?'

I tilted my head. *Maybe, maybe not.* 'Perhaps I was asleep, in the lateness of the hour and my tiredness. Maybe I dreamed.'

'What did you see?'

'I dreamed I did indeed see dancers on this rock on which the castle now stands. They danced about a man with light on his head. And there were tens of thousands of people holding torches, lining that ridge, and that, and that,' I said, pointing. 'But it was an illusion, no doubt.'

'Doubtless. I am a man of the sun. Stephen was always lurking about in the moonlight.'

'Yet,' the earl continued, 'I, too, dream of such things …'

'What things?'

He was looking to the peak of Pen Cerrig-calch again. 'Of dark things, Maeb. Of the never-ending screams of hell, and of the Devil, come to snatch me. I dream I will lose everything I have ever worked for. Lose it all, to hell.'

I was horrified. 'My lord! You surely have no need to fear the Devil!'

'You have *no* idea what I have done in my lifetime. No idea of what alliances I have made. No idea at all.'

I did not know what to reply. His face had closed over, become rigid and unknowable, and I felt a shiver run down my spine.

Then he blinked, and turned his eyes from the mountain to me. 'I have frightened you, Maeb. Ah, I am sorry for it, for I should not have spoken the meanderings of my thoughts aloud. Forgive me.'

'Done, my lord.' Yet still I had to repress the desire to take a step backward, to remove myself from him, just a pace or two. I realised we stood right against the parapet and that with a twist or two of his strong arms he could dash me to the ground below.

'Did you love Stephen?' he asked, once more looking over the inner bailey. 'Speak the truth, for I will know otherwise.'

'Yes.' I could barely speak the word, so wary was I of the earl right now.

'Did he speak of me on his deathbed? Again, speak truth only.'

'No,' I said. 'He spoke of Edmond, and of the honour Stephen had at spending his youth within the king's household.'

'You have a harsh tongue for truth, Maeb.'

'It was what you asked for, my lord.'

I had taken that step back now.

'Do you think to use me to return to the king's court, and the king's regard?'

'How can that be?' I said. 'It was not I who proposed this marriage.'

His mouth curved in a small smile. 'No, it was not.'

'My lord, I am walking into a marriage that I think you have constructed to punish me.'

'It is not meant to punish you.'

'The deaths of Stephen and Rosamund and John will always lie between us, forever keeping us cold and distant if I cannot find your forgiveness for what I did. It was such a sin, my lord, I know it, but I would do it over again. They suffered so much. Stephen —'

'I have never blamed you for their deaths, Maeb. I blame myself. If only I had not taken the path I have … if only I had returned a day or two earlier … if only …'

'You could not have saved them, my lord. No one could.'

'They should not have died!'

I said nothing, but took yet another surreptitious step away.

'They should *not* have died,' he said again, much softer now, striking softly at the top of the stone parapet with his fist. 'Their deaths were an arrow meant for my own heart. As yours was also meant to be.'

I did not understand his words. 'My lord, Stephen dreamed as he died. I had the same dream.'

'What dream?'

'My lord, it was terrible. We both dreamed that the Devil came for us. A giant, hulking, monstrous presence. Sir … I have not the words to describe the terror I felt, and which Stephen doubtless felt, too.'

'I know of it, Maeb. Continue. What did the Devil want?'

'I do not truly know, my lord. He took me by the throat, and shook me, and demanded to know where it was.'

'Where what was?'

Tears came to my eyes as I remembered the terror of that night. 'I don't know! He just asked over and over, shaking me, where it was, what had I done with "it"!'

'And Stephen had this dream, too?'

'Aye. His was worse, I think. And after … after, bruising appeared on his throat, as if the Devil had caught him in the same way.'

'*Damn* him, for so hounding my son! Did he truly think *Stephen* had it? He knew I would hear of this, and knew how cruelly it would wound me. Damn him!'

'My lord?' Now he spoke in riddled circles.

'I speak nothing but the rantings of a grieving father.' The earl leaned back against the parapet, looking thoughtful. 'Some say, Maeb, that this plague is Devil-sent —'

'That I can believe!'

'Sent by the master of hell to seek something, something he has lost.'

'Then I hope he finds it soon,' I said bitterly.

'Ah,' said the earl softly, 'mayhap we should not wish so hard for that.'

'Why not?'

He gave a shrug of the shoulders, then a small, cold smile. 'What is this, Maeb? I swear a few minutes ago we were standing close. Now look at you. A half-dozen paces away. Do I frighten you so greatly?'

'Very often, my lord. You say things I cannot understand, and I fear that you are always angry at me.'

'You should not seek to understand me,' he said. 'You might not like what you discover. But to other, more delightful, matters. You are looking much better, Maeb. Perhaps the day after tomorrow we can speak the vows of betrothal. I see no reason to wait. Then shortly after, we may marry.'

I tried one more time, simply to quiet my mind. 'My lord, why *me*? You could have the choice of any noble lady. You could pick up wealth and estates and alliances simply by riding your way to court and snapping your fingers at those highly ranked women looking for a husband. Why me?'

'Have I not said enough, Maeb? You are a woman, and I need a wife. If you want more, then I will say that you are a lovely woman, and it will be no trouble on my part to bed you. Is that enough for you? If not, then I regret it, for there is nothing more to say. Now, take my arm and do not be afraid. I will see you back to the solar, where I will set you back in your chair and you will be safe once more.'

There was just a little amusement in that last, so I stepped forward and took his arm, and the earl saw me safe back to the solar.

CHAPTER SIX

I sat up late into the night, stitching the earl's gift, hoping it would be good enough to please him. The earl had set the date for our betrothal for the day after tomorrow, Saint Swithun's Day, and I needed to have the gift finished. Evelyn and the two other women were making good progress on the kirtles and chemises. All would be ready. From Saint Swithun's Day I could be a reasonable apparition of an earl's betrothed.

I still had fears regarding the marriage, and the earl's motivations for it, but I tried to set them to one side. I had little choice in the matter and only hoped that I should not be a wife to embarrass my husband, his name, or his titles and influences. I had always wanted marriage, I had always wanted a good marriage, and now that I had moved past my startlement at *how* good a marriage I would make, I resolved to do my best.

While I sat up late stitching, remembering what had happened on the roof of the great keep (were all the stranger days of my life to be delineated by rooftop conversations?), I prayed to the Blessed Saint Virgin Mary to guide me, as also to the departed souls of Stephen and Lady Adelie. I prayed to Stephen for his forgiveness, and hoped that from his place in heaven (where surely he must be) he would not think I had stepped on his dead back to reach the higher prize of his father. To Lady Adelie I prayed for guidance in my life ahead, as also forgiveness for what I had done to her children, and that I was to take her place in her marriage bed.

I stitched prayer and hope into my gift for the earl, and wished that he would accept the gift in the spirit in which I stitched and gave it.

Saint Swithun's Day dawned clear and bright, a good omen for the day, and my new life, ahead.

The betrothal ceremony was to take place in the solar in the late afternoon (I should have to wait all day!) and then there would be a celebratory feast in the great hall of the castle. I still had not attended an evening dinner in the great hall (let alone a feast), as Lady Adelie had never done so. Then the plague had struck and in the chaos of its aftermath and my own feebleness, I had not been to any of the dinners in the hall hosted by the earl. I was looking forward to the evening feast, if only because then I could relax after the high nerves of the betrothal ceremony … but even then that feast held traps and fears as I remembered how I had only barely avoided disaster during the feast I'd attended at Rosseley Manor.

The betrothal would be my first public act as countess-to-be. I did not want to spoil it with some unwitting muddle on my part. I drove Evelyn to irritation by my constant questions about protocol, what I should say and do, when I should smile and when not, and what rank, in courtly terms, did a woman of no rank but soon-to-be of high noble rank hold between betrothal and formal marriage? Who should I dip in courtesy to after betrothal but before marriage, and who not?

We spent the morning in my bathing and the protracted business of washing my hair. It was so thick and long that it took Evelyn, together with Sewenna who arrived to help as well, most of the morning to wash, dry and anoint it with rosewater and sweet smelling herbs. When it was fully dry and combed out it was so glossy, soft and thick I thought I would never manage it.

Should I wear it loose as befitted my virginal state?

'No,' said Evelyn, 'leave that for the marriage mass.'

Then what?

Evelyn was grinding her teeth by this point, I am sure. In the end we decided to comb the mass of hair over my right shoulder, loosely plait it down to my waist, then leave the hair to flow free again down to my knees, securing the loose plait with a length of black ribbon that exactly matched my hair. Sewenna went down to Owain's herb garden, found some purple and scarlet flowers, and we wound those through the plaited section.

The flowers matched the purple and scarlet in the embroidery about the neckline and sleeves of the emerald silk kirtle. This kirtle was so fine, so beautiful, that I had to be persuaded to wear it. I thought I would feel more comfortable in the plainer scarlet woollen day kirtle, but Evelyn would not hear of it.

'You will wear the green,' she said.

'I should save it for the wedding,' I responded.

'We will have something finer for you by then,' Evelyn said, winning the argument.

Finer than this emerald kirtle? I could not imagine it. But I allowed Evelyn and Sewenna to lace me tightly into the silk kirtle. I had lost much weight over the past few weeks, and the slender, richly dressed figure in the mirror left me speechless when first I looked.

I could barely recognise myself.

'You need jewels,' Evelyn said, 'but I suppose they will come soon enough.'

I thought jewels would overwhelm me, and was glad I had none. Evelyn had made a scarlet girdle, stitched about with the gilded golden thread, and she wound that about my waist and hips so that it emphasised the soft roundness of my belly.

'You are very beautiful,' she said. 'Every knight, serving man and torch bearer will envy the earl tonight.'

Then she smiled. 'You still look like the wood dryad with that hair of yours and your green eyes.'

I tried to smile back, but my nerves would not allow it. I was desperate not to misstep today and wished that somehow I could be transported instantly through the terrors of the afternoon and evening to the time when I could lose this finery and slip gratefully into bed and close my eyes against the day.

Late afternoon arrived. I had not been able to eat anything all day, and now, whenever I tried to sit still, I found that my hands trembled imperceptibly. My stomach was a knot of nerves.

From our chamber with its thin wooden partition walls we could hear the build-up of voices close by in the solar.

Sweet Jesu, how many witnesses *had* the earl invited? I had thought two or three — why bother with a crowd — but, as I moved from the women's dormitory to the solar, it became very evident that the earl had determined on a crowd.

I paused at the doorway, hiding one last time in the shadows, taking comfort from them, then raised my head and stepped through into the solar, Evelyn a step behind me.

Dear sweet Jesu, there was a multitude of people.

Later, when I had the time to sit down and sort through them by name, I realised that there were only some twenty people in the solar, but to me, at first sight, it looked like hundreds.

They all turned to look at me virtually the moment I stepped into the chamber.

My stomach turned over, my heart likewise, and I wondered what I was doing to have agreed to this. Then I realised I had never actually formally consented, and for one wild instant my brain considered the possibility of just running from the chamber shrieking denial.

And then I smiled, inclined my head slightly, took a deep breath and stepped forward.

There were only men in the chamber, no women. I recognised d'Avranches, Gilbert Ghent, Taillebois, Owain and several knights from the garrison. Then to my shock I saw Walter de Roche, the Earl of Summersete, whom our party had left at his castle of Walengefort on our way to Oxeneford.

What was he doing here?

Beside him was the earl, dressed in a fine tunic of scarlet and blue, heavily embroidered with golden silk in the heraldic symbols of Pengraic, and wearing a jewelled sword belt and scabbard.

Suddenly, gratefully, I did not feel overdressed and was glad I had donned the finest kirtle after all.

To one side of the earl, as the crowd continued to part, I saw an even more richly dressed young man of about my age.

He was tall, almost as tall as the earl, and of good strong features with curly brown hair and warm brown eyes. I lingered a little at his eyes, for they somehow seemed familiar to me, then I caught myself and lowered my own, for this was obviously a young man of rank (another earl, I wondered? Or de Roche's son?).

The earl, my earl, Pengraic, stepped forward and held out his hand. His eyes, too, were reassuringly and somewhat unusually warm, and he gave me the smallest nod of approval.

'My lord,' I murmured, dipping in courtesy. With Pengraic still clasping my hand, I turned in Summersete's direction, as the next senior ranking man in the chamber, and dipped to him as well.

'Mistress Maeb,' Summersete said, his entire face alive with sardonic humour at the idea that a girl he had last seen travelling as the least of Lady Adelie's women was now about to take the lady's place.

Then, obviously, the young man. I was feeling more confident now. I had made a decorous entrance, and had thus far greeted everyone in seemly order.

Nothing could go wrong.

'My lord prince,' Pengraic said, and my heart suddenly sank in horror. *Prince. Oh sweet Virgin, this was one of Edmond's sons. No wonder those eyes had looked familiar.*

And I had ignored him in favour of Pengraic and Summersete when his rank demanded that I should have greeted him first.

'My lord Prince Henry, this is Mistress Maeb Langtofte, in whose honour we all gather this afternoon.'

'Mistress,' said the prince, taking my hand from Pengraic's and holding it gently as I dipped again, my face flushing in my humiliation.

'I am sorry, my lord,' I said, mortified that the first true words I spoke had to be an apology, 'I did not know —'

'It is of no matter,' Henry said. 'You could not have known me.' He let my hand go. 'By God, Pengraic, no wonder the haste!'

There was a ripple of polite laughter about the chamber.

Pengraic managed a small, tight smile, and I realised that he did not like Henry overmuch, or perhaps resented his presence.

Why is he here? I wondered, realising that Pengraic did not invite him willingly. And Summersete? Both of them suddenly appearing?

'Perhaps we might get on?' Pengraic said.

'By all means,' Henry said. 'The sooner we progress to the feast the better.'

Pengraic led me, Henry and Summersete just behind, to a table where a large parchment lay.

I realised that another humiliation lay before me.

'These are the jointure documents, Maeb,' Pengraic said, 'drawn up by Owain who was clerk enough for the duty. They convey to you the manors of Cogshall, Shiphill, Wharton and Hexthorpe as your jointure, your support and sustenance in the event of my death. We both need to sign them, and my lord prince and Summersete will witness.'

With that Pengraic picked up the pen, dipped it in the ink, and signed his name with a flourish.

Then he handed the pen to me.

I took it, hesitating.

I could feel Pengraic tense, perhaps thinking I was about to refuse (or, worse, ask for more).

'I can make a mark only, my lord,' I said softly.

'A mark is as legal as a name,' Pengraic said, as if utterly indifferent to the matter. 'That is why we have witnesses for such things.'

Immensely grateful to him, I dipped the pen in the ink then, at the place he indicated, drew a shaky X.

I stepped back, Henry taking the pen from me, signing his name with a flourish, then Summersete.

'And now the vows,' Henry said cheerfully.

Pengraic took both my hands in his, our wrists crossed in the traditional vowing manner.

'Before these witnesses,' Pengraic said, 'I swear I will willingly take Mistress Maeb Langtofte of Witenie to wife.'

Eyes turned expectantly to me.

'Before these witnesses, I swear I will willingly take Raife de Mortaigne, Earl of Pengraic, to husband.'

'Done!' said Summersete, moving toward a manservant who held a tray of full wine cups.

'Not quite,' said Pengraic.

He reached behind him to another servant who held something wrapped in a sky-blue cloth. Pengraic picked it up then turned back to me. 'To my betrothed,' he said, 'as symbol of my good faith.'

I had not expected a gift, but at the same time was not surprised by it. Acceptance of the gift would be as legally binding as the vows spoken prior. I was glad also, for this now would make my own gifting far less awkward.

I quickly checked for Evelyn … good, she was standing close.

Then I gave a little dip and took the bundle from Pengraic. 'I thank you, my lord.'

I unwrapped it, gasping in unfeigned wonder as I beheld a stunningly worked girdle woven with gold wires and links and set with pearls, diamonds, emeralds and rubies. It was a magnificent thing — I had never seen the like, nor ever expected that I should receive such a gift.

I looked at Pengraic. 'You do me great honour,' I said. 'Thank you.'

He gave a smile and I thought I could read him well enough now to see that he was pleased with my reaction.

'You must put it on,' said Henry, and stepped forward as if to take the girdle and fix it himself.

I was too quick. I held the girdle out to Pengraic. 'My lord?'

Evelyn was at my back, undoing the girdle she had so carefully stitched. She slid it from my hips, then I stepped closer to Pengraic and held out the girdle to him.

He took it, stepping close so that he could wrap the central and most exquisitely bejewelled portion of the girdle about my waist, handing the ends to Evelyn. She crossed them over behind my back at my waist, clipping them together, then handing the ends back to the earl. He draped them low on my belly, loosely knotting the ends of the girdle so that it sat snugly.

'It is beautiful,' I said.

'For what you did for my children,' he said, very low.

My eyes flew to his. Others may have heard what he said, but they would not have known the significance.

I collected myself and turned slightly to Evelyn. She handed me my gift to the earl, wrapped in fine lawn. I handed it to him.

'My gift to you, my lord,' I said as I dipped in courtesy.

He looked surprised, but pleased, and his mouth curved in a smile as he unwrapped it.

He stared at the gift, then his smile widened slightly and he looked at me with what might have been some real warmth in his eyes.

'It is lovely, Maeb. Thank you.'

I smiled in sheer relief that at least he had not hated it.

'What is it?' Henry said, stepping close.

'It is a belt purse,' said Pengraic, holding it out so those near him could see. 'Exquisitely worked.'

The belt purse was of plain leather, but I had stitched a cover for it. For the background stitching it had a dark forest, much like that depicted on the walls of the castle chapel, while in the centre and foreground was a depiction of Pengraic Castle. Above the battlements I had stitched a fanciful sun and moon.

'If the sun and moon ever come that close to this castle's battlements,' said Henry, 'then I would think it a most unhappy event.'

'Indeed,' Pengraic muttered, then he stepped forward and kissed me.

It was not a deep kiss, but it *was* the first time he had kissed me and I was more than a little startled by its warmth, for I think I had only ever imagined a cold, hard kiss from the man. Maybe he meant it to convey his thanks for the purse.

'It is a most exquisite design,' he said, 'and I thank you most deeply for it, and for the thought behind it.'

My heart still raced, but now with relief that my gift had gone down well.

'Well,' Henry said, 'they are now betrothed, the gifts given and received. Surely we should drink to their health, and then proceed down to the great hall for our entertainment and feasting?'

CHAPTER SEVEN

Despite Prince Henry's obvious desire for haste, we tarried in the solar for an hour or two more, drinking spiced wine and exchanging pleasant conversation. I admit I downed the first cup of wine a little too quickly, but it did relax me and I was careful with later cups.

Summersete cornered Pengraic and kept him in low, serious conversation. Prince Henry stayed by my side, exchanging inconsequential words as, one by one, the other men within the chamber came up to greet the prince and to wish me well.

Eventually, the prince managed to steer me into a clear space where we might not be overheard easily.

'A meteoric rise, mistress,' he said, his affable manner sliding away. His eyes had lost their warmth, and with that I thought he had lost all in him of his father.

'It was not of my doing, my lord.'

'I had not known, when I arrived here this morning, that I would be asked to witness Pengraic's hasty new marriage. I was an admirer of Lady Adelie and sorrowed to hear of her death when Stephen's message arrived at court.'

'I also admired her, my lord.'

'My father mentioned you, before I left Oxeneford.'

'He did?' Already on my guard because of the prince's cooling manner and his questions, his words now confused me.

'He told me to watch for Lady Adelie's attending woman, Maeb. He said you were very beautiful. He was not wrong.' The prince glanced about to ensure we were not being observed, then he slid a finger of his right hand under my girdle, against the soft mound of my belly.

Maybe he *was* his father's son, after all.

'I had thought to dally with Lady Adelie's beautiful attending woman, but alas, I cannot see now how that might be without creating further crisis in the realm.'

'Then by all means, let us avert the crisis,' I said, drawing back so his finger slipped away from my girdle. I felt sullied and wished he were not here.

'Your presence has quite startled me, my lord,' I said, 'for I had heard no rumour of your arrival.'

Instantly I regretted the last. Maybe Pengraic had known Henry and Summersete were on their way, but did not judge me of enough consequence to be informed.

'We had thought to surprise Pengraic,' he said. 'But your betrothed husband is a difficult man to unsettle.'

He thought this might be news to me? 'Why the need to unsettle him?'

'Lord God, woman, you need some tuition in the skills of courtly conversation. Such direct questioning.'

'*She* has the skill to unsettle *you*, it seems,' Pengraic said, coming up behind us.

Again, there he was, having obviously heard much of our conversation.

I hoped he had not seen the finger under the girdle.

Pengraic took the empty cup from my fingers, handed it to a servant, then took my elbow.

'It is time for us to descend,' he said, 'and feast.'

Confined by the dimensions of the keep, the great hall of Pengraic was somewhat smaller than the one at Rosseley, but it was still impressive. It had two fireplaces: one at the southern end of the hall, one in the eastern wall, and both were chimneyed to keep the air clear. At the northern end of the hall stood the dais holding the lord's table; there were several braziers set behind the table to keep those at the high table warm.

The floor was of stone, its surface smooth and neatly joined. Hangings covered the northern, eastern and western walls, the subject matter reminding me again of the paintings in the chapel. Heraldic pennants and lamps hung from the panelled ceiling and torches lined the spaces between the hangings.

As at Rosseley, two long tables ran down from the high table. Most of the diners were already here, enough to fill both tables, but yet sparse enough in number that there was ample space between each diner. The plague's shadow still hung over life at Pengraic.

Despite the shadow, there was a minstrel playing, and servants to carry ewers of wine and platters of food.

The music ceased and all stood as we entered.

I was reminded starkly of the feast at Rosseley when Edmond had attended. Then I'd been a naïve girl from the country, watching with wide eyes as the king and nobles processed up the hall.

I was little changed from that person, although life and death had marked me in the meantime. Yet now I was among the great nobles who strode up the centre of the hall, if not yet one of them, and eyes followed me, watchful, wondering, calculating.

It was unsettling. It would have been unsettling enough with Pengraic, but I was not walking with Pengraic.

As senior woman present (or close enough to my marriage to be so thought) I accompanied Prince Henry, the senior nobleman. We led the procession into the hall, slowly walking up the centre of the hall to the high table. To either side people bowed, their heads low as we passed.

I was very tense. Not so much because I had at my side a prince, but because of what that prince had revealed of himself. No wonder Pengraic did not like him.

I would need to watch my tongue tonight, and I hoped that the prince would be a few places from me.

It was not to be. As host, Pengraic sat at the centre of the table facing into the hall, myself on his right and Prince Henry on my right, so that I was positioned between the two men. Summersete sat on Pengraic's left, d'Avranches beyond him and Owain (his place at the table surprised me) sat on Prince Henry's right.

Servants hastened to offer us bowls of water to wash our hands and then towels to dry them. The wine servitors then filled our cups, and Henry led the hall in a toast to Pengraic's and my betrothal. He managed it courteously enough, and once the cheers and good wishes and the *drinkhails!* had died down, servants set fine plate and platters of food before us.

Pengraic filled my plate for me, taking the choicest of morsels to set before me and, as Saint-Valery had so many months previously, took care to keep the lip of my wine cup clean by wiping it with his napkin every so often. He offered me salt from the ornate silver salt cellar, and I nodded my thanks as he tipped it from his knife to my plate.

Every time a new course was served, the servants waiting behind us leaned in to clean the table, straighten the table cloths as much as they could, and gave us fresh napkins and plates or trenchers, whatever the course demanded.

It was all very formal, and very courteous, and I made sure to only sip at my wine and nibble at the food, keeping my responses to either Pengraic or Henry as brief as possible. Every so often I looked to Evelyn for reassurance. She sat a little way down the table on my right, and each time she caught my glance her way she smiled and gave me a small nod.

I slowly relaxed.

For a time the conversation was convivial and courteous. Most of the men concentrated on their eating, only asking polite queries of others as they ate and drank. The minstrel strolled about the centre of the hall, singing songs of nobility and adventure and, each time he came nearer me, foolish romantic ballads that had me blushing — more from the attention than the words.

Time passed. I relaxed more and, even though I had but sipped at the wine, I'd had enough to start to think that I may have been mistaken in forming a poor initial opinion of Henry.

Eventually the men sat back, their appetites sated. Pengraic gestured for the man serving the wine to step forth and refill all the cups.

'My lord prince,' I said to Henry, who was leaning back slightly in his chair and looking sleepy with wine, 'what brings you to Pengraic? On my oath, I did not expect to meet with one of Edmond's sons when I stepped into the solar this afternoon!'

Henry gave a little shrug of his shoulders. 'Summersete and I were riding on my father's business to the Bishop of Hereford, when, in Monemude, we fell to thinking we must make sure that Pengraic was still well. We had heard the plague was here and that Lady Adelie had died, and we were concerned.'

'Your concern, as always, does me great honour,' Pengraic said in a voice that indicated Henry's concern did everything but.

'It was truly a terrible time, my lord,' I said to Henry. 'The death …'

'All of your children dead, I hear,' Henry said, speaking over me to the earl. 'Even those not at Pengraic. No wonder you are so anxious to get yourself a new heir. Losing … what was it … five sons if we count the one dead with Adelie? Such bad luck.'

The hairs were rising on the back of my neck. There was an under-conversation going on here. I could sense it, but could not understand what it might be.

'From five heirs to none in the space of a few weeks,' Summersete added from the other side of Pengraic. 'The lordship of Pengraic itself hangs by the thread of a single heartbeat.'

Suddenly I realised the true purpose of this conversation, and of Henry and Summersete's visit. Pengraic was a very wealthy man, controlling vast estates, here in the Marches as well as elsewhere in England. It was not just that he was a powerful nobleman, but a powerful *Marcher* Lord, almost independent of the king, controlling his own lands as if he were their king — Edmond had little power over Pengraic's lands and wealth. It was possible, then, that Henry and Summersete had detoured to Pengraic to see what Pengraic was doing.

Or, more probably, to seize the castle and perhaps the Marcher Lordship if Pengraic had perished in the plague, too.

So much power to be seized had Pengraic been dead. The lordship could have been anyone's. Henry's most like, if it had reverted to the Crown.

By God, they, and perhaps even Edmond, must be whetting their lips with anticipation knowing all of Pengraic's heirs were dead!

What disappointment Henry and Summersete must have felt, then, to see Pengraic striding about so obviously well.

I wondered what they thought of this marriage. The matter of who I was, a low-ranked woman who formerly had been grateful for her modest place in the household, was of little concern. What must be of concern was that Pengraic appeared to be set on the business of acquiring a new heir as soon as possible.

212

Henry had been watching my face. 'Ah, mistress, you have just realised how important your womb is. By Jesu, all you are, truly, is a womb with limbs and a pretty face attached. No wonder the gift of the girdle, given it frames your womb perfectly. Its filling is all Pengraic cares for. *When* did you say the marriage was to be, Pengraic?'

It was a hateful little speech and I was mortified by it, not in the least because I suspected it held more than a grain of truth. Wasn't that what Pengraic himself had said? *You owe me a family, and you shall deliver me a new one.*

'Edmond wants you back at court, Pengraic,' Summersete said. 'You left Elesberie without his permission in order to return here. Now might be politic to regain your king's favour. Marriage and bedding can wait.'

Everything about the entire night had changed. By now I was staring down at my lap (and trying not to notice that the way the girdle was tied did, as Henry had said, frame my womb perfectly). The noise of music and conversation and dogs barking from the body of the hall was strangely muted, as if it were miles away. There was only Prince Henry, Summersete, Pengraic and myself, enclosed in a sphere of hostility.

For better or worse, Saint-Valery had said, my position within the Pengraic household would draw me into the dealings of court. Now, on the eve of marriage to Pengraic, I was at the heart of it, and wishing I was anywhere but here.

"Tis most uncourtly of you, my Lord Henry, to treat Mistress Maeb with such ungraciousness,' Pengraic said, his tone mild. 'If you wish to land a blow on me, then land it honourably, my lord. Do not use the body of an innocent woman to shield yourself.'

'My apologies, Mistress Maeb,' Henry said. 'What must I do to make amends?'

'This castle is still wrapped in grief, my lord,' I said. 'All of us are easily wounded. Be a gentle lord, if you might.'

'Your reprimand is received, mistress, and taken to heart. I have treated you poorly. You must have witnessed such horrors during the time of the plague.'

'Indeed, my lord. It was truly dreadful.'

'Yet you managed to escape the plague?'

'No, my lord. It gripped me, too, but somehow I survived.'

'Then you are truly remarkable, mistress! I am sure your betrothed hopes you pass your strength to your children. Tell me of Lord Stephen's death and that of the other children. Did you witness those?'

Sweet Jesu, where was he going with this? 'I did, my lord.'

'The burning must have torn at your heart, as it must continue to tear at my Lord Pengraic's.'

'They did not —' I stopped, appalled.

'They did not burn?'

Everything about the prince now focused intently on me: his eyes, his manner, his body.

His questions.

Pengraic made to say something, but Henry held up a hand, silencing him.

'Mistress Maeb,' Henry said, 'I can understand that maybe one among them may have died of heart failure before the flames consumed him or her, but *all* of them? That speaks for the weakness of the Pengraic heart, surely, or of, how may I put this courteously, some intercession to ensure they died more peacefully?'

He knew. *He knew.*

Henry was staring at me, his eyes intense, his tongue hovering about his lips, as if he knew his prey was trapped.

'The plague as it found its way into Pengraic, was a variant form,' Owain said, from further down the table.

My heart pounded so violently I could barely hear him.

'Many of its victims died before they could burn,' Owain continued.

'How fortunate for them,' Henry said softly, his eyes still riveted on me.

I could not look at him, but was staring at my hands clasped white-knuckled in my lap.

He had likely seen those, too.

'What part did you have in those deaths, Maeb?' Henry said, softly.

'I —'

'Enough, Henry!' Pengraic said. 'I say again, why torment Maeb when your issue is with me?'

Henry's eyes still had not moved from me. 'Because I think I have found a delicious morsel to take back to court with me,' he whispered, so low I do not think Pengraic could hear him.

But *I* did. *I* did.

Henry leaned back, waving a hand as if all this talk were nothing. 'My father is displeased, Pengraic. He wants to know when you return to his side. He has uses for you, yet you are not there to achieve them.'

'Edmond well knew my reason for riding back to Pengraic,' the earl said. 'I cannot think he has forgot it so quickly. I will return once the castle and the lands surrounding it are secured. I have yet to hear news of Madog and while the garrison here remains under-manned, I will not move. The Welsh upstart remains a threat. Do you want Welsh rebels flooding into England? If not, then may I suggest I serve Edmond's best interests by remaining here to secure his western door.'

'You serve *your* best interests,' Summersete muttered.

'In this instance,' Pengraic snapped, 'both my and the king's interests marry.'

'Speaking of which,' Henry said, 'Summersete and I might as well stay for the marriage mass. You surely cannot be thinking of tarrying over the matter?'

If Pengraic was thinking anything even remotely similar to what I was, he'd be planning the marriage mass for tomorrow morning, if it meant he'd be rid of these two.

'Within the week, I think,' Pengraic said, 'now that Maeb makes good recovery from her illness.'

'That is well,' Henry said, picking up his napkin and dabbing at his lips. 'I am sure you can organise entertainments enough for us in the meantime. Now, I have had enough of this feast, even though it turned out even more pleasurable than I anticipated.'

He glanced at me as he said this last, and I knew he had not forgot his 'delicious morsel'.

Henry stood up, and with that, the feast was over.

Sir Gilbert Ghent escorted the Earl of Summersete to the northern keep, where Summersete would be quartered, but Pengraic led myself, the prince and Evelyn back up the stairwell into the solar. Here, the prince said his goodnights pleasantly enough, and disappeared into the privy chamber, which Pengraic had given over to him. Pengraic nodded to Evelyn that she should go through to the chamber we shared in the female dormitory, then Pengraic pulled me aside for a quiet word.

'My lord,' I said, desperate to forestall what I assumed would be angry words. 'I am sorry for what I said before Henry. I did not think. And now ...'

'Now he has something he thinks he might use against me,' Pengraic said. 'Be wary of him, Maeb. He will not use this yet, but should we return to court, expect a dark rumour to surface sooner or later, when Henry thinks to wound me.'

'I am sorry, my lord.'

He gave a little shrug. 'If not that, then he would have found something else with which to bark at my heels. Tell me, have you given confession to Owain?'

I nodded.

'Then all you need say is that your conscience is clear. Maeb,' he looked back toward the door to the privy chamber, checking it was shut, 'there is something else you need to be most wary of. Did you understand the thrust of Henry's remarks about needing an heir?'

'Edmond distrusts your power, and the power of this castle and the lands it commands. He would not hesitate to seize it if he could. I am sure Edmond would prefer not to see you sire an heir.'

'Very good, Maeb. Your perception pleases me, although I think it is more Henry's ambition than Edmond's we need to fear. Henry is the danger, not his father — Henry is using his father as a front for his own purposes. You think perhaps that I am in danger, but Henry and his factors will not move against me so openly. Not yet. The danger is against you.'

'My lord?'

'Maeb, Henry will waste no opportunity to ensure that there might be every doubt about the paternity of any child you conceived within the next few weeks. It would be in his best interests that there be doubt.'

It took me a long moment to realise what he meant. I think I must have gone very pale, because Pengraic took my arm, as if to steady me.

'I will be putting a guard outside the door to your sleeping chamber,' Pengraic said. 'A senior man, one who will not be intimidated by Henry and against whom Henry would be reluctant to draw sword.'

'My lord, he would not dare ... surely?'

'Aye, he would dare. During the day, if you are not in your chamber, Maeb, then you walk escorted. Do not be lax in this regard. You must be wary.'

I nodded, unable to speak for fear.

'Send word to me if you wish to walk abroad, and I will send an escort if I cannot come myself.'

Again I nodded.

Pengraic's voice softened. 'You did well tonight, Maeb. That table was littered with teeth.'

'And I was bit. Hard. My lord, again I apologise for creating suspicion in Henry's mind. It has left you vulnerable.'

'Henry is a dangerous man, but he does not know what he truly faces if he thinks to tilt his ambitions my way.'

'He does not seem his father's son.'

'Edmond can be a dangerous man, too, Maeb. Do not forget that. And … Maeb? Thank you for this purse. I do greatly value it.'

He smiled, surprising me with its apparent warmth, then escorted me to my chamber. As he said goodnight, d'Avranches appeared, nodding to me as he took up a position just down from my door.

'Your safety for the night,' Pengraic said.

As I turned to enter my chamber, the earl stopped me with a light touch to my arm.

'Maeb … I like the way you have dressed your hair today. Wear it that way more often.'

Then, with a small bow, he was gone.

CHAPTER EIGHT

We married within ten days. I spent much of that time sequestered within my chamber, although each day I did take a walk outside, accompanied, if not by Pengraic himself, by d'Avranches or Taillebois or one of the senior knights as well as Evelyn.

I felt the most chaperoned woman in England.

I met Henry on several occasions during those walks and we passed pleasant, courteous words that said nothing. Always Henry had a look of sharp amusement in his eyes that sent shivers up my spine.

Sweet Jesu, he knew about Stephen and the children! Not the particulars perhaps, but he knew that I'd somehow had something to do with their 'dying more peacefully'. I dreaded to think what he might do with that information.

The time spent in the chamber was, if somewhat confining, at least less dangerous than the outer world. Evelyn, Sewenna, Tilla and myself spent the time sewing. We made two new kirtles: another day kirtle of pale apple-green woollen cloth with embroideries rich enough to allow it to do duty at court, and a far richer silken kirtle of deep wine red that I would wear for the wedding. As well, we stitched ribbons, more chemises, a cloak from heavy wool, gloves and hose.

No one could say we were not industrious.

I only saw Pengraic on the few occasions he accompanied Evelyn and myself on our walks. Our conversations were brief, and touched only on trivial matters. His thoughts seemed to be elsewhere. I was most pleased, however, to note that whenever I saw him he wore my purse on his belt. I was so unsure of the earl that this simple gesture of his pleasure in something I had done for him reassured me extraordinarily.

We spoke of something deeper only once, when I asked him when he thought it would be necessary to return to Edmond's court.

'Necessary?' he arched an eyebrow. 'It is necessary now. Every day I delay my enemies will be trying to turn Edmond against me. I do not want to give them any more opportunity than I must.'

I wondered how I could rephrase the question without him becoming irritated. 'Then why do you delay, my lord?'

It was direct, but I hoped it would not anger him. Even though I was now betrothed to the man, I still stepped carefully and as delicately about him as I might.

'The garrison needs to be fully manned,' he said. 'It will take several more weeks before enough knights and soldiers have come from my other estates. Thank Christ d'Avranches survived the plague, for I would be lost without him.'

'And then to court?'

'You seem most desirous to get to court as quickly as you might, mistress.'

'I press only because I understand the danger posed by your enemies there, my lord.'

He stopped, and looked south as if he could see over the great keep. 'I want to know where the plague got to,' he muttered. 'I want to know how far it travelled down this valley, and where it stopped, and why.'

Why do you need to know that, my lord? But I did not ask that question; I knew my limits. 'You cannot send a party of men to discover?'

He gave a slight shake of his head. 'They would need to travel deep into Welsh territory. I fear they might not return.'

'And you do not wish to deplete Pengraic of a party large enough to travel safely.'

He looked at me then, a glint of amusement in his eyes. 'Had you been a man, Maeb, you would have made a useful general.'

I laughed — the first time I had ever freely done so in his presence — and was rewarded by a deepening of the amusement in his eyes.

I tried to think of some witty remark to make to counter his, but my mind failed me, and we stood there a moment, the amusement fading to awkwardness. Eventually the earl gave a small bow and we parted.

* * *

As had my betrothal day, my wedding day dawned fine and clear. This was a far less formal occasion than my betrothal, which had seen the formal legalities signed, spoken, exchanged and witnessed, and there was to be only a short mass in the church, an afternoon meal to be taken in the solar with a few guests, and then the commencement of married life, with its adventures, worries and drudgeries.

While I had many fears and insecurities about marrying Pengraic, one of my most prominent thoughts was that I was glad this day had come if only because we would see the back of Henry and Summersete.

I dressed in the kirtle of wine-red silk that Evelyn, Sewenna, Tilla and I had stitched over the past week, wearing Pengraic's golden girdle and leaving my hair to flow free as indication of my virginity. Evelyn made a small circlet of flowers which she placed on my head. D'Avranches escorted me to the chapel where there was a group of witnesses waiting, Henry and Summersete among them. Pengraic was already there, standing before the altar with Owain. The earl was looking a little awkward and more than a little impatient. I dipped in courtesy to Henry and Summersete, then did the same to Pengraic as I stood by his side.

Owain conducted the ceremony and mass with remarkable brevity — possibly acting under instructions from Pengraic. Pengraic presented me with another gift, this time a lovely, delicate, twisted gold ring set with tiny pearls whereupon we kissed perfunctorily. Then Henry and Summersete stepped forward, said the modicum of polite phrases, and both kissed me briefly on the lips.

Everyone was back out in the sun before noon.

I had expected that Henry and Summersete would join us for the celebratory meal in the solar, but to my surprise — and delight — their horses and escort were waiting as we exited the chapel.

'Do not forget that my father waits for you,' Henry said to Pengraic. 'It will go the worse for you the longer you delay.'

Then he gave me a smile. 'My lady,' he said, kissing my hand.

With that he was gone, Summersete's goodbye consisting of a grunt that my husband (how strange it seemed to be thinking of him as such!) and I had to share.

The column clattered out the main gate without a backward glance.

'For sweet Christ's sake,' Pengraic muttered to d'Avranches, 'set a man atop the parapets to watch so he can reassure me they rode all the way out of the valley. And have the gates locked.'

We went to the solar where, with Owain, d'Avranches and two other of the senior knights, including Gilbert Ghent, we ate a light repast of cold meats, fruits and cheeses. Evelyn stood to one side, ready to attend me if needed. The air seemed thick with people muttering 'my lady'. It was very strange, watching Evelyn hover beyond me, listening to others address me, trying to come to terms with the realisation I was now a countess and wed to one of the most powerful nobles in the realm.

And yet, here we sat talking of inconsequential things and nibbling on cheeses and meats and dried figs.

Generally, the earl and d'Avranches kept conversation going with a prosaic discussion of repairing the garrison keep from the damage the plague fires had wrought. Eventually, they both decided they needed to inspect some work that was being done on the upper floors of the garrison.

Such was my marriage feast. The earl told me we would have a light meal in the evening, again in the solar, and then he and d'Avranches departed with the other knights. Owain stayed a few minutes longer, then he, too, left.

Evelyn and I were on our own.

We passed the afternoon in desultory manner, stitching away at yet more garments. I spent the time mostly thinking and worrying about the night ahead. I was no stranger to what went on between a man and a woman: having lived my childhood in a village, I had spent enough time, along with other children, with my eye glued to cracks in planks of barns and other outbuildings where young lovers chose to cavort.

If I had been as other village children I would have chosen a lover as a young woman and only married when I was breeding my first child.

But my life had taken a very different course, and here I was, noble wed, awaiting my marriage night. I was nervous enough of Pengraic without wondering how he might expect me to behave in bed. What did he want from a wife? Quiet compliance? Screaming enthusiasm? I didn't know.

Given that I had known his former wife, though, I could make some suppositions. Adelie would doubtless have been quietly compliant (unless she presented her husband with a very different side than she showed to everyone else). She had herself told me that the earl was demanding of his marital rights, and that she was always glad when she was breeding so that she might evade such demands. Is that what the earl liked? Or had he kept a mistress who had provided him with the bed sport he truly desired?

Sweet Jesu, did he have a mistress? At court, perhaps? I had not once thought of this possibility, and I had not been with the household long enough to know. Did Evelyn know?

I could not ask her.

I just wanted it to be over. My marriage night was merely something to be got past, something where I wanted to know what was expected of me that I might do my best to comply. Perhaps I would start breeding soon and then, like Adelie, I could find a reprieve from my husband's demands.

As always, the unknown assumed a more terrifying guise than what turned out to be reality.

We had our supper, and then I retired to the privy chamber with Evelyn to get ready for bed. I suppose that had this been a marriage made in more usual times, the ceremony would have been more elaborate. As it was, it was utterly perfunctory.

I was beyond relieved to see the bed had been replaced, and that there were new hangings on both the bed and at the window. The bed had even been shifted to another part of the commodious chamber. There were bad memories still in here, but at least the new and rearranged furniture made it easier.

Evelyn and I did not talk much. I was too nervous and she, I think, too uncomfortable at the new relationship between us: I cannot imagine Evelyn had ever thought of us as lady and attending woman. We laid aside my kirtle, brushed out my hair, and then Evelyn gave me a light wrap to put over my chemise so I could wait for the earl.

I did not know whether to climb into bed or wait in a chair by the fire.

In the end, I chose the chair by the fire. Evelyn left me, saying she would return in the morning.

For now, and for the rest of the night, I would be alone with my husband.

I sat for what felt to me a very long time, but which in reality was likely only a brief period. I think the earl must have been in the solar, waiting only for Evelyn to leave.

When he came in, I rose hastily, and dipped in courtesy. He walked over and gave that small strange smile of his and, a little hesitant himself, ran a gentle hand behind my neck.

'I do not require such formality in our bedchamber, Maeb.'

I felt vulnerable at the touch of his hand, but relieved at the mention of requirements. 'I do not know what you want, my lord. I do not know how to please you, or what pleases you.'

Again, that small smile. He brought up his other hand, running the fingers slowly through the bulk of my hair before he gently kissed my forehead. 'Get into bed,' he said, 'while I disrobe, and then we can talk.'

I walked to the other side of the bed as the earl disrobed. Should I offer to assist him? No, he had told me to get into bed. Somewhat self-consciously, for I had never before been naked before a man, I set my wrap to one side before stepping out of the chemise.

I slid into bed, trying not to hurry as I drew the coverlets over my breasts. My hair was so long it caught behind me, and I pulled it over my shoulder, using it, as well as the coverlets, as a form of defence.

The earl undressed unhurriedly, then slid into bed beside me.

We sat there, my stomach knotting.

'I know that my decision to choose you as a wife, particularly after the manner in which I spoke to you on that day we met, has been a surprise to you,' he said.

I made a noncommittal noise, desperately unsure of what to say.

He shifted so he could look at me directly, and the knots in my stomach increased. 'My opinion of you changed as you settled into my household, although I was never happy about the regard in which Stephen held you, nor, indeed, that which you felt for him. I had heard reports of how you rode together much of the way to this castle, and that angered me.'

The earl lifted a hand and brushed a small amount of hair away from my shoulder. 'I spent half my time being angry at you, Maeb, and the other half being grateful you walked into Rosseley. You twist me both ways.' He sighed, his hand still stroking at my hair, gently touching my shoulder now and again. 'I worry that my desire for you might deflect me from my purpose. I worry that you might be my undoing.'

'My lord, I —'

'Perhaps I should not have remarried,' he continued, giving me no chance to speak. 'There are such pressing matters ahead I need to focus on, and such dark times, that it would be simpler for me without the burden of a wife and a family. Better without the temptation of such a lovely girl in my bed. On the other hand, a wife would be a comfort to me. *You* would be a comfort to me. Should I have married you? I don't know, perhaps not, but it is done now, Maeb, and we shall both have to make the best of it.'

Hardly reassuring words, although his voice was gentle. He worried that I would be his undoing? He referred to Henry, obviously, and how my witless naïvety might make the earl vulnerable.

His hand slipped behind my neck, very slowly stroking. 'Maybe we might have a marriage where we can both be of comfort to each other. Do you think we might manage that?'

'I will try, my lord.'

'Call me Raife, in this privacy. We hold equal rank now. You should learn to wield it.'

'I am too unsure to wield it!'

He laughed and its genuine amusement startled me. 'You will become more comfortable, in time. Call me Raife, now. Say it.'

'Raife.' It felt strange.

'It will become familiar to you,' he said, leaning forward to kiss my neck. His hand went to my shoulder. 'Come now, lie down.'

I lay down, he sliding down to accompany me. I prayed this would be over soon and that he would not be too displeased. Then I could close my eyes and move toward tomorrow when everything, I was sure, would be easier.

'Do you know, when I married Adelie, we were both so young. I was fifteen, and Adelie only fourteen or so.'

I smiled, a little tremulously.

'On our wedding night she spent three hours on her knees on that side of the bed,' he nodded to my side, 'praying fervently.'

Sweet Jesu, is that what he expected me to do?

'No, fair Mae,' he said, kissing my shoulder now, 'I do not want you sliding away from my warmth onto the colder orbit of the floor. Stay right where you are. But, oh, that night, I was full of righteous lust, Adelie of pious duty. I fear she did not enjoy herself. But ... that was Adelie. This is you. Perhaps we can manage all kinds of excitements between us, you and I.'

My mind instantly leapt to the dark whispers I'd heard among women of the village: that some men liked to obtain their pleasure with knives and bindings, even with fire and blood.

My fear must have shown on my face, for the earl chuckled.

'No, Mae! I do not intend to beat you! Nor harm you in any way. I would never do that. Never. Tell me you understand that.'

I liked the way he used the diminutive of my name. It reassured me, somehow. 'I know that you would never harm me, my ... Raife.'

'If only your voice carried conviction, wife, but I can live with the mere words for the moment. Time will bring trust. I *will* never harm you, Mae. Never. Whatever you may come to think of me. You are the one person I could never want to harm.'

I rolled my head over to look at him, knowing my eyes still mirrored my doubt.

'Oh, Mae ...' He kissed me, very deeply, his hand caressing my body. I was still uncertain of him, but I tried to relax as he touched me intimately.

'Just trust me, Mae.'

'Yes.'

'Whatever happens.'

'Yes.'

I *was* relaxing now, and astonishing myself by realising that I enjoyed the touch of his hand. He rolled me over to face him, and I leaned in, pressing my breasts against his chest, for the first time recognising the power of my own body and of my own sexuality as I heard his breath catch.

We kissed again, more passionately now that I was a little more at ease, and he pressed me the length of his body.

'You are full of surprises,' he whispered, kissing me on my cheek and chin, and a sweet, sweet spot on my neck that made me shudder. 'So full of surprises. I must beware of you.'

All I heard was the desire and wonder in his voice rather than the words themselves, and I did not think any more on what he said.

Thus was my marriage night. I shall not speak more of it for modesty's sake — I have already spoken too freely. But it was not what I had expected, and certainly not what I had feared.

I had hoped only that I would please him. I had not thought that I, also, would find pleasure in him, and from him.

CHAPTER NINE

Thus I became the Countess of Pengraic. A new circumstance and an uneasy one. Previously I had watched the world from a lowly rank, and I was comfortable there. I knew my place. But suddenly I was transported to the very highest of ranks within secular society. I had to relinquish so much of my understanding of the world, and virtually all of my learned and comfortable behaviours.

I no longer knew my place. All I could do was rely on Evelyn, to a lesser extent on my husband, and from my memories of how Adelie had behaved. But I had only known Adelie a short time and what I learned from my memories of her was limited. How did I command? I did not know. What were my rights — and my courtesies — in command? I did not know. For instance, Evelyn was now my attending woman rather than my friend. We both found that adjustment uncomfortable.

I wanted, as a gesture to Evelyn, to ask her daughter to join me as an attending woman as well, but did not know how to go about this. Did I ask my husband? My instinctive feeling was that yes, I should ask him ... but was that instinct a relic from Mistress Maeb, low-ranked attendant? Did Pengraic have any care as to who my attending ladies were? Should I just ask Taillebois to organise her transport here and be done with it?

But would that antagonise de Tosny, in whose household Evelyn's daughter currently resided. Did I need to ask him? As a countess, did I need to 'ask' a lower ranked noble ... or did I just take? I didn't know! Again, my gut instinct was to ask de Tosny's permission, to be courteous, but my head argued a countess did not need to 'ask permission'.

There were other doubts and considerations. Did I need more than one attending lady, when I had no children? Was two an extravagance? Wasteful? Indulgent? What would Adelie have done?

It was such a simple matter, one which I am sure would have concerned my husband not the least, and which Adelie would have solved and acted upon within an instant. But I spent days, *weeks*, worrying over it and, in the end, did nothing.

I had not been raised to be a noble. I did not know the order and manner of things in such a life.

I struggled.

I worried about my struggles, because this was but life at Pengraic Castle which, while formal enough, was nothing as compared to life at court. I started to hope that when my husband finally surrendered to Edmond's wishes and returned to court, he would leave me behind. Adelie had remained behind at Rosseley; might not I at Pengraic?

In the meantime I managed as best I could and hoped I did not embarrass my husband. My new role as wife was much easier than my role as countess. Pengraic did not ask much of me. At night we shared a bed and, most nights, we coupled, and I became far more confident in that aspect of my new duties.

As I had discovered on my marriage night, I found love-making surprisingly enjoyable. Surprising because I had never thought of Pengraic in terms of 'lover', and I had supposed that sharing a bed and my body with him would prove to be as awkward (and sometimes as frightening) as so often were our conversations. After all, that was what Lady Adelie had led me to expect with her sighs and talk of her husband's 'demands'.

But, no. I did not struggle to be self-assured in bed, as I did out of it.

I quickly grew to enjoy my husband's attentions, and grew to trust in my own abilities as his sexual partner. I had never thought I might enjoy love-making so much, or grow to look forward to it. From what my husband said on the matter (and even more from his undoubted enthusiasm for our bed sport), I realised that my lack of inhibitions (as compared, I supposed, to Adelie's) pleased him and that gave me ever more confidence. I was careful not to be too presumptuous, and to always defer to my husband — I did not want him to think me the harlot — but I was relaxed and accommodating, even at times a little forward, and our bed was one of the few places I ever heard my husband laugh spontaneously.

I pleased him and that left me with a warm sense of accomplishment.

He was gentle and courteous in bed, when he was so often not when out of it, and that pleased me even more. It allowed me to be more tolerant with his moments of ill-temper during the day. I also came to realise that when he was uncomfortable he retreated behind his mask of indifference, at times hiding behind anger and snappishness.

Gradually I grew to know my husband better.

Over several weeks our life settled into an increasingly comfortable routine. We rose early and we broke our fast and generally shared few words over a frugal meal in the solar. My husband (the words slowly rolled ever more easily from my tongue) then spent the majority of the day within the castle, overseeing the task of rebuilding (where necessary), restocking and re-manning the castle, and restoring morale. He sometimes spent a few days at a time away at neighbouring towns and villages; Ragheian and Monemude, Tretower and Crickhoel.

I spent the days within the solar sewing, or within the chapel praying or chatting with Owain with whom I maintained a friendship, even after my elevation to countess. The nights, if my husband was home, we spent dining within the great hall in some informality. These were often cheerful evenings, especially if an itinerant minstrel was passing through, or even players or jugglers. Other guests might be present, such as travelling friars and monks, messengers, merchants, pilgrims, all of whom added their own interest, news and tales to the evening. We oft had dancing — the minstrels taught me of the newer dances in favour at court — and even courtly games to while away the evenings. And thence to bed, which, for its lack of formality, my husband's laughter and the sport we shared, was the part of the day I always looked forward to most.

I enjoyed the closeness and warmth of our privy chamber. I also enjoyed the fact that my husband preferred to share our chamber at night with me alone. Most nobles had a servant or two sleeping on a truckle bed, or on a cot at the foot of the main bed, but not the earl. I was grateful for it, that we could enjoy our bed sport, and each other, without fear of what my husband's valet, Charles or, heaven help me, Evelyn, might be thinking as they listened.

* * *

One day, while my husband was off with d'Avranches, I decided I was sick of the solar and was not in a mood for Owain or the chapel. With Evelyn left behind in the solar, I walked out to the stables in the outer bailey. I had often thought of Dulcette, and wondered if she had survived the time of chaos when the plague hit the castle. Perhaps I might stroke her nose and dream of riding her … as part of my insecurities as countess I did not know if I could request to have her saddled, or if it was proper (or even safe) for me to ride out by myself.

I would just content myself with stroking her nose, and feeding her an apple I had taken from the fruit tray in the solar.

And, if she had been lost when so many horses roamed untethered, then the mere walk to and from the outer bailey would amuse me and keep me entertained for the morning.

The outer bailey was a foreign land to me. I had not had a reason to visit here previously and I halted just inside the bailey after I'd walked through the tunnel under the northern keep. It was a bustle of activity. To one side was the kitchen for the garrison, men coming and going with baskets and carcasses.

The blacksmith, Sewenna's husband, was hammering away by a roaring fire, his face and torso red and sweating in the heat. Several men were washing horses down in one corner. In another a group of children played. Yet somewhere else a group of women, wives of the craftsmen and soldiers, stood and chatted. Soldiers sat in the sun and mended and polished saddlery and weapons.

I hesitated, not sure where to go. I knew the stables were here, but suddenly I felt very self-conscious. Would my presence cause problems? Should I be here at all?

'My lady?'

A soldier, in middle-age with a grizzled face and sun-browned arms, had appeared at my side.

'Where might the stables be?' I asked, wondering what I should call the man.

'The stables, my lady?' While he had doubtless understood the question, he was obviously struggling, trying to find a reason I might want to visit the stables.

'There is a horse, Dulcette, a grey mare, who I wondered about. I rode her here to Pengraic, and I wondered if she were well.'

Sweet Virgin, I sounded like a simpleton!

'Dulcette?' he said.

'The stables,' I said firmly, and suddenly all was well. Just the change in tone, from query to command, had put the man at his ease.

'My lady,' he said, now quite happy, and led me toward the north-eastern wall.

Here was a large stable block, as much a hive of activity as the rest of the outer bailey. I thanked the soldier as he left me at the main doors, then I stepped inside. A man grooming one of the horses put down his brush and, having learned from my mistake with the soldier, I asked in a confident tone that, if there were a grey mare here called Dulcette, might he show me to her.

Instantly he led me down the ranks of horses and there, to my delight, was Dulcette.

She whickered in recognition when she saw me, and I hastened over to her, patting her neck and stroking her nose, and feeding her the apple which I had kept hidden in my skirts. I was glad to see her, and a little guilty that I had left it this long. In her turn, Dulcette appeared pleased to see me and blew warm air over me as she butted her face into my chest.

'I am about to ride out along the spur to Pen Cerrig-calch. Join me.'

I looked up.

My husband was standing in the aisle of the stable, holding the reins of his bay courser.

'Truly?' I said, and the earl smiled slightly at the delight in my voice. He called to one of the grooms to saddle Dulcette, and in a few minutes we were leading our horses out into the sun.

Although it was a bright day I was wearing a mantle borrowed from the stable: my husband … Raife … had insisted I wear a mantle as the top of the mountain would be cold.

'She'll pull hard today,' Raife said as he helped me mount. 'She's not been exercised since you arrived apart from a turn about the outer bailey now and again.'

'Then if she runs away with me I shall reach the top of the mountain before you,' I said, grinning in anticipation of the ride.

I was also absurdly pleased to realise that we were riding without an escort. There would just be Raife and myself.

Oh, that was such a morning. I look back on it now, so many years later, and think what a glorious day it was. We rode out the northern gates of Pengraic and took to the track that curled around the spur connecting Pengraic Castle to the greater mountain of Pen Cerrig-calch. My husband was more relaxed than I had ever seen him. Both horses pulled hard, and eventually we gave them full rein, laughing as the horses surged ahead, putting down their heads and blowing away their high spirits on the climb to the mountain peak. The wind blew away the hood of my cloak, then unravelled the loose plait over my shoulder that I'd taken to wearing after Raife told me how much he liked it, and my black hair streamed out in the sun. My husband looked over at me and the look on his face made me happy, so happy.

From the mountain peak the view took my breath away. The land lay before me, brilliantly coloured in the bright, bright day. The castle was far below, and even further the gentle winding river, and the wide valley stretched as if into eternity. Behind us mountains and thick woods.

Between us, nothing but smiles and occasional laughter. I don't think I'd ever seen Raife this light of heart before. We sat our horses, both close, our legs bumping now and again as our mounts moved beneath us.

All of creation was ours that morning. No troubles lay between us, all was open and shared, nothing was amiss. I could forget that I had ever feared the Earl of Pengraic.

Raife pointed out many of the features in the landscape — the mountains, the villages, the fields, the winding roads and the river.

I thought about that night when Stephen had taken me to the top of the northern keep and I had seen the mountain and hill tops alive with torchlight, and, suddenly, my husband brought it up, too.

'I remember you telling me that Stephen had brought you to the top of the northern keep so that you might see the dancers in the moonlight,' he said, 'weaving their way about a man with light on his head.'

I nodded, wondering where he was going with this.

'It is easy to believe in the old legends,' he said softly, his eyes faraway as he gazed at the view, 'on a day like this, with the sun in our faces, and the world laid out before us.'

'It is,' I said, enjoying his relaxed mood. This was a man I so rarely saw out of the confines of our bed.

He turned his face my way and gave me such a gentle smile that my heart gave an unsteady beat.

'You have such a lovely, enchanting old soul,' he said, 'and I have to fight so hard to guard my own against you. Sometimes I worry that you threaten everything I am, and all that I want and have fought so damned, damned hard for.'

My old anxiety that he was somehow angry at me resurfaced, but then he pushed his bright bay courser close to Dulcette and gave me a kiss.

'Mae, promise me something.'

'Anything, my lord.'

'Trust me, blindly if you have to, but trust me. Sometimes it may seem as if what I propose is wrong, or leads down some dark path ... but always, always trust me, and I promise I will never mean you harm, nor lead you to harm. I will do nothing, *ever*, to harm you.'

I remembered that on our marriage night he had asked me the same thing.

'Of course I will trust you,' I said. 'Always.'

He kissed me again, deeper this time, until only the movement of the horses broke our mouths apart.

Ah, that bright, bright morning, laughing atop Pen Cerrig-calch, my hair blowing in the wind, my husband at my side and nothing between us but the joy of the day. I held its memory close, for many years. I was falling deeply in love with my husband by that morning, although I did not yet recognise it.

We were, I suppose, about halfway down the ridged spur leading back to the castle. Of necessity we were riding slower than we had ascended, for it was far easier for the horses to slip on descent than ascent.

We had been chatting about light matters. Suddenly Raife's attention was caught by something in the valley. He had remarkable sight, for all I could see was the movement of horses and the bright sparkle of metal.

It was, he later told me, that sparkle that warned him. He pulled his courser to a halt, standing in the stirrups for a better view, shading his eyes against the sun.

Then he swore, softly, violently.

'What is it?' I said.

'An armed force,' he said. 'A hundred men, perhaps, riding to Pengraic. Come, kick Dulcette forward, we must make haste.'

'Who?' I said, concerned at the worry in Raife's voice.

'The Welsh,' he said. 'It can be no one else. There is no other force west of Pengraic that can command those numbers. It must be Madog.'

The Welsh prince! Heart in mouth, I urged Dulcette down the slope after Raife.

CHAPTER TEN

The northern gates clanged shut behind us and I heard the sound of them being bolted and barricaded. Raife rode straight through the outer bailey, through the high-arched passageway under the northern keep and into the inner bailey.

I followed as close as I could. I was intensely relieved to be inside the castle, but terribly anxious about what was to happen. Were the Welsh about to lay siege?

Raife jumped down from his horse, letting it skittle about in nervousness as he raced to the steps leading to the parapets and guard towers by the main gates. I pulled Dulcette to a halt, not sure what to do, and was relieved when Owain came over and helped me to dismount.

'What is happening?' I said to him.

'A Welsh column,' he said. 'Some hundred men, heavily armed, Madog at their head.'

'How did they get this far?' I said. 'There are castles, men, further down the valley, are there not?'

'Only one small fort,' Owain said, 'and that poorly manned as the earl has brought most of the men back here to help replace those lost to the plague. They would have watched Madog ride past and not attempted to prevent his passage. No wonder Madog feels he can ride this far with such impunity.'

'What is he doing here? Is he laying siege?'

Owain shrugged.

I looked up. Raife stood with d'Avranches and several other knights at the top of the northern gate tower. They were looking to the east, down the road which doglegged its way up the slope to the castle.

Sweet Jesu, was the Welsh prince already at the gates? I wondered if the outer bailey was a safe place to stay.

Pengraic was now engaged in conversation with d'Avranches and the knights. He gestured emphatically, making his point, and d'Avranches and the others nodded, several times.

Then d'Avranches and the knights clattered down the steps to the outer bailey, calling for their horses, as well as for several other knights to join them.

Owain wandered over. I hesitated, then followed him.

'What is happening?' I asked d'Avranches as he belted on weapons with sharp, hard movements.

He spared me a single glance. 'Madog has approached under the flag of truce. I am leading a party out to see how honestly he means that flag.'

'Many say Madog is an honourable man,' Owain said mildly, and d'Avranches spared him a longer, harder glance.

'With a sharp sword and a penchant for revenge,' d'Avranches said, fastening his helmet. Then he turned, shouting for his knights to mount and grabbing the reins of his own horse.

I stood back hastily as they booted their horses toward the main gate. Guards opened the wicket gate for them, then slammed and bolted it as soon as the last rider was through.

Again hesitating, then reminding myself I was the countess, I walked over to the wicket gate, which had a small eye-level window in it.

'Is it safe to see?' I asked one of the guards.

He nodded, opening the little door that covered the barred window, and I stepped close.

The Welsh had halted just where the road to the castle doglegged before turning into the final straight stretch to the main gates. They were well ordered, armoured and weaponed in maille and helmets, shields, and carrying either spears or lances as well as their swords. All wore red tunics under their maille. At their head sat one man on a horse, holding the flagstaff, a white flag fluttering at its head.

Next to him sat another rider.

His entire bearing, his armour, his accoutrements, spoke of his authority. Madog ap Gruffydd, Prince of the Welsh.

I felt Owain at my shoulder, and I stepped aside so he could see.

'It is Madog,' he said, somewhat unnecessarily, 'and his Teulu.'

'Teulu?'

'His personal bodyguard,' Owain said. 'He can also call on men from lands under his rule to serve in his army when and if he needs it, but his Teulu stay with him always.'

'Could he not have come to surrender?' I asked. 'The white flag …'

'He has no reason to surrender,' Owain said. 'This is more like the flag of truce. Gruffydd wants to talk and that is why d'Avranches has gone. To find out what he wants.'

'Isn't that dangerous?'

'Yes.' Owain stepped back, letting me see again.

D'Avranches and his party had reached the Welsh, halting some six or seven paces away from Madog.

'He is so vulnerable,' I murmured.

'If the Welsh attacked,' Owain said, 'yes. But the Welsh themselves are within arrow strike of the castle and you can be sure your husband has several score of arrows trained on them right now. If the Welsh attacked d'Avranches and his men, they would not escape unscathed. But I do not think they mean to attack.'

Every so often, as the wind blew our way, I could hear snatches of voices, if not distinct words. Eventually d'Avranches looked up to where Raife stood atop the walls, and made a gesture. He waited, obviously for some response from Raife, then looked back to Madog, giving a single nod.

Madog pulled his horse to one side, and d'Avranches and his party rode forward, being absorbed into the Welsh ranks.

I stepped back to let Owain have a view. 'What is happening?' I said.

'Madog wants to talk,' Owain said. 'D'Avranches and his men stay as hostages for Madog's safe return. The Welsh are returning down the road — they'll wait at the foot of the mountain. Stand back now, my lady. Madog approaches.'

I retreated hastily, just as the guards opened the wicket gate.

Madog clattered through.

He turned his head to look at me almost immediately — I was closer to him than any save Owain — and I suddenly realised that I must look like a wild wood maid, with my hair loose and tangled about me.

I could not see his face, for he wore a helmet much like those in Norman fashion and it obscured most of his face, but otherwise he had an exotic feel about him — his tunic was a rich, deep red like that of his men, and the designs on it and on his shield — hung behind his saddle — were unfamiliar.

Then he was past me, and halted before my husband, who had come down from the parapets.

Madog dismounted, and he spoke with Pengraic quietly. The men came to some agreement, each nodding, and they turned for the great keep, Madog unbuckling his helmet and taking it off as they did so.

Again I hesitated, not knowing what I should do, but Raife turned, made an impatient gesture to me, and thus I hurried after them.

They strode through the central courtyard of the great keep and up the stairwell into the solar. I had to hurry to keep up with them, and by the time I stepped into the solar I was breathing deeply, wishing that I could have had but a few moments of time alone in which to tidy my hair.

Madog dropped his helmet on the top of a bench, making a loud, startling clattering sound in the solar. He turned slowly, taking in his surroundings, eventually coming face to face with me.

I was shocked by his commanding presence. I had always thought of Madog as a savage, a rebel lurking amid the wild, misty hills of Wales, and this darkly handsome clean-shaven man, elegant and assured, was not what I had expected at all. His black hair was very short, close-cropped to his skull, and it accentuated the strong bones of his face and the darkness of his eyes.

He must have been surprised by me. Both the richness of my kirtle and my presence in the solar with them indicated high status.

My wild tangled hair — well, sweet Christ alone knew what he made of that.

I had an urge to dip in courtesy, but forced myself to restraint.

'My lady,' Madog said, his voice holding the faintest note of question, as he stepped forward to take one hand to kiss it.

'My wife, Maeb,' Pengraic said.

Madog did not let go of my hand. His eyes were warm, very dark, glittering with something I thought may have been amusement. 'This lovely countess is not the one I remember,' he said.

I had thought he would have a coarse accent, but his voice, like his appearance, was well modulated and sweet, and he spoke courtly French well, with no hint of difficulty.

'Adelie died in the plague,' Raife said.

'And took her comb with her,' Madog murmured to me, low enough that Raife, standing by the hearth, would not have heard.

'A tragic loss,' Madog said, in a louder voice, dropping my hand and walking over to Raife. 'But I hear loss was extreme at this castle. Your children?'

'Dead,' Raife said. 'What do you want?'

'Not even wine with which to smooth our reacquaintance?' Madog said.

I moved to the table, where stood a pitcher of spiced wine and wine cups, serving both my husband and Madog. Then I moved away, walking briefly into the privy chamber to fetch my comb before returning to the solar, sitting on a chair slightly distanced from those about the hearth, and combing out my hair as I listened to the men talking, watching to see if they needed more wine.

There were few pleasantries exchanged. They talked about the plague, Madog pressing Raife for information about how badly the plague had struck the castle, Raife just as assiduously avoiding giving him any information.

'But it must have been bad,' Madog said, 'if its toll including the tragic loss of your wife and children.'

'It was bad enough,' Raife said. 'And you, Madog? How did your lands fare?'

I remembered my husband's earlier keenness to discover how far the plague had travelled into Welsh territory, and I listened carefully for Madog's answer.

'The death scarcely brushed us,' Madog said. 'God's punishment only extended to the English, it seems.'

'I heard hundreds died in this valley alone.'

'Then you heard wrong. Less than a dozen died in the Usk Valley and none deeper into my lands.'

I could hear no deception in Madog's voice and looked to my husband. One of his hands was idly stroking his chin as he studied Madog, and I thought I saw some uncertainty in his eyes.

'But I thank you for your concern,' Madog said, waving his cup about.

I rose and fetched the pitcher, refilling Madog's cup as Raife grunted in response to what he had said.

'My lady,' Madog said as thanks, and for one moment I was stilled, spellbound by his powerful eyes.

'But to the point,' Madog continued, as I returned the pitcher to its table top. 'The devastation of the plague is why I am here. Surely you have guessed my anxiety?'

Pengraic raised an eyebrow as I sat down once more.

'My wife,' Madog said quietly. 'My son. Are they still living?'

His wife and son? Why should my husband know about them?

'I do not know,' Raife said. 'My concern was always for *my* family, not yours.'

'And yet you have had as guest recently Prince Henry. He said *nothing*?'

I was entirely lost in this conversation.

'We had other things of which to speak,' Raife said, and, so far as I knew him by now, I knew he was dissembling.

'My lady,' Madog said, suddenly swivelling in his chair so he could look me in the eye, 'perhaps you might have sympathy on a fretful husband and father.'

'My lord,' I said, 'I have no idea —'

'You have no idea of what I speak? My lady, do you not know that your countrymen keep my wife and my son locked in some dark dungeon? That your king and your new-wedded husband conspire to keep my —'

'I have nothing to do with it,' Raife snapped, 'which is why I know not if they have succumbed to the plague.'

'Where are they?' Madog demanded, turning once more to my husband. 'What jail now confines them?'

'I don't know *what* Edmond has done with them!'

'Edmond has my Lord Madog's wife and children?' I said, helplessly, endeavouring to understand.

Madog once more swivelled to me. I was beginning to think that maybe I should move my place, simply to prevent Madog from succumbing to dizziness.

'My lady,' he said, his voice softer now he addressed me, those magnificent eyes of his just as compelling, 'in this month last year, the bastard Earl of Chestre led a raiding party into my northern lands, taking my wife and the infant son she had just birthed into captivity. Since then, Edmond has been using them as bargaining tools, hoping, I think, I might hand him Wales in its entirety for my wife's and son's return.'

Now his voice hardened again. 'Chestre — Ranulf de Gernon — is, as well you realise, close kin to this castle's garrison commander, d'Avranches —'

I had no idea, but did not let my ignorance show on my face.

'— and from that connection I have no doubt your husband knows full well where my wife and son are, and how well they are, if they live or not. You have compassion in your eyes, my lady. Can you not persuade your husband to show me some, as well? All I want to know is whether or not they live, and where they are, that I might send them a message of my love and care.'

I had moved to another chair now, closer to the men, that Madog might not have to spend his time swivelling to and fro.

'My lord,' I said to my husband, 'surely knowledge of whether or not they live can bring no harm?'

He just looked at me, his eyes narrowed and cold.

I knew he was angry at my intervention, but I also felt for Madog, and for his wife who had been imprisoned through no fault of her own, and with a tiny baby. How frightened she must be, so far from her home! And from her husband, who cared enough to risk his life to learn of her fate.

'It would be a charity, nothing else,' I said. Then, emboldened by stupidity and little else, I looked at Madog. 'My lord, perhaps if I find myself in court, and if I find myself close to your wife, I might visit and let her know of your concern? She must be frightened, alone in a strange land. I pray she and your son have survived the plague, my lord. It has been so terrible here. This castle alone lost most of its garris—'

'Enough, you witless girl!' Raife said, his voice a snarl, and I looked at him, startled into silence and not a little frightened by his tone and expression.

Madog chuckled. 'You should have poured the wine yourself, Pengraic. But I thank you, my lady, for you have served me well. Aye, if perchance you find yourself close to that dark and rank prison where my lady wife lies disconsolate, then —'

'Maeb, leave,' Raife snapped. I stood up, almost blinded by tears at my own stupidity, and stumbled into the privy chamber, shutting the door behind me.

I sat there, cold, shivering from time to time, until the late afternoon. I heard Madog and my husband talking for another while — I could hear their voices but not their words — before I heard sounds of them leaving.

I went to the window. I had to crane to see, but I made out Madog riding from the castle and d'Avranches and his party riding back in.

Madog turned to ride down the mountain and, as he did so, he looked up to the castle and saluted.

I may have been imagining it, and I likely was, but it seemed to me that he had seen me at the window, and that salute was meant for me.

After a while I heard voices in the solar again. My husband. D'Avranches. Several other knights. They talked a short time, then the door to the privy chamber opened and Raife walked in.

He slammed the door shut.

'I have no idea why I took you to wife!' he said, his voice loud enough for the words to be clearly distinguishable in the solar beyond the door.

I winced, and said nothing.

'What did you think you were doing?' he said. 'I stopped you just before you gave Madog a list of who died and in what state the castle garrison currently lies! As it is he knows now we are vulnerable. Sweet Jesu, Maeb, are you in his employ?'

I dropped my eyes to my lap, humiliated that d'Avranches and the others heard this, too.

Raife stalked to a far wall, standing staring at it as if the stonework contained something fascinating.

'I felt compassion for him,' I said softly.

'For Christ's sake, Maeb, the man has been raiding English territory for most of his life,' Raife said, now pacing in short, hard steps about the chamber. 'Hundreds — *including* innocent mothers and babies — have died. The fact that Chestre had the nerve to capture his wife and son means that, for the time being, Madog's raids have ceased as he does what he can to win their return.'

Thankfully his tone had moderated a little now.

242

'I didn't know,' I said.

'No. You didn't know. In future, when you "don't know", then refrain from commenting! Your duty is to support me, not undermine me!'

'My lord, I am most sorry for what I said.'

Raife grunted.

'I will keep my counsel in future.'

'You are my wife. I say again, your duty is *not* to undermine me. Remember it!'

I nodded, still feeling humiliated and not a little fearful, wondering that I could so easily have wrecked the trust we had begun to build between us.

This morning had been so golden, full of laughter. This afternoon, my thoughtlessness had shattered everything.

'We will sup early, and thence to bed,' he said, and I nodded again.

Raife was cool but relatively courteous throughout the rest of the evening, and I was absurdly grateful for it. I was even more grateful to d'Avranches who, when Raife left table for a short while during the evening meal, told me to not take his anger to heart.

'He speaks hotly, but cools quickly,' d'Avranches said. 'You are a wife, not a general, and should not be expected to think with the mind of a general.'

'Thank you,' I said, and he gave me a smile.

That night Raife treated me kindly enough in our bed. I was grateful, and sought hard to please him. Eventually, we lay curled together tightly, not sleepy, just content to lay silently, when his hand slid over my belly.

'When is the child due?' he said.

I tensed immediately. I had not told him and now he was angry. I should have known that he must have learned the early signs of breeding from Adelie's numerous pregnancies.

'Around Lady Day next year,' I said.

'Why did you not tell me?'

'I was afraid …'

'Of what? Maeb, of what?'

'That I would need to leave your bed.' I was almost in tears now. First my reckless stupidity of the afternoon, now my foolishness in not telling Raife as soon as I had become confident I was with child.

'Why did you think you would need to leave my … ah.' He gave a soft grunt. 'Adelie. She always gratefully absented herself from my bed when she was breeding. But I gather from your words that you do not wish to thus absent yourself.'

I could feel his mouth curve in a smile against my skin. 'A greater compliment a wife never paid a husband. You do *not* need to be Adelie, Maeb. We make of this marriage what we will.'

I smiled, immensely relieved that he was not angry and that he did not demand I leave his bed. I enjoyed lying close to Raife at night. It was far more than just having a body to warm me — I'd had that with Evelyn — it was … well, I was not sure exactly what. But lying there with him, comfortable and relaxed with each other, brought me great joy and contentment.

'We will return to court soon,' he said, 'now that you are breeding.'

PART FOUR

———⟨∞⟩———

THE CONQUEROR'S TOWER

CHAPTER ONE

Ihad hardly dared allow myself to think about the child, nor think about the reasons I did not dare. The relief I felt when Raife laughed off my concern that I should need to leave his bed because of the child was overwhelming.

I did not dwell on the reasons for the depth of that relief. I was simply relieved. Leaving Raife's bed had been Adelie's personal choice. It need not be mine.

Now that Raife knew, I allowed myself some measure of joy about the child. I did not want to anticipate too much — so many children were lost during pregnancy, and many, many more during the first year of life — but I did allow some happiness to suffuse my life. And I was pleased that I had bred so quickly. Now Raife need not worry that he had a barren wife.

My principal task was to breed him sons. I prayed, morning and evening, that this child would be a boy.

The next morning, as Evelyn helped me dress for the day, I told her about the child.

She grunted. 'I had wondered when you were going to tell me.'

'Does everyone realise?' I said, disgruntled that even Evelyn had known.

'Given that you have not yet taken to spewing your dinner across high table, no, but anyone who has seen you naked would have known. I am assuming from your words that the earl knew, too.'

'Yes.'

Evelyn gave a little laugh. 'He was well-practised with Lady Adelie's pregnancies. He was pleased enough, I am sure.'

I was still out of sorts. 'Yes. Pleased enough. He said, also, that now we can go to court.'

Evelyn laughed more fully now. 'And that pronouncement followed on directly from your news, eh?'

I tried to remember. 'Close enough.'

'The earl thinks you will be safer from the king if you are with child.'

'Oh, Evelyn, surely not!'

In return, all she gave me was a long look. She finished tightening the laces on the back of my kirtle, remarking that she and Sewenna would have to sew in extra panels now, then combed out my hair, braiding it in the loose plait over my shoulder that Raife liked.

'What is court like, Evelyn?'

'I don't know. I have never been.'

'Never been?'

'Adelie did not like court and would not attend. She spent her time at Rosseley when the earl was at court. Maybe Edmond had propositioned her once, too.'

'But you said that you and Edmond ...'

'Like you, I met him at Rosseley. There was a time some years ago when he was a regular summer visitor, often staying at one of his manors close by. It was during one of those summers that we became lovers. I met him when I could, where I could.'

'So we shall both be there for the first time.'

I wondered where Edmond was now, where he held his court; whether at his palace at Westminster or if he still kept to his manor at Elesberie because of the plague.

At dinner that evening in the great hall, I asked Raife.

'Edmond's court?' Raife picked some tender pieces of veal from the plate of meats we shared and put them into my trencher. 'I hear he has left Elesberie and returned to London. He will keep court at his palace at Westminster, I assume.'

'What is it like? Edmond's court?'

'It is full of men and women all trying to gain preferment and lands and wealth for themselves, by whatever means they can.' He gave a little shrug. 'It is a useful enough place.'

'It sounds terrifying.'

'We shall have time away from it. I have a house in London and you may prefer to spend much of your time there rather than at court.'

I reflected that I knew almost nothing of my husband's wealth and landholdings. A house in London? I felt a kernel of excitement. My father had told me many things about London, about its bustle and excitement, the foreigners who thronged its streets and its markets.

A house in London. Where I could hide from Edmond — and Henry — if need be.

'What news of the plague?' I said. 'It must have abated if Edmond has returned to Westminster.'

'Aye, it has abated.' Raife paused. 'There are few reports of it. A death here and there, but the major sweep of the plague appears to be over.'

'Praise the saints,' I said.

Raife chewed his food slowly, thinking. He swallowed his mouthful, then drank some wine. 'This plague has been most strange,' he said.

'It has been most *malignant*,' I said.

'It seems to have died out,' Raife said, 'early in the season. Most plagues ravage all through summer, only releasing their hold on mankind in late autumn as the colder weather sets in. But this ... this seems to have abandoned its grip most early.'

'I do not think it a matter to complain about.'

'It is unusual. I do not understand it. It has not done what I ...'

For one moment I was sure he had been going to say *needed*, then I dismissed the thought as fanciful. But I remembered my husband's keenness to discover how far the plague had penetrated Wales. 'You think too much on the plague,' I said.

'It is my duty.'

'*Duty*? How so?'

Raife wiped his mouth with his napkin, then gave me an affectionate smile. 'How is it we managed to veer onto such dark matters when we began by talking of the gaiety of court?' He leaned back a little, narrowing his eyes as he looked on my kirtle.

It was not my most beautiful, but nonetheless I thought it fine — a rich red material, heavily embroidered by Evelyn and Sewenna — and I squirmed under his regard, thinking he was about to find fault.

'I have sent word ahead to my house steward in London,' he said, 'to have some rich fabrics awaiting us for our arrival. And seamsters to stitch and embroider.'

'But Evelyn and Sewenna can —'

'They work well enough, Maeb, but they cannot do the fine work needed for court. I shall make sure there are some rich mantles, kirtles and linens awaiting our arrival.'

I could not help but feel a thrill, even though I felt mild insult on behalf of Evelyn and Sewenna. I had by now completely forgot our strange conversation about the plague. 'When do we leave, my lord?'

'In several weeks. There are still matters here I should pay heed to. We will travel gently, unlike the rush Stephen took to get you safe inside Pengraic. I do not wish to risk the child.'

I nodded, thinking of the journey ahead, and thinking of all the places I had only heard about and which now I would see.

'You will also need another lady, Maeb. One is not enough for court, and particularly not now you are with child.'

Raife had broached that issue which had worried me ever since my marriage. 'I had thought I might ask for Evelyn's daughter, my lord. She is of an age now when she can —'

'No. Not Evelyn's daughter.'

His abrupt dismissal of the idea caught me short. 'Why not? She —'

'This is an opportunity for us to grant favour to some noblewoman at court, Maeb. An opportunity to indebt some family to us or to reinforce ties to someone powerful. And you will need a woman who is familiar with court, who can guide you. Neither Evelyn nor her daughter can do that.'

The thought momentarily terrified me. A noblewoman as an attending lady?

Raife gave me a small smile. 'Maeb, you underestimate yourself. You will do well enough.'

'I shall have to watch every word I say.'

'Maeb, you will need to watch every word you say in any case. Your first lesson of court. Trust no one.' His smile broadened. 'Except your husband, of course. Our bed can be the only place you may speak freely.'

* * *

Despite what Raife had said about the seamsters working in London, Evelyn, Sewenna and I spent much of the next two weeks sewing. We worked on undergarments and travelling kirtles, and also sewed extra panels for the kirtles I had already so that they might accommodate my growing belly.

Three days before we were due to leave, Evelyn and I began the task of packing my clothes into a chest for the carts (elsewhere the household was being packed up likewise, as all plate and linens were to be carried to London as they had once been carried from Rosseley). Even with all the clothes I had acquired since my marriage, only one chest was required, which we packed carefully.

'Finer clothes than those you wore when you first rode in the main gates,' Evelyn remarked. 'What do you wish to do with your old kirtles and linens?'

She had picked up that small bundle of clothes I had brought with me to Rosseley and was sorting them.

'Perhaps give them to one of the women in the village of Crickhoel?' I said, and Evelyn nodded.

'A good idea. You will create much goodwill with the gesture. We can ... what in the world is this?'

Evelyn had found a small bundle of cloth.

'Oh!' I smiled. 'I had almost forgot that!' I reached for it, then gently unfolded it and held it out for Evelyn's inspection. 'What do you think?'

Evelyn frowned. 'It is very old, and very worn. And the stitching is of a kind I have not seen before.'

'Aye. But I treasure it, even though the embroidery is so old and the cloth almost rags.'

Evelyn was obviously not taken with the piece, but, because I had said I treasured it, was not quite sure what she could say.

I laughed, and folded it up again. 'After my father died, our old steward, Osbeorn, gave it to me, saying my father had wanted me to have it. My father had only been home from his travels a few short weeks before he died.'

'Travels?'

'My father had been living some years in Jerusalem.'

'Your father was a pilgrim to Jerusalem?'

'Of a kind,' I said. 'He left after my mother died, and spent years there. Our manor steward Osbeorn and his wife were the ones who raised me for the years while he was gone. When my father returned, he was almost a stranger to me.'

'I did not know that, my lady. What adventures your father must have had!'

'Indeed.' I looked down at the bundle of worn cloth. 'I will take this, too. It is one of the few things I have left with which to remember my father.'

CHAPTER TWO

I went to the chapel early in the morning on the day we were to depart. I wanted to pray at the graves of Lady Adelie, Stephen and the children. In the past few months I had barely thought of them, and I was overcome with guilt that I should now be going to court when, truly, they had been better suited for such a life.

The chapel was brightly lit with candles. I took one of them, walking quietly down the centre of the nave to where Stephen lay buried under the heartstone of the chapel.

I stood there a long while, praying, and in contemplation of Stephen. What would Stephen think, to see me married to his father? And carrying his brother or sister? What would he have said, knowing that I had loved *him*? I still felt great guilt that I had survived and he not.

Tears threatened, and I stepped back, whispering a goodbye, before moving to Lady Adelie's grave in one of the aisles. What would *she* have thought, seeing me take her place in her husband's bed, assuming her titles? I could imagine her saying something gracious, but with internal reflection shadowing her eyes. I think she would have feared that I might fail in my duty, somehow.

In turn I visited the gravestones of the other children: Alice, Emmette, Rosamund and John.

I prayed for them all, and for me, for three of them had died from my own hand.

'Lady Maeb.'

I turned about, wiping the tears from my cheeks. Owain approached, looking weary and wan, as if he had been up all night, praying. I suddenly realised how much I would miss him. Owain had become a true friend and I would be the worse for lack of his counsel in London.

'I will miss you,' I said.

'And I you. Remember, always, that Pengraic is your home. Your true home. Do not be seduced by the wonders and gaiety of court.'

'Court terrifies me,' I muttered, then spoke a little louder. 'Owain, I bear so much guilt.' I gestured at the graves of the two little ones, and Stephen. 'I wonder what will become of me, what tragedies I must bear, to atone.'

'You did what was needed, Maeb. Those who died would have thanked you for it. I carry no guilt for what I did, which was no more than you — rather, much worse.'

'But I worry God will never forget, despite my confession and penance and your absolution. I fear I will be damned.'

Owain looked as if he struggled with himself, trying to find the right words to say. Finally, he spoke. 'There are many others who weigh the goodness and the evils of souls, Maeb. You acted out of love. That will always stand as your defence.'

I shrugged, thinking Owain's words only falsehoods meant to comfort me. 'I fear I will lose this child, as punishment for what I have done. Or lose Raife.'

Owain stepped forward and placed his hands on my shoulders, giving me a gentle shake. 'You will *not* be called on to atone for what you did, Maeb!'

I still did not believe him, but I spoke out of love for him and also that he would not worry for me. 'You are a comfort to me, Owain. What shall I do without you?'

'There are priests aplenty in London and Westminster.'

'But none of them are you.'

'No. None of them are me.'

Owain started to say something else, but just then there was a step at the door.

We turned to look. It was three women from the village — I knew their faces but not their names. Two were young, my age perhaps, but one was older, carrying a basket, and it was she who stepped forward.

'Priest,' she said, 'we have an offering. May we enter?'

'Of course, Eada,' Owain said. 'You are always welcome.'

She smiled at him, and then at me. 'My lady, you are most welcome here, too. You have that way about you.'

I was so astounded by this statement that I could not reply. I managed to give the women a nod and a smile as they passed, then turned to Owain. 'What —?'

He put a finger to his lips. 'Shush, Maeb. Just watch a moment.'

I was still struggling to understand why Eada should have said *I* was welcome here — by God, I was the countess of this castle and, apart from my husband, there was no one with more right to be here.

Then I went stiff. The three women had gone straight to Stephen's grave, to the ancient heartstone of the chapel. There Eada set down her basket and the women took out meadow flowers, kissing each one before laying them down gently, one by one, to form a circle about the stone.

'What are they doing?' I murmured to Owain.

'Honouring Stephen, as also the Old People,' he said.

I remembered he had said once that the village people liked to come and lay flowers here. But at the altar, surely?

And then I thought: this heartstone is their altar, not the Christian stone under the cross.

The women had finished laying out their flowers now, and paused, bowing their heads as they laid their hands over their hearts.

I was touched. 'They know that is Stephen's grave?'

Owain hesitated, then nodded. 'They honour Stephen as much as they do the Old People,' he said.

Then Eada reached into the basket and, to my horror, lifted out a dead cockerel and laid it in the very heart of the stone.

The bird was only freshly killed, for blood oozed across the stone where Eada had laid its corpse.

I opened my mouth to speak, to voice my horror, but Owain caught me by the arm and squeezed it tight as the women, now done, approached us.

Eada's mouth twitched as she saw my appalled face. 'For the wolves, my lady. For the wolves.'

And then she and her companions were gone out the door.

'For the *wolves*?' I hissed.

Owain nodded toward the walls. 'You remember the wolves in the paintings. I told you that in ancient times people believed that the wolves were their protectors. The villagers still believe so, and like to appease the wolves in the mountains that Crickhoel may be spared their angry ravages.'

I remembered then the dream I'd had when I was dying, of the wolves who snapped at my heels and prevented me moving completely into death.

'They are no protectors of mine,' I said.

'Do not fret. I will remove both flowers and cockerel.'

'Just the cockerel, perhaps,' I said.

He laughed, then leaned forward and laid a gentle kiss on my forehead. 'Go in peace, Maeb. Do not worry about the ancient legends. Look after that child and husband of yours. And remember that Pengraic always waits here for you as refuge, should you need it.'

We travelled to London by the same route we had, so many months previous, travelled from Oxeneford to Pengraic. As Raife had said, we journeyed more slowly than when Stephen had led us westward, partly because Raife did not want to risk the child, and partly because our train was so large — ten carts, a hundred and sixty soldiers, knights, servants, grooms and two minstrels Raife had contracted to entertain us along the way.

Additionally, the further east we travelled, we acquired almost a score and four of pilgrims who travelled with us for the protection we afforded. Three parties were travelling to Saint Edmund's Burie and then on to Walsingaham; another party to the tomb of Edward the Confessor in Westminster; others yet much further afield, to shrines in Europe, and even Jerusalem. All were glad to have the protection offered by the earl's column as it travelled toward London, and the pilgrims themselves provided us with much entertainment in the evenings as they told us their tales.

But in many places it was grim travelling. On our journey we passed two villages which had burned entirely to the ground, most of their residents carried off by the plague. In other places, a house here and there may have burned, but most buildings still stood, even if many of the buildings, or the whole village, were now deserted.

It was not unusual to see flocks of sheep, pigs or cattle left to fend for themselves, or stray, starving dogs that the soldiers had to beat away from our column. There were people, too, on the road, who passed hollow-eyed and thin, their clothes worn and ragged. They rarely gave us a glance, and did not respond to greetings, as if they had lost any connection to this world, even though they still lived within it.

The monks in the monasteries where we stayed, or the lords of manors who offered us shelter for the night, warned us of parties of brigands. Men left desperate after losing everything during the plague, and now resorting to stealing and thieving to feed themselves. Despite the warnings, we were never troubled by them. I think the sheer size of our column, and the number of soldiers and knights who travelled with us, meant that any brigands kept to the forests, perhaps coveting our riches with their eyes, but not daring to attack.

Many of the towns we passed through had been damaged by the plague. Monemude and Glowecestre both had swathes of their housing blackened and burned, although the majority of their towns had survived.

Circecestre, however, was almost totally ruined. Here it was easier to count the houses left standing, not the ones lost. We rode through the town in absolute silence, everyone overcome with the horror of what had happened, everyone imagining what it must have been like — the plague triumphant, and the town afire. Here and there men made the effort to rebuild, but I thought it would be a lifetime before the town existed again in any measure of normality.

Thus sorrow marked our journey. Everywhere we rode the plague reminded us of its grim toll. Everywhere we stayed we heard more stories of the suffering. Every family house and monastery we overnighted at was the lesser in number because of the plague than it had been when we'd passed through on the journey toward Pengraic. There was one monastery which offered Raife and myself a bed for the night — the bed was scorched although still sound, and it sickened us so much we slept on the floor.

Saints knew what lived in its mattress.

It was if we travelled to London along a vast, open wound which still suppurated anguish.

I prayed that the plague had indeed worn itself out. That, having taken what it wanted, it had now slunk back to whatever hell had spawned it. I did not think the country and its people could survive another onslaught.

After we'd passed Oxeneford, the land was better off. Here the plague had bypassed the hamlets and peoples, and most appeared bright and well. Peasants were in the fields bringing in the harvest, or driving their pigs into the forests to gorge on acorns before the Christmastide slaughter. Here was another world, the world I had forgot, and even though I had my concerns about court, somehow these contented lands relaxed me and I became happier the closer we came to London.

I allowed myself to believe that all my troubles lay behind me. I allowed myself to believe that I had a future as Raife's wife. I allowed myself to dream of a life bouncing his babies on my knee, and watching them grow untroubled and beloved in a bright, unshadowed meadow.

I was very young then, and naïve.

The day we approached London was dark and gloomy and cold, for autumn had started to descend. By the time we rode through the tiny hamlet of Hamestede and neared the city, the occasional showers of earlier in the day settled into a steady drizzle that soaked through our mantles and froze our hands. I was half agog to see London ahead of me (drifting in and out of the rainclouds) and half desperate to find a warm chamber with a roaring fire.

Raife, riding close, looked at me in worry. 'You are exhausted,' he said.

'It has been a long day,' I said. As it had. We had risen at dawn and left not long after in the effort to reach London before dark. Now it was approaching dusk.

'We will ride straight to my house on Cornhill,' he said. 'Another hour, two at the most, and we will be there. The steward has been warned of our arrival and will have the house bright and warm and a meal awaiting.'

Thank the saints for stewards, I thought. But an hour or two more? That meant we would not arrive until well after dark.

'Which way is Westminster?' I asked, trying to show some enthusiasm for Raife's sake.

He pointed almost due south. 'That way. On Thorney Isle. Edmond has a goodly enough palace there.'

'We should not ride there first, as a courtesy?' I desperately hoped not. I *was* exhausted, and I did not think I could cope with the complexities of court, nor with being polite and courteous, when I felt so fatigued and sore and sick to my stomach. Today my pregnancy wearied me immensely. I had not been able to keep any food down, and my temper was snappish and hot.

Raife shook his head. 'No. We will go straight to the house. It is too late to pay Edmond a visit now. Time enough tomorrow for courtesy.'

I was so relieved I almost wept. Dulcette had a sweet pace, but right now I only wanted to get off her back and collapse onto a bed. Food and fires be damned ... all I wanted was the bed.

Raife reached across and briefly laid a silent hand on my shoulder. That gesture of care was enough to undo me, and I spent the rest of the ride to London snuffling childishly and surreptitiously wiping away my tears.

We entered London through Lud Gate. Despite my exhaustion I roused enough to gaze about me. I had never seen the like of this! Immense red-brick walls punctuated by high towers surrounded the city, and as soon as we were through and riding up Lud Hill my gaze was drawn to a space further up the road, atop the hill, where arose what looked to be the unfinished building of a cathedral.

'Saint Paul's,' said Raife as we rode by. 'It burned down a generation ago and is only slowly being rebuilt. But there is enough there now, a nave and the choir, to worship. One day it will be numbered among the greatest cathedrals of Christendom.'

We rode on. I was amazed by the number of streets, the buildings — both timber and stone — that rose everywhere, the churches, the markets, the warehouses. I had never imagined anywhere so huge! At this time of night, and in this weather, there were few people on the streets, but I imagined that during the day there would be a constant bustle of people. Once past the cathedral we turned onto a long market street — West Cheap, Raife informed me — until eventually we came to a fork where three streets joined with the Cheap. We took the middle street, climbing a gentle hill and then, wonderfully, just over the crest of the hill, we turned into the courtyard of a large stone house and we were at the earl's home in London.

I was so stiff I could barely move and Raife had to lift me bodily from Dulcette's back. He held me about the waist on the ground as I tried to get my balance, and only reluctantly let me go when I said I was all right.

The courtyard was a-bustle with men, horses, dogs, and servants emerging out of the house. A man came up to Raife almost immediately, bowing and welcoming him into the house.

'This is Robert fitzErfast,' Raife said to me. 'The house steward.'

'Welcome, countess,' fitzErfast said, bowing. 'Your chamber is ready for you, and a meal if you wish.'

He led us inside, first into a small enclosed porch, then into a hall that, while nowhere near the size of those at Rosseley and Pengraic, was nonetheless commodious with a lovely high ceiling. At the far end of the hall we went through another door, climbed a circular stone staircase, and, after moving through several other chambers and a large solar, finally found ourselves in a spacious privy chamber, its fire blazing and a bed enticingly draped and hung with soft woollens, linens and embroideries.

I sat down on a chair with a thump, pulling off my mantle with tired, jerky movements. 'I have a woman, Evelyn Kendal,' I said to fitzErfast. 'She cannot be far away. Can you have someone find her and send her to me?'

'Immediately, my lady,' fitzErfast said, and started for the door.

'FitzErfast,' Raife said, just before the steward vanished, 'send also one of the servants to Westminster Palace to let the king know, either now or when he rises in the morning, of my arrival. I am sure he is well informed anyway, but the servant will be a courtesy.'

FitzErfast hesitated. 'The king is not at Westminster, my lord earl,' he said.

'Not at Westminster? Lord God, fitzErfast, do not tell me we have ridden all this way for naught!'

'Not at Westminster,' fitzErfast said, 'but at the Tower.'

'The Tower?' Raife hesitated, staring unbelievingly at fitzErfast for a heartbeat, then he strode over to the chamber's window and flung open the shutters.

Despite my fatigue, I rose and walked over to see.

There, in the not-so-far distance across some fields, a commanding square tower rose into the night, lights gleaming from behind its narrow slit windows.

'He has gone to the Conqueror's Tower,' muttered Raife. 'Why? Why?'

CHAPTER THREE

I rose in the pre-dawn darkness, wrapping myself in a soft woollen coverlet as I made my way to the privy set into the thick stone walls of the house. When I came back to bed and slid once more under the warm covers, Raife pulled me close, complaining sleepily about my cold skin. We lay for a while in silence, both of us awake, before Raife spoke.

'How do you feel this morning, wife?'

'Better for the night's rest,' I said. I hesitated. 'Do we need to go to court today?'

His arm tightened about me momentarily as he gave me a gentle hug. 'I will go, but you may stay here and rest if you wish. I will pass onto Edmond your flatteries and excuses.'

I laughed softly. 'Thank you, husband.'

'You must eat today.'

'I will, I promise. A day spent in a chair rather than on Dulcette's back will work miracles on my appetite.' I was touched by his kindness (and relieved that I did not have to attend court), and turned over in his arms to kiss him softly.

'You will delay my attendance at court,' he murmured.

'Good,' I said, and kissed him again, more deeply this time.

Later, when he was dressing, I propped myself up on an elbow and waited until his valet, Charles, had stopped fussing. Raife was garbed in a magnificent tunic, a jewelled sword belt I had not seen before (and with my purse attached to it, I was glad to see), and a mantle of such richness that, had I not been so languid from our travelling, and our early morning love-making, I would have been hard pressed not to have risen from our bed and buried my hands and face in it.

'What is the Conqueror's Tower?' I asked.

Raife sat down in a chair while Charles handed him his shoes. (I had seen none of this clothing before, and thought that Raife must keep it exclusively in this house for court wear.)

'It is the tower that William the Conqueror had built in the north-east corner of London,' he said, pulling on one shoe then reaching for the other. 'You will see it clearly once you have risen and can find the energy to walk to the window.'

His eyes crinkled in amusement as he said this, and I knew we were both thinking of our earlier ardent activity. It had not been easy to find time for love-making during our travels as either I was too fatigued or we shared a chamber with too many others, and to find ourselves once again with the privacy of our own chamber was a luxury we had taken full advantage of. I blessed again Raife's somewhat unusual habit of not having any of our servants or attendants to sleep at the foot of the bed.

'And Edmond being there is unusual?' I asked, remembering Raife's reaction last night.

'Yes. It is a great palace, but usually Edmond, as other kings before him, prefers the more commodious palace at Westminster. But the Conqueror's Tower is far more defensible.' Raife paused, the final shoe half on, half off. 'I wonder what he fears ...'

He shrugged and pulled the shoe on, then came over and kissed me. 'I will not stay for the evening's entertainment, but will be back to sup with you. My worry for you shall be excuse enough for Edmond. Ask fitzErfast to fetch the chest of new clothes I ordered for you — that should keep you and Evelyn happy enough until I return. And rest. And eat.'

'Yes, my lord,' I said, and then he was gone, shouting for his knights and companions to accompany him to the Tower.

A few minutes after he left I rose, opening the shutters of the window. I was just in time to see Raife's party ride out. Thirty or forty strong, it comprised some of Raife's most senior knights, their squires, and about ten ordinary soldiers. Everyone was dressed in their best, and at the head of the column rode a young man with the Pengraic pennant fluttering from a staff.

Raife rode just behind the young man with the pennant, and I watched until he grew too distant for me to make out his features.

I lifted my eyes to the Tower. It was massive, rising some three levels above ground and composed of grey-brown stone with creamier stones delineating its corners and narrow windows. Four towers rose from each corner: three square and one round. It looked impregnable.

A curtain wall, looking to be of somewhat newer construction than the Tower, ran about it, and a moat outside that.

I looked down. There were mostly fields, dotted with only a few houses, between the Tower and where this house stood just off the crest of Cornhill. A tournament field had been set up in one of the fields closest to the Tower.

I looked for Raife and his escort, and saw them cantering down a track that led through the fields.

He was going to be there in only a few minutes.

I raised my eyes to the Conqueror's Tower again.

There waited Edmond.

I spent the day quietly, but in a welter of worry for what was happening at court. I remembered Henry's antagonism for my husband very clearly, as well as Saint-Valery's words about how Edmond distrusted Raife, and I hoped, quite desperately, that Raife would return safe and well at the end of the day.

After I had prayed and then broken my fast with Evelyn, fitzErfast sent to my chamber the chest of clothes Raife had caused to be made.

I thought the silken kirtles I, Evelyn and Sewenna had sewed in Pengraic were rich and beautiful, but they were as nothing compared to these. The silk fabrics had been delicately stitched with intricate patterns of flowers and leaves in threads of gold and silver, crimsons, emeralds, turquoises, azures and creams. One gown had golden figures of dancers and minstrels about its hem, another figures of stags and horsemen. They were astounding, rich beyond belief.

Evelyn smiled wryly as she delicately folded them back into the chest. 'The earl makes a grand statement with these, Maeb, as he does with you.'

'What do you mean?'

'His power,' she said. 'His wealth. The beauty he commands. Poor Lady Adelie never cut a fine figure at court, but you …'

'Lady Adelie was beautiful!' I said, remembering how she had looked the night of the royal feast at Rosseley.

Again that wry smile from Evelyn. 'Not as you are, Maeb. You shall outshine everyone there, even Edmond.'

'Surely not,' I said, thinking that would be a dangerous thing to do.

Evelyn chuckled. 'Wait for a night of grand feasting, Maeb, and, you will see … Raife and yourself shall *groan* under the weight of the jewels the earl can summon!'

I shivered, and for a moment wished I was the wife of a minor nobleman who did not have to play such courtly games, nor attract the envious and bitter gazes of those who wished to strip my husband of his power and seize his wealth for themselves.

Later in the day fitzErfast showed Evelyn and myself about the house. While smaller than Pengraic Castle, of course, it was nonetheless impressive. The house was divided in two by a stone spine wall. Down one side of this wall ran the hall; on the other side of the wall, over two levels, ran store rooms on the lower level, and a solar and various privy apartments on the upper level. Underneath the whole was a vaulted crypt, one part of which was arranged as a small chapel, the other as storage. As at Pengraic, the crypt also held large cisterns of water collected from the roof.

Outside was a sizeable courtyard bounded by the kitchen, a well, dormitories and stabling — accommodation for a large number of men and their horses. Beyond the courtyard, fitzErfast said, were several fields, an orchard, and a training ring for men and horses.

All in all, it felt like a small, wealthy estate, but one held within the walls of a city.

'You will need to learn to play the lady, fast,' said Evelyn.

The afternoon I spent resting, then bathing in a large wooden tub Evelyn had caused to be brought to the privy chamber, draped with linens, and then filled with hot water. I luxuriated in the soak, washing away the grime and stink of travel, and Evelyn washed out my hair before combing it through with oil to make it shine.

That evening, to my relief, Raife returned. 'I have found you a friend at court,' he said. 'She shall be waiting for you tomorrow.'

CHAPTER FOUR

I stood, smoothing the fine linen kirtle over my body, feeling as nervous as I had at my betrothal. It was a warm day and this, combined with the fact that it was not a feast day or other special occasion, had dictated my choice of kirtle. This one, a beautiful cornflower-blue embroidered with crimson, gold and green, was rich and opulent in its own right — more magnificent than anything I'd ever worn previously — but was not among the most splendid of the gowns available to me.

I wore also the lovely jewelled girdle Raife had given me on our betrothal day, its gold and jewels reflecting the embroidery on the kirtle. Evelyn had plaited my hair again in the loose plait over my shoulder, the braiding ending at my waist so that a mass of hair hung freely to my knees. The braid was interspersed with golden jewelled flowers, glinting amid the blackness of my hair.

I felt a pretender. Some fool woman who thought she could attend the court of the king and pass herself off as the Countess of Pengraic.

'You will do well,' said Raife, giving me a smile and kissing my hand in courtly style.

'I have no idea —'

'Lady Alianor will guide you,' he said.

Lady Alianor de Lacy, wife of the lord of Bouland and of Blachburnscire. A powerful neighbour in Raife's lands in the north of England. An ally. Lady Alianor was to be my friend at court, my guide through its intricacies, and my mentor in its dangers.

'I will not always be able to be with you,' Raife had told me last night, 'but Lady Alianor can be. Let her guide you.'

'Can I trust her?' I asked my husband now.

'Almost completely,' he said, stepping to one side as he drew on his gloves. Evelyn came to help me with my mantle, brushing aside my trembling fingers to fasten it with a large bronzed brooch.

'*Almost?*' I said as Evelyn left the chamber.

He gave me a significant look. 'There will be some matters best kept to yourself,' he said. 'Remember always that your loyalty is to me first, even before Edmond.'

'Yes, my lord.'

'There will be people who will come to court you today, flatter you and all the while hunt for your secrets,' Raife said. 'Be wary of them all. You are the road to me, the doorway to my vulnerabilities. Keep that door closed.'

He took me by the shoulders. 'Maeb, you and I ... there has grown an affection between us, I think. It is comforting, and makes our nights the sweeter, but I fear it also, for how easily it could undo me. Be careful, Maeb, for in holding my heart in your hands you also hold the power to create such havoc ...'

Dear God! I silently thanked him for undermining my confidence with his unfathomable words. What if I betrayed Raife in my first nerve-ridden babble of conversation with some meaningless, thoughtless remark born of my unease? I had been so grossly indiscreet with Madog ap Gruffydd, a man I had already been uncertain of, what might I do at Edmond's court?

'Ah, I am sorry,' he said, leaning forward to plant a kiss on my forehead. 'Thus speaks my nerves, only. Just be careful today, Maeb, eh? Now, come. We shall go to court and I am sure you will do me proud.'

And thus poor orphaned Mistress Maeb Langtofte, left by her father with no dowry and nowhere to call home had, by a set of remarkable and tragic events, found herself the Countess of Pengraic, off to court to meet the king.

We approached the Conqueror's Tower slowly. Yesterday Raife had ridden with his escort at a full canter. Now we proceeded with grace and elegance at a leisurely pace. Behind us rode a half score of knights and their squires, and a squad of some sixteen soldiers, and enough banners and pennants to decorate a great hall. Overhead the sun shone, about us various riders and walkers stood to one side and watched with curiosity as we passed, and a group of knights practising with their swords on the tournament field came to a halt, turning to peer at us with their hands shielding their eyes from the sun.

I felt ill, but could not blame the pregnancy for it. Raife — as resplendent as I — gave me a concerned glance, but said nothing.

As we approached the outer curtain wall, I swallowed and squared my shoulders. I would cope and I would make Raife proud.

There was an enormous gate, protected by a square tower, in the western aspect of the wall, and we approached it across a long stone bridge that gave access over the deep moat.

'The wall is new,' I said, speaking not so much for the sake of discussing the wall, but to let Raife know that my mind was not completely consumed by my nervousness.

He gave a nod. 'Edmond has spent much of his reign extending the defences of the wall, as well as building new quarters and a new great hall within the inner bailey. That inner building is still underway, we shall have to content ourselves with the great hall within the tower, but one day, perhaps in five years or so, this tower complex shall be a great glory to the king and to England.'

We were clattering under the gate now, guards standing back and saluting with their long-handled axes and lances, and then we were in an outer bailey. Most of the area was grassed, with two stands of trees, but I saw several large wooden buildings to one side that were likely barracks for soldiers as well as falcon mews and hound kennels.

I looked up at the tower, which we now approached.

This close it was massive, its huge walls punctuated by the slit windows, and corner towers rising even higher than the walls connected by battlements and parapets. I could see guards, their weapons glinting in the sun, pacing slowly along the parapets.

We rode toward an inner wall — not such a massive construction as the outer curtain wall — and yet another gateway.

And then we were in the inner bailey, and a richly dressed man was striding forth to greet us.

'Chestre!' Raife said, and I could hear the false cheer in his voice.

We reined in, and Raife dismounted, leaving a groom to assist me. I tried to remember where I had heard the name before. Chestre … ah, yes. Ranulf de Gernon, Earl of Chestre, close kin to d'Avranches … and the man who had seized Madog's wife and son … yes?

For a brief moment I remembered that the Welsh princess might well be secured somewhere close by, then I put all thought of her to one side as Raife brought Chestre over to meet me.

He was a big, dark burly man, reminding me of a bear, with a beard so bushy it kept catching in the fine embroidery of his tunic.

'Lady Maeb,' he said, surprising me by leaning forward to kiss me on the lips. 'The court is happy to welcome a Countess of Pengraic back into the midst of its pleasures. Lady Adelie was always so shy.'

'My lord earl,' I said, almost dipping in courtesy until Raife's fingers tightening about my arm stopped me just as one knee began to bend.

'Edmond has asked to see you both privately,' Chestre said, 'before court commences.' He glanced at me. 'He is keen to re-make the countess' acquaintance.'

Raife slid his arm through mine as we walked toward a wide wooden set of stairs that led from the grass up to an enclosed porch on the first floor of the Tower's southern wall. We talked of inconsequential things as we walked … the brightness of the sun, a knight who had died yesterday by toppling off the parapets while drunk, the wife of a baron who had just given birth to twins — a remarkable event.

'I have heard you are breeding yourself, my lady,' Chestre said as we reached the top of the stairs.

'Yes, my lord,' I said.

He glanced at my belly. 'Well, you are not yet far enough along to keep you from courtly sport,' he said, and waved us through the doorway ahead, leaving me wondering what he meant.

We entered a great hall running north–south (I discovered later that this was known as the lesser hall). It was a large chamber, easily taking up one half of the entire level, and with twin rows of columns running down either side, creating shadowed aisles. There were several score people inside: knights, guards, serving men, and many nobles and noblewomen. But even this number could not fill the hall, and they were scattered about in groups, talking, playing at dice, drinking, or just sitting on the benches that ran along the walls, looking and noting. There were several fireplaces in the hall, two of them with fires burning, and both of these with small groups standing before them, chatting and laughing.

It did not seem so intimidating after all, and I relaxed a little. Chestre led us down the hall, our way lit by thin shafts of light from the narrow windows and torches on the walls. As we proceeded, individuals and groups stopped chatting and turned to us, bowing and dipping in courtesy as we passed.

Their eyes were watchful, careful.

Raife occasionally acknowledged someone with a nod of his head, but otherwise we passed silently and steadily down the centre of the hall to the end, where Chestre indicated a doorway in the eastern wall of the hall. Just as we reached it I noticed two men standing to one side.

One was Saint-Valery. I had a start of surprise, and he smiled at me, bowing graciously.

I wondered what he was truly thinking, seeing me now as Raife's wife. Perhaps that I had my sights set far higher when he had asked for my hand and that was why I had hesitated over him?

Another man was standing with Saint-Valery. He was very tall, with short-cropped, thick dark hair and a hard face. Unlike everyone else in the hall, he was dressed plainly in a simple white tunic with no embroidery or decoration of any kind.

He stared at me, his eyes hard and uncompromising, and I looked away quickly, grateful for the door.

We walked through into another, smaller chamber and from there Chestre led us to a narrow, dark stairwell in the north-eastern tower. We climbed slowly, emerging into a lovely gallery that overlooked the northern fields. Here we turned almost immediately into a doorway on our left, entering a large chamber that was clearly the king's privy quarters.

There were perhaps a score of people in this chamber, and, with another start, I recognised Prince Henry among them. He had not seen either Raife or myself, and was standing with another man dressed in a plain white tunic, laughing with him as they drank wine.

Then two of the noblemen in the room moved, and I saw Edmond, sitting in a chair by the fire.

He was looking directly at us, as if he had intuited our entrance the moment we'd stepped through the door.

He rose immediately, waving aside the nobleman he'd been talking to and those who turned to him as he moved toward us.

'My lord earl,' he said by way of greeting to Raife, then he turned to me.

I dipped low in courtesy, remembering how I'd fallen that day I'd first met the king, and praying my balance would not give way again.

'My Lady Maeb,' Edmond said, once more extending his hand to me that I might rise safely.

I looked at him fully, then, the first time I had done so since entering the chamber. He was much the same as the last time I'd seen him, with the short-cropped wiry hair — now with a little grey in it — and the olive-skinned face more suited, I remember thinking from my first glimpse of him, to a more ordinary man. But, as at that first meeting, it proved to be those warm brown eyes that were so compelling.

He was dressed in good but serviceable clothes — not the magnificence I had been expecting.

'Pengraic said you were not well from your journeying to London,' the king said, as he stepped forward and, as Chestre had done, planted a kiss on my mouth. 'He said that you were with child, and early in your breeding. I pray you are recovered now?'

It amazed me that Edmond actually appeared to be genuinely concerned, and, of course, I wondered at the reason behind that concern.

'All I needed was a little rest, my lord king,' I said. 'I am quite recovered now.'

He still had not let go my hand, as he had also lingered over my hand that first day we'd met, and his eyes still had not let go of mine, as also on that first meeting.

'You look well as a countess,' he said, 'but I sorrow at the reason for it. I have heard that you suffered deeply.'

I was aware of everyone else in the room staring at us, silent in their regard, waiting for every word that they might discuss it later.

'I lived,' I said, fighting to keep the tears from welling up at the warmth and apparent sincere care in his voice. *Damn him.* 'Many others, much beloved, did not. I sorrow for my lord,' I glanced at Raife, 'who lost so many.'

There was a soft grunt of amusement from someone, and to my horror I realised it was Henry.

I saw Edmond's eyes flicker to his son, then they were back on me. 'We will talk more,' he said, 'when we dine this afternoon. But for now,' he finally let go my hand, and addressed Raife, 'your lord husband looks as though he needs some exercise and fresh air. Come, my lord,' he gave Raife's chest a hard slap, 'we must lose those fine garments of yours, and ride to the hunt. My valet will find you something of more durable wear for the chase ... I cannot have you looking finer than me.'

Edmond sent me a faint wink at that, as Raife gave a small bow.

'The exercise will do me good, my lord,' he said, and I thought him the liar, for we'd had nothing but exercise this past three weeks to reach London, and I think we were both heartily sick of it, 'but if I may have a moment to leave Maeb in safe hands?'

'There are *un*safe hands at my court?' Edmond said, giving a chuckle, then he waved us away. I dipped again, and Raife bowed, and then Raife led me across the chamber, passing Henry, who gave us a sardonic nod, toward a woman standing against a series of archways that looked as if they led into a chamber mirroring the hall below in size and scope.

'Alianor,' Raife said, 'this is my wife, Maeb. I pray that you shall be careful of her amid this vast nest of vipers.'

Lady Alianor dipped in courtesy to him before switching her gaze to me.

I liked her instantly. She was some fifteen years older than me, of warm beauty and with a ready smile. She dipped — I was overcome with yet another deep sense of unreality seeing this aristocratic lady humble herself before me — and then reached out both her hands to take mine.

'We shall be friends,' she said, her smile so amiable I found it hard to believe it had any artifice behind it at all. And yet, as I squeezed her hands, I wondered how deeply I might trust that smile and the woman who wore it.

CHAPTER FIVE

—◆◈◆—

'A re you quite overcome yet?' Lady Alianor said to me as we moved to one side, allowing a trio of noblemen to pass through the arch into the great hall beyond.

I gave a wan smile. 'I dare hardly speak, lest I betray my unease.'

'You will become used to it.' We had our arms linked, and she patted my hand. 'Do not fret about it. Every young girl is overcome when first she arrives here. But you ... my dear, *everyone* was agog at the news of the earl's marriage! The loss of Adelie and her children, especially Stephen, may the saints hold him close, was the most dreadful news, but to have Henry return to court with the news that Pengraic had wed again, and so quick —'

'And to someone of no name and no dowry.'

She chuckled. 'And that, too. Well, the court has been hot with rumour and conjecture ever since. What Henry did not tell us was that you were so beautiful. And the king, too, has been keeping such knowledge close ... for I believe you have met prior?'

I nodded.

'Now that I see you, and now that all of court can see you, there will be no more reason to wonder. Sweet Jesu, Maeb, you shall set all the tongues here a-wag!'

Her tone became more serious. 'And you must learn to use that, as you must use the fact that most will think you a country naïf.'

'I *am* a —'

'As of this moment, no, you are not, Maeb. You are the Countess of Pengraic. Apart from Queen Adelaide, and apart from any of the princes' wives, you are now one of the highest-ranked women in this land. Your husband stands among the most wealthy and powerful. You will find both flatterers and assassins fawning at your feet. Use them both, but do not allow yourself to be used by them.'

'There is so much to learn.'

'Aye, and that is why the earl asked me to care for you. Do not worry, Maeb. I shall not leave your side today, and shall guide you through whatever treacheries occur.'

Any fears I'd had about court mostly evaporated during the morning. Alianor proved a pleasant and reassuring companion. From the king's privy chamber she took me out to the gallery, where we lingered to enjoy the view. In the far distance, to the east, where spread light forest, we could hear the shouts and horns of the hunting party, although we could not see them.

'If the king returns with a good boar, he shall be happy,' she said.

'If my husband returns with his life intact, then I shall be happy,' I countered.

'Why do you fear so, Maeb?'

I told her what I'd learned from both Saint-Valery, Summersete and Henry — that Edmond feared my husband's power.

'All kings fear their high nobles' power,' Alianor said. 'They fear their wealth, and the armies they can raise from their lands, and yet most high nobles still walk about with their heads attached to their shoulders. Henry and Summersete?' She gave an elegant shrug. 'They are most likely envious of your husband's easy grasp of power. It makes them dangerous, yes, but they are unlikely to move against him.'

'And Edmond?'

She thought, looking out over the expanse of green that ran east. 'Edmond may well worry about Pengraic, but Pengraic has never done anything to threaten the king. Pengraic appears a man happy with what power and wealth he has, and does not covet more.'

She ended that last with a questioning lilt to her voice, and I merely raised my eyebrows slightly at her.

She gave me a little nod, as if approving, and carried on. 'I think that, rather than fear him, Edmond is oft frustrated by Pengraic. Your husband rarely jumps to Edmond's will like other noblemen and that irritates Edmond.'

'Yet Raife agreed happily to the hunt today, when *I* think he would have rather desisted.'

'That is such a small thing, Maeb. It is in the larger matters that Pengraic oft acts on his own behalf. Not against the king, just on his own behalf.'

I glanced back inside the privy chamber, where I could see Henry continuing his talk with the man in the white tunic.

'Henry bothers me,' I said, low.

'Henry bothers many people. He will be your most dangerous opponent at court, for he hates your husband and covets his power — and his independence from Edmond. Come, let us descend to the lesser hall, and we shall parade along its length, and gather you admirers.'

We carefully traversed the narrow spiral stairs to the lower level — Alianor showing me, unasked, where the privies were on the way (she had borne seven children, she told me, and understood the needs of the woman carrying a child) — and into the lesser hall. Here we spent the next few hours, taking seats before one of the fires, sipping small beer and picking at the tray of fruits and cheeses presented for our pleasure, as one by one or two by two, the noblemen and women of the court came over to introduce themselves. I felt as if I were holding court and I would have been ill at ease, save that Alianor's presence gave me courage and her continuous whispered commentary gave me the knowledge to deal graciously and easily with the never-ending procession.

At one point, left to our own devices for a short while, Alianor leaned close and touched my loosely braided hair. 'Why do you wear it so, Maeb?'

'I wore it thus one day, and Raife commented that he liked it so much that I have continued ever since. Why? Is it unbecoming for court?'

She gave a soft laugh and squeezed my arm. 'No! I had thought it the most artful piece of politic cunning when first I saw you! Here you are, your hair dressed so simply, and yet so glorious in its richness and gleam, and, while all the men of court admire it — it is true! I have seen all their eyes slip to it sooner rather than later — all the women regard it with envious eyes. They have thickened and lengthened their braids with horsehair and ribbons and pins and beads and baubles and bells so that they drag on the floor, and yet here you sit, glorious in your natural beauty, your hair outshining all of their wily tricked braiding. Wait and see, Maeb, for the next time you return to court I swear you will see a number of these women here discard their horsehair and baubles, and try to emulate your simplicity. And when you see that, Maeb, *know your power.*'

We chatted a little while, watching people moving about the hall.

I asked Alianor where was the queen, for I had thought she would be at court with her husband.

'Adelaide suffered a bad miscarriage not a month past. She is old for childbearing and the loss was ruinous to her health. She, and Edmond's two younger sons, remain at their manor at Elesberie.'

'Oh, I am sorry,' I said, meaning it. I would vastly have preferred the queen to be here.

Then I thought I would surprise Alianor with a very different question.

'Which of these women present,' I said, 'have been my husband's mistresses?'

Alianor looked shocked and I think it was genuine. 'My sweet lord, Maeb, you are not such the country naïf after all! Well, as to your question, that woman standing there in the red kirtle, and the lady in the far corner, with the blue ribbons through her braids.'

I felt the stab of a terrible jealousy, almost physically hurtful, and I wished I had not asked the question. Both women had talked to me in the past hours — and they had shared Raife's bed? I felt sick.

'But they are long-past mistresses, Maeb. I think you have no need to worry. I have seen how Pengraic looked at sweet Adelie, and I have seen the way he looks at you and, no, you have no need to fret.' She smiled a little. 'I admire you for the courage of asking the question, and am heartened that you *knew* to ask the question.'

I wanted to ask her more, but just then two men wandered over. It was Saint-Valery and the tall, dark, brooding man in the plain white tunic.

'Ah,' said Alianor, 'our court poet, as well as my lord d'Ecouis.'

Saint-Valery bowed, then took my hand and kissed it. 'Jewels suit you, my lady.'

I blushed, wondering if criticism underlay the remark. 'The world has turned upside down since last we met, my lord.'

'And my heart inside out. We shall need to talk of it later. My lady, I believe you have not met Sir Fulke d'Ecouis. Forgive his plain apparel — he is of the Templars and has foresworn frippery.'

The Templars. My heart gave an uncomfortable flip. I had half lifted my hand, expecting d'Ecouis to follow Saint-Valery's example and kiss it, but d'Ecouis stood his ground, not even giving me a nod, let alone a bow.

'Countess,' he said, grinding the word out as if under torture.

'There was another of your brothers upstairs,' I said, if only for words to utter.

'Ah, you spotted him,' said Alianor brightly. 'That is my husband's kinsman, Gilbert.' She waved a hand in the air. 'Lord of some vast estate somewhere or the other.'

Alianor's kinsman by marriage was a Templar? My heart sank. I did not trust the Templars, for I blamed them for keeping my father too long in the Holy Land, and our family's difficulties because of it.

Suddenly d'Ecouis' patent disapproval of me and his boredom at having to endure being presented to me, spurred my anger. 'My father rode with your Order for some years,' I said to him. 'It was too much for him, and he died well before his years.'

Finally, I had caught d'Ecouis' attention. 'To die within the Order and at its work is to be assigned a place at God's right hand,' he intoned sententiously. 'May I enquire as to your father's name?'

'Godfrey Langtofte,' I said, meaning to say that he had not died *in* the Order's service, but was stopped precipitously by the look on d'Ecouis' face. He had gone completely white, almost as white as his spotless tunic.

'You are Langtofte's daughter?' he said. 'I —'

'My lady,' Saint-Valery said, 'the king's household chamberlain is seeking your attention.'

I looked to where he indicated, and saw a man standing by the entrance to the chamber beyond the hall gesturing at me.

'It is time for us to go, my lords,' said Alianor smoothly, standing up and sliding her arm through mine as I, too, rose. 'The king has returned.'

'I hope we have time to speak at more length later, my lady,' Saint-Valery said, and I gave him a smile, shot d'Ecouis a more ambiguous glance, then walked toward the chamberlain with Alianor.

'Your father was a Templar?' Alianor murmured.

'Only for a few years. After my mother died he went as a pilgrim to Jerusalem and stayed, joining the Order as a sergeant. Then ill-health plagued him, and he came home and died soon after.'

'Does your husband know this?'

Did Raife know? Raife had never asked about my father, save on that very first day we'd met. I couldn't imagine that he cared overmuch and, besides, my father had never held any office of importance within the Order — he had done little but count the Templars' coin from one table to another.

'I doubt he cares,' I said.

'Mention it to him,' Alianor said, and then we were at the chamberlain, who waved us through into the king's privy chamber.

The hunting party had returned, and were filled with jovial humour and much flattery as each praised another for their bravery and skill in the heat and blood of battle. Alianor and I shared a glance, laughed, and rolled our eyes.

'The ladies dispute our skills!' said Edmond. He was standing by a small table on which stood a bowl of water. Both he and Raife, standing with him, had stripped back to their linen braes and hose and were splashing water over their chests and faces as they washed away the sweat of the chase.

A servant handed each of them a towel and they dried off with rough, impatient strokes.

'You mistake us, my lord king,' said Alianor. 'We were so overcome with the joy of seeing you safe after your dangerous adventure our eyes rolled as we near fainted in relief.'

Raife had donned his linen shirt, and, taking his richly embroidered tunic from the servant, pulled it on as he walked over. 'Did you spend your morning well, wife?' he said.

'Very well, my lord. My Lady Alianor has been a good friend.'

The skin about Raife's eyes relaxed a little.

The king had similarly donned his tunic — he was garbed as richly as Raife now — and walked over. 'We dine at nones,' he said. 'My lady countess, will you do me the honour of accompanying me at table?'

Such a suggestion, even early this morning, would have had me in a tremble of nerves, but after the experience of the past hours, and Alianor's gentle instruction, it did not frighten me overmuch. I dipped in courtesy.

'I thank you, sir. You can tell me how my husband managed at hunt.'

The king smiled. 'He may tell you himself now, and then I shall tell you later, and you can decide for yourself how well the two accounts marry. Pengraic, we wait an hour or two until we dine. Why don't you show your wife the chapel?'

As much as I liked Alianor, and had grown somewhat easier with the number of people at court, it was a relief to spend some time alone with Raife. We walked arm in arm out to the northern gallery, then toward the north-east tower where we turned down the eastern gallery which led to the chapel.

'You encountered no problems today?' Raife said as we came toward the entrance to the chapel.

'No,' I said. 'Alianor has proven a good friend. Thank you for her introduction. And I have kept my tongue well, my lord.'

He gave my arm a soft squeeze. 'Thank you, Maeb.'

We walked through into the chapel, and we stopped as I took in a deep breath.

It was stunning. A large vaulted chamber of cream stone that glowed in the sun streaming through its upper windows. A succession of thick columns created two aisles, and supported a large gallery above. The walls and columns were painted in bright colours, as were the two rood screens. Candles flickered at the altar where gilt and gold glowed, and somewhere incense burned.

'The chapel of Saint John the Evangelist,' Raife said. 'Often the one peaceful place to be found within the tower.'

We walked slowly through the aisles.

'What did you discover this morning,' he said to me.

'Two of your mistresses.'

He stopped, looking at me. 'Long past, now.'

'Good,' I said. 'I also found a Templar, of uncertain temper.'

Raife chuckled as we resumed our slow pacing.

'I did not know they were in England,' I said.

'They arrived a few years ago. They have a church on Holbournestrate but are petitioning Edmond for a parcel of land just outside Lud Gate. Their wealth and influence grows. I do not like them. Edmond does not like them either — their loyalty is to the pope, not to him. But I fear we shall have to endure their presence.'

'My father was a member.'

'Your father?'

We had stopped again, and now Raife looked at me curiously.

'After my mother died he went on pilgrimage to Jerusalem. There he joined the Templars.'

'He was in Jerusalem? Among the Knights of the Temple?' Raife's interest had sharpened.

'Not a knight, and I do not know if he was at the Temple. He was a sergeant, involved only in coin counting, and I believe he soon became disenchanted with the Order. He returned home, where he died soon after.'

'The Order is rigorous, and not for all.'

'I think he missed his home.'

Raife had lost his interest in my father now, and began pointing out the devices on some shields hung on the walls. I asked him if he had enquired of the king why he was at the Conqueror's Tower rather than the palace at Westminster, and Raife said that the king had felt it necessary to stay in London while the plague threatened the country.

'To show his people that he does not run and hide,' Raife said. 'And also, probably, because if there is civil unrest in London, as there has been in the south-east of the realm, then Edmond is more directly placed to respond to it.'

We talked a while longer, and then left the chapel and returned to the king's privy apartments, where Alianor introduced me to her husband, and the four of us sat chatting in a quiet corner until it was time for us to proceed in to dine.

CHAPTER SIX

I accompanied the king in to dinner, which was a great honour, and then sat at his side to eat, sharing a platter with him. I was cautious of what I said, and possibly over-watchful of my table manners, but Edmond was a calming companion and, unlike his son, I did not feel I had to watch every word I said.

I would lie if I denied that sitting at the king's hand to eat and sharing his platter while the eyes of the court were upon me, did not give me some small pleasure and thrill of excitement. I looked at the lower tables, at the many noble men and women, dressed in such richness, eating from the gleaming gilt and pewter of the king's plate, and wondered how it was that I had come to this means.

Raife sat down the end of the high table with a bishop and Henry (I did not envy my husband his company, and was grateful that Henry was seated so far from me), while on my side of the table sat the earls of Warwick and Pembroke, Roger de Beaumont and Gilbert de Clare, and their wives, who were pleasant company.

I soon relaxed and ate daintily, both through not wanting to appear the pig before Edmond (and the watching eyes) and because my stomach had recently become queasy, and I did not want, as Evelyn had once so delicately put it, to spew across high table. Most of the time, I used my old silver eating knife to cut my meat into ever smaller pieces, moving them about the plate, and occasionally lifting a tiny morsel to my mouth.

The initial stages of the meal were spent sipping wine and sharing general conversation with those near me, the earls and their wives to my left, and Edmond and a bishop (I forgot his name and titles as soon as I heard them) to my right.

But, as the platters of food began to arrive in earnest, Edmond became my exclusive conversational companion.

Our conversation was of the most ordinary kind at first, then Edmond asked me to describe for him what it was like at Pengraic when the plague struck.

I had just sipped from my cup of wine. Now I put it down and, my eyes gleaming with tears, told him as much as I could without veering onto the nightmarish subject of Stephen's, Rosamund's and John's deaths. Edmond was a sympathetic listener, stopping me occasionally to seek further detail from me.

I felt comfortable with him. Edmond's manner was warm and sympathetic, and he had a way of putting me so completely at ease that the fact he was also King of England receded completely from my mind. All the gossip I had heard about him — and had intuited about him previously — as a man always on the hunt for a new mistress, also receded completely.

I felt as I did with Owain. That he was a friend and that I could say to him anything I wished.

Still, I was careful.

'I cannot imagine the pain you have been through, Maeb,' Edmond said. 'The terror. Pengraic thought the castle safe, as did I, and when the news came …' He broke off, shaking his head. 'It cut many hearts open, Maeb.'

'It has been terrible for many people, my lord. On the ride to London Raife and I saw so much suffering, the burned villages and towns, the deserted fields, the people on the road. In the south-east of the country, I believe it was also bad?'

'Yes. Devastating. The counties from Dovre through south of London … by God, Maeb, in some areas there is nothing left save the burned stubble of crops that will never be harvested, and of homes and churches that will never have foot step in them again. Those people left may not ever recover.'

'You had to send my husband there to quell unrest?'

Edmond nodded, signalling to the servitor to replenish our cups with more wine. 'There was panic and commotion as people tried to flee the plague yet only spread it further. Thank sweet Jesu it did not reach London. By God, I do not know what will happen if it strikes again, or if it travels further. The harvest will be small this year as so many crops have burned, or have been left to perish unheeded because there is none left to harvest them.'

He stopped, fiddling with his wine cup, his eyes roaming over the hall. 'Much of this autumn and winter court, Maeb, will be spent trying to plan and prepare for spring and summer, when the plague is likely to rise again. It is why I wanted your husband here so badly. Pengraic commands much land in England, and many men, and he is a wise man, and moderate and unambitious when I am surrounded by many immoderate ambitious men who offer me advice designed only to advance their own means.'

He gave a small grunt of amusement. 'Whatever you may have heard, Maeb, I trust your husband as I do very few men.'

'Yet others say you distrust him, and fear his power.'

Edmond looked at me, his gaze keen. 'I think your husband has his eye set on other prizes, not my throne, Maeb. I need not fear him.'

'What other prizes?'

'Ah,' Edmond smiled, and supped at his wine, 'he is your husband. Ask him yourself. Some men covet forgiveness, some sainthood, some have dreams that exist nowhere but their own minds. All I am sure of is that Pengraic is a driven man, but not, praise the saints, driven to acquiring my throne. He has secrets I cannot know, but I do not feel threatened by them.'

He pulled off a few tender bits of swan breast and put them on my plate. 'You should eat more.'

'My lord, it is the child. I dare do little more than nibble.'

'You know, Maeb, when word came to me that Raife had married you, I, as many people, was somewhat surprised. *I* would have bedded you, I would *not* have married you. Pengraic could have had any great heiress in this country. Why you?'

Now, suddenly, the conversation had turned very personal. I said nothing, pushing the pieces of meat about my plate with my fingers.

'Your beauty, that I can understand. But that can be enjoyed with a bedding, it does not demand a marriage. Pengraic has had mistresses in the past, why not yet another one? So I asked myself — why Maeb? And I have finally found that reason, through my conversations with you tonight, and with others.'

Alianor, I thought. Edmond sent me off with Raife so he could talk to Alianor.

The thought that she had been used to discover information about me made me feel somewhat sad, but not particularly surprised.

'And that reason is … my lord?'

'You do not realise?'

'No.'

'Well, no, you wouldn't.' Again that smile, those warm eyes radiating friendliness. 'It is your complete artlessness, Maeb. Your trueness and honesty. You say what you think. Ah — I see the disbelief on your face, for I am sure you have secrets, as does everyone. Secrets aside, to have the freshness, the lack of guile, the honesty and the spirit, all combined with great beauty, is a heady mixture indeed. You do not come from a noble background and your elevation to countess must have been difficult for you, yet you sit here and converse with a king with ease.'

He paused, fingers tapping slowly on the table. 'You are a complex woman, Maeb. An unexpected treasure. Did Stephen want you as well?'

That sudden question startled me. I opened my mouth, but did not know how to answer.

Edmond narrowed his eyes. 'Your reddened cheeks and your wordlessness answers me well enough, Maeb. Is there any man who has not yet fallen under your spell?'

'Many, my lord,' I answered.

'My son among them,' Edmond said, surprising me with *his* honesty. 'Be careful of him, Maeb. Try not to be artless about *him*.'

I wondered what Henry had been saying to his father, and it made me wonder why Edmond had asked me to describe what had happened at Pengraic when the plague struck. Was he seeking to trap me over some minor detail? Discover a means to make me confess to Stephen's, Rosamund's and John's murders?

'Thank you, my lord,' I said.

Edmond studied me seriously, then gave a nod. His eyes, normally so warm, were now watchful, wary.

'Be careful, Maeb. I am not your enemy and I will protect you as much as I am able. But even I cannot guarantee your safety.'

'Why do some hate me, as you intimate?'

I knew the answer even before he spoke it.

'Because you are the route to Pengraic, Maeb. Many covet, or fear, his wealth and power. Pengraic loves you. That may well prove his downfall.

'Ah, but why do we discuss such bleak matters? Tell me, do you like the minstrels who entertain us this day? They have come from Normandy, and are reputed to be among the best.' Then he gave a sigh. 'But, oh, how I wish they would sing of something other than the Holy Grail and those who quest for it. I am heartily sick of quests and grails.'

After that Edmond and I fell back to discussing inconsequential things, and eventually he turned to the bishop on his other side and I to Pembroke and his wife who were closest to me on my left. The afternoon wore on toward early evening and the atmosphere in the hall was convivial as diners consumed more wine and the music livened. Benches were pushed back from tables, and people moved about the hall, talking to others sat distant from them.

I saw Raife move down to talk earnestly with the Earl of Chestre and a woman who must be his wife, and had a nasty jab of surprise when Henry rose from his seat and walked behind his father to the back of my chair, laying a brief hand on my shoulder. But he moved on immediately, not saying a word, and I watched him walk down the right side of the hall to talk to none other than the two Templars, Gilbert de Lacy and Fulke d'Ecouis. The three men talked for a few minutes, their heads close, then as one they turned and looked at me.

My stomach turned over as I instinctively shifted my eyes away, and I wondered what they were talking about. Why had d'Ecouis reacted so strangely when I'd mentioned my father's name? Was Henry telling them of his suspicions regarding my part in some of Raife's children's deaths?

'My Lady Maeb.'

Edmond had turned to me again, and I blinked and smiled at him, trying to forget the other three.

'The musicians are going to play an Estampie. It is time we had some dancing, eh? Will you join me?'

I smiled somewhat wanly, and rose, taking Edmond's hand. I did not know the Estampie well — it was a new dance from France that several of the minstrels who had played at Pengraic had taught me, but I had never performed it save in the relatively safe atmosphere of the great hall at Pengraic.

I prayed that the dance those minstrels had taught me would prove to be the same dance the king's court knew — the same dance the *king* knew.

The Estampie, like so many dances, was a line dance, save this differed in that it involved two lines, and each dancer had a partner in the line opposite them with whom they began and ended the dance. During the dance each of the lines interwove, people moving in and out, catching hands with those dancers from the other line they met along the way. It was not a particularly fast dance, for which I was grateful, but one of grace and elegance — and one where the dancer had to concentrate, lest they find themselves out of step and out of place.

The twin lines formed, and each dancer bowed or dipped in courtesy to their partner. No one else seemed surprised that the king had joined the dancing — he must do it routinely — but again I found eyes directed my way as I took my place opposite him.

The horns, pipes and drums began, and we all dipped and bowed again and the dance began. To my relief it was the same as I'd been taught, and as the dance moved forward I began to enjoy myself. Alianor was among the dancers, and we smiled widely as we passed each other briefly, clasping hands as we did so. People at the tables called encouragement, or clapped in beat with the music, and I allowed my smile to remain, taking pleasure in the moment.

Finally it was over, and the twin lines reformed facing each other, the dancers miraculously finding themselves opposite their partner again. The music ended in a series of wild chords, and yet once more we bowed or dipped to our partners.

Then, suddenly, came the difference with the Estampie I'd been taught. All the dance partners stepped toward each other and kissed, in a final display of courtliness. Edmond smiled at what must have been a look of panic in my eyes, and he came to me, took my face in his hands, and kissed me deeply.

'I hope Pengraic takes good care not to lose you,' he said, very softly as he raised his face from mine, 'because then I shall have to come find you and keep you myself.'

I was somewhat breathless from both dance and kiss, and I excused myself to go to the privy where, for a short while, I could have some time to myself. When I returned along the north gallery, Henry and the Templar d'Ecouis were waiting for me.

I stopped, my heart thudding. I would have turned and sought to escape into the eastern gallery and thence into the chapel, but they were too quick for me.

'My Lady Maeb,' Henry said, grabbing my wrist and pushing me roughly against the exterior wall of the gallery, 'how fortunate to find you.'

D'Ecouis took position at my other side and together the two men pressed me against the wall.

'I discover from my lord d'Ecouis that you had a most adventurous father, Maeb,' Henry said.

I did not reply, so fearful I could barely draw breath. Their nearness, their tone and the way they held me against the wall was not merely discourteous, it was immensely threatening.

'To Jerusalem and back,' Henry murmured. 'And I'd always believed he was a man of no spine. He joined the Templars, d'Ecouis tells me.'

'Yes, my lord,' I managed. I looked about, but even though the music and conversation and laughter of the great hall wafted out into the gallery, the gallery was deserted apart from the three of us. There was no one I could appeal to for aid.

'During his time with us,' d'Ecouis said, his mouth close to my face, 'we think Langtofte became privy to secrets he should not have discovered. He was a money sorter, nothing else, but we think he listened at too many doorways.'

'My lords, I do not know what —'

'The Templars are privy to *many* secrets,' Henry said. 'They are trusted by His Holiness the Pope when no other is. What my friend and I would like to know is … did your treacherous father pass these secrets to *you?*'

'I have *no* idea of what you speak!'

'The Order think that perhaps your father made off with … some of their wealth,' d'Ecouis said. 'With the *Church's* wealth. We can think of no one else who may have taken it. Such a sin, my lady. What did he leave you after his death, Lady Maeb? Some gold, perhaps? Jewels? A bauble or two?'

'He left me nothing save rags and his blessing,' I said. 'I had nothing from him. All his property went to the Order, as you should know.'

'And yet how sweetly you have done with that "nothing", Maeb,' Henry said. 'From destitute waif to Countess of Pengraic in less than a half year. Now, we are sure Pengraic was taken with your pretty face, but we wonder why *else* he married you. What dowry, Maeb, what *secretive* dowry did you use to buy yourself into Pengraic's bed?'

'None save my sweet charm,' I snapped, 'of which you evidence little.'

'The Templars want back what was stolen,' said d'Ecouis. 'We —'

'I say again, I have *no* idea of what you speak!' I said. Then, miraculously, a knight appeared from the east gallery, walking toward the door to the great hall.

'Good sir!' I called out, wrenching my wrist from Henry's grasp. 'Can you escort me back to table?'

As I was walking off, I heard Henry say to d'Ecouis, 'Do you think she knows?'

I was struggling not to cry from shock when I sat down at the table. The servitors were handing out sweet custards, but I knew that if I so much as put a spoonful to my mouth I would vomit it forth again.

'Maeb?' said the king, who had turned to me as I sat down. 'What is the matter?'

'Nothing, my lord king.' My hands, resting in my lap, gave the lie to my words by their treacherous trembling.

Edmond glanced at them. 'Maeb?'

'Nothing, my lord king.'

I saw a movement, and then Raife was with me. He also must have seen my face as I had sat down although he was further along the table.

'Edmond,' Raife said, and I registered through my shock how familiarly my husband addressed the king. 'Edmond, my wife is unwell with her child, and is over-tired from her first day at court. May we have your permission to retire?'

Edmond gave it with a nod, then reached out with one of his hands, laying it over mine, still a-tremble in my lap. 'Maeb?'

My tears spilled over now, both from my continued upset and from the care in his voice.

'I *am* tired, and unwell,' I said, 'as Raife has said. I am sorry, my lord, that I —'

Edmond put his hand briefly to my lips, silencing me, then looked to Raife. 'Rest a while in my privy chamber. I will send a man to get your horses saddled and to collect your retinue.'

'Thank you, my lord,' Raife said. He aided me to rise, and I dipped in courtesy before the king, who was still gazing at me with watchful concern, then we left the great hall and entered the king's privy chamber via one of the connecting arches — I silently thanked sweet Jesu we did not have to use the gallery.

There were people about in the privy chamber, but there were silent, private spaces, too, and Raife sat me down on a bench in one of them. He sat close to me, and took my hands.

Still distressed, but more relieved than I can say to be with Raife, I allowed the tears to flow freely, and for some time all I did was weep as Raife tried to dry my tears away.

'For God's sake,' he said, 'what has happened?' He paused. 'Maeb?' he said, with the same amount of frustration as the king.

I swallowed my tears and, somewhat haltingly at first, told him of the conversation with Henry and d'Ecouis.

'They think your father became privy to "secrets"?' Raife said. 'That he made off with something, some jewels?'

I nodded.

'What did they mean?' Raife said.

'*I don't know!*' I replied.

'Your father did not return from the Holy Lands with any jewels? Of any description? He did not leave you any "baubles"?'

'No. He left me nothing save some rags and a good enough name to join your household. There were no jewels. No secrets. *Nothing.*'

Raife sat back a little, one of his hands resting on the purse I had stitched for him, his fingers tapping, looking at me although I could tell his mind was far away. Then, just as he was about to speak, one of the king's men appeared before us, saying that our horses and retinue awaited.

CHAPTER SEVEN

We arrived home. I was exhausted and fraught. I could see Evelyn wanted to know what had happened, but I did not want to tell her and she kept her peace. All I wanted was my bed and Raife to hold me for the night.

In the morning I lay abed as Raife dressed. Once garbed, he waved Charles away and sat on the side of the bed.

'You will stay quiet for the day,' he said.

I nodded. There was nothing I wanted more.

'Edmond will want to know what happened,' he said.

'Tell him,' I said. I had not wanted to talk with Edmond last night because I knew I would do little more than weep, as I had with Raife, but there was nothing about that conversation I needed to hide, nor wished to. I still had no idea what Henry and d'Ecouis wanted, or what they meant.

Once Raife had gone I summoned Evelyn, and she helped me dress. We prayed, then broke our fast in the solar. I felt better now, and I gave Evelyn a lively account of what my day at court had been like, leaving out only that time Henry and d'Ecouis had me trapped in the gallery. I did not want to answer questions about it, and I feared that Evelyn would have nothing but advice for me, which I could not stomach. I said that the day had wearied me and that I had felt indisposed, which is why I'd been so pale and silent the night before.

The house steward fitzErfast came to speak with me mid-morning to arrange some household matters, and then, almost as soon as he had left Lady Alianor de Lacy arrived.

Her cheerful face was welcome, and I rose to kiss her as she came into the chamber.

Evelyn, who had been sitting with me, now gathered her needlework and left us alone, and Alianor and I spent the morning chatting, and recalling yesterday's events. She, too, wanted to know why I had left so precipitously, and I had no hesitation in telling her. I did not know why Henry and d'Ecouis accused me, or even of *what* they accused me, but I wanted word to spread through court of my indignation and innocence before they could spread rumour of whatever sin they imagined me guilty.

I had learned yesterday's lessons in court-craft well.

'Alianor,' I said, 'I have no idea what the Templars want of me, or of what they suspect me. Do you know?'

The direct question, and its indirect reference to her kinsman Sir Gilbert, the other Templar we had seen at court yesterday, surprised Alianor.

'No,' she said, 'I do not know. I can make gentle enquiry of Sir Gilbert. Maybe *he* knows. But he is more a Templar, and far less a de Lacy. He will remember his loyalty to them first when he answers.'

Thus her answer. The de Lacys were not likely to shed any light on the mystery. I nodded, and accepted it. I'd had no expectations of Alianor on this matter, but I had wanted to remind her that I knew how close by blood she was to the Templars.

I *had* learned yesterday's lessons in court-craft well.

Close to sext, when a servitor brought us a light meal, fitzErfast came to tell me a knight from Edmond's retinue had arrived and would I see him.

Curious, I nodded, and a short while later fitzErfast escorted a handsome and well-dressed young man of my own age into the solar. He bowed deeply before me, and introduced himself as Roger de Douai. He was so good looking and had such an open air of honesty about him, that I liked him instantly.

He sat at my invitation, withdrawing a small fabric-wrapped parcel from a pocket deep within his surcoat.

'My lady,' he said, extending the parcel to me, 'please accept this small gift from my lord king, who has asked me to attend you today.'

'A gift?' I said, hesitating to accept it.

Alianor caught my eye and gave an imperceptible nod.

I reached out and took the parcel from de Douai.

'My lord king wishes you to know of his concern,' de Douai said. 'He is worried that you were somehow discomposed at his court, and also worried for your health and that of your child. This gift is a token of his concern, and wishes that you will accept it as such only.'

That 'only' carried with it an entire conversation's worth of words. He was concerned, and it was concern only which prompted this gift. It was not meant to bribe me into his bed.

It was also not an apology on behalf of his son who, if Raife had not already told him, Edmond must have suspected of having some hand in my distress.

I was genuinely touched by Edmond's concern, and understood the lack of apology on behalf of his son. I untied the ribbon holding the fabric and slowly unwrapped my gift.

Nestled into a delicately embroidered square of fine woollen cloth was the loveliest mantle clasp I had ever seen. Made of gold, it was intricately worked and twisted, embedded all about with garnets and tiny pearls.

It was a precious, precious gift.

I stared at it a long moment, then looked to Alianor. She was also gazing at it with round eyes, and her surprise made me realise that Edmond did not routinely lavish gifts such as this on women of his court.

I wondered where it had come from, for Edmond certainly could not have caused it to be crafted in the space of a single night.

'The clasp once belonged to Edmond's lady mother,' de Douai said, as if he had read my mind, 'who my lord king honoured and respected.'

Now I was truly shocked. This clasp had once adorned a queen. That gave it wealth and meaning far beyond its value in gold and gems.

Again I glanced at Alianor, and saw that she was now quite stunned.

This clasp was an astounding gift.

I wondered what Henry would do if he saw me wearing it at court.

'Sir Roger,' I said in a voice surprisingly calm, given my deep emotion, 'I cannot thank my lord king enough for the gift and the care and concern that lies behind it. This must have been a treasured piece, and to gift it to me … please tell him I am deeply, deeply honoured, and will cherish this clasp.'

De Douai's face relaxed a little and I realised that he — and the king — had held some concern I may not have accepted the clasp. We passed a little while in idle conversation, de Douai refusing an offer of wine, and then he made a gracious withdrawal.

Once he had left the solar, Alianor took a deep breath. 'My Lady Maeb … that is an extraordinary gift.' She paused. 'It shows such uncommon favour …' Again she paused. 'Maeb, be careful. That gift will win you as many enemies as it will flatterers.'

'Perhaps I should not wear it.'

'Oh, you must wear it. Edmond will expect it. Besides, word of this will have already spread. The choice of de Douai as its bearer was a careful decision by Edmond. De Douai may be a favoured knight in the king's retinue, but he is also known as an idle gossip. When Edmond wants word of something to spread, he uses de Douai. There are so many layers of meaning to this gift, Maeb.'

I stared at the clasp in my hands. After what Alianor said, I knew that this was not 'only' a gift of concern. It was also an amulet of powerful protection.

Harm her, it said, *and you harm me*.

Once de Douai had departed, Alianor and I ate lightly of a platter of fruit, nuts, bread and cheese that one of the servitors laid before us, and finally Alianor came to perhaps the real reason of her visit — apart from her genuine desire to discover how I was after my distress at court, of course.

'My lord earl has told me you need another attending lady,' she said.

I inclined my head, and wondered, *who?*

'May I suggest a kinswoman?' Alianor said. 'I have spoken to the earl about her and he approves.'

What choice I, then?

'Your kinswoman?' I said.

'Isouda de Lacy,' Alianor said. 'She is widowed now, and with no children. She is only a few years older than you, but versed in matters courtly, and,' Alianor broke into a wide smile, 'she is a most amiable woman. You shall adore her.'

Indeed I might, but I doubted I'd trust her.

'She shall do well, then,' I said. 'Is she at court now?'

'She is not far. She can be here within the week.'

Alianor phrased the last as a question, and I nodded, giving my assent. I wondered what Evelyn would make of her.

When Raife returned later that afternoon I told him of Alianor's visit, and the offer of her kinswoman as my new attending lady.

'She said you approved,' I said.

He gave a noncommittal nod.

'The de Lacys must be powerful allies,' I said.

'And so will you trust her as you do Evelyn?'

'No.'

Raife nodded. 'Good. The de Lacys *are* powerful allies. Having the Lady Isouda as your attending woman will be fine for that alliance. Nonetheless ...'

'Nonetheless,' I said, and we were in agreement.

'Raife,' I went on, 'Edmond sent me a gift today.' I showed him the clasp.

Raife looked almost as shocked as Alianor had. 'I remember this from Edmond's mother's mantle. Sweet saints, Maeb ...'

'It is a powerful gift.'

'Beyond powerful.' Raife handed it back to me, studying me carefully. 'How shall you thank Edmond?'

'Not by betraying you.'

Again, a long look, then he gave a nod, accepting it. 'Maeb, I am going north for a few weeks. I need to visit my estates and lordships there, and this is the last chance I will get before the worst of winter.'

My face must have shown my complete dismay, for Raife suddenly laughed, and leaned forward to kiss me.

'And that look did more than your words to reassure me that you will not betray me,' he said.

He sat on the bench beside me. 'Mae, do not worry. These weeks shall pass quickly, and then I will be back. I *must* be back, for Edmond will hold winter council and wants me here for it.'

'I shall hide in this house.'

'No. You must not do that. Attend court, several times a week if you can. Other times open up the hall here, that *you* may hold court in the afternoons and evenings. You have high rank now and, between them, Edmond and de Douai have made certain the knowledge of your favour in Edmond's eyes. You need only sit, and be gracious, and let people come to you.'

'I fear that I will unwittingly betray you, or embarrass you.'

'The de Lacys, Alianor and Robert, will be at your side often, Lady Isouda almost continuously. But do not look past fitzErfast. I trust him completely, as few others, and he knows the court, its alliances and feuds, as also this city, like no other. He can get a message to me fast, if needed. Pembroke is also an ally, and will aid you if he can. And, as much as it pains me to say this, I think you can trust Edmond, too. At least some of the way.'

'So long as I do nothing to threaten him.'

A slow smile. 'You have learned fast, Maeb. You will do well enough while I am gone. Just be wary always of what you say and do.'

'But *where* are you going? I know nothing of your northern estates. I cannot come?'

'I will be riding fast and hard, Maeb. It will be no ride for you, and most certainly not in the north, where the autumn gales have already begun. As for where, to Eurvicscire first, where I have lands abutting those of the de Lacys. They are my most northern lands. Then on the ride south I go to Lincolescire and Sudfulc. Then back to you, and the delights of Edmond's winter court.

'Maeb, be careful always. Watch your every word, guard your every action.' He leaned close, and kissed me. 'Be here for me when I return.'

He kissed me again, deeper, cradling my head in his hand, and I wished desperately that he would not leave.

CHAPTER EIGHT

Raife took me back to court one more time before he left. This was not a formal visit: rather than dine, or pass the hour in idle (yet watchful) chatter in the lesser hall, we spent the day attending military and equestrian games in the fields to the west of the Conqueror's Tower. It was a fine day, but cold, and we were chilled further by a persistent wind from the north, and thus I wore a thick mantle, secured by Edmond's gift.

I saw Edmond only briefly, but I dipped graciously before him, touched the clasp, and said but two simple words: *Thank you.* I did not need to say further. They were enough. Edmond gave me a nod, we passed a few words, and then Raife and I took our seats on the large raised dais on which Edmond sat. We sat next to the Earl of Pembroke, Gilbert de Clare, and his wife Isabel. Raife had told me Pembroke was to be trusted — I had already met the earl and his wife during my dinner with the king — and both the earl and his countess went to some lengths to assure me that they would keep me good company while Raife was away. They also kept a London house, some distance from ours, and this day spent in their company gave me much confidence about the forthcoming weeks.

Gradually, I was building friendships at court.

I enjoyed the games, despite the shouting, the jostling, the violence, the blood and the single death. I thought it as if all the hidden intrigues of court had, for just one day, come to life on the green swath before me. The games were, indeed, a courtly dance — if enacted with drawn weapons — and by the end of them not a few lords had tripped over their own feet as they lost the beat of the discordant music.

As Alianor had predicted, on this day I saw two other women wearing their hair braided loosely and over the succeeding weeks I saw many others take up the fashion.

It was, indeed, a lesson in power.

The next day Raife left. I cried, even though I had not meant to, and now I was on my own.

The first week passed pleasantly enough. Lady Isouda de Lacy arrived and she was installed in my household as my attending lady.

Evelyn did not like her. I was not surprised. Evelyn's and my friendship had cooled somewhat since I had become the countess; it cooled even further when she was joined by a woman of much higher rank than herself. Lady Isouda instantly became my senior companion, the one who had closest contact with me, who woke me in the mornings, who knelt at my side during prayer, and who kissed me goodnight at the end of the day. Evelyn was relegated to my low-ranking companion, who always walked behind, and who shouldered the burden of tedious tasks when, formerly, she had been my closest companion.

Isouda was a charming, pretty woman, much like Alianor with her warmth and ease of manner although they were not blood kin. I found her company restful and she was, as Alianor had said, a woman to whom I could turn for all manner of advice and knowledge.

In most things I knew I could trust her. I knew also, however, that sometimes I would not be able to trust her, or depend on her loyalty, and I kept myself watchful for these times.

For the moment, Isouda became a good friend, and I relied on her immensely.

I kept court myself — entertaining honoured guests in the solar during the day, and, after nones, keeping a larger company in the hall. Here nobles, knights and squires came, as well as jesters and jugglers and minstrels and poets, filling the hall with their chatter and sweet music. I did this latter only when I knew Edmond did not keep court — that he had spent the day hunting, or travelling to a nearby priory or manor, and would not be keeping formal court later in the day. I did not want to compete. The de Lacys and the Pembrokes were frequent visitors, as was the Earl of Chestre and his wife, and sundry minor nobles.

Thankfully, Henry and the Templars kept their distance; they never attended court at my house, nor did I see them at Edmond's court.

One of my visitors was Ranulph Saint-Valery. He came one day when Alianor was with me, but she sat at some distance away in the solar, working on her stitching, to give us some privacy to speak.

'I had hoped I would be the man to wed you,' Saint-Valery said with a wry smile.

'I am sorry, Ranulph,' I said. 'Life was turned upside down and before I knew it my lord Pengraic had determined we should wed.' I gave my own wry smile. 'I had little say in that matter.'

'But you are happy.'

Now my smile was far more genuine and wide. 'Yes. He is a good husband to me.'

'I remember once that you feared him.'

I gave a soft laugh. 'Once, if I had known I would become his wife then I would have fainted with terror! But he *is* a good husband and I regard him well.'

'Better than well,' Saint-Valery said. 'Lady Maeb, I would have married you, and honoured you, even when you were but Mistress Langtofte.'

'I know, Ranulph,' I said. 'I am sorry.'

He gave a nod, and our conversation turned to more general matters. From then on, Saint-Valery became one of my good friends at court and he came to visit two more times, when he knew Alianor to be with me.

I went to the Tower frequently, as Raife had asked. Largely because both Henry and the Templars were absent (where, I wondered?). I enjoyed myself there. Edmond showed me much courtesy, often sitting me at high table, although not again at his side — not without my husband present. I made deeper acquaintance with many of the other nobles, secular and clergy alike, and slowly found my way about this gallantry of aristocrats with a degree of confidence. Edmond and I spoke often, although usually only in generalities, and I became more comfortable with him, too, and often I would find our eyes meeting across some crowded space and a gentle smile exchanged.

Alianor continued to be a good friend and companion. Together with Isouda and Evelyn, as well as Alianor's women and various attendants, we sometimes wandered the markets and streets of London, or visited the churches. I also spent time at the Pembrokes' house, as I did at the de Lacys'. Alianor graced me with a most beautifully crafted and jewelled eating knife, and I accepted it gladly, giving the one I'd had since childhood to our house steward, fitzErfast, as evidence of my regard for his service.

My pregnancy continued well, for which I thanked the Virgin Mary every day. From time to time I was indisposed, but I found that much of my energy returned now that I was past the first few months. My belly had rounded out, its plumpness pleasingly displayed by the jewelled girdle that I wore often. I spent much time in prayer, asking that my confinement would not be injurious to either myself or the child, and that the child would prove a son and healthy. Alianor and Isabel both suggested good midwives they knew in London, for it appeared I would not return to Pengraic before the birth.

Overall, the weeks that Raife was away passed pleasantly enough and with little to note, save for three incidents, the last of which, occurring the night before Raife returned, destroyed my hard-won complacency.

The first incident I put behind me quickly. It was the second week that Raife was away, and I lay fast asleep in our bed. As Raife liked, so I had come to like, and I had no sleeping companions, either in my bed or in the chamber: Isouda and Evelyn both slept in a chamber nearby.

I woke, suddenly. I thought I could hear snuffling in the chamber, as if a snotty child was rummaging through one of the chests. I could also smell something horribly malodorous — like dog droppings left to steam in a puddle of water in the sun. I was so confused by this, the soft noises and the terrible odour, that I sat bolt upright.

'What's this?' I said, peering into the blackness.

There came a bang, as if of a chest slamming shut, then a slight scuffling sound, then nothing. I sat, terrified, my heart pounding, the bed covers clutched to my chest.

'Who's there?' I cried, louder this time, my voice thin with fright.

There came a banging from outside the door, and it suddenly opened.

It was one of the house servants who slept in the chamber beyond. He carried a candle.

'My lady? What is wrong?'

'There was someone here!'

The man shouted instantly for aid, and within moments two guards had appeared, weapons to hand.

They looked about, but there was no one. No place to hide and the shutters on the window were securely closed and bolted on the inside.

'There is no one, my lady,' one of them said.

My heart had ceased pounding now.

There was no one.

Even the odour had vanished.

'I must have had a dream,' I said. 'I am sorry for disturbing your rest, but thank you for coming so quickly.'

Isouda and Evelyn had appeared by now, too, their faces worried as they clutched robes about them.

By now I was feeling severely embarrassed. 'A dream only,' I said again. 'A night vapour.'

'Would you like one of us to stay, my lady?' Isouda said.

'No, no,' I said. 'Go back to your beds.'

I lay awake once everyone had gone, but I convinced myself as I had the others that it had been nothing but a dream, and I drifted back to sleep within a short while.

Three days later I was at court when I found myself talking with Maud de Gernon, wife to the Earl of Chestre. We had been taking part in a lively game of bowls down the centre of the lesser hall and now sat drinking small beer by one of the fires.

'I have heard,' she said, as we watched two squires further down the hall start pushing each other in the chest over some slight, 'that Madog ap Gruffydd came to parley with your husband.'

'Yes,' I said, 'it was a tense day.'

Maud laughed. 'I can imagine! His name is cursed in our Marches. He has caused such terrible dismay and destruction.'

'So Raife has said.'

'Thankfully most of his raids have stopped now that we have his wife.'

Instantly, my interest in the Welsh princess was renewed. 'Where is she now?' I said.

Maud looked at me with round eyes. 'Here! Beneath our very feet! Both Edmond and my husband felt it too dangerous to keep her within the

Marches — saints alone know what Madog might have been capable of if he thought she were near — so now she lives in an apartment on the ground floor of the Tower.' She gave a little shrug. 'It is commodious enough, and airy, and less chill than her Welsh homeland.'

Here? Beneath our feet? Our conversation turned to other matters, but my mind kept worrying over the presence of the princess below.

Later I had opportunity to speak with Edmond privately.

'My lord king,' I said. 'You know that Madog came to parley with Raife?'

He gave a nod.

'Madog spoke of his worry about his wife and son, and now I hear they are confined to an apartment on the ground floor of this tower. I said, perhaps foolishly, that if I could I would let his wife know of his love and care. May I have your permission to visit his princess?'

Edmond studied me, and I could see he struggled between the yea and the nay. 'Be careful she does not use you, Maeb. You are not yet as studied in court-craft and intrigue as she is.'

'I will be careful, my lord.' I hesitated. 'My lord, I am a young wife, and I know the fears and uncertainties that go with that. I can imagine her fear as she is confined so far from her husband and her worries over her child.'

'The boy died last spring.'

'Oh! Then she must be in need of comfort and —'

'Maeb, *be careful!*'

I thought he was warning me only of the princess, and I did not, *could* not, think through other dangers. Despite all my new-found confidence at court, I *was* still a novice at court-craft and intrigue and could not see the trap.

I contented myself with looking at the king appealingly, and eventually he sighed.

'It is against my better judgment, Maeb, but if you wish, then go. But, by God, be careful what you say and do! Do not trust her, do not carry anything out for her, nor anything in. *Nothing.* Yes?'

'Yes, my lord,' I said happily. 'Thank you, my lord.'

I went to see the princess the next day. I learned her name was Mevanou, and that she was not much older than myself.

A guard escorted me down the narrow stairs of the north-eastern tower to the lower level that was partially above, partially below ground. Here the large spaces had been partitioned into store rooms, dormitories for soldiers, and even a few cells for prisoners, but the guard led me past all of those until we reached the south-western portion of the tower where the space under the chapel crypt had been redesigned into a spacious apartment for the Welsh princess.

I admit to some nerves as the guard fumbled with the keys to the lock of the door, but when he opened it and announced my name in a gruff voice I put a smile to my face and walked through the door confidently.

I found myself in a commodious chamber, well furnished and most comfortable. It was lit by two narrow windows that looked onto the inner bailey, and in the far wall I could see a door into a privy chamber. The air felt a little damp, but there was a brazier burning to one side, and wraps enough to keep anyone warm.

A woman stood just before one of the windows, in a shaft of light. She was very small, and somewhat thin, and as she moved forward a step, out of the light, I saw that she had a pale complexion, her nose scattered with freckles, and dark red hair.

'My lady?' I said. 'I am Maeb, Countess of Pengraic. I have come on behalf of your husband, that you may know of his love and concern for you and …'

I stumbled to a halt.

'Our son?' she said. Mevanou did not speak French so well as her husband, and her voice had a heavy accent. 'Our son is dead, murdered by the malignant air within this prison. My husband's love and concern is no longer of any use to *him*.'

'Then may I offer it to you.' This conversation was not going the way I had thought it might. 'I spoke with your husband recently enough, and he —'

'Most likely misses me not. He has mistresses and bastard sons a-plenty to keep him warm.'

'But he has ceased raiding since you were seized. He must hold you in great affection!'

'If he has ceased raiding then there will be other reasons for it. The nearness of the plague, perhaps. Madog values *his* life before any others.'

'Then I am most sorry for you, my Lady Mevanou, to be so far from your homeland and so great a distance from any love and care. Would you like me to stay? I can share the gossip of the court, and —'

'Go,' she said. 'I have no interest in you, nor in your sympathetic cause, and most particularly I have no interest in the idle wife of one of the bastard Normans who keeps my land under a foreign yoke.'

Her voice was harsh and unyielding. I tried to summon yet more sympathy for her, but I felt as if I had been slapped in the face.

'Then I will bid you good day, Lady Mevanou,' I said, inclined my head slightly, and turned for the door.

Having been rejected so utterly, I did not go to see Mevanou again. I worried for her, and thought her forthright rudeness most likely a product of her grief and fear, but I did not want to thrust myself on her, nor suffer the sharpness of her tongue again. A few days later Edmond asked me what had happened and I told him.

'She is a vicious witch,' he said. 'I think sometimes that Madog is grateful Chestre took her. So is your crusade of sympathy over, my lady?'

'I am afraid so, my lord,' I said ruefully. 'It took her but a few brief moments to learn to hate me, and I do not want to anger her further by visiting her again.'

'You took nothing to her, nor carried anything hence?'

'No, my lord king, I was most careful.'

'Good, but it is best if you speak of this to no one.'

'Yes, my lord.'

The third incident still leaves me, after all these years, shaking in fear.

I had woken in the middle of the night and could not get back to sleep. The weight of the child was bothering me, I had a deep ache in my head and my legs cramped continuously. I decided to rise and walk a little, perhaps go down to the chapel and pray, and then return to bed to see if I could find some sleep before dawn.

I slid out of bed, shivering in the cool night, and slipped into a warm, loose robe. I opened the door, walking into the chamber beyond mine. Here slept always one of the household's servants, and a candle always kept burning.

I used the candle to light another, my slight noise rousing the servant from his sleep.

'I am just going down to the chapel,' I said. 'I am well, but cannot sleep. Stay where you are.'

He nodded, fell back to his bed, and was asleep again almost instantly.

I moved as silently as I could through the house. It was very quiet, although there was soft noise coming from the hall where a couple of the knights or squires who slept there must have been talking softly. I crept past the entrance to the hall and down the tight circular stairs to the crypt beneath the house, where lay the chapel.

As I padded down the steps I thought I heard a slight noise from the chapel, but thought little of it. It might have been someone else visiting the chapel at night, it might have been a rat … it might have been the result of any number of innocent actions. I simply did not think for a moment it might be something malevolent.

Vicious.

I reached the last step into the crypt and then turned to my left toward the part that was used as a chapel.

And stopped dead, so terrified I could not move, nor utter a sound.

The candles were burning in the chapel and I could see clearly.

An imp from hell, standing with his back to me, pissing against the altar, whistling some devilish tune softly through his snout.

I knew what it was instantly, for it was a perfect brother to the one I had seen in the palace in Oxeneford. It had the same lumpish body, the same forked, snaking tail, the same thin, stick-like limbs.

And, as it turned at the slight sound I had made as I gasped in horror, the same round, pig-snouted, sharp-toothed visage.

It hissed when it saw me, then it shook its cock free of dribbles, and turned to face me fully.

'The master's bitch,' it said, its forked tongue glistening as it slipped in and out of its mouth during speech. I backed against the wall in horror. I wanted to flee, but for the moment my limbs were frozen and I could not move.

The imp took a step toward me. 'Bitch,' it said again. 'Hell awaits all murderers!'

Terrified, sure it was going to drag me down to hell then and there, I finally rediscovered my capacity for movement and, throwing the candle at the horror, I turned into the stairwell and scrambled up, screaming for aid.

Men came tumbling out of the hall.

'My lady! My lady! What is it?'

'The chapel,' I managed to say. 'The chapel!'

Half a dozen men piled down the stairs. I could hear them below, searching and shouting.

Eventually, several of them returned.

'There is nothing, my lady,' one said, 'except a terrible odour.'

I felt coldness seep through me. As soon as the man had mentioned it, I remembered that I, too, had smelled the stink as the imp stepped toward me.

It was the same stink I'd smelled in my chamber the night I'd woken thinking there was someone in the chamber.

There *had* been someone in the chamber with me.

The imp. Snuffling through one of my chests.

I bent over, and was sick.

I told no one of what I had seen. I remembered how Raife had asked me not to speak of the imp that we'd seen in Edmond's palace in Oxeneford, and so I held my silence this time, too.

I did not wonder why the imp had called me 'the master's bitch'. All I could think of was that it had promised me hell for what I had done.

For the rest of that night I had Evelyn sleep with me in my bed.

CHAPTER NINE

Raife arrived the next day in the late morning. There was much clattering of horses' hooves in the courtyard, and men and dogs milling about, and I tried not to rush down the stairs to reach him. He smiled as soon as he saw me — a wide genuine smile — and I thought I'd never been so glad to see anyone in my life as I was to see Raife.

He came over, clasped my shoulders, and kissed me soundly. 'How do you, wife?'

'I do well, my lord,' I said, wanting only to speak to him privately. 'Perhaps —'

'The child?'

'The child does well, too, my lord. Can we —'

But Raife had turned away and was shouting at one of the grooms to take care of his courser.

It seemed to take half my life for my husband to escape the clamour of the courtyard, traverse the hall (where countless squires, knights and sundry nobles seemed to want his attention), up the stairwell and into our private apartments. There I had to engineer the departure of Charles, Isouda and Evelyn and fitzErfast as well as a small boy who seemed to be scrambling about directionless.

But, finally, I had Raife alone.

He came over, smiling, kissed me, and laid a hand on my belly. 'The child has grown handsomely in my absence, I see by the size of your belly.'

'Raife —'

He kissed me once more, deeply and passionately, and I realised he had missed me perhaps as much as I had missed him.

I pulled my face away. 'Raife, twice while you were gone an imp has been here.'

His face went white. Both his hands gripped my upper arms. '*What?*'

'Once I woke and the vile thing was snuffling about my belongings, and last night,' my voice was rising into hysteria but I could not help it, 'I went to the chapel late and one was pissing on the altar. Sweet Jesu, Raife! What is happening?'

Raife just stared at me. I think he was so shocked that he could not say anything for the moment.

'They were just like the imp we saw in the palace at Oxeneford.' I had not actually *seen* the one in my chamber at night, but I was not going to split hairs over the issue. It *had* been an imp.

Now I burst into tears — I was still terrified from the previous night. 'What is happening, Raife? Why are they in our house? Do they follow Edmond?'

He gave me an odd look at that, but quickly replaced it with one of concern, then held me tightly in his arms.

'It is Hallow's Eve today,' he said. 'Perhaps the gates between hell and our world have opened. I will have a priest reconsecrate the chapel, and bless this chamber. That will keep them at bay.'

He leaned back, looking me in the face and using one hand to wipe away my tears. 'These are bleak times indeed, Maeb, if imps scramble about unhindered. Maybe it is simply because of All Hallow's Eve when the borderlands thin between our world and that of the dead. Perhaps the imps are here to spread plague ... we need to take care and keep good watch.'

They might be here to spread plague? Jesu!

'I did not tell anyone about the imps. Not even Isouda or Evelyn.'

Relief suffused his face. 'You are a true wife to me, Maeb.' He kissed me, then hugged me tight to him once more. 'It is best if we keep this to ourselves as we did the other imp. In this court, who knows how it could be used against us? Oh Maeb, I won't leave you again, I swear.'

'Raife, it said ... it said that I would go to hell for what I'd done to ... to ...'

'Shush, shush. It said that only to torment you. Has not Owain taken your confession? Have you not done penance? Perhaps, to be certain, we can donate some gold to Holy Trinity Priory in your name. What more can we do? Maeb, do not worry on it. You will not go to hell. You will *not*.'

I hugged him tight, allowing him to reassure me. 'It *stank*, Raife!'

'I know, sweetheart, I know,' he murmured into my hair, and then he kissed the crown of my head, and rocked me back and forth.

'Dear sweet God,' I thought I heard him whisper. 'What did it want, if I were not here?'

'Raife?'

'Nothing,' he said. 'I will keep you safe. From everything. Trust me.'

We had thought to spend a quiet day. Raife had been riding hard to get home and I wanted to compose myself after the previous night. But in the afternoon, just as we were about to go to the hall to dine, the Earl of Pembroke, Gilbert de Clare, arrived and asked to speak with us privately in our chamber.

I thought perhaps he wanted to speak with Raife, and so spoke to excuse myself, but Pembroke waved me to sit as well.

'Fulke d'Ecouis has reappeared in London,' he said without preamble. 'I saw him riding toward the Templar church in High Holborn earlier today.' He paused. 'I have been informed, very privately, that he has been in Witenie these past weeks.'

Pembroke looked at me and I felt a flush of guilt redden my cheeks even though I had nothing to be guilty of so far as Witenie and my father were concerned.

'The village where I was born?' I said. 'By all the saints, Gilbert, what was he doing there?'

'Making enquiries about your father, Maeb,' Pembroke said. 'And about you. It is said he begged hospitality at the house once owned by your father ... the Templars had leased it to a knight from Oxeneford.'

'And no doubt d'Ecouis searched it from top to bottom,' I said. 'I have *no* idea what he wants of me!'

Pembroke looked enquiringly at Raife, who told him briefly of the conversation Henry and d'Ecouis had had with me and of the manner in which they had frightened me.

'They seem convinced that my father had stolen from the Templars,' I said, 'and that I now have whatever it was they imagine my father took. Gilbert, I cannot speak for what my father may or may not have done while within the Order at Jerusalem, but if he did steal — which I dispute, for my father did not have that within him — then he did not hand the booty to me. I received nothing from him save his name and the clothes on my back. Rags and a bloodline. Nothing else.'

Pembroke sighed. 'It is hard to know what the Templars want,' he said. 'Their Order has grown extraordinarily since it was founded a few years ago. They answer to no one save the Pope. Even Edmond has no power over them. They come and go as they want, collecting ever more wealth and land as each year passes. They hold their secrets close, more so than most clergy.'

When Pembroke had gone, refusing politely an offer to dine with us, Raife asked me if there was anything my father could have given me that the Templars might covet.

'They seem to want gold and jewels,' I said. 'My father had *no* gold and jewels. No precious objects. Raife, when I say he left me nothing but rags, then rags was all he left me.'

When we retired that night, we lit the chamber with candles. We would sleep among light, lest the spirits and demons use the darkness of Hallow's Eve to slide across the divide from their world to ours.

The light cheered us, and I discovered what pleasure it could be to make love with my husband amid the flickering shadows of the candles.

PART FIVE

—◆●✧●◆—

CHRISTMASTIDE

CHAPTER ONE

Raife had hurried home for what Edmond liked to call his Advent court, some ten days of celebration, hunting, feasting and games before the commencement of Advent on Martinmas. Advent, the weeks leading up to Christmastide, was a quiet time of reflection before the celebration, feasting and fun of the Christmastide court. Edmond, renowned for his hospitality and the cheer and festivity of his Advent and Christmastide courts, expected all of his leading nobles to attend both celebrations.

Today, Hallowmas, was the first day of Advent court. Raife was tired from his hard ride back to London, I was fatigued from the events of the past two days, but nonetheless we rose before dawn, dressed and, without breaking our fast, left the house just as the eastern sky was lightening to ride for the Conqueror's Tower. Many of the household came with us: Raife's valet, Charles; Isouda and Evelyn; fitzErfast; many of the knights and squires of Raife's court; grooms, pages, soldiers, falconers, servants; Raife's head huntsman Wulfsige; his Master of Horse, Ludo; Raife's hunting dogs and his three gyrfalcons with their attendants.

To all intents and purposes we were moving our household (or an attenuated version thereof) to the Conqueror's Tower for Advent court (and as we would also for Christmastide court). Advent court was to be so packed with activities and feasting that running to and fro, often in the dead of night, between the Tower and our house was simply impractical, so Edmond had assigned us generous quarters in one of the new buildings within the inner bailey.

Although I felt weary already at the idea of so much feasting and fun, I was glad to leave the Cornhill house for the time being. While we were gone, Raife had arranged for the prior of the Holy Trinity Priory to bring in priests to bless each room and reconsecrate the chapel.

It would feel clean on our return.

I could not bear the idea of birthing a precious, tiny baby in a house where imps roamed.

When we arrived within the inner bailey we immediately dismounted and left our household to settle us and them into our apartments while Raife and myself entered the Tower. We were greeted by Edmond's Constable of the Tower, Alan de Bretagne, the Earl of Richemont. He led us directly to Saint John's Chapel on the top floor of the Tower, where Hallowmas was to be marked with a service, and the participants in today's planned hunt were to be blessed.

The chapel, ablaze with candle and torchlight, was already crowded, people shuffling and coughing and rubbing hands beneath mantles in the cold air, and I think the crowd was much relieved when Edmond arrived. Prince Henry accompanied him, to my disappointment, for I had hoped he may have found something else to occupy himself this Hallowmas, but I suppose I had to expect him to attend Advent court. Also accompanying Edmond were two younger men, one only a boy, who, by reason of resemblance, were immediately apparent to me as his younger sons, Richard and John. I looked about for Adelaide, Edmond's queen, but if she, too, was attending Advent court, then the lucky woman must still be snuggled in her bed.

Once mass and prayers and blessings were done, we moved to the great hall, where lay food with which to break our fast. We did not sit down, but rather moved about, picking what we wanted, and supping of small beer and weak ale as we chatted with acquaintances, discussing the day ahead.

There was a buzz of excitement in the hall. Today was to be a festive hunt in the forests to the east of London. Almost all of the court, save the infirm, were to attend. When Raife and I (and our household) had ridden through the outer bailey earlier it had been a bustle of activity as huntsmen, grooms, falconers and houndsmen were moving their charges from stables, kennels and mews into the outer bailey ready for their masters to ride out.

I had never ridden to the hunt before, and was slightly anxious, but excited also.

'It will be more of a gentle ride through the fields, marshes and forests than a true hunt,' said Alianor, standing with me, and warmly wrapped in a fur mantle. 'Can you imagine this lot setting off at a gallop from Ald Gate? We would frighten any game into France within moments!'

'Then I am certain the men will be disappointed,' I said, 'for surely they would relish the opportunity to display their hunting prowess to their lady folk.'

'They will find something to slaughter,' Alianor said. 'No one will enjoy the day until a little blood be spilt. We will ride gently, my dear, in honour of your baby, and at the earliest opportunity will make our excuses and guide our horses to that field chosen for our picnic. There we shall make ourselves comfortable by the nearest brazier, sip spiced wine and, when our menfolk arrive, shall make loud praise about their prowess.'

I laughed, and prepared to enjoy the day.

We rode out not long after. We made a procession down the stairs, through the lesser hall, and then down the wooden stairs to the inner bailey where grooms held our horses for us. By now the sun was risen and the moisture of the night steamed from walls and cobbles. To my relief I saw that it was a cloudless day. It would be cold — this was the first day of winter — but it would not rain, and the sun would be welcome.

Raife was clearly looking forward to the day and the hunt. He jostled and shouted with the rest of the men, heated by excitement. As we rode out, Alianor on her pretty bay palfrey by my side, he came over with Gilbert Ghent.

He greeted Alianor, then looked to me. 'Are you well, wife?' he asked, and smiled at my nod.

'Ghent will ride with you today, to make sure you are kept safe,' Raife continued, his courser skittering beneath him, eager to be off.

I looked at Ghent, who was trying — and failing — to keep the disappointment from his face. No doubt he'd have much preferred to have ridden with the rest of the nobles at full chase.

'I am most glad of your company, sir,' I said, and gave him a sweet smile which I hoped was some compensation for his duty this day.

We rode in splendid procession out from the Conqueror's Tower and then north through the fields to Fenechirche Street, ignoring Tower Gate though it was the closest gate for us to exit London. Instead, Edmond wanted to ride in procession through eastern London and depart via Ald Gate. There were, I believe, several hundred among us: nobles, knights, squires, grooms, various huntsmen and falconers, servants accompanying the oxen-trundled carts that carried the tents and tables and food for our field feast, spare horses and, of course, the dogs, both hunting hounds and pleasure dogs, the latter running up and down the column of riders, barking with excitement and in constant danger of being trampled by horses over-excited by the noise and desperate to run.

As well as numerous, we were colourful. Everyone wore the best clothes they could that were also suitable for hunting. As the sun rose higher it glittered from buckles, jewelled sword belts and mantle clasps (I wore Edmond's gift). Pennants and banners fluttered from staffs. The horses were clad in their best harnesses and bright cloths covered their rumps. Dulcette was resplendent in scarlet leather and rump cloth embroidered with gold and turquoise. Her mane and tail had been washed yesterday and were left to wave and flow in the sun.

It was impossible not to enjoy myself. Many Londoners had come out to line Fenechirche Street and wave us on our way — their enthusiasm no doubt fed, as their stomachs were, by the meat pies Edmond had caused to be handed out. Horns sounded, bells rang, pipes and drums played, and gaiety filled the air. I sat Dulcette, Alianor by my side, and we smiled and dimpled and waved at the people lining the street. Even Gilbert Ghent overcame his disappointment at having to stay by my side and straightened in the saddle, doing his best to look like one of the Arthurian knights riding out on some romantic, idealistic quest.

We rode down Fenechirche, past Holy Trinity Priory (whose occupants I hoped were even now in our house, delousing it of imps), through Ald Gate (draped in huge banners depicting the king's devices), and past Saint Botolph's without Ald Gate, and thence down the road that led into the forests to the east.

As we reached the forest, the column halted, and split into two: those who would take their falcons down to the marshlands abutting the Thames to hunt heron, and those who wished to hunt boar, and perhaps even deer, in the forests. The wagons carrying the equipment and food for our field feast went with the heron hunters, for the field chosen to host our feast bordered both forest and marshlands.

Here Alianor and I split, too. Alianor loved to hunt with her falcon, and so she peeled off to join the hunting in the marshlands. I had hesitated, but eventually decided to stay with the main group who headed into the forest — to Ghent's evident relief.

Alianor gave me a quick kiss on the cheek and said we should meet up in the field later, and then she was off, calling to her falconer to join her.

Dulcette and I headed into the forest. This was relatively lightly wooded land, but with trees that were from ancient times. They stood all about us: elm, beech, oak, chestnut, and many others, mostly unleaved now, their ancient trunks twisted and gnarled and thick, their branches arching and winding overhead to provide a canopy as fine as any stone vault I had ever seen. The ground underneath was thickly carpeted in autumn leaves. Sunlight streamed from overhead in many-splintered sunbeams, piercing the thin morning mist which was still trapped among the trees.

I had never seen anything so beautiful, nor so peaceful.

I reined in Dulcette, letting the hunting party stream ahead, the dogs baying, the riders shouting. I just wanted to enjoy this mystical, ancient, comforting forest.

I rode for a while, grateful that the horses and their riders and the dogs had gone far ahead — I could just make them out at the limits of my hearing. Dulcette seemed content to pace along at an extended walk — I think she, too, revelled in the calm and peace of the forest.

Poor Ghent rode his horse behind me. I could hear the despondent thudding of its hooves into the soft carpet of leaves, and I thought both Ghent and horse must have wished desperately to be riding with the hunt.

I looked over my shoulder. Ghent and his horse, riding ten or so paces behind me, were bathed in bright dappled sunlight, so much so that I could barely make out any features of either horse or rider.

'I am most sorry, Gilbert,' I said, 'to be such a sluggard at the hunt.'

He made a deprecating gesture with his leather-gloved hand, managing to convey that somehow he, too, was enjoying the peaceful, sunlit ride. Happier, I turned back to the path, sitting so relaxed that I thought I could almost doze in the comparative warmth of the forest.

After a while I *did* actually catch myself dozing, and thought that perhaps I should make my way to the field where we were to feast. Hopefully by now the servants would have set up braziers and chairs, and I could doze in more safety there than on Dulcette's back in the forest.

I turned again in the saddle. 'Gilbert,' I said, 'which way to the field where we are to dine?'

He was still bathed by the bright sun which glinted from every piece of maille that he wore, his concealing helmet, and his gold and silver surcoat. Strange, I had been sure that Ghent had been wearing a blue surcoat earlier, and certainly no maille or helmet, but maybe I had been too excited to take true note. I thought he said something, though I did not quite catch it, but he pointed to the south, turning his horse that way, and so I likewise turned Dulcette and we made our way through the trees.

Ghent rode by my side, now, at a similar distance as he had ridden behind. I had a clearer view of his horse from this perspective, and realised that it was completely white, and that its wavy mane was so long and thick it trailed upon the ground, catching at the leaves. The mane appeared to have diamonds woven through it, as did the horse's flagged tail.

Strange I had not noticed that before and I wondered where Ghent had found such a courser, and where he had obtained the fistfuls of diamonds that littered its tresses.

We rode on. Often trees separated us, and we wove in and out of the ancient forest like partners caught in some sunlit, silent dance, our only music the soft hoof-falls of the horses, our only guide the path laid down by the sunbeams. Sometimes I blinked and thought there were other riders with us, too, noiselessly weaving their way in and out of the trees. Other times I thought a silver wolf, his coat rippling with light, walked majestically with us, but when I opened my mouth to mention the wolf to Ghent, the wolf vanished.

Maybe it was all a trick of the bright light.

I felt an amazing peace. I had Ghent to watch over me, and his presence comforted me immensely. At one point I thought he said something to me about the deaths of Stephen, Rosamund and John, that they were safe and contented and there was no guilt nor burden for me to carry over the manner of their passing. But when I turned my head to answer Ghent (being somewhat surprised that he should talk to me of this), I saw that he was almost twenty paces away, his horse still weaving silently in and out of the trees, in and out. As he was too far away for conversation, I thought I must have dreamed it.

Maybe the voice was a construct of my conscience, and its interaction with the tranquillity and beauty of the forest and its almost unearthly light.

Yet, somehow, even now I can still hear the voice, and am sure *someone* must have spoke the words.

I know that this ride cleansed my soul of guilt, and that from this day forward I remembered Stephen, Rosamund and John with uncomplicated love.

Eventually, too soon for me, Ghent reined in his magnificent horse and nodded ahead, and I saw that beyond the trees lay a field festooned with colourful tents, pennants fluttering at their peaks.

If ever you need me, he said, *call for me. I will always protect you.*

I sighed, deeply reluctant to give up the serenity of this ride, and thanked Ghent for his trouble and the companionable nature of his guardianship.

But he was gone and I frowned in puzzlement. How could he have vanished so quickly? Had he been so anxious to rejoin the hunt?

I rode from forest to field, shaking off my almost dreamlike state, and raised a smile as I saw Alianor standing before a brazier, warming her hands.

'How was the hunt?' I asked her, as a groom hurried to help me dismount. She grimaced and said that the herons had flown away from the marshes during the night, and there were none left to hunt.

Even the falcons were sulking.

We settled in chairs, taking the warmed wine a servitor brought us. Most of the other falconers had returned as well, and the field was bright with colour and chatter and movement.

'Look,' said Alianor, 'here come the forest hunters!'

I turned in my chair slightly, and there, indeed, came a procession of riders out of the forest. At their head was Raife, riding his horse hard.

Gilbert Ghent was just behind him. Raife was shouting something, and only after a moment did I realise it was my name.

Someone, a falconer, pointed to where Alianor and I sat, and Raife rode over to us at such an abandoned pace that servants and cooks and other dismounted hunters scattered to avoid his steaming horse.

'Maeb!' Raife jumped down from his horse. 'You are well?'

I frowned. 'Of course. Raife, what is this fuss?'

'You vanished from the forest and this … this bastard cur of a dog,' he indicated Ghent, who was standing behind looking deeply chastened, 'had misplaced you. We feared you were still lost among the trees!'

'Well, as you can see, I am perfectly safe and well, and was enjoying the peaceful sun until you rode up. But what is this about Ghent? He accompanied me all the way to the forest edge.'

I looked to Ghent to confirm this, and with a sudden drop of my stomach realised he was, indeed, wearing a blue surcoat.

Not the gold and silver surcoat of my companion.

Ghent wore no helmet or maille, unlike my companion.

His horse was a chestnut, not the white, diamond-gilded mount of my companion.

'My lady,' Ghent said, 'I did not. I lost you soon after we entered the forest.'

'But …' I said.

'Maeb?' said Raife. 'What is it? Did someone follow you?'

'A knight accompanied me,' I said. 'I thought it was Gilbert, but the sunlight made it hard to see properly. I was *sure* it was Gilbert! But he wore a gold and silver surcoat … not that blue that Gilbert wears now.'

Raife and Gilbert exchanged glances, Gilbert giving a slight shake of his head.

'I have seen no one wearing a surcoat of that description,' said Raife. 'Alianor?'

She gave a shake of her head also.

'What did he say?' Raife said. 'What devices did he wear?'

'He said nothing. And the sun was so bright … it glinted so from his maille, his surcoat, his helmet, that I could make out no devices. I … I was so certain it was Gilbert that I did not look close, nor question him. He led me straight here.'

I paused. 'It could have been anyone,' I said, 'among all this crowd.'

But no matter how much I looked about while we dined that day in the sunny field, I saw no knight wearing a silver and gold surcoat, nor dressed in helmet and maille.

CHAPTER TWO

When we returned from the hunt we partook of a light and informal meal in the great hall, then Raife and I retired to our private chambers in the new buildings in the inner bailey. We were both weary and looking forward to some time to ourselves.

Our chambers were spacious and well appointed, on the first floor of a large building that looked over the inner bailey to the wooden stairs leading into the Conqueror's Tower. We sat in the solar by a window, drinking ale and watching people come and go from the Tower. Most of the hunters had by now either retired to the chambers or dormitories Edmond had appointed for them, or had left the Tower for lodgings or homes elsewhere in London.

Evelyn, Isouda and Charles had left us alone, going for their meal in a hall directly below us.

'What happened today?' Raife said.

'I don't truly know,' I said. 'I was riding in the forest, and I had reined Dulcette back so I could enjoy its tranquillity and beauty. A knight rode with me. I was *sure* it was Ghent, even though I thought his surcoat different and his horse too fine.'

'Describe the surcoat and horse.'

'The surcoat I could not distinguish to any degree, save that it glittered with gold and silver thread. His horse … oh, Raife, it was magnificent. A white courser, his mane dragging on the ground, and with diamonds twisted throughout. Now, of course, I know that it could not have been Ghent, but then I was in such a dream and so trusting.'

I had thought Raife might have been angered with me, but he was not.

'He did not speak?'

I thought of the words I'd thought he'd said, and of his promise that he would be there to protect me whenever I needed it, but were they true words, or not?

'No,' I said, 'he did not speak.'

Raife was looking out the window, as if transfixed by what was happening in the inner bailey, but I knew my husband enough to know that the twitching in his jaw meant he was thinking deeply.

'There are legends,' he said, speaking slowly and turning to look at me again, 'that sometimes mortals wander onto the paths of the Old People. The ancient, lost falloways of this land. Mayhap that is what happened to you.'

'I became lost down one of the ancient paths of the Old People? One of these falloways?'

'Perhaps.'

I pondered that. The falloway had felt so peaceful, so enchanting.

'Are these ancient paths, these lost falloways, dangerous?' I said.

'Did you feel in danger?'

'No. I felt utterly safe.'

'Well, then.' Raife gave another slight, almost disinterested shrug.

'And the knight?'

'A guide perhaps?'

'Raife, what do you know of the legends of the Old People? I heard some of them while I was at Pengraic Castle, and saw three of the village women lay flowers and … and a dead cockerel on Stephen's grave. Owain said that you allowed that. You must know some of the legends.'

'Are you interested?'

'Yes. Yes, I am.'

'The legends of the Old People still hold powerful sway over the folk of the west of this isle, Maeb. Not so much in England, not in these southern and eastern Christian lands, but in the west, in the mountains and the forests, where the Church has a weaker grip. I was raised with these legends along with my nurse's milk, at Pengraic.'

'What are these legends, Raife? Who are these "Old People"?'

'The Old People are supposed to be an ancient, and somewhat mystic, race who lived in harmony with the mountains and forests and the beasts who lived within, as well as with the circling of the sun and moon and the stars in the heavens above. As for the legends, they are mostly that the Old People never really left this land, nor died out, they just vanished down these lost falloways. A long, long time ago. Many hundreds of years, maybe even thousands. No one knows why. The legends say that sometimes the Old People can reach out to us, or that we can somehow touch them. But they are legends only, Maeb.'

'But still powerful in people's minds.'

'Yes, thus I allow the villagers at Crickhoel to visit the ancient sacred heartstone in the chapel at Pengraic. It is of no consequence, Owain does not mind and it gives some peace to people who often find little enough of that in their daily lives.'

Owain and the villagers, I thought, possibly worshipped the Old People as much as they did our sweet Lord Jesu.

'Raife, why did you inter Stephen under the heartstone?'

Raife sighed, and looked out the window as if distancing himself from the question.

'It was the most beautiful place I could think of for him,' he said finally, very softly.

My eyes filled with tears. I always had known that Raife loved Stephen, but this …

'Raife —'

He rose from his chair. 'Come, wife. We shall retire early. Edmond has us up at dawn for yet another day of games.'

We were in our bed shortly thereafter. Raife went to sleep almost immediately, but I lay sleepless for hours. I was deeply fatigued and badly wanted to sleep, but my head was still full of thoughts about what had happened today, and as well both my back and head ached, my bladder complained, my legs cramped, and the baby twitched as if it still enjoyed the hunt.

At some point, deep into the night, and when all noise from the inner bailey had ceased, I grew tired of laying still in bed, trying not to move lest it wake Raife, and so decided I would rise, don a warm robe and shoes, and perhaps stroll about the inner bailey for a while. Maybe that would make me sleepy.

I rose cautiously, trying not to wake Raife, but my efforts were in vain.

'Maeb. Are you going to the privy?'

'I am going for a walk outside, Raife. I cannot sleep, I ache and I need some air.'

'Maeb —'

'I will take Evelyn with me. Raife, we cannot possibly be safer than we are here, within the Conqueror's Tower. Do not fear that the Old People will snatch me!'

He chuckled a little, and mumbled something else, but made no further protest, and I think he was fast asleep by the time I opened the door of our privy chamber and crept through into the solar.

Here Isouda and Evelyn slept, and I shook Evelyn awake, and told her I needed her to accompany me for a short walk.

She muttered complaints under her breath all the way out to the inner bailey.

The inner bailey was frosty and silent. Guards stood at the gate into the outer bailey, but otherwise there was no one else about. I tugged my mantle tighter about me, taking deep breaths, enjoying the stillness and the frost.

Evelyn muttered something, and I shushed her. I just wanted to walk and let my thoughts drift.

'My lady, I am *cold*,' Evelyn said.

'Then stand in the doorway until I am done,' I said tersely, nodding to the deep porch over the door leading to the building which housed our chambers.

Happier now I was on my own, I did several circuits of the inner bailey, murmuring a greeting to the guards as I passed them. My leg cramps eased, and my head and back aches almost disappeared, and I was just about ready to go back indoors when I heard a slight sound from a window close by.

I stopped. I was standing right by the southern wall of the Tower, and I realised with a little start that these windows must belong to the chamber where Madog's wife, Mevanou, was confined. I stepped closer, hugging my mantle ever tighter.

'Mevanou?'

I thought I saw a glimpse of a white face.

'Mevanou?'

Then nothing. The face vanished.

Silence.

I sighed and decided it was time for my bed. I walked back to the porch and accompanied a grateful Evelyn back to our chambers.

We woke in the hour before dawn. I was stiff and cold after only a few hours' sleep, and now it was my turn to moan and complain as we rose. We dressed, but did not break our fast.

Edmond had planned a dawn meal and bonfires in the fields beyond the outer bailey to celebrate All Souls Day.

I thought he was mad.

But at least there would be bonfires.

We proceeded to the field beyond the outer bailey on foot, as it was not far. Once we were across the bridge we could see the bonfires Edmond had caused to be made, and other nobles arriving on horseback from London.

Raife and I made for the nearest bonfire.

Edmond was already here, moving among the groups standing huddled about the fires, looking cheerful. Evelyn and Isouda, who had accompanied us, moved elsewhere and to my surprise I saw Evelyn talking briefly with Prince Henry.

I thought that I would later ask her of what they spoke, but also reminded myself that she possibly knew him from the time she had been close to Edmond.

Henry of Blois, the Bishop of Wincestre, led us in prayers for the dead and then, official duties done, we were free for revelries for the day.

For most of us, that started with warm food and an even warmer place by one of the bonfires.

I had just taken a trencher filled with a stew of meat, and was congratulating myself on a good place by a fire, when there came a distant shout.

It took me a moment to orientate myself. Then, following the direction others looked, I turned to the Tower.

It rose, gilded almost pink in the dawn light, its parapets picked out by the first rays of the sun.

Something was happening on top of the Tower.

I heard Edmond shout something, and I saw soldiers, who had been standing about, race for the Tower.

I quickly sought out Raife for reassurance — he was standing not so far from me — then looked back to the Tower.

Soldiers on the parapets were chasing someone ... a woman I thought by the flying hair behind her. She ran from the north-western tower along the parapets toward the south-west tower.

But there, suddenly, soldiers appeared and the woman stopped halfway. She desperately turned this way and that, and then, horribly, she leaned over the parapets and, just as a soldier grabbed at her, fell.

I watched her tumble over and over all the way down, my heart in my mouth, my trencher of food now splattered on the ground before me, only losing sight of her as she fell beneath the height of the outer curtain wall of the outer bailey.

Silence.

Then people started running and shouting.

Raife was beside me. 'Who?' he wondered aloud.

I did not need a close inspection of the body to know who it had been, for her red hair had floated out behind her all the way down to the ground.

'Mevanou,' I said. 'Wife of Madog.'

Soldiers were scrambling about the outer bailey, into which Mevanou had fallen. Raife and I were among the first to arrive into the outer bailey. Like everyone else, we hurried over to where Mevanou had fallen.

Immediately I wished I hadn't. Mevanou had first fallen onto the roof of the falcon mews, and then slid onto a grassy patch to one side.

Her face and upper body were covered in blood, her limbs lying at odd angles.

She was not moving.

People gathered. The scene was made even more gruesome by the shrill cries of the falcons in their mews, disturbed as they had been by the terrible bang on their roof.

'Who —' someone asked, and I opened my mouth to answer, but Prince Henry spoke before I could.

'It is Mevanou, wife of Madog ap Gruffydd.'

'But how did she escape her chambers?' Edmond said, stepping forward.

Henry looked straight at me. 'I think we should ask the Countess of Pengraic that,' he said.

Everyone looked at me, then, but in my shock I saw only one face and registered its expression.

It was Edmond, and his face was swathed in reluctant suspicion.

CHAPTER THREE

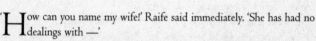

'How can you name my wife!' Raife said immediately. 'She has had no dealings with —'

'I am afraid she has, Pengraic,' Edmond said. 'While you were away tending your estates I know she visited Mevanou on at least one occasion.'

Raife turned to look at me, his face equal parts anger and worry.

'And again last night,' Henry said, 'she went to the Welsh princess' window. Did the countess pass Mevanou something? A key?'

'No,' I said, 'I was walking the inner bailey only.'

'And yet you went straight to her window,' Henry said. 'Why?'

'I thought I heard something,' I said. 'I looked and realised it was Mevanou's window, and thought I saw her face, so I went over.'

'Murder and death follow you everywhere, don't they, countess?' Henry said, and I felt cold fear slide down my spine.

'We take this inside,' said Edmond. 'Now.'

'You went to see Mevanou?' Raife hissed at me as we climbed the wooden stairs into the Tower. He had his hand tight about my elbow and I gave an experimental tug to see if he would release me.

No.

'Once only,' I said. 'How can Henry accuse me of —'

'And last night?'

'As I said, Raife! And as I told you last night! I was walking to relieve my cramps and aches, when I thought I heard —'

327

We had reached the top of the steps and Raife pulled me almost roughly into the lesser hall. In front and behind us tramped what I thought was a horde of people. Whatever Henry wished to accuse me of, it did not seem as if it would be before any lesser number people than had been outside.

'God's mercy,' Raife muttered. 'Henry would not have come into the open with his accusations if he didn't have certain intelligence. What does he *know*, Maeb?'

'I don't know!' I said. 'I don't know!'

'I had trusted you not to betray me, Maeb. *Trusted* you!'

I wanted to reply, or defend myself, but Raife dragged me down the hall, then to the stairs inside the north-eastern tower. It was dark and close inside, and I was beginning to feel very sick.

It was a relief to step into the gallery on the third level.

We went straight to the great hall. Edmond led us to one of the fireplaces and gestured me into a chair before it. Raife stood just behind me, a hand on my shoulder. People gathered about, a few score, maybe even more. There were many nobles present — Alianor and her husband Robert de Lacy (Alianor looking worried), Chestre, Pembroke, Richemont, the Bishop of Wincestre, and many others. Fulke d'Ecouis was here, too, and somehow I was not surprised.

Henry stood to the fore, looking calm and certain.

'What is this about?' Edmond said.

'The Countess of Pengraic,' Henry said, 'had become close to Mevanou, wife of Madog ap Gruffydd. She —'

'That is not true —' I began.

'Peace, my lady,' Edmond said. 'You shall have opportunity for your say in turn.'

'The countess had promised Madog that she would look after his wife and aid her in every way she could,' Henry continued. 'The countess was much taken with Madog, with his handsome face and sly, cunning manner. One must wonder what she promised him.'

Where had he heard this?

I knew. I knew almost as soon as I thought the words and my heart sank. Henry would know almost everything.

'The countess stood close by Mevanou's window last night. She dismissed her attending woman so she could do this alone. Did she pass

Mevanou a key? Most probably, for Mevanou let herself out this morning, and —'

'Let me speak to the guard at her door,' Edmond said, and we waited in stiff silence until the man was fetched.

He was pale and sweaty, as he thought he had every right to be.

Everyone else in the hall knew differently. The guard would not be carrying the blame for this.

'Soldier,' said Edmond. 'What happened at the Lady Mevanou's door this morning? How did she manage to leave her chamber?'

'I went to the kitchens to bring her food so she could break her fast,' the soldier said. 'When I left the door was locked and there was no one else about. When shortly I returned, the door was standing open and the lady had fled.'

'Can the door be unlocked from the inside?' Edmond asked.

'Yes, my lord,' said the soldier.

Next Edmond called for the two guards who had stood at the gateway between the inner and outer baileys last night.

They confirmed what Henry had said, that Evelyn and I had walked about the inner bailey together, then I had sent her to the porch, while I walked over to stand close by Mevanou's window.

'My lady,' Edmond said to me, 'had you anything to do with the Lady Mevanou's escape?'

I stood. 'No, my lord king. I did visit Mevanou once, as you know, out of obligation because I had said to Madog that I would seek her out and pass to her his love and concern. But I did not linger, for Mevanou found my visit unwelcome, and she was most impolite to me.

'I did not return a second time. As for last night, I rose to walk as I was sleepless, and my limbs and back were cramped and achy. I thought a soft walk in the night air might make me sleep. So I went outside with my woman Evelyn, and we walked. But Evelyn did not like the cold, thus I said she could wait for me under the porch leading to our chambers. Then, as I walked once more about the inner bailey, I thought I heard a noise at one of Mevanou's windows, and I thought I saw a face, so I thought it only courteous of me to wish her a good night. When I reached the window no one was there, so I returned, with Evelyn, to our chambers.'

Edmond looked to Henry, giving a slight shrug. 'Who is right?'

'It is not the first time the countess has been too close to death,' Henry said. 'Her husband, the earl, lost his entire family to plague, most of them at Pengraic. While no one disputes that his children *caught* the plague, there is dispute and rumour that some of them — Stephen, Rosamund and John — died, not by the plague, but by the countess' hand.'

'By God, Henry,' Edmond said, 'this is a most terrible accusation. If all you rely on is rumour, then this is a truly blackhearted thing you do.'

Henry held his father's gaze. 'Not just rumour, my lord father. I have a witness who states that the countess, or Mistress Maeb as she was then, confessed to her that she smothered the earl's two youngest children, as well as his eldest, Stephen. Within weeks she was betrothed to their father. Madam,' now he looked direct to me, 'how say you in this matter?'

'My conscience is clear.'

Henry's lip curled, then he looked to his father. 'My lord king, I have a credible witness to these murders — she will stand forth if needed — and no one can deny that the countess stands ill-placed for the Lady Mevanou's escape and subsequent death —'

'I did not push her over the parapets!' I said.

'So you admit aiding her escape?' Henry shot back at me. He gave me no time to reply, switching his attention to Edmond again. 'My lord king, according to the Westminster assizes, the law of the land requires that anyone who shall be found to be accused or notoriously suspect of having committed murder must be taken and put to the ordeal of fire.'

'No!' shouted Raife, but his voice was drowned out in the tumult that ensued.

CHAPTER FOUR

The hall was in an uproar. Many people were shouting. I know my husband, the king, Henry, Saint-Valery, and even the Templar, Fulke d'Ecouis, were doing so.

Eventually, Edmond managed to restore some order.

'I stand forth as witness for this woman,' said Alianor, literally taking a step forward. 'I attest to her good character and to her innocence.'

I was amazed. I had not thought it of Alianor, and her public support brought a film of tears to my eyes. She was a truer friend than I'd thought.

'And I,' said Saint-Valery, also stepping forward, and again I was somewhat taken aback at his support.

Another friend, truer than I'd ever given him credit.

There was more uproar.

I held up my hand. 'I am willing to take the ordeal of fire,' I said.

'No!' Raife said and, grabbing my elbow again, pulled me a little way distant so he could speak to me privately.

'Maeb, for mercy's sakes! You are with child ... we can easily appeal to have any ordeal or even further questioning put off until you have given birth, and by then ...'

'By then the rumours shall have grown larger,' I said, 'and more potent, and will be viewed as truth by most of England. This is an attack on you, my dear lord, and I shall not allow it. I know you have always feared that marrying me might somehow undo you, and —'

'This is not what I meant!'

'But what else, my lord? Do not fear for me. These accusations are false.' I pulled my arm free, and turned back to the crowd.

'I am innocent,' I said. 'My conscience stands bare and unstained before God. I shall take this ordeal of fire. Now. Before my Lord Henry can spread further false rumour to besmirch the Pengraic name.'

I met Henry's eyes boldly as I said this, and I was pleased to see a little uncertainty flower in his.

'My lady,' Edmond said, 'you do not have to do this.'

There was sadness and pain in his eyes, and I dipped before him, in acknowledgement of it.

'I do, my lord king,' I said. 'I have no fear.'

'Edmond,' Raife said, 'for Jesu's sake, *stop* this!'

'Do you fear your wife's guilt, Pengraic?' Henry said, the certainty back in his face now. 'Do you fear her ... burning?'

'Enough, Henry!' Edmond said. '*Enough!*'

'The lady consents to the ordeal,' Henry said. 'I suggest for her peace we get this over as quickly as possible. D'Ecouis, will you administer the —'

'No,' I said, 'not him. I wish the Bishop of Wincestre to administer the ordeal, if you please.'

Henry shrugged. 'Wincestre then. Will someone send for the blacksmith? And a brazier?'

'And I would ask that all the court who are close by attend this ordeal,' I said. 'I want to demonstrate my innocence in front of as many people as possible.'

Edmond nodded, and sent several squires scrambling to spread word.

Raife took me to one side again as Wincestre sent someone to fetch his book of rituals, someone fetched the blacksmith, and several guards set up a brazier, fetching hot coals from the fire.

'Mae ...' Raife said.

His voice was agonised, and I took both his hands in mine. 'Raife,' I said quietly, 'I will be safe. Trust me in this.'

'This is nothing but —'

'This is a chance for me to put a stop once and for all to the rumours. Henry has undoubtedly been voicing them far and wide. I have to do this, Raife. I *must*. I *will* be safe.'

He pulled his hands from mine and took my shoulders, so tightly he came close to hurting me. 'Maeb,' he said, almost hissing in his intensity, 'listen to me and *let me finish*. I can put a stop to this here and now. You have *no* idea of the power I can unleash if I have to. I will give up everything, Mae, for you. Everything. I cannot see you suffer. I *cannot*. I will throw away my dreams and all they mean to me to keep you safe!'

'No,' I said calmly. 'I cannot let that happen, and I *will* not.'

'Maeb, I *can* stop this. We *can* walk away from this. I have estates in Normandy. We can go there.'

I was horrified. Ruin everything, for me? No. *No*. This was what he had always feared I would do to him, and I would not allow it.

'I will *not* see you ruined,' I said, pulling myself away from him. 'Please, sweet Jesu, *trust* me!'

Wincestre came over. 'My lady countess,' he said, 'I offer you the choice of the boiling water, the hot iron, or the burning gauntlet.'

'The burning gauntlet,' I said.

Raife hissed. '*Maeb!*'

'Will you say a prayer with me, countess?' Wincestre said.

'Surely, my lord,' I said, and I bowed my head as he made the sign of the cross before me, and began a prayer.

At that moment I prayed more fervently than I have ever prayed before in my life.

But I did not pray to God, nor to his crucified son, nor to any of the saints in their heavenly court.

I prayed to my companion knight, and prayed that he had truly meant it when he'd said to me that he would always protect me.

'This has to stop!' Raife said, once Wincestre and I had finished our prayers. 'This *has* to stop!'

He moved away, seeking support from among the crowd, but Edmond grabbed him by the upper arm and pulled him back.

'No,' Edmond said, 'now this must go ahead. Your wife has consented. It *must* go ahead. God help me, Pengraic, *I* do not want this either, but even I cannot prevent it.'

Alianor came over and gave me a hug. 'God be with you,' she whispered.

I kissed her cheek. 'And with you, Alianor. Thank you.'

* * *

The ordeal was set up within the hour. Wincestre was already garbed in his clerical robes from the dawn ceremony, and needed only his ritual book. Two soldiers placed a brazier in the centre of the great hall and filled it brimful of coals from the fireplace, one of them fanning the heat with a small pair of bellows. The blacksmith arrived with several pairs of tongs and leather grab patches.

'My lady has chosen the burning gauntlet,' said Wincestre. 'Does anyone have —'

'Take mine.' Fulke d'Ecouis stepped forward. He held out a maille gauntlet, its upper surface covered in metal plates cunningly attached to the maille. 'I have large hands,' he said. 'The countess' delicate hand shall easily slide inside.'

Wincestre took the gauntlet, showed it to me and, at my nod, handed the gauntlet to the blacksmith who plunged it into the coals using a pair of tongs.

We waited. I looked to Raife, and tried to smile for him, but I could not quite manage it.

He looked agonised.

I looked also to Edmond.

His face was not much better.

The number of people in the hall continued to grow until it was full. Eventually Edmond had to command the guards at the doors to close them against latecomers.

Apart from the hiss of the coals, it was almost silent in the hall.

Up to now my anger had been sustaining my confidence.

Now doubts crept in and I felt nerves flutter in my belly. What if I was not right? What if the knight could not protect against *this*?

I looked about and caught Henry standing with d'Ecouis, both men regarding me with confident smiles on their faces, happy that at the very least they would be causing me agony, even if my wounds healed enough that Wincestre could declare my innocence.

To one side a man carried a bowl of water, salve and bandages to a small table. My hand would be bound at the end of the ordeal and, if the wounds had healed within three days, then innocence was mine.

If they weren't …

But I hoped that the bandages and salve would not be needed. I hoped …

'Madam?' Wincestre said, and I took a deep breath and nodded.

The bishop began the ritual, blessing those present, blessing the brazier and the now glowing gauntlet, and finally blessing me. He began a long rambling prayer, and, as he did so, I lowered my head and closed my eyes and prayed to the knight.

Help me, help me, help me now.

'Madam?'

I opened my eyes.

Wincestre stood before me, his prayers done.

There was utter silence.

I nodded, then stepped forward as the blacksmith used two pair of tongs to lift the glowing gauntlet from its bed of coals and hold the maille open about its wrist, so that I might slip my hand into it.

The blacksmith stepped forward, the gauntlet held out before him.

It glowed a dull red.

He was three paces away, but I could feel its heat even from here.

I closed my eyes again, praying now quite desperately.

A pause, then I lifted my head and opened my eyes.

There, at the very top of the hall, standing on the dais so I could easily see him over the heads of the crowd, was the knight on his magnificent courser.

Again I could not distinguish his features, for the light streamed through the archways from the windows in the gallery bathing the knight in an ethereal light, but I could make out the slight nod of his head.

I walked over to the blacksmith and, without any hesitation, slid my right hand into the gauntlet.

The top of the gauntlet came halfway up my forearm and I smelled the burning of the sleeve of my kirtle.

There was a collective gasp about the hall.

The knight led me down to the shores of a viridescent sea, the hoof-falls of his courser muffled in the packed, damp sand. I held on to his stirrup, that I might not fall nor lose my way.

The sea mist swirled about us, and I could not see the knight's face.

How damp and cool it is, the knight said, and I nodded, breathing in deeply of the salty air.

'Who are you?' I said, and I *sensed* a smile, but could not see it.

He did not answer.

The waves crashed and pounded, and the sea's spray wet my face and hair and soaked the hand and arm that held on to the knight's stirrup.

Eventually he sighed.

You must return.

Sweat poured down my face and body, sticking my clothes to my flesh. I could smell the stink of burning, hear the sizzling heat of the gauntlet.

'Enough!' cried Edmond, and I pulled my hand from the glove.

I hugged it to me for a moment, then held it out for all to see, palm outward.

My flesh was unmarked, my skin as white as when it had entered the gauntlet. My sleeve hung ruined from my arm, but my flesh was untainted.

Murmurs began, then cries of disbelief, and soon the hall was in as great a tumult as when Henry had first demanded the ordeal.

My whole body was shaking, but still I moved slowly forward, showing the unblemished hand and arm to any who would see it. Raife came to me, put his hands on my shoulders, begged me to come sit, but I shook my head and kept moving through the crowd.

I returned to Wincestre, and he inspected my hand, raising his face to mine in utter astonishment.

'Innocent!' he declared, and the hall once more erupted. I could see Alianor crying with relief, but there was one man I truly needed to face.

I walked to Henry.

'See,' I said, holding my hand up before him as Edmond shushed the crowd. '*See*. I am unblemished. Where lies the guilt *now*, Henry?'

Then I pulled back my shoulder and delivered the mightiest open-palmed blow I could to Henry's face.

He staggered back, then gave a sharp cry, clutching at his cheek.

Steam rose from between his fingers, and blood seeped down.

D'Ecouis grabbed at Henry's hands and pulled them away and, yet once more, the crowd gasped and moved.

The distinctive weave pattern of maille was burned deep into Henry's cheek.

'God has spoken,' I said, and turned away.

CHAPTER FIVE

❖⋘❀⋙❖

Raife hugged me to him so tightly he squeezed my breath away. 'Thank God,' he muttered over and over. 'Thank God.'

Edmond came over, resting a hand on Raife's arm to make him release me, if only slightly, and looked me direct in the eye.

'*Are* you well, Maeb?' he asked quietly.

'I am, my lord, if my husband can be persuaded not to crush my ribs.'

He gave a slight smile, then turned to the crowd.

'Hear me now,' he said, and his voice was angry and austere. 'Today God has judged the Countess of Pengraic of her guilt or innocence, and he has found her innocent. On that authority, should I ever hear another man or woman of this court spread vile rumour about either the Earl or Countess of Pengraic, then I shall hand them over to God's judgment *by the same means as was forced on the countess here today*. The slightest rumour, the slightest blackening of her name, and this gauntlet awaits.

'Blacksmith, cause a bracket to be made, and hang that gauntlet above the central fireplace to remind all who inhabit this hall, and enjoy my cheer, of my intent.

'D'Ecouis, you were glad enough to hand that gauntlet over for the ordeal. I can only assume you will be glad enough to lose it completely to this just cause.'

Edmond walked over to Henry, his anger evident in his stiff gait and upright body. 'You are a *fool!*' he hissed, grabbing at his son's chin so he could the more easily inspect the brand on his cheek. 'That mark shall never leave you now, even your beard will not grow over it. You have shamed my name this day, boy. Get you gone from my sight until I can find it within my ability to stand your presence again.'

He gave Henry's chin a wrench, making Henry stagger to keep his balance.

Henry shot me a glance full of hatred. 'Witch!' he hissed as he straightened.

Edmond took a single step forward and dealt Henry such a blow that the prince was catapulted several paces across the floor.

Then Edmond whipped about to Wincestre. 'Bishop,' he said, 'can that accusation stand?'

'No, my lord king,' Wincestre said. 'No witch could have endured both the prayers and the ordeal conducted under God's name. By God's grace and judgment, the Countess of Pengraic is a woman true and innocent.'

'Then get that churl out of my sight!' Edmond said to two guards standing nearby.

They hesitated an instant, then came forward, grabbed Henry under his arms, and half dragged, half supported him from the hall.

Edmond came over to me, took the hand that had endured the gauntlet, and kissed its palm gently.

'My lady,' he said, 'you grace my court and my heart.'

Raife took me back to our chambers. I was weak-kneed and shaking after what had happened, and needed rest, and I barely made it back to our privy chamber on my own legs.

But I could not rest immediately.

Isouda and Evelyn came to me as I sat in a chair, but I asked Isouda to wait in the solar for a while.

When she had gone, I turned to Evelyn.

She would not look me in the face.

'Why?' I said.

Evelyn dropped to her knees, weeping. 'He threatened my daughter, my lady. I beg you to forgive me.'

I looked over Evelyn's bowed form to Raife, standing arms crossed and leaning against a wall.

He shook his head slightly.

'He said he would see her cast out from de Tosny's household,' Evelyn continued, her words falling over each other, 'and that he would see to it that she would not be accepted elsewhere. My lady, she would have had to wander the streets, and —'

'Enough, Evelyn,' I said, wearied beyond measure. I felt for her, and even understood why she had betrayed me. Henry commanded the power to have done as he threatened — and Evelyn loved her daughter. I wished now I *had* asked Evelyn's daughter to serve with me, because then she would have been safe, and Evelyn not vulnerable.

But I also knew Evelyn would not have betrayed Adelie in this manner.

'You could have asked either myself or the earl for aid,' I said.

'Forgive me,' Evelyn said.

Perhaps I could find it in my heart to forgive her, but I would never trust her again. I rued that our friendship had come to this, but Evelyn had never been comfortable with my elevation from the lowest of the countess' attending women to the rank of countess, and maybe the friendship had died months ago.

I did not know what to do. I looked over to Raife.

'You will not serve my lady again,' Raife said, his voice hard, emotionless, 'nor any lady, for I shall ensure that word of your action spreads.'

I could see the back of Evelyn's head tremble, and her hands clutch together.

'But I also know my wife holds you in affection,' Raife continued, 'and for that reason alone I shall not cast you out without hope. I shall settle on you a cottage and some land in Donecastre. I am patron of an almshouse close to there and you may serve the master and help as you might.'

Poor Evelyn. She was to be sent far north, where she might never see her daughter again. While her keep was assured, with the cottage and land and position under the master of the almshouse, another place serving within a noble household was now beyond her. No one would take her after what she had done to me, nor would they take her from an almshouse, from where most would fear she might carry disease.

'Now leave,' Raife said. 'FitzErfast will see to the arrangements.'

Evelyn rose, sending me one single glance as she did so, and then she was out the door, and out of my life.

I missed her; missed her companionship and our memories of shared life together within Adelie's household.

She was almost the last reminder I had of my life as Mistress Maeb Langtofte.

Isouda came and helped me disrobe, and put me to bed, promising to return with a warm herbal to drink. Raife waited until she was gone, then he came over to the bed, sitting down by me.

He picked up my right hand, tracing one finger about its palm before enclosing it between both of his hands.

'My God, Mae,' he said. 'I have never known such terror as I felt this morning.' His hands tightened about mine.

'Raife, I knew that the —'

'Don't say it,' he said suddenly. 'Don't. I know what happened.'

'You do?'

'You have a powerful protector,' he said. There came a significant pause. 'In God.'

I studied him, somewhat perplexed. I thought for a moment he referred to the knight, but then to add the 'In God'?

He lifted one hand to lay his forefinger on my lips. 'I *know*,' he said. 'You trod the paths.'

I nodded, slowly. He did not wish me to speak of it, and used his own voice to lay a false trail. Why?

He bent down and kissed me, slowly, sweetly.

The door opened, and Isouda came back, bearing a steaming cup of something that smelled sweet.

'Drink this,' said Raife, 'and then sleep.'

CHAPTER SIX

William inter was colder than it had been for many years. The period from Martinmas to Christmastide was one of storms and icy sleet interspersed with snow. Edmond's Advent court celebrations turned to indoor activities, and the sudden cold snap appeared to dampen even those celebrations, for the mood of the court often turned as grey as the skies outside.

I certainly did not enjoy the remainder of the Advent court so much. This was likely due more to the lingering effects of my ordeal than the weather. People were cautious around me, not so much due to Henry's accusations, but because anyone so obviously God-touched as to emerge from the ordeal of the burning gauntlet completely unmarked was someone, apparently, to avoid; lest perhaps I slapped their faces, too, and God marked the guilt (from whatever misdemeanour or sin) in maille weave on their cheeks.

Partly as a result of what she had done for me on the day of the ordeal, and partly because others were more careful of me, my friendship with Alianor de Lacy became stronger and truer and I spent much of my time at court in her company.

Henry vanished from court. I do not know where he went, but I was deeply thankful he *had* gone. I did hear that, as his father had foretold, his cheek scarred deeply during healing and he would remain marked for the rest of his life.

His cheek would serve to remind Henry constantly of his humiliation that day.

I knew that, whereas Henry had been my enemy beforehand, now he was my bitterest of foes. I prayed often, either to sweet Jesu and all the saints, or to my miraculous knight protector, that Henry would heed his father's warning and tread more lightly about me.

After Advent court Raife and I took our household back to Cornhill. I stepped inside the house cautiously, wondering how it would feel. Thankfully, it *did* feel cleansed, and I breathed a sigh of relief as I walked through the hall, past the stairs down to the crypt, and up to the first floor to our privy chambers. The house felt empty without Evelyn, though. I thought of her often, and wished that our friendship had not been so soured, nor sundered by betrayal.

In her absence I had acquired not one but two more women. Ella Peverel was a Norman woman of good family, who came to attend me alongside Isouda. Gytha was a girl just past sixteen, but known throughout London for her ability to dress hair. She had already served in two noble households and now came to me. I liked them both, but felt more warmth toward Gytha who almost never spoke but would glance at me shyly as she worked wonders with my hair.

After Henry's attack on me in court, Raife appointed Gilbert Ghent as my permanent escort. If I so much as stepped foot outside then Ghent was by my side, and there he stayed with almost religious fanaticism after what he perceived as his failure to keep me in sight in the forest that day of the hunt. If Ghent would have preferred some more manly duty then he never showed it. He became a good companion, a friend, and trailed uncomplainingly behind me as Alianor and I sought out ribbons and baubles in the covered stalls and shops of West Cheap.

On the second last day of Advent, the day before the Vigil of the Nativity of Christ, a raging storm blew in from the ocean. Our household spent the day huddled about fires, windows tightly shuttered, listening to the roaring of the wind and the thunder of the rain outside. I was glad of the safety of a stone house, and thought those who sheltered in wooden or wattle and daub houses must be truly terrified.

We escaped unscathed, save for some minor water stains where rain had leaked in through cracks in the roof, but when we emerged the next morning, the Vigil of the Nativity, it was to see that the storm had wreaked much havoc through the city.

Raife sent soldiers and servants to give aid (as did most of the noble households currently resident in and about London), and our kitchen cooked bread and pease pudding for those whose fires had been dampened by inundations. As the day drew on, we heard reports of much damage from around the city: much of the building work on Saint Paul's had been undone; many houses in East Cheap and Rother Lane had been blown completely apart and their beams and debris littered both streets; the wharves along the Thames had been affected and much merchandise lost after an exceptionally high tide driven by the winds had invaded some of the warehouses. Miraculously, in this Christmastide season, no one had lost their life.

Along the Thames itself, from London to Westminster, the high waters and winds had damaged many craft. Scores of barges and boats, however tightly secured along the banks and flats of the river, had been wrenched from their moorings by the wind and waves and, as the tide receded, were borne down the river to London Bridge where they wrapped themselves about its piers and struts. There was such a chaos of splintered timbers now lodged under the bridge, so I heard, that much of the flow of the river was impeded and, in the absence of the storm, the water upriver of the bridge had become almost a still pond.

It would take months to clear the mess, and that not likely to start until after the celebrations of Christmastide.

Later that day, Raife and I once more embarked with a large part of our household to take up residence in the Tower chambers Edmond had assigned us. Now it was Christmastide court, a chance for Edmond to demonstrate his largesse to those he invited — mostly the greater nobility of the country but also most of the aldermen and the more powerful among the merchants and traders of London.

The memory of my ordeal had faded somewhat, and most gossiped now about the storm and the damage done to London and various villages along the Thames to its mouth. Christmastide court, Edmond's Advent court, passed amid cheer and celebration, with much feasting, plays, dancing and games.

The Christmas Feast held in the great hall of the Conqueror's Tower was memorable. The hall was decorated in greenery, holly and mistletoe, with ribbons strung all over. I was dressed in such finery, and Raife, too — oh, we were splendid! Raife had given me a beautiful coronet (he wore one as well), all gold and precious gems, and Gytha had outdone herself, twisting my hair in intricate weaves through the gold of the coronet and then down my back with gems glittering within the complicated braiding.

Edmond sat Raife and myself at high table. We sat to either side of him, which was a great honour. That afternoon and night was filled with feasting and games and dancing. The king gave us both stunning gifts: for Raife a salt cellar in the shape of a unicorn, delicately worked in gold and silver, and for me a beautiful deep-green, fur-lined mantle … 'To go with the clasp,' he said as he gifted it to me.

Both our table placements and our gifts signified to the court as nothing else in what affectionate favour the king held us.

It was such a merry night of wassailing: I drank perhaps a little too much posset — a rich, thick drink of ale and egg, honey and spices — but no one seemed to mind that my smiles became a little freer as the night wore on. The Yule log hissed and spat in the fireplace, the multitude of candles burned bright, everyone in the hall exchanged kisses of friendship, and all seemed so well with my world.

The storm seemed to have cleared winter of much of its early malice, and, while it was still cold, the wind and rain and sleet had stopped. Thus — once we had quite recovered from the richness and excess of the Christmas Feast! — we were able to enjoy jousts and races and games on the fields abutting the Conqueror's Tower. Everyone was wrapped up in one, or even two, thick mantles and furs (I, of course, wore the king's gift), and with hoods drawn close about our faces we made the most of the entertainment, the wine and food and the cheer. I was now far enough into my pregnancy that all queasiness of stomach had passed, and I did not tire so much, and I truly enjoyed the twelve days of festivity.

Toward the end of Christmastide court, Edmond suggested to many of the noblemen that they embark on a hunt through the forests and woodlands east of London. Edmond had manors to the east, as did several other noblemen, and Edmond proposed a hunt extending for scores of miles with nightly rests and feasts at various manor houses.

The men thought it a splendid idea (those whose manor houses were to be engulfed by a royal visit, and its expense, managed to keep their sinking stomachs to themselves). Their wives, also, thought it splendid, for we suddenly envisaged a quiet week or so of gentler entertainments after the excitement of court.

Raife was as eager as the rest about the prospect of a winter hunt through the crisp, white landscape. He was somewhat anxious about me, especially after the incident with the imp the last time he had left me alone in the Cornhill house, but when Alianor suggested that I stay with her and Robert de Lacy in their manor hall in the meadows north of Holbournestrate, just outside London, he greeted the idea with relief (and I with considerable enthusiasm).

Thus it was that, on the day after the Feast of the Epiphany, while our men rode with the hounds and their hawks to the east, the de Lacys and I (along with Ghent, four other soldiers, my three women, and several servants and grooms) rose westward out of London along Holbournestrate. We were doubly lucky on that journey, in that the sun shone bright but the chill air froze the roadway mud beneath us. I nestled inside my fur-lined mantle, its hood about my head, and relaxed on Dulcette's back. We rode along at a sedate pace, mindful of the horses' footing on the icy road. Dulcette seemed to know of my pregnancy, for she stepped sure and smooth, and did not tire me by pulling on the reins.

The fields were frozen under a layer of white, the rooks distinctive black smudges as they sifted through the snow to find worms and insects. Everything was quiet. It was too cold yet to work in the fields and most people were, I imagine, content to rest after twelve days of Christmastide indulgence. To the north of us the stalls and pens of Smithfield market stood empty — just a few cattle and pigs left to forage for food in the pens before trading began anew in a few days. The only sign of life came from the nearby Saint Bartholomew's priory and hospital, where smoke rising from chimneys suggested warm fires and kitchens.

As we rode further along Holbournestrate we came to a newly built church on the southern side of the street. It was entirely round, very solid, and had many outbuildings: a hall, dormitories, stables, kitchens, bakehouses and a brewery. Behind the complex I could see a fishpond and an orchard, both currently as white and still as the rest of the fields, the branches of the orchard's trees bleak and thin in the winter air.

'What Order is this?' I asked Alianor curiously.

She gave me an amused glance and chuckled. 'It is the Temple — the Templar's church,' she said.

We pulled the horses to a halt, looking over the church.

'I very much doubt your curiosity will get you entry,' Robert said. 'The Templars are known women haters.'

I grunted. Fulke d'Ecouis certainly seemed to have taken a dislike to me.

Then — as if thought had given flesh to name — d'Ecouis and another, older Templar, walked out of the Church and halted as they spotted our party in the middle of Holbournestrate, staring at them. Immediately they came toward us, leaping smoothly over the roadside ditch, as sure-footed in the treacherous conditions as I suppose only men of God can be.

'My lady countess,' d'Ecouis said to me, then greeted the de Lacys. He turned slightly, indicating his companion.

He was an older man, his hair silvered but his body still wide with muscle. He looked at us with a bright blue gaze that was both bold and curious.

'This is Hugh of Argentine,' d'Ecouis said. 'Our newly arrived Master of Temple.'

We all inclined our heads to the master, as he did to us. We passed a few minutes in idle conversation — the storm, the coldness of the air, our destination — then d'Ecouis indicated me as he spoke.

'Master,' he said, 'the countess is the only child of Godfrey Langtofte.'

Instantly, Hugh's eyes became keen, penetrating, and he stepped forward to lay a hand on Dulcette's neck, as if to prevent me riding away.

'Your father was a member of our Order in Jerusalem,' Hugh said. 'I recall him well.'

I sighed inwardly. 'He was a sergeant, I believe. He came home the winter before last, only to die within weeks.'

'We must remember him together sometime,' Hugh said.

'I have done my grieving for my father,' I said, 'and would prefer not to rekindle it.'

Hugh's eyes narrowed. 'Perhaps so,' he said, 'but there are matters left untended and —'

'They are not my matters,' I said, 'and not my worry.'

Hugh and d'Ecouis exchanged a glance, then Hugh tipped his head, as if the matter was of no concern.

'Indeed,' he said. 'Perhaps we shall see you at court?'

'Perhaps,' I said.

'Master,' said Robert, 'we must ride on. The countess is with child and this cold does her no good.'

'Indeed,' the master said once again and inclined his head in farewell as we turned our horses back to the road.

'I have lost the immediate threat of Henry's malice,' I muttered to Alianor, 'only to be left with that of the Templars. What in sweet Christ's name can they *want* from me?'

With that unanswerable question hanging between us, we resumed the ride toward the de Lacy manor and hall.

CHAPTER SEVEN

The de Lacy's manor hall sat atop a rise amid meadows and fields not far from the banks of the Fleet River. I imagined that in spring and summer it was a delightful place, with views right down to London, Westminster and the curving Thames, but now, in this January freeze, their lands were as cold as anywhere else.

Their hall, however, its lower floor built of stone, its upper of wood, was warm and comfortable. I settled happily, enjoying the company and the respite from the busyness of London and the excitement and intrigue of court. My stay here was meant to be quiet, spent in front of fires, with gentle conversation to amuse me, but on my third day there came news that a fair day was to be held on the morrow on the Thames, upriver from the bridge, to mark Plough Monday.

Since the day of the Great Storm, which had seen scores of barges and boats crash into the bridge, creating a dam of splintered timbers, the waters upriver from the bridge had become almost completely still and for the past weeks the river had been freezing over, the ice growing ever more thick. Now the watermen of the Thames had declared the ice safe enough for man and beast alike to gambol over.

The Londoners, not ones to miss the opportunity for combining money-making and fun, had decided to hold a festival and fair. There were to be sports, dancing, hare chasing, dog races, bonfires, outdoor feasts, contests of all descriptions, mummers and players, troubadours and minstrels — and all on the ice.

Gilbert Ghent, who brought us this news, stood before myself, Alianor and Robert, his eyes a-gleam, and I had to smile at the hope in his face.

'My lady?' said Robert. 'It is but a short ride away.'

'There will be tents full of benches and braziers a-plenty for the ladies to sit and rest, if needed,' Ghent said.

I did not need to be persuaded. 'A gentle ride there,' I said, 'and we shall see on our arrival if we wish to stay, or return to our fires here. So long as tomorrow is not full of sleet or rain, then I say we should go.'

The day dawned fine and clear. Even the chill in the air seemed to have moderated. We rose at our leisure, said prayers in the de Lacys' tiny chapel, broke our fast, and then decided to dare the ride to London.

We entered the city through Lud Gate, turning our horses toward Baynard Castle on Thames Street, running along the riverbank. It was mid-morning, and there were a goodly number of people moving through the streets toward the river, all intent on merry-making. Once on Thames Street we pulled our horses to one side of Baynard Castle, gazing in wonder at the river.

Where once had been flowing greenish water was now creamy ice. It appeared quite solid, for there were horses and laden carts trundling over its surface, as well as men, women and children walking, dancing, running.

Along the centre of the ice were two lines of tents, gaily coloured and with flags and pennants flying from their pinnacles. The de Lacys pointed out some of the standards and devices: some were of inns and taverns, now set up with trestle tables on the ice; some were for various of the guilds and crafts of London, there to sell their wares; some represented nobles, who had set their own tents; others marked bands of players or musicians, and there were the tents of vendors plying food and merchandise. Also, Alianor indicated to me in an undertone, privy tents where we could retire should the need take us.

In front of, and behind the twin rows of tents, were various areas marked out for dancing, racing, games and sports.

There were already crowds of people on the ice, and much noise and jollity.

We left the horses with our grooms and proceeded to a hastily built set of wooden steps leading down to the ice. Robert helped down Alianor, while Ghent took my hand and aided me down the steps.

I was tentative at first, not trusting my weight on the ice nor my footing on its surface, but my confidence grew as I walked further out into the ice fair and soon I was walking with only a light hand on Ghent's arm.

There was activity everywhere. In one open space two knights were demonstrating sword play to a thick crowd of admirers. In another, a score of boys kicked a leather ball to and fro, trying to get it through large hoops that had been set up fifty or so paces opposite each other. Yet somewhere else a small racing circuit had been established, its bounds fenced with woven hurdles. Here, hares raced, carrying with them the bets of the wildly cheering crowd which had gathered.

One resourceful man had affixed a small sled to a pole which was itself affixed to a central gearing mechanism so that the man could push sledfuls of shrieking children round and round and round at ever faster rates. Elsewhere, adults, well-fuelled by ale, had set up circles on the ice to play Bee in the Middle.

People were selling hot nuts, dried apples, sweetmeats of every description, alcohol — whatever your heart could desire and whatever could be carried easily down to the ice (there was even one tent of whores, though Ghent hurried me past that all too quickly, despite my curiosity).

At one point our group stopped by an archery field set up in the very centre of the river, and it was not long before Alianor and I persuaded Ghent and Robert to show us their skills with the bow and arrow. Gytha watched with wide eyes (I had brought my three women with me), and when Ghent won a ribbon for his skills he presented it to the blushing girl.

I thanked him for that, for it was a sweet and courtly thing to do for a girl who had, I think, seen little pleasure in her life.

We wandered for hours, stopping now and then to rest at one of the tavern tents where we drank small beer and feasted on hot beef from one of the roasting oxen. The ice was such a novelty, and the scene so festive, that none of us truly wanted to leave.

By the late afternoon we had walked closer to the bridge. Here the ice was rougher, for the tides underneath the ice could the more easily pull at its edges, and we did not linger. We could see, also, the tops of the piles of jumbled timbers, poking through the ice and mush, that so obstructed the flow of the river that this ice pond had become possible.

There were groups of boys here who, I think, had imbibed a little too heavily of cups of full ale, for they were loud and raucous and too uncaring of the danger on the rougher ice. Several of them had brought along the smaller bows that boys often learned with, and were running about with arrows dipped in oil and set alight, that they might shoot them a little too close to their friends for comfort.

We left, lest they started shooting those arrows in our direction.

'We should make our way back to the stairs,' Alianor said, 'and then make our way home.'

I nodded, and there was general agreeance. It had been a full and most enjoyable day, but I was tired now, and content to begin the gentle ride home to rest before a fire.

Everyone was weary, I think, for there was little conversation as we wandered back toward the stairs by Baynard Castle. My head slowly drooped, and, as I leaned ever more heavily on Ghent, I found myself studying the strange patterns in the ice. Occasionally objects had been caught and then frozen into the ice. There were muddy brown fish, and some flotsam and jetsam. An infant rabbit, its jaws wide open in an ever silent scream, its black eyes staring.

That made me shudder, yet I did not look away, for I was strangely fascinated by these objects that had become caught in the ice.

A few steps later I saw what looked like the partly decomposed hand of a man in the ice, its black hairs still clearly visible on its upper aspect, its wrist ragged and thick with putrid pus where the hand had been torn from its arm.

I began to feel ill, yet *still* I did not look away.

A few paces on I saw an entire body under the ice. It was blackened, yet red raw in places, and looked as if it had been burned. The layers of ice above it distorted the corpse, so that it appeared as if it had a short, thick body and impossibly long, thin limbs. Even its tail looked as if —

My heart started thudding. I stopped, staring, unable to look away.

Deep under the ice, the imp's head swivelled so it looked up at me.

It grinned, its mouth gaping red and broken-toothed.

I opened my mouth to scream when Ghent exclaimed, 'Mother of God! Look to that! Look to the bridge!'

The bridge? The bridge? He was worried about the bridge when underneath our feet an imp —

I blinked, and the imp was gone and there was solid ice under my feet once more. Still, I felt sick to my stomach, and had to battle the urge to void the nuts and sweetmeats I had nibbled on these past few hours.

Everyone about me was exclaiming, and I finally looked up to see what had happened.

London Bridge was afire.

I couldn't understand what I saw for a few heartbeats, for my mind was still consumed with the vision of the imp. But the leaping and roaring of the flames and the crackling of the timbers — heard even from this distance — finally penetrated the fog that had overcome my mind, and I gasped in horror.

Those boys must have shot one of their damned flaming arrows into the jumble of timbers about the base of the piers.

'Everyone off the ice,' Ghent said, his voice curiously flat. 'Now.'

He began urging us toward the stairs, still some distance away.

'Be still, man!' Robert de Lacy said. 'We need to see if those flames are going to enter the city!'

'My lord,' Ghent said, 'the ice is no longer safe. If the bridge collapses it will break the weir of timbers beneath it, and likely all this still water dammed upstream will rush downriver — the ice will break apart if that happens.'

Before any of us could answer, one of the central spans of the bridge crumpled in a shower of sparks, and heavy, burning beams collapsed into the jumble of ice and timbers beneath it.

There was a momentary pause, and then we all saw the timbers and ice give way.

Even this far distant we all felt the slight shudder in the ice underfoot.

'The stairs. *Now!*' Ghent said.

We hesitated no longer. We all moved toward the stairs as fast as we dared, Ghent holding onto my arm and half pulling me across the ice.

Every so often I glanced back to the bridge. It burned even fiercer now, and two other spans collapsed as we walked and slid our way to the steps.

Most of the crowd on the ice were staring at the bridge, even moving closer to it to catch a better glimpse.

'I hope those small boys drowned in the cursed water,' Ghent muttered, and I could not find it in my heart to condemn him for his uncharitable thoughts.

Suddenly there came a distinct tremor under our feet, and we heard cries of fright behind us.

'The ice is breaking up!' Alianor said, and unfortunately her words carried, and the people nearby panicked and rushed for the stairs.

Our way was now more difficult, for so many pushed and pummelled us, fighting to get off the ice, that we found it ever harder to move as fast as we wanted. People fell in the crush, and at one stage Ghent had to lift me bodily over a tumble of three people fighting to get up.

I looked about me, desperate to see that Isouda, Ella and Gytha were close, and felt immense relief when I saw they were near behind. If Ghent felt responsible for me, then I felt responsible for them. Their faces were panicked, as I supposed mine was, too, and the smile I tried for them failed before it even began.

'Maeb! *Climb!*' Ghent said, and suddenly, thankfully, there were the stairs, Ghent pushing a way through for me, and reaching behind for Alianor and my three women. Robert de Lacy lent his strength, too, and I have never felt anything so good as those solid steps underneath my feet. Above I heard the grooms we had brought with us crying our names, and shouting something about —

The stairs trembled and then fell through the air.

The ice had collapsed at their base!

We clung to railings and steps, whatever we could manage to grasp and, achingly slowly, painfully, we clambered up the now vertical steps as if they were a ladder.

Praise sweet Jesu their upper joints had stayed fastened to the wharf.

Always there was Ghent at my side or beneath me, pushing me up, supporting me, saving my life.

I was sobbing with fear — I could hear Alianor crying, too — and every moment I expected to be pulled or pushed from my precarious hold by the terrified people about me. I feared the steps would collapse with the weight of the people remaining on it. I feared one or all of my women had fallen into the river below — the ice now deadly splinters churning amid the rushing waters.

I feared the imp would not let me go, and would reach up from the ice to drag me down.

But somehow, somehow, we all managed to reach the wharf alive, our grooms reaching down to haul us up the final few feet. Even my women clambered up securely, as did the de Lacys, and we stood shaking in fear, hugging each other as we wept.

I turned to Ghent, and in my joy and relief forgot all propriety and hugged him tight, kissing his mouth, thanking him with all the strength left in my voice, for without him I know I would have died.

We were among the last to have found safety.

As I clung to Ghent I turned my head and looked over the river.

Even now I can barely describe the horror.

Almost all of the burning bridge had now collapsed, and in the doing it had destabilised the weir that had held back the waters of the Thames. Everything had been swept away, bridge and weir, in the maddened rush of water downstream.

Upstream from the bridge the ice pond had collapsed, taking with it people, horses, tents, everything and anything that had sat on its surface. Now sheets of jagged ice surged and tumbled through the water, and I could see bright flashes of some of the gaily coloured tents as they rose suddenly through the churning waves and then were sucked underneath.

I saw the flailing limbs of people, as they too were sucked and spat through the torrent.

Hundreds, *thousands*, were dying.

I turned away, unable to look, and realised that only two score or so of people had made it up the stairs from the ice.

So many. Dead.

I was wracked with sobs, and Ghent lifted me into his arms, then put me atop his own courser, mounting behind me, keeping me safe with a strong encircling arm. He shouted to the others to mount, to ride away as safe as they might, that the fire was spreading into the city.

Ghent did not wait for them to mount. Instead he kicked his courser into a canter, sending it up through the streets of London, and then out Lud Gate, the first gate we encountered. His courser shied and panicked amid the shouting people in the streets and from the smell of fear on his riders, but even with one hand Ghent controlled him with little effort, and

I have never breathed so easy as I did once we were out of the city and riding northward toward the de Lacys' hall.

There was a white flash by our side, and I saw that someone had loosed Dulcette, and she had followed us through the gate.

Our group reformed outside the city and we stopped, far from London, on the rise leading to the de Lacy's hall.

None of us spoke.

The entire south-western corner of the city was ablaze.

We sat our horses for a long time, watching, and then, with a sigh, Ghent turned our horse for home, and everyone followed.

CHAPTER EIGHT

———◆◇◆———

I stayed abed the next day, and only heard what news there was to be had when Ghent came to see me in the mid-afternoon.

He sat by my bed. 'Are you well, my lady?'

Too often now these queries after my health could be roughly deciphered as, 'Is the Pengraic heir you carry safe, my lady?' But when Ghent asked, he sounded truly concerned for my own welfare.

'I am, Gilbert. I am merely fatigued.'

He smiled, and I thought once again how good-looking he was.

'I am glad,' he said.

'How goes London, Gilbert? Have you heard?'

He nodded. 'It is said that near eight thousand perished in the river.'

Sweet Lord Jesu! I could not begin to comprehend such numbers, nor the terror they must have felt in their dying.

'The fire,' Gilbert went on, 'has been devastating, destroying many shops, homes, taverns and warehouses — even scorching Saint Paul's — but it has taken relatively few lives. Sixty-three, so one of the aldermen has said. The loss of the bridge is disastrous, for it shall take many months to rebuild, and in the meantime Londoners shall need to rely on ferries for their transport to and fro the Thames.'

'My lord's house in Cornhill?'

'The fire did not come anywhere near, my lady.'

'Praise the saints. Can you send one of the grooms or servants, and instruct fitzErfast to offer what assistance he can? There must be homeless, and people need to be fed.'

Ghent nodded. 'I have word also that Edmond is returning, together with his hunting party. They should be back within London by early tomorrow morning if they ride hard.'

'I will return to Cornhill tomorrow, I think.'

Ghent looked concerned. 'My lady —'

'We will ride slow, and I will be well enough, Gilbert.'

I hesitated, then held out my hand.

He looked long and hard at it, then took it, closing his fingers gently about mine.

'Gilbert. You saved my life. You saved *all* of our lives. I thank you, and shall tell my husband of your actions. I hope that he will reward you with more than mere grateful words.'

Ghent flushed slightly, but he nodded, and smiled.

I allowed my own smile to widen. 'You have more than redeemed yourself for losing me in the forest. You are my saviour, Gilbert.'

He could hardly be held responsible for losing me to the dream falloways of the Old People in the forest, but I knew that Ghent felt that failure deeply.

The next morning we set off just after dawn. I knew that Raife must be either barely arrived at the Cornhill house, or close to, and I wanted to reach him as soon as possible. I knew he would be worried about me.

We avoided the western gates of London. A thin pall of smoke still hung over the south-western quarter of the city. We rode through the northern fields and orchards outside the city to Bishops Gate, where we rode down the street to Cornhill and thence to the house.

Raife had just arrived — so recently that he was still in the courtyard of the house, handing the reins of his courser to a groom.

'Maeb!' he cried as he saw me. 'Praise God you are safe!'

He reached up to me, helping me to dismount, then enveloping me in a bear hug. 'I pray you kept safe at the de Lacys' hall.'

I glanced at Ghent, who had dismounted just behind us.

'My lord,' I said, touching his face, feeling such a rush of pleasure at seeing him that I could hardly bear it. 'My lord, we were not. We had gone to play on the ice with the Londoners, and, sweet Jesu, were on the river when the ice broke apart. Were it not for Gilbert then I would have died, and my ladies, and the de Lacys besides. He saved our lives, first from the ice, and then from the flames. Without him ...' My voice broke, and I could not continue.

Still holding me tight, Raife turned to look at Ghent. 'By God,' Raife said, in a voice thick with emotion, 'I shall see you do well for this. I thank you, from the depths of my heart. I could not bear to lose my lady.'

'And you, my lord?' I asked. 'How do you?'

'We heard of the disastrous misfortune of London early yesterday,' Raife said. 'We rode through the day and then the night to reach the city. By God ... by *God*, what calamity!'

I thought of the imp under the ice. I would not tell Raife, I decided. Maybe I had dreamed it; maybe the vision of the imp was some instinctive part of my being warning me of the river disaster. Raife had enough concerning him without my adding to those worries.

Raife gave me another long hug, and we went inside.

Everyone in London — king, the royal household, nobles and Londoners — spent the next week to ten days involved in helping those left homeless, those needing food, and beginning the reconstruction efforts. There was no court, nor entertainments, nor intrigues. There was only the effort to be put into restoring as much of the city and its citizens to rights with all due haste.

We took in two score and five people who had been left homeless by the fire, housing them partly in the dormitories and courtyard outbuildings, partly in the hall where we set up bedding for them.

But warehouses and houses and shops could be rebuilt. The loss to the city of the eight thousand who had died in the river was almost unbearable. Near a third of the city's stall holders and traders had perished, many nobles had died, hundreds of craftsmen and tradesmen and artisans and their apprentices, a handful of aldermen and, crucially, the city's portreeve. Many families had lost someone, and many, many families had vanished entirely. It would take the city longer to recover from that loss than it would from structural devastation.

Edmond did what he could. With so many aldermen and the portreeve lost, he stepped personally into the chaotic aftermath of both river and fire disasters, directed relief and aid, used the soldiers and guardsmen stationed at the Tower to help in the aid effort for people, but also to pull down dangerously leaning, half burned buildings and cart away the rubble. He rode through the city each day with the Constable of the Tower, Alan de Bretagne, seeing for himself what needed to be done and setting the Constable to sort it out.

Ten days after the tragedies, the king stopped for refreshment at our house before riding back to the Tower. He looked fatigued and drawn, and sat down heavily in a chair in our solar, inching it closer to the fire.

I poured him some spiced wine, and he thanked me for it as I handed it to him.

'The damage, to buildings and spirit, is ruinous,' Edmond said, drinking heavily of the wine before handing the cup back to me to refill. 'Half the craftsmen needed for rebuilding died in the river. The other half are mourning wives or children or parents who died.'

He sighed. 'Much of my work seems to be shaking people out of their shock in order to rebuild or aid others. How goes the families you have housed here?'

'We have only a handful remaining,' Raife said, stretching out his legs as he took a chair opposite the king. 'Some have gone to family in outlying villages, or back to their home villages. Some have taken, for the moment, those houses left standing empty because their former occupants died in the river.'

'It is an ill day, indeed,' Edmond said, 'when one tragedy gives hope and opportunity for those caught in the next tragedy.'

'I've heard word that of the ships destroyed in the river,' Raife said, 'the greatest loss has been the —'

He was interrupted by the sight of fitzErfast, who had entered to stand just inside the door and look anxious.

'What is it, man?' Raife said.

FitzErfast came over and spoke quietly in Raife's ear. Raife gave him a hard look, then nodded. 'Let him enter.'

Then he looked to Edmond. 'A rider, with urgent news,' he said, 'for you, my lord.'

A young man, probably a squire, although it was hard to tell from the travel stains and the wear on his clothes, hurried into the chamber and bowed before Edmond.

At the king's nod, he spoke, his voice harsh from his fatigue. 'My lord king, I bring you greetings from the Earl of Summersete, currently resident in Walengefort Castle.'

'Yes, yes,' said Edmond. 'What has Summersete to say?'

'My lord, he sends news that the plague is flourishing once again, from Monemude to Glowecestre, and from Cirecestre to Oxeneford, and many hamlets and villages along the way. It began with small outbreaks during Advent, but since Christmastide has spread farther, as well as deeper, within each community. My lord king, my lord of Summersete begs you to watch and plan for an outbreak in London, as the pestilence now draws close and shows no sign of abating, and he begs you to watch over your own health and that of your family.'

We stared at the man, almost unable to take in the news of this further horror.

Then Edmond swore, soft and foul, before apologising to me. 'Sweet Jesu, Pengraic, the plague? *Now?* In the middle of winter. How can this be? No plague flourishes during winter! Isolated cases, yes, but ravaging outbreaks … No!

'Man,' he said to the squire, 'have you word of the numbers who have died?'

'Many hundreds, sire,' said the squire. 'My lord of Summersete only received word of this two days ago, and I have ridden hard to get this intelligence to you in London.'

'It has likely been brewing many months,' Raife said, his voice soft. 'We know from its last outbreak that it can live within a community for many weeks, even months, before it begins to show its vicious claws. By that time, by the time we *know* of its presence, then it is too late, for hundreds have been infected.'

'Perhaps *you* brought it with you,' Edmond said, his voice hard, 'on your journey from Pengraic.'

'I can assure you *not*,' Raife said. 'Pengraic was quite free of the plague for months before we left.'

Edmond waved a hand in apology. 'I am sorry for the slur, Pengraic. Dear God, what have I done that my realm must be wracked with so many disasters!' He swore again, this time omitting any apology to me. 'I will call a council meeting for the morrow, Pengraic. You will attend.'

He rose, handing his once more empty cup to me, gave me an unreadable look, and then was clattering down the stairs and calling for his horse.

CHAPTER NINE

When the morrow arrived, it was to discover that Edmond wanted me to attend the council meeting as well. He sent word that Hugh of Argentine, the newly installed Master of the Temple, would be attending, along with Fulke d'Ecouis, and that the two Templars wanted me there.

'And so also,' said Roger de Douai, who had brought the news, 'Edmond wants you there, my lady. If there is to be further charge against you, then it shall need to be made to your face.'

I looked at Raife in despair. '*What* can they want of me?' I said.

'I would not worry overmuch, my lady,' de Douai said. 'Edmond has said he also wants the maille gauntlet used in your ordeal to be placed in the very centre of the table. As a reminder.'

'I am *tired* of being blamed for all that is wrong in this world,' I muttered.

Raife put a hand on my shoulder, and addressed de Douai. 'I would be grateful, de Douai, if you could murmur in the master's ear that I will personally cut off his balls if he lays a single accusation at my wife's feet or threatens her in any way.'

'I will so do,' said de Douai with a small smile.

Edmond held his council in the great hall at the top of the Conqueror's Tower. A large trestle table had been set up near one of the fireplaces, then covered in fine linens, and then topped with ewers of wine and cups as well as platters of breads, dried fruits and cheeses. Edmond's council, Raife told me on the ride to the Tower, was usually composed of his leading nobles, top officials and the high ecclesiastics, but today, well, it would be composed of whoever could be there at such short notice, or who hadn't fallen into the ice among the eight thousand.

As we walked into the great hall, it was to see that a goodly number *had* managed to be here. The Bishop of Wincestre, together with Tedbald du Bec, the Archbishop of Cantuaberie. The two men stood well apart, their hatred of each other known to all. The bishopric of London was vacant, awaiting Edmond to name a successor to the bishop who had just died, so his place was filled by Gervase de Blois, the abbot of Westminster.

The Constable of the Tower was present, as was the castellan of Baynard Castle, Geoffrey de Mandeville, and the Earl of Exsessa, along with the earls of Pembroke, Lincolie, Chestre among others. There were also several aldermen from London, as well as the high officials from Edmond's household and Edmond's second son, Prince Richard, who was some sixteen or seventeen years of age.

The two Templars, Hugh of Argentine and Fulke d'Ecouis, were here also. Edmond entered from the archway leading into his privy chamber at the same time as Raife and I came through the door from the gallery, and after he greeted us, he drew us aside for a quiet word.

'My lady,' he said to me, 'do not be afraid. Hugh reassures me that he has no accusation against you.'

'Then why does he want me here, my lord?'

'Who knows? But I am glad enough of your presence, Maeb, not merely because the very sight of you soothes my eyes, but because you have lived through the plague whereas most of the men in this chamber have not, and your insights may be of use to me.'

He turned to stride over to the chair placed at the top of the table.

'My lords, we begin,' he said, and as he sat so everyone in the chamber took their places at the table. I sat with Raife close to the head of the table, the two Templars about halfway down the other side.

Many of those present shot me curious glances as they sat, but no one spoke up to ask the reason for my presence.

The council began with reports from the aldermen present about the current state of repairs, rebuilding (such as had been started) and the people of London. While most of the burned buildings had been pulled down and the sites cleared, rebuilding would take months if not years, and could not begin properly until the winter snows and rains were past.

As for the bridge — that would take at least a year of construction to have a viable structure in place.

Most everyone who had lost their homes had been re-housed. The bigger dilemma was replacing so many of the citizens, and their skills, who had been lost in the river. That, one alderman remarked glumly, would take years, and would affect the rebuilding programme within the city, trading and the city revenues due to the king.

Then to the plague. The intelligence that it had reignited and appeared to be headed directly for London was dismal news, particularly following so close on the heels of the twin tragedies of river and fire. Edmond discussed briefly with the council what could be done to prepare the city, and asked me to add any insights I might have to the council about the table.

'Only, my lord king,' I said, 'that those suffering be moved away from their own homes into hospitals or buildings made of stone. Our priest, Owain, offered the use of Pengraic's chapel to hold the dying, that their mortal scorching might not devastate the entire castle. From my own observation, so much of London's buildings are wooden, and …'

'As we have seen,' Edmond concluded dryly, 'fire tends to spread rapidly.' He spoke to the aldermen, asking them to identify and prepare stone buildings now, whether they be churches or warehouses, to take in the sick and dying.

'I can offer my house,' said Raife. 'Both it and its outbuildings are of stone, and close enough to Holy Trinity Priory that the brothers might use it as an extension of their own hospital.'

'Then you must accept my hospitality here,' said Edmond, and Raife nodded.

I admit I breathed a small sigh of relief. I did not wish to be trapped within the crowded city if plague broke out. The Tower, somehow, was more comforting.

'My lord king,' said Hugh of Argentine, 'if I may speak? What I need to say intimately concerns the plague.'

Edmond inclined his head.

'Before I speak, I need to seek assurances from all present, to be spoken as if they stood before God himself, that no word I utter is to be spread beyond the chamber walls. My lord king, if I might request that we can serve our own wine from this point?'

Edmond nodded and waved the servants away.

Hugh then asked each of us in turn to agree not to spread gossip of what we heard, and we agreed solemnly.

Several of the earls and all the clergy looked irritated, however, and I imagined they were annoyed not only by the intrusion of the Templars into this privy council, but also Hugh's dramatic insistence on oath-taking.

Once we were done, Hugh began speaking in a deceptively calm and moderate voice.

'My lord king, my lords of soul and land, my lady. What I speak of now is gathered from knowledge contained within the innermost circle of the Templars, as those secrets conferred to us by the Pope. It is terrifying, and I beg you to keep your wits sound while I relate it.

'Some time ago, in recognition of our Order's service to God, and His pilgrims in the Holy Lands, the Pope granted us exclusive access to the ancient Temple of Solomon within the precincts of Jerusalem. In recent times, as the pestilence ravaged Jerusalem, our brethren discovered within its crypt —'

'Saints save us,' said Edmond. 'I pray this is not yet *another* tale of the elusive Holy Grail and its dark magics!'

There was a subdued twitter about the table, and Hugh shot Edmond a black look.

'It is not, my lord king,' he said.

'Then reach your point speedily,' said Edmond, 'for I have better things to do than settle about this fire and listen to Templar tales all day.'

Hugh took a deep breath, and I could see he struggled to control his temper.

'Then if I may be blunt,' he said. 'What my brothers found scrabbling about in the temple's crypt was an imp from hell.'

There were gasps and murmurs about the table, and I froze. Eventually, once my initial shock was passed, I risked a glance at my husband — his face was impassive.

'This vile imp was searching for something,' Hugh continued. 'One of our brethren, braver and faster than the others, seized the imp before it had a chance to vanish, and he threatened it most menacingly with his sword and demanded of it what it sought. It hissed, and spoke many foulnesses, but eventually my brethren learned it searched for a crown of some description.

Our brothers learned no more from the imp, for so soon as it spoke those words it disintegrated into a vile-smelling pile of decomposing flesh.

'Our brethren dug, they sifted the rubble from one end of that crypt to the other, but they could find nothing. Most certainly nothing resembling a crown. In the end we thought no more of it and continued our aid to those crusaders caught in the grip of the pestilence until, God be praised, the pestilence speedily moved on.'

Hugh paused to take a sip of wine, and Edmond tapped his fingers on the table in irritation at this delay.

'No doubt you wonder how all of this is connected, my lord,' Hugh said to Edmond. 'I will say so, but will make my account brief, lest I try your patience further. Our Order in Jerusalem did not connect the two concurrent horrors, imp and pestilence — both of which occurred at the same time — until someone informed Pope Innocent II. He then called to his presence our new Grand Master, Robert de Craon, and told him a most terrifying tale.'

'Which you are doubtless about to tell us, eh?' Edmond said.

His ill-temper was growing by the moment.

Hugh inclined his head.

'Innocent told de Craon that, many years ago,' Hugh said, 'before even the time of the Viking attacks up and down the coasts and rivers of Europe, a monk vanished from among his small order of brethren in the wilds of Anatolia. Greatly disturbed in his mind, but of powerful vision, the monk made his way down to hell, from whence he stole the Devil's favourite diadem. The monk returned to this mortal world, where he wandered for years carrying the diadem, listening to its fateful whisperings. Eventually, maddened, he hid the diadem just before his death.

'We, both Innocent and the Templars, believe that the Devil now wants his diadem back.'

'Is that what the imp searched for within the Temple?' Wincestre asked.

'Aye,' said Hugh, 'we believe so. We think this monk must have hidden the diadem within the Temple's crypt, the Devil had discovered this fact, and sent his imp for it.'

'And so who has this diadem now?' asked my husband. 'I imagine, that once confronted with a tale of such a powerful and rich icon, you have searched everywhere for it.'

Hugh gave a small smile. 'Well, my lord of Pengraic, we believe that, likely only quite soon before the imp searched for the diadem, someone *else* found it and removed it from the Temple precinct. Where is it now? Well, we have some idea, but the Devil had none. Thus he sent the pestilence onward to *sniff* out its location.'

There was a loud murmur about the table.

Again I glanced at Raife. His face remained impassive.

'My lords, hear me out,' said Hugh. 'We have deduced all this from a number of careful observations, and I would like to lay them out before you. My lord king, this concerns your realm, and it concerns your highest magnates, so do *not* toss me that impatient glance again lest you want your realm to vanish entirely!'

For one moment I thought Edmond was going to thump his fist on the table and shout at the Templar master, perhaps even have him expelled. Edmond's fist clenched, his face tightened and flushed, but he collected himself and gave Hugh the smallest, tightest nod possible.

'My lords,' said Hugh, 'let us leave the matter of the diadem momentarily and discuss this plague. It began in the land of the Ghaznavids, where it tormented the people, and then spread rapidly into the Holy Lands. From there, as you all know, through the lands of Europe and then into this realm.

'But this plague did not travel like other pestilences. It followed a narrow path, devastating towns and hamlets in a thin corridor that led from the Holy Lands, through the Byzantine empire, the Germanic lands, northern France, Normandy and then to England. Everyone outside of this slender path has been spared. What other plague has spread this way?'

No one answered him.

'And once it entered England,' Hugh continued. 'What did it do? Again, that relatively narrow path across the southern and central parts of your realm, Edmond. As if it were following a *scent*. It travelled in a straight path.

'Straight to Pengraic. Where it stopped.'

'What do you intimate?' said Raife. 'That I have been harbouring some devilish —'

Hugh held up a hand. 'If you please, a moment, my lord. Now the plague has reoccurred. How is it travelling? May I ask?'

'It is travelling from Pengraic straight toward London,' said Richard, Edmond's son.

Hugh smiled, staring right at Raife. 'Ah. It is travelling in a direct line from Pengraic right toward London.'

'It is following the earl?' Edmond said, his voice thick with disbelief.

'I believe not,' said Hugh. 'I think, as does my Brother Fulke here, that it is following the earl's wife, the Lady Maeb.'

Raife sprang to his feet, thumping a fist on the table as he did so. 'What new accusation is this cast at my wife? Eh? You asked her here under false pretences, monk!'

Hugh spread his hands. 'Hear me out. None of this made sense to us, until I arrived in England recently and Brother Fulke here told me that final piece of information which *did* make sense of everything.

'A few months before the pestilence and the Devil's imp's arrival in the Holy Lands, one of the Order's sergeants, Godfrey Langtofte, left both the Order and the Holy Lands and returned to his native country.'

I felt cold.

Hugh gave a slight shrug. 'Sometimes we lose people back to the sinful life. It happens. At the time we thought nothing of it, and *I* had continued to think nothing of it until I arrived here in London and Brother Fulke informed me of both the path of the plague here in England, *and* of the identity of the Earl of Pengraic's new wife.'

He paused, and I looked at the table top, unable to look at him or anyone else about the table.

'The Lady Maeb,' Hugh said. 'Godfrey's daughter.'

I closed my eyes momentarily at the sudden buzz of murmuring.

'*What are you saying?*' Edmond hissed through the low voices.

'We think now that someone found the Devil's diadem within the crypt of the Temple of Solomon, and stole it, fixated by its beauty. We believe that person to be Godfrey Langtofte — he is the only member of our Order in Jerusalem at the appropriate time, who had access to the Temple, and whom we cannot account for. That he fled Jerusalem with little reason given to us is damning. As is the fact the plague trails at Langtofte's daughter's heels, from one side of this realm to the other, town by town as she rides through, and then back again. It does not deviate.

'Lady Maeb's father stole the Devil's diadem from the crypt within the Temple at Jerusalem,' Hugh said again, his voice as calm as if he discussed the clouds in the sky, 'then brought it to England, where he gave it to his daughter Maeb before he died. As the pestilence follows her every move, then Lady Maeb must have the diadem.'

'I have not!' I said, looking to Raife for support.

He was gazing at me with an unfathomable look. *Sweet Jesu! Did he believe this?*

'I do *not* have any diadem,' I said as forcefully as I could.

'This is truly some fantastical tale,' Edmond said slowly, but even he was regarding me speculatively.

I felt increasingly ill with fear. Was this why the imps had been in our house at Cornhill? But I did not have any diadem! I did not! I closed my eyes briefly, praying that Raife did not mention the imps.

'Did your father give you anything before he died?' Edmond said.

'How many times must I say this?' I said. 'My father gave me nothing but a few rags to wear and the name of his house. That is all. Sweet Jesu! He left everything else in his will to the Templars! *You* have it, Master Hugh! You must have! Perhaps buried in the crypt at your round church on Holbournestrate. Has your Brother Fulke neglected to mention it to you?'

'We have searched your father's old estate carefully,' Fulke d'Ecouis said. 'There is nothing there.'

'Then I give you full permission to search my chests and chambers, Brother Fulke. You may search my body, too, lest you think I secrete the diadem in this belly.' I struck my belly with my hand.

'You may have hidden it anywhere,' d'Ecouis said. 'You've had long enough.'

'I do not have the damned thing!' I cried, and the note of hysteria in my voice finally brought Raife to my support.

'My wife has no diadem,' he said. 'I know her belongings as well as any. She does not harbour the diadem. If what you say is true then my wife must be carrying it about, hither and thither, but yet I have not seen it, nor have, I wager, any of her attending women. Believe me, if she was secreting the Devil's diadem then I think *I* would know it.'

'I have nothing to hide,' I said, still emotional and frightened. 'Search what you will. You have my entire permission. Ask my women! Search! I dare you to find this thing!'

I was so angry that I found myself weeping, and Raife put a hand on my shoulder.

'If the plague is, as you suggest, coming now to London,' he said to the Templars, 'then you must believe that the diadem is here, now, in London. Then come search my house, I beg you, and let this matter rest.' He paused, then thumped the table with his fist. 'Lord God above, I am heartily *sick* of these attacks on my wife! How often must she prove herself innocent to you?'

'I stand with my lord of Pengraic on this issue,' said Edmond. His voice was calm, but very authoritative. 'The countess has already been venomously attacked and proven by God and before all to be innocent. This is a truly fantastical tale you weave, Master Hugh, and on what? Mere supposition?'

'How many other people have been through Jerusalem and then back in England in the past few years?' Raife said. 'If the diadem is here — if it exists at all — then anyone might have brought it. Thousands of pilgrims and crusaders have been to and fro this realm and Jerusalem in the past years. Why fixate so on my wife?'

'Because, unusually for a mere sergeant, her father had access to the crypt before he vanished from our Order so precipitously,' said Hugh. 'We kept stores of gold there, which he accounted for.

'Because the plague clearly follows your wife's steps. And because of your wife's sheer damned luck over the past year — she survived the plague, and rose from obscurity to sit at the king's right hand as your wife. I find that ... fascinating.'

'My horse, Dulcette, might be harbouring the diadem,' I said. 'The plague could as easily have been following her as me.'

'Think not to use wit to —' Hugh began.

'Enough!' Edmond said, raising both hands. 'I have heard *enough* of this! It is a fine tale, master, but I cannot yet believe it. I have a city half burned and de-populated, a people terrified by the renewed ravages of the plague, and here you sit prating of strange jewels and devilish pestilences and accusing one of my court of harbouring a crown so vile that it surely must have stained her hands black with venom had she ever handled it. Yet I see no stain, Master Hugh, not on her hands nor on her character.'

He threw his hands up in the air. 'What will the Countess of Pengraic be accused of next? Crucifying Christ himself?

'Enough, I say. Now all I want to hear from this table are practical measures by which we can aid those affected by fire and drowning, as those by plague who are either in its grip or in its path. Speak, if you will.'

'Raife, look. This is all my father ever gave me.'

We were back in our privy chamber in the Cornhill house. Soon my ladies would be with me to aid me pack for our removal into the chambers in the Tower. But for now, Raife had wanted to see *what* precisely I had from my father.

Raife held the old, ragged folded cloth in his hands, fingered it to make sure it was not concealing a diadem, then he shook it out and looked at it.

'It displays a somewhat poorly worked depiction of the Last Supper,' I said.

He nodded, laying it back in the chest from whence I had taken it. 'It is nothing but tapestry,' he said. 'There is nothing else?'

'No, he gave me nothing else. Most of what I brought with me from my childhood home have been passed on. Two kirtles and several chemises and ribbons. The ribbons I still have, there,' I pointed to where they lay atop my new chemises, 'and the kirtles and chemises I gave to two good wives in Crickhoel before we came to Edmond's court. After your generosity, I had no further need of them.'

'You are *sure* your father gave you nothing else?'

'I am *certain*!'

Raife sighed and sat down. 'What are those Templars on about?'

'I do not know why they fixate on my father.'

'He brought nothing back with him from the Holy Lands?'

'Raife, how am I to know? He might have brought Christ's crown of thorns with him for all I know, and buried it somewhere along the way. I was not his keeper. I do not know where he went or what he brought here or there! All I know is that I do *not* have this diadem and I saw no evidence of it in my father's possession in those few months at Witenie before he died. He made no mention of any such thing.'

'And the Templars have your father's lands and manor at Witenie.'

'Yes.'

'Perhaps I should ride there …'

'And search for this piece of Templar fabrication? You cannot believe this story!'

He gave me a long, considering look, then a small smile. 'Of course not. Now, send for your women that they may pack your finery, and we shall be off to enjoy Edmond's hospitality once more.'

As our house was to be prepared to take in victims of the plague, should it arrive in London, we moved much of our household into the apartments Edmond gave us at the Tower. There Isouda, Ella and Gytha and I unpacked and tried to make our chambers as homely as possible. I felt safer here, not so much from the plague that approached, but from the Templars.

I wondered if Henry was behind their accusations. It seemed that those who plotted against me, having failed to prove me the murderess in God's eyes, had now moved to making me the consort of the Devil — or at least of his diadem.

I might have laughed away their accusations, their fanciful tale, but for one thing.

Those imps who seemed to follow me. Had not one of them been searching among my linens? Had not one of them followed me when I'd got lost within Edmond's palace at Oxeneford? God's truth, one had even secreted itself under the ice, no doubt to see if I had hidden the diadem under my skirts!

Why did they believe this of me? I had *no* diadem!

I did not speak to Raife of these doubts. He had been late in my defence when the Templars had related this tale in Edmond's council, and I think he had truly been considering riding to Witenie to find this mythical diadem himself. I had also never mentioned the imp under the ice to him, so could hardly bring this matter up now.

So I sat, and worried, and wondered what fate, or God, or even the Devil, had in store for me.

CHAPTER TEN

‹‹‹◦⟨∞⟩◦›››

I tried to put the Templars and their accusations behind me. The days passed. I kept mostly to our chambers within the Tower complex. My child was growing heavier, I needed to rest more and, as Edmond was so concerned with London, there was no court to attend. I saw little of Raife, as he spent most of the days out in London, helping where he could.

When I did see him he made no mention of what had been said in the council chamber. Beforehand, he had been so adamant that he would defend me from any more accusations, but now one had been made he was strangely silent.

We did not speak of it, but from time to time I found him looking at me speculatively.

No one else spoke to me of this diadem, either. I do not know if de Lacy had told his wife, but I had not seen Alianor since leaving her hall. She had returned north to her husband's estates in Blachburnscire while her husband Robert rode with the Queen's funeral procession. I missed her company.

I grew bored. My women and I sewed garments for the baby, and we made what arrangements we could for my confinement within the Tower, as it seemed I would give birth there, but I did little else save stroll about inner and outer bailies, and sometimes, with the gentle Ghent at my side, along the moat outside the outer curtain wall.

One morning I rose very early, well before dawn. I had spent another uncomfortable night — alone, as it happened, as Raife had sent word to say he was staying overnight in the Cornhill house. Uncomfortable, cramped and achy, I decided to visit Saint John's chapel to pray.

Ella came with me. She had been lying in bed, too cold to sleep, and was happy to accompany me (Raife had forbidden me to wander about beyond our chambers alone in the dark). We wrapped ourselves warmly and set out across the inner bailey.

The Tower was very quiet. Guards on the staircase into the lesser hall on the first floor allowed us entry unchallenged (both of us were well known about the Tower now). The hall was comfortably warmer than outside, all its fireplaces roaring, stoked by the boys set by each one to maintain them overnight. People lay huddled about wrapped in mantles, cloaks and covers. A few dogs nosed around looking for scraps.

'You stay by the fires here, Ella,' I murmured as we walked through the hall. 'I would like to pray by myself. I cannot have you loitering to your death in this cold in the gallery outside the chapel.'

'Are you sure my lady?'

'Certain, Ella. Look. There is a stool by that fire. Take it now, and I shall know where to find you on my return. I shall not be long.'

Ella nodded, grateful for the command, and she left me for her place by the fire. I hugged my mantle closer, walking through to the north-east tower stairs and then up to the southern gallery and into the chapel.

It was freezing in the chapel, and I thought I would not spend long at my prayers at all; the walk was what I had wanted more than anything else. I walked toward a statue of the Virgin Mary where I thought I would kneel and ask for her intervention during my confinement that both I and the child might survive.

I stepped about a pillar — then gasped and took a step back in shock.

'My lady, I did not mean to startle you.'

Edmond was sitting on the floor of the chapel, his back against the pillar. I did not know if he was drunk, or ill, or in despair, for I had never seen his face look so terrible, or his posture so slumped.

I knelt down, ungainly in my pregnancy. 'My lord? Are you ill? Should I summon —'

He waved his hand. 'Not ill. Raddled with guilt.'

'My lord? What is wrong?'

He let out a deep breath. 'News came during the night. Adelaide is dead.'

My mind was so fogged it took me several heartbeats to remember who Adelaide was.

'Your queen is gone? God rest her soul, sir. May the saints watch over her.'

Another wave of that hand. 'May the saints watch over her? *I* should have been the one watching over her, Maeb. Instead I let her slip further and further from my mind. I did not realise how ill she was … I never thought.'

'I had heard she miscarried a few months ago.'

'Aye, and she continued to bleed from that miscarry until it killed her, and yet none thought to tell me. Yet neither did I think to enquire. I sent messengers occasionally to spout hackneyed words regarding her welfare, but I have not truly *thought* of her in months. Is that the fate of all wives, Maeb? Is this what husbands do to you all? Do we all swagger our way through the concerns of the wider world and thus leave you to die alone and forgot in our thoughts?'

I did not know what to say. I thought banal words of reassurance that he had not treated Adelaide badly would be met with irritation, and so I did not speak them.

'Many times, my lord, yes,' I said softly.

Tears had formed in his eyes, and he wiped them away with one hand. 'I will show her the respect in death I should have done in life,' he said. 'Adelaide shall be buried in Hereford Cathedral whose building she championed throughout her life; she told me once she wished to rest there. But that deed shall not atone for my neglect during our marriage. Oh God, Maeb, what shall I do?'

It distressed me to see him so melancholy. 'You could rise from this cold floor, my lord king. That would be a start. I am near-encased in ice sitting here with you.'

'Jesu God!' he said, getting to his feet and holding out his hands to assist me to rise. 'Here I am wallowing in my own self-reproach and letting you sit amid this frozen lake of a floor! What more do I need to prove my neglect of those about me?'

Even with his support I struggled to get to my feet, and both of us were smiling at my ungainliness by the time I stood before him.

'Pengraic should have defended you more in council,' he said. 'I was angry at him for not speaking out earlier than he did.'

I shrugged my shoulders.

'I would have spoken out far more boldly had I been your husband,' Edmond said.

'You did speak out boldly, my lord.'

'And you may be sure, Maeb, that not a day goes by that I wish I was, indeed, your husband.'

Now I truly did not know what to say.

'But how could you want me,' he said, so soft, 'when you know already what a poor husband I be?'

I knew well before he laid his mouth to mine that he would kiss me, but I did nothing to evade it. The kiss was very gentle, yet deep, and I found myself leaning in to him, allowing him to run his hand behind my head, down my back, over my hip.

The baby kicked suddenly, and I pulled back.

'I must not,' I said.

'And yet you did.' Edmond touched my face, running tender fingers from my temple down my cheek to my mouth. 'And even now, having found your resolve, you do not run.'

'How could I?' I asked. 'In this state.'

We both smiled, and Edmond gave me another, quicker kiss. 'One day, Maeb …'

'One day is very far away.'

'I wonder,' he said, his fingers and eyes back on my mouth. 'I wonder.'

PART SIX

THE BEARSCATHE MOUNTAINS

CHAPTER ONE

I had been exceedingly unsettled by that chapel visit, and was glad when Edmond departed within two days for Elesberie manor where lay his wife's corpse. He said that he would be attentive to her in death as he should have been in life, and meant to give her the burial she wanted — before the altar of the recently completed Hereford Cathedral.

Richard and John went with their father. Of Henry there had been no word. No one knew — or if they did were not saying — where he was. It worried me more than a little. Henry was a bad enemy to both me and Raife, and we would have preferred him in plain sight.

It was not a good time to leave London, but Edmond was insistent. His guilt over his lack of care for Adelaide ran deep indeed. He left Raife as Constable over all London to direct the rebuilding and reorganisation of the city, as well as its preparations for the plague which came closer every day. My husband, who I think may have preferred to have returned to Pengraic, was thus stuck in the city. Much of the court went with Edmond, too. There was to be a stately funeral procession from Elesberie through the counties of Bochinghamscire, Oxenefordscire, Glowecestrescire to Herefordscire and then two weeks of mourning and funeral ceremonies at Hereford Cathedral.

Every day news grew of the plague drawing closer. It had reached, and consumed, Oxeneford, and now moved along the roads which led to London.

It took the precise path Raife and I had taken on our journey to London. It took no detours. This plague wanted London, and nothing else.

No one who had heard Hugh of Argentine speak could put his words out of their minds. When those few left in the Tower who had heard his words — Alan de Bretagne, the Constable of the Tower, the Bishop of Wincestre, those city aldermen who occasionally came to speak with Raife — passed me within the Tower, or held conversation with me, I could see the speculation in their eyes.

Does the Countess of Pengraic have this diadem? If she admitted it, and handed it over, then could this Devil-sent plague be averted?

I felt like screaming at them that if I *did* have the diadem then I would throw it from the top of the Tower to any who would catch it, if they thought that might help.

I could see the question shadowing Raife's eyes, too, and I felt it created a distance between us, as if he no longer trusted me.

I felt marked by the Devil, although I had never wittingly allowed him near.

I wished I could raise my father from his grave to either set these rumours to rest once and for all, or to say where he'd left the damned diadem, if he had, indeed, taken it.

I cursed the Templars daily, and wished I had any other birth name than Langtofte.

Raife and I spent most of our time apart. He was consumed by London and its troubles, and spent many nights away from our bed, claiming he kept such late nights at London's problems, and such early mornings, that oft times it was easier for him to bed down somewhere in the city, even in our house on Cornhill. In my darker moments I imagined him tearing that house apart while I was not there, looking for the diadem. I don't know why he could have wanted it … perhaps to save me from the persecution of the Templars, or perhaps for power, which all nobles lusted after.

I was big with child now, and I feared my body had grown unattractive to my husband. On those nights we did spend together Raife said he was weary and was not interested in love-making.

Images of his former mistresses swam through my dreams. Both were still in London, and I wondered *where* he spent his nights, truly. I suppose I suffered the anxieties and insecurities of every wife at some time or the other, but even if I tried to reassure myself of that, it did not help me sleep better at night.

Edmond found me desirable enough, even big with child. Why not my husband?

I could not even remember the last time Raife had kissed me.

One night, again spent on my own, I could not sleep. I worried about Raife and his absence. I worried about the Templars. I worried about the plague. I worried about whether or not my father had died in unconfessed sin, wearing the mantle of a thief. I carried the weight of the world on my shoulders that night, I think. I rose sometime, late, and wrapped myself in a gown to make the journey to the privy which, in these apartments, was far down the end of a corridor. I slipped through the solar, pausing to tell Isouda — who had waked as I opened the connecting door between my chamber and theirs — that I was only going to the privy, and made my way to the cubicle set into the outside wall of the building.

On my return, walking along the corridor, I heard my husband's voice.

I stopped, astounded and delighted. He had returned after all! I stood still, trying to locate him — he was speaking very low — and then walked several paces further to a small chamber which was used to store our household plate and linens. I did not even wonder why Raife was holding a conversation with someone in there, or why at such a late hour.

I was simply happy that he had decided to come back to me this night, after all.

I knew at some deep level that it was all wrong even before I had pushed the door open. The foul stink would have registered at some level, but it didn't register soon enough to make me stop pushing the door fully open, nor soon enough to stop me stepping into the chamber.

I surprised them. I caught them totally unawares, which meant that I saw Raife, sitting on a chest, completely relaxed, half smiling, engaged in a conversation with the imp who stood, equally at ease, leaning against a wall.

It was that sense of friendship and utter relaxation between them which, on later reflection, I found almost as shocking as the sight of my husband engaged in a conversation with an imp from hell.

They both stood straight when they saw me.

Raife's face registered profound horror, the imp's complete disdain, even hatred. It hissed, so violently that spittle flew across the room, and reached its clawed hands forward.

'Begone!' Raife said. '*Now!*'

I don't know who he was speaking to, me or the imp, but we both took action.

The imp took a step back and dissolved into the stone wall behind him, and I turned, my hand on the door, mouth open, about to shriek as I ran into the corridor.

Raife seized my wrist and dragged me into the chamber, closing the door behind us and leaning against it so I had no hope of escape.

I could hardly breathe. I was shocked, frightened, and the imp's stink still thickened and fouled the air.

'By God, Maeb, why did you disturb us?' Raife said, and I thought I heard his voice break.

I turned my head, retching, and Raife caught me to him, trying to support me.

I twisted to one side, fighting him with my fists, wanting only to get away.

'Maeb, *listen to me!*'

'No! Release me! Release me!'

He seized both my wrists, and wrestled me to stillness.

'You have been talking to these imps?' I said. 'Why? Why?'

'Maeb —'

'They've been following *you* all this time! Not me! Always in your house … and that imp in Edmond's palace was about to meet you when I —'

'Maeb, *silence!*'

I stared at him, terrified. I kept trying to pull my wrists away but he had them in such a grip that I knew by morning they would be bruised.

If I was still alive.

'Who are you?' I whispered. '*What?*'

'Damn you for disturbing me! *Damn you!*'

I was so terrified that now I was weeping. I knew he was about to kill me. I sobbed, wretched convulsive sobs that tore through my body.

Raife cursed, then grabbed me to him, trying to comfort me.

I could not be comforted by him. Not by him, not now.

'Why? Why? Why?'

'Maeb, you must not speak of this. I —'

'No! You want me to keep silent about *this*? I saw you talking to that imp as if … as if you were brothers! What is happening Raife? What?'

'Maeb, you *must* keep this silent!'

'No!' I screamed the word, and Raife had to grapple with me and slap his hand over my mouth so that I did not continue to scream and wake the entire household.

'For God's sake, woman, calm yourself! You are with child, and you might harm the —'

'What have I got in my belly, Raife?' I said, managing to wrench my mouth away. 'What are *you*?'

He took a deep breath. 'If I tell you, will you keep calm?'

I did not reply.

'God's justice, Maeb, if I tell you *will you keep calm*?'

I gave a terse nod and his grip on me relaxed somewhat.

'Sit down here, Maeb.' He indicated a dusty stool, and I sat, noting that Raife still kept his back to the door.

My hands were shaking, and I gripped them to try and ease their tremble.

'Whatever I say now, Maeb, remember that once I asked you to always trust me completely. *Whatever* happened. You agreed.'

'Fool that I was,' I muttered.

'Please *trust* me, Maeb.'

I did not answer, and Raife sighed.

'The Devil has sent his imps to find this diadem,' Raife said.

I gave a nod. This the Templars had said already.

'Thus the Devil has also sent the plague to —'

'Sniff the cursed crown out. Yes, I know.'

There was a silence, and I looked at Raife. He was struggling with himself, and I realised he needed to force out the next words.

'The Devil has also sent me,' he said, 'to retrieve the diadem once the pestilence has sniffed it out.'

I did not at first take in his words. I just looked at him, my mind trying to rearrange what he'd said so that it made better sense than 'The Devil has also sent me'.

'The plague is to show me where the diadem hides,' he said, 'and I am to retrieve it and take it back for the Devil.'

I remembered Raife's preoccupation about how far and to where the plague had spread. All his maps.

I remembered how he had worried so that his love for me might deflect him from his purpose. Then, I had thought it the usual aristocratic ambition, but now …

And that time so recently, when I was to undergo the ordeal, and Raife had said that I knew not the power he commanded that he could bring to bear to save me.

So many things, that I had misinterpreted at the time in my innocence.

Sweet Jesu, the signs had been there all along that Raife was no true man!

'You come from hell?' I said, my voice not working as it should. 'Are you … an imp?'

'No. I am a man. A sinner sent to hell for my misdeeds. Over the centuries I have worked my way to being the Devil's most trusted lieutenant. Maeb … *please trust me.*'

'Trust you? Trust you?' Then the import of what he'd said a moment earlier sunk in. 'You married me because you thought I had the diadem? Is that why?'

Is that the only reason he took me to wife, because he thought I had the diadem?

Pain and hurt knifed through me, so deep, so sharp, I once more found it difficult to breathe. All those sweet words. Lies. All those tender kisses and caresses. Pretence.

Sweet Jesu … sweet Jesu … sweet Jesu …

He dropped down on his knees before me, grabbing at my hands. 'No! I married you because I loved you, Maeb. What the Templars said was as new to me as it was to you. I had no idea, oh God, Maeb, I have never loved any as I love you. Trust me, please, God, *please!*'

'You hated me the moment you saw me! You always have!'

'Do you want to know why I snarled at you in that damned, *damned* dirt hole of Alaric's? *Do you?* It was because I had just walked to that door, and I had seen the way Stephen looked at you and you at him. God, I was jealous beyond redemption —'

'You are far beyond any redemption!'

'This is God's truth, Maeb, nothing else! I had loved you from the instant I first set eyes on you. All I had wanted was you!'

'And thus you set your entire family to die so that you could have me?'

'No! *No!* The Devil was supposed to spare my family. I had asked it of him and he had agreed. Oh God, Maeb, I love you, I loved my children, I wanted to see none of you die. I had truly thought you would all be safe at Pengraic! I could not believe he'd set the plague on them. Maeb, Maeb, I have done nothing but love you from the moment I first beheld you.'

'Get away from me.'

'Maeb —'

'Get away from me!'

'Maeb, you promised you would trust me. I ask you to keep that promise now.'

'I shall keep no promise to the Devil's spawn. Get away from me!' I said that last on a rising shriek, and he let go my hands and stood.

I noticed that he was shaking, too, and I thought it because he feared I might reveal him to all.

But how could I do that? How could I walk out that door and reveal that I had taken the Devil's servant to my bed, that I was carrying his child? Accusations of witchcraft would again be raised, and this time people would believe them.

Everyone would think that I had survived that ordeal through the Devil's graces, not God's.

I would be burned. Not even Edmond could save me.

Not even Edmond would *want* to save me.

And all for this 'man' who had betrayed me in the worst possible way.

'Get away from me,' I whispered. I felt sickened, tainted, my belly filled with vileness.

I had loved this man. I had given him everything I was without question, without any price.

And look now what wickedness and depravity he returned to me.

CHAPTER TWO

––•••❦•••––

I returned to our privy chamber, not answering Isouda when she lifted her head and remarked that I had been a long time in the privy and was I well?

I am not too sure how I managed to get back to that chamber on my own legs, nor when precisely Raife let me go. I know he pleaded with me to trust him (how could I?) and to keep silent (how could I not?).

To be honest, I did not even know how I continued to breathe.

My husband. Servant of the Devil. Come to earth from hell. Here to do the Devil's work.

And I tied to him as wife. My *fate* tied to him. I could no more plead for help from an ecclesiastic or noble than I could command the sun from the sky. No one would believe I had not also been in league with Raife, particularly not after all the seeds of doubt Henry planted in people's minds, nor after my miraculous ordeal.

Sweet Jesu, one way or another he would drag me to hell along with him.

And he wanted me to *trust* him?

I don't know where Raife went after that terrible time in the storage chamber. Maybe he went to weep on the imp's shoulder. I don't know. I didn't care.

I sat in the dark in our privy chamber, shaking with fear and cold and shock, not knowing what to do.

At dawn, Isouda and Gytha came in, and rushed to my side, no doubt seeing from my face that I was not well.

'My lady!' cried Isouda. 'What ails you?'

'I am not well.'

'My lady? Should we call the midwife?'

I gave a shake of my head. 'I have had the most terrible nightmare,' I said. 'It almost seemed real.'

Isouda hugged me — she was not one to hide her emotions. 'Then we shall see you washed and dressed and set to rights with the morning sun,' she said.

If only, I thought. If only the morning sun could set all to rights.

She chatted over me as she aided me to wash and garb myself, Gytha, silent as always, attending to my hair.

I did not know what to do with my day. It was if my entire life had come to a halt and I could not see what step to take next.

Raife walked into the chamber just as I was dressed and sitting again, staring vaguely into the chamber, trying to think what I needed to do.

'Leave us,' he said to Isouda and Gytha.

'Stay,' I said to them.

His face tightened, and I knew he was angry. What could he do against my disobedience? Call on me the fires of hell?

'As you wish,' he said, his voice grating through his teeth.

Isouda and Gytha sensed the tension, and backed into the shadows, their eyes watchful.

'I have decided,' Raife said, 'that it would be better for you to go to —'

'Pengraic,' I said, suddenly realising that I wanted to be there more than anywhere. I could pray over Stephen's grave. Talk to Owain.

I could talk to Owain when I could talk to no other.

'Have you lost your wits, woman?' Raife said.

'I have lost all else I hold dear,' I shot back at him.

'You cannot undertake a journey like that! You are near to your confinement, and —'

'Adelie did it. What she did, so can I.'

And look what happened to Adelie. I could see it writ over his face.

'It is winter!' Raife said. 'The roads will be icy and treacherous!'

'Better than spring and the roads thigh deep in mud.'

'By God, woman, you risk both yourself and the child on the way!'

'Don't you dare speak of God's name to me,' I said, low. Then louder. 'I will go. Ghent can escort us and I have no doubt you will send a suitable company with us and coin enough to pay for us to sleep under cover at night.'

'The plague is —'

'We can avoid areas of the plague.'

'And you want to drag Isouda and Gytha and Ella through this?'

'They can come with me or not as they please,' I said. 'I shall not hold it against them if they do not wish to come.'

'I will come,' said Isouda.

'And I,' said Gytha.

I smiled, feeling as if there was some worth left in this world after all. 'Thank you, my friends.'

Raife was furious. I could see it in the way he held himself and in the tightening of his face.

He was losing control of me.

Good.

He could see his damned diadem vanishing before his eyes.

Good.

'I want to go home to Pengraic,' I said, 'and so I shall.'

'Have you no idea what will follow you?' he hissed.

The plague? I raised my eyebrows at him. 'Then I shall save London, shall I not?'

He hissed again, then whipped about and struck a goblet so viciously it flew from its platter halfway across the room.

Even in their shadows I could see Gytha and Isouda jump.

'I have said everything I have to say to you, husband,' I said. 'Please see to the arrangements, or at least allow Ghent to make them in your name.'

'I asked you once to trust me,' he said. 'Now I ask it again.'

I was so furious I almost rose to strike him. He *dared* ask me to trust him? After what he had revealed?

After what he had *hidden* from me all this time?

'And I have given you my answer,' I said. 'Now, will you aid your wife to return to her home, or shall I be forced to beg charity from Bretagne?'

He glared at me, then turned on his heel and stalked from the chamber.

I let out a soft breath of relief, both that he had gone, and that he had not struck me.

Pengraic. I would go home. I would have time and space there to think and reflect, to talk with Owain, and to birth this baby.

* * *

My husband allowed me to go. He had no choice, really, for to demand I stay in London when the plague approached and when I wanted to leave would have seemed ... odd. Likewise I could not speak out to anyone of his true nature, because then the charges of witchcraft and murder would rise again as sure as the sun rises each morn.

He left all the arrangements in Ghent's hands along with a goodly purse of coin to pay for what was needed. Poor Ghent. He was confused by the sudden iciness between the earl and myself. He did not like it, but he said nothing. All he did was his best, as he always did, and that best was more than good enough.

We left London four days later.

CHAPTER THREE

••►◄(◎)►◄••

We travelled in as small a company as possible. It was still deep winter over the south and middle of England and, with the spring crops a long way distant (and a bad harvest the previous year because of the plague), many places might find it impossible to offer food for a large group. What we ate might well mean hunger for someone else. Thus, together with myself and my three women (Ella was also happy to leave London) and Ghent, there were just nine horsed soldiers, and two grooms. We did not travel with any of the Pengraic household plate and linens that normally accompanied a countess or earl to and fro their abodes, but only our clothes and some warm covers. Pengraic had plate and linen enough for my needs, I did not require the gold and silver and pewter.

My husband the earl could keep it for his daily needs.

I travelled in a cart together with Gytha. I was too big with child now to ride safely, although I did insist Dulcette came with us. Tied to the back of the cart with a loose rope, Dulcette ambled contentedly along, no doubt happy to undertake a journey free of rider and harness.

Ghent and I had plotted out a journey that would take us to the north of the usual route to Pengraic. We wanted to avoid the plague areas. If, as the Templars had proposed, the plague always travelled in a narrow strip following my footsteps, then I could be confident that if we strayed only a short distance north we could avoid the plague completely. Ghent was less sure — he had not heard what Master Hugh had said — but I tried to reassure him as much as possible that the northerly route would be safe for us.

I was torn over this decision though. Although I had survived the plague once, and would be unlikely to catch it again, as countess I had a responsibility to those who travelled with me. I should not risk exposing my women, none of whom had been in contact with the plague, nor the soldiers and grooms who travelled with us. But in doing this, and if Master Hugh was correct in supposing the plague followed me, I would be exposing villages, towns and communities which otherwise would have remained pestilence free to the horrors of the disease.

Whatever I did would see innocent people die. Even if I had stayed in London, then that city of tens of thousands would be ravaged, whereas now I hoped it would escape.

I did not sleep well at night.

On the day we left, my husband came to farewell us in the inner bailey of the Tower. He spoke for a good while with Ghent, then stood to one side, silent, as my women and I either climbed into the cart or mounted our horses.

Only once we were all set, and Ghent about to wave us forward, did he come over to my cart.

'Travel safely, wife,' he said.

I gave a nod.

'Send word once you reach Pengraic.'

I gave another nod.

'For God's sakes, Maeb …'

'I wish you good luck in your quest,' I said. 'It will be quite the relief to me once it is all done.'

And you returned to hell.

My husband's face tightened. 'You have no idea of what you speak,' he said.

'If I *still* have no idea then it because you have spun yet more lies to me.'

Everyone in our column was now completely silent, the earl's and my words ricocheting about the inner bailey.

My husband stepped back. 'Journey well, Ghent. Keep my wife safe.'

Then he was striding back inside the building which housed our chambers, not waiting to see us gone.

I was close to tears, not only because the depth of ill-feeling between my husband and I was unsettling, but because everyone had heard that ill exchange. Poor Ghent, his back was as stiff and as straight as if he was tied to a lance.

As we rumbled out of the outer bailey, I turned on my cushions and looked behind me.

The Conqueror's Tower rose grim and silent in the early morning, dusted with snow, the skies low and grey above.

My eyes filled with tears, and I turned my face forward, looking to the journey ahead.

We travelled as fast as the icy roads and winter conditions would allow. Our first day's travel was on roads well kept because of their proximity to London, and we made Sancti Albani by nightfall, where we were welcomed by the abbot of the church and fed and housed comfortably. It had been a long day, and I slept solidly despite my worries, and we did not start the next day until well into the morning.

From Sancti Albani we turned north-west to follow a route that would take us a comfortable distance north of the plague-affected towns. In two days we reached Elesberie, where so recently Queen Adelaide had died. Here we stayed at the royal manor, almost ghost-like now that Edmond had departed with his wife's corpse for the journey to Hereford cathedral. He was ten days or more ahead of us.

Ghent thought we should try to catch up as we would be travelling for much of the way along the same route. Edmond would be travelling slowly as he had half of his court and household with him, and because his was a mourning procession.

I did not wish to catch up with Edmond. To Ghent I argued that it would mean speedy and risky travelling along icy roads in bad weather for us to make up those ten days, and I did not wish it, nor did I wish to suddenly find myself among the court again when I was so great with child. Privately I simply did not want to see Edmond. I was certain that he would know almost instantly that something was badly wrong, and his sympathy and charm (and his sheer dogged persistence) might well worm it out of me.

I did not want Edmond to think badly of me or risk him withdrawing his support when I needed it so badly. Because of me his eldest son, his heir, had been humiliated in front of the entire court and had subsequently vanished.

No. I could not risk losing Edmond's support.

We would not catch up to his procession.

To make certain, we stayed in Elesberie some three days, during which

Ghent's impatience grew at the same rate his temper heated. He wanted badly to get me to Pengraic as quickly as he might — the last thing Ghent wished was for me to go into labour in the cart.

Finally he managed to get me back in my cart, and we set off once more.

From Elesberie we wandered across the back of the realm, though Wodestoch and Chinteneham and all the hamlets in between, until, finally, after some two weeks of uneventful if bone-chilling journeying, we reached Saint Mary's Priory and monastery at Derheste on the Severn. The monastery here was only small, and while Ghent, myself and my women were housed in the monastic dormitories, the soldiers and grooms had to make do with the chillier loft above the stables.

My women and I went into the church to pray before our supper. Once done, I wandered about the beautiful, ancient church. One of the monks accompanied me, a man named Thomas, who pointed out the ancient font covered with strange spiral carvings as well as many of the other carvings in the church.

I came across one set of carvings that made me furrow my brow.

'What beasts are these?' I said, touching the stonework, so ancient it had worn quite away, making the original lines of the carving difficult to decipher.

'Ah,' said Thomas, touching them almost in reverence, 'some say these represent wolves, some dragons. The people hereabouts believe them their protectors — whether dragons or wolves — and come to church to rub the figures with their fingers, and pray to them for safeguard.'

'That is most un-Christian,' I said automatically, but I remembered a similar story that Owain had told me, the wolves in my dream when I had died and the silver wolf who had wandered with my protector knight.

The wolves, always.

Thomas shrugged. 'It can be difficult to wean people away from their ancient beliefs. The stories of the Old People are still told in the forests about here, and this church is very, very old. Built when respect for the Old People was strong.'

And now the Old People again. I thought of my sun-drenched knight, and wondered if he would still protect me even knowing I was wed to one of the Devil's servants.

* * *

After Saint Mary's Priory and Derheste we travelled through increasingly dense forests as we wended our way west. We were close to Wales now, only a week at most from Pengraic, and I looked forward to reaching the castle. It would be good to cease this travelling, and relax, and think.

The forests protected us from the worst of the wintry weather which still battered the country. Even then, some days we could not travel because of the storms, and had to wait out the winds and snow in some tiny hamlet or monastic outpost. Eventually we crossed the Wye at Godric Castle, and there enjoyed the hospitality of its castellan, Godric of Mappestone.

Godric was a goodly fellow, and happy for the company. We arrived at midday at his castle, and thus had time for rest before we enjoyed dinner about the fires of his large hall. Ghent and I sat at his high table, while Godric went to great lengths to ensure that the wife of the powerful Earl of Pengraic was well fed and entertained.

He was curious — and somewhat cautious — about our planned route through to Pengraic. 'The forest of Depdene between here and Bergeveny is thick and dark this time of the year,' he said. 'The snow will be lying in great drifts on either side of the road and, in some places, even over the road. Your soldiers and groom may have to lay aside their weapons for shovels. I shall give you some, that you not be caught unawares.'

Ghent thanked Godric and asked if there were any other dangers.

Godric looked uncertain, flashing a concerned look at me.

'If I must endure it,' I said, 'then I may as well hear it now, my lord.'

Godric sighed. 'You must be careful to keep your company together, Ghent. The pickings in the Black Mountains have been poor this winter, and at least three packs of wolves have come down into the forest, hunting. They are thin and dangerous, and may attack any isolated outriders.'

'They would surely not attack our company?' I said.

Wolves? What was this — legend come to life?

'Not if you stay together, my lady. And be sure at night, wherever you stay within reach of the Depdene, to keep your horses well stabled, for the packs *will* attack a horse.'

I shuddered, thinking of Dulcette.

'We shall be careful, my lord,' I said. 'Thank you for your care.'

* * *

We rested with Godric for two days while poor weather blew over, then rode further into Depdene forest. Godric, worthy man that he was, had supplied us with not only shovels, but stores of dry food and cured hams in case we had to overnight within the forest at any point.

I hoped we should not have to do that, for I had taken to heart his warning of the wolf packs.

But we had to be careful. We were travelling on forest tracks rather than populated roads, and on our first day out we saw no one the entire morning of our travel.

We stopped for a brief meal about noon, then continued on our way, hoping to make Skenfrith Castle by nightfall. Despite our best intentions, our travel was slow. The track was poor, making it difficult for the two carts to travel at any speed. We twice had to stop so the soldiers could dismount and clear a path for us through the snowdrifts.

By late afternoon, as we travelled as quick as we might along the track, we could hear the baying of wolves.

'They are far away,' Ghent tried to reassure me, and, yes, at first they were. But they quickly drew nearer, and a little time later it was pointless to assume anything other than that a pack of wolves had scented our horses, or had heard our laborious passage through the forest, and were firmly on our track. Despite all the old stories and myths I had heard about the wolves being protectors, I was frightened. It was easier to believe these howling hounds were vicious predators than supernatural protectors.

Ghent bunched us together as tightly as possible, positioning soldiers to either side of my cart, riding close himself, sword drawn, eyes darting this way and that.

The howls of the wolves were now close in among the trees to either side of us, and sometimes I thought I could see a flash of their bodies as they ran. But soon even those flashes vanished as the weather set in, and a cold, grey mist enveloped us.

Ahead I could just make out that the forest drew back a little, and that we were coming to a clearing.

'Perhaps we could stop here?' I said to Ghent.

He shook his head. 'No. We have to continue on. We cannot stop. We keep moving until we reach Skenfrith Castle. The moment we stop we are vulnerable.'

I hugged my mantle closer, calling out to Isouda and Ella, who rode horses, to keep as close to the cart as they could, and trying to reassure Gytha who sat white-faced and round-eyed next to me.

She must have been wondering at the wisdom of leaving the streets of London for the wilds of the Welsh Marches.

We trundled into the clearing, and I breathed a little easier, thinking that while we were so far distant from the trees the wolves would stay back.

But as soon as that thought crossed my mind, I heard Ghent exclaim, and our company ground to a halt.

I half rose, to see what obstructed our path, and froze as I saw.

A knight sat his courser fifteen or so paces before us, half obscured by the mist.

It was a magnificent white courser, its mane trailing on the ground, its tresses woven with diamonds which glinted but dully in this light.

I stared, realising that Ghent, as everyone else, could see him as well as I.

A wolf appeared out of the mist behind the knight, trotting up to sit by his courser.

It was a huge beast, silvery-grey, with pale, piercing eyes.

Then another wolf trotted out of the mist to sit with the knight, and another, until ten or twelve of them sat about the knight.

Ghent kicked his horse forward, his sword still drawn.

'Ghent —' I called, but either he did not hear me, or he ignored me.

Several among the wolves snarled as Ghent rode up to the knight but did not otherwise move. He pulled his horse to a halt some two paces from the knight, stayed still for several heartbeats, then he abruptly sheathed his sword, and rode his horse up to the knight.

They both reached out, grasping each other's forearms in greeting.

Sweet Jesu, what was going on? I looked at the ground, wanting to get down and walk up to them, but I could not climb out by myself, and none of the soldiers would look at me, even when I spoke, so possessed were they by what happened up the track.

Muttering to myself, annoyed that I could not get out of the cart, I balanced precariously, Gytha holding onto one of my hands as I tried to see or even hear what was happening.

From what I could see, the strange knight — his face hid now by tendrils of mist rather than by bright sun — and Ghent were simply sitting their horses, looking at each other.

Then the knight leaned forward, clapping Ghent on the shoulder, and both knights spent a long moment, heads bowed, foreheads almost touching, in some strange, silent communication.

The knight leaned back, Ghent nodded, then abruptly the strange knight wheeled his courser about, and he and the wolves vanished into the mist.

I felt resentful. He had paid me no attention.

'Gilbert?' I called.

Ghent's shoulders and back moved as he visibly pulled in a deep breath, then he pivoted his horse about on its hind legs and rode back to me.

'Please sit down, my lady,' he said. 'You will topple out if you do not sit.'

I sat, irritated. 'Gilbert? What did that knight want?'

'You did not hear our conversation?'

'No. I did not. What did he say?'

Ghent frowned, as if I had disappointed him. 'Well, he talked of the bear, and how he may not trespass on the bear. The bear is sacrosanct, and he may not interfere.'

I almost hissed in frustration. 'Gilbert, what does that *mean*?'

Again Ghent frowned. 'You do not understand, my lady?'

I was about to snap at him, then realised that Ghent was still lost in another world. 'What else did he say, Gilbert?'

'That we face trials ahead. That he will do what he can.'

Trials?

'My lady,' Ghent said, hesitating a long moment before he continued, 'how may I say this?'

Again, a pause.

'There are trials ahead. There is blood ahead. There is nothing you can do, nor could have done, to prevent it. Do not grieve too much.'

And with that unsettling, obscure statement, Ghent turned his horse and waved our company on as he rode forward.

No matter how much I pressed him later that night, when finally we arrived at Skenfrith Castle, Ghent did not elaborate. Indeed, he barely spent a word on me, and I realised he was still adrift into whatever dream the knight had dragged him.

CHAPTER FOUR

We started early the next day. It should be an easy day's journeying through the last of the forest until we reached Bergeveny, but we did not want to take risks.

From Bergeveny, just one short day's travel to Pengraic.

We were almost home, and I allowed myself to rest. I had taken enormous risks travelling when I was so big with child, but we would reach Pengraic in good time.

Or just enough time. Already I could feel the child moving downward, settling itself for birth, and I had begun to experience annoying pains in my back, hips and legs. It would not be long, now.

It was a bright day, and everyone seemed cheered by the appearance of the sun. All save Ghent, who seemed lost in his own world. I found it barely possible to get a word out of him, and his continued dreaminess was beginning to annoy me. I wanted to reach Pengraic, and I didn't want a dawdling, dreamy Ghent to hobble our progress.

We began well enough, but by mid-morning our progress had slowed as we encountered yet more snowdrifts. By mid-afternoon tempers had frayed from our stop–start progress and when we came to a massive tree that had toppled across our pathway, I am afraid I hit the side of the cart with my fist in frustration. I was tense, achy, my back pained me, and all I could think about was Bergeveny and a night's rest there before making for Pengraic as early as possible the next day.

Ghent dismounted from his horse and waved the soldiers into action. We had shovels, but only one axe, and swords were of little use against this mighty tree trunk. While the horses and riders could easily have gone round the tree, the carts could not. The trunk had to be cleared from the path. Ella and Isouda had dismounted from their horses, and sat in the cart with Gytha and myself. We talked desolately, none of us able to raise much of an interest in anything, when Gytha suddenly gave a small shriek.

She was looking round-eyed at something over my shoulder, and I turned grumpily, wondering what could be going wrong now.

What I saw sent a chill of fear through my body.

Two score or more of armed men in maille over dark red tunics were kicking their horses from the forest, and even now were upon Ghent and our soldiers.

My escort had no chance. Most had laid aside their weapons to struggle with the tree, and they did not have time to reach them before they were struck down by the flashing weapons of our attackers.

Two soldiers survived long enough to land several blows, but were then cut down.

Ghent, turning too slowly to face the riders, was felled by a hard blow to the head.

It was all done within moments. I had a hand to my mouth in shock, my women were crying out.

Our two grooms had fled.

Suddenly the attackers surrounded my cart. Several of them flung themselves off their horses, hauling a shrieking Isouda, Ella and Gytha out of the cart. The men spoke in a strange language, and it took me a moment to put the language and red tunics under the maille together and realise who they were.

These were Madog's men. His bodyguard, the Teulu.

Two of the riders climbed into the cart, reaching for me.

I cried out, trying to struggle, but they were too powerful for my pitiful strength. One tied my hands together at the wrists, the other gagged and blindfolded me.

Then one of them grabbed my ankles and pulled me roughly down so that I lay along the floor of the cart.

Covers, blankets and cushions were thrown over me, then something heavy that left me feeling stifled.

For some time nothing but some muffled speaking and a few shouts. I heard something being tossed into the other cart.

I wondered what had happened to my women, then tried not to think of it.

I could easily imagine what was happening to them.

Madog may want me, but he had no use for my women.

After a long time the heavy cover that stifled me was drawn back, and I heard and felt maille hauberks being tossed in the cart, some of them covering my legs, then some cloth — the red tunics, probably.

'Lady Maeb,' said a voice in good French, 'you will lie there quiet. We are taking you now to our lord. You will be kept safe. But while we are moving you will stay still and you will not try to cry out. We have your companion Ghent in the other cart and we will not hesitate to kill him if you try to attract attention. Do you understand me?'

Ghent was still alive? I remembered the sound of something heavy being thrown into the other cart.

'Do you understand me?'

I nodded, wishing I could speak so I could request to be moved into a more comfortable position, or even given some water.

But the man pulled the heavy cover over me once more, and I was left in the darkness, hardly able to breathe, and with the weight of several hauberks lying on my legs.

The cart lurched, and we moved on down the now presumably cleared track.

We travelled for many hours. What was originally discomfort for me eventually became searing pain as my muscles cooled and seized. The movement of the car buffeted me to and fro, and the weight of the maille on my legs became almost unbearable. I could barely move, nor to change my position, and certainly not make any kind of noise to attract attention, even if I had wished. The rope about my wrists cut into the flesh, and my hands swelled so that after a while I could no longer feel or move my fingers. My back and hips ached more powerfully than ever.

But of all the aches and pains, nothing distressed me so much as the fact that after some time I could no longer control my bladder. Urine soaked through my chemise and kirtle, and I wept with the humiliation.

I would be dragged before Madog in this disgusting state, dishevelled, soiled, bleeding.

And then? I did not fool myself that he wanted me alive. He would want something from me — I could not think what unless this was a design only to humiliate my husband — and when he had that he would kill me. This treatment now indicated that he had no interest in keeping me alive once he'd done with me.

The tears collected under my blindfold until the entire wretched thing was soaked, making me even more uncomfortable.

I prayed to my knight, my protector, but he did not come.

I remembered what he had said to Ghent.

There are trials ahead. There is blood ahead. There is nothing you can do, nor could have done, to prevent it. Do not grieve too much.

I wished I had never left London.

We passed through a town at some point, almost certainly Bergeveny. I could hear the street noise, the clatter of carts down the streets, the sound of people talking, laughing.

People living normal lives, not knowing that in the cart rumbling by them a woman lay in agony and in fear of her life.

I wondered if Ghent was still alive in the other cart, and if my women, too, were alive or if they had been slaughtered by now.

I hoped they were dead, if only to end their suffering and humiliation and fear.

Oh sweet Jesu, why had I insisted on this journey?

We travelled through until well after nightfall. I could not see the light from behind my blindfold and the heavy layers that covered me, but gradually I felt the air grow chill, and I shivered from the cold.

The cart also slowed as we travelled along increasingly rougher and steeper tracks.

We were moving uphill. I guessed we were into the hills and mountains on the other side of the Usk Valley from Pengraic if we had passed through Bergeveny.

We travelled long into the night, the movements of the cart increasingly violent as the terrain grew rougher. Occasionally, I heard one or two of the men speak, the language coarse and unknown to my ears.

When the cart lurched to a sudden halt, I moaned in pain through my gag.

There were more voices, raised in obvious greeting, and I knew we had arrived at our destination.

I trembled with fear and felt so unsettled in my stomach I worried I would vomit into my gag and choke myself.

Suddenly the heavy cover over me was wrenched back, and icy air rushed in about me.

The voices were louder now, laughing, close.

The hauberks were hauled off my legs, and then someone climbed into the cart and lifted me under the arms, sliding me down the cart until I half fell out.

My legs could barely support me, and I swayed to and fro, sure I would fall.

Someone caught me by the arm to steady me, and said something in a derogatory voice at which many men about me laughed.

Not before, or ever after, have I ever felt so humiliated. I knew I was dishevelled, stained, ungainly with my belly and numb limbs, and my clothes stank vilely. I must have looked like a street whore down on her luck.

There were fingers at the back of my head, and my gag fell off.

I heaved in a breath, desperate for water but not wanting to beg lest I set off the laughter once more.

Then the fingers were at the back of my blindfold, and it fell away.

For a long moment I could not see. It was deep night, very black, but there were five or six fires roaring fiercely, throwing leaping light about and highlighting the shapes of men walking to and fro.

There were two men standing in front of me, perhaps four or five paces away. I blinked, trying to focus, trying to make out their faces in the fractured light.

Then my vision cleared, and I saw standing before me Madog ap Gruffydd … and Henry, son of King Edmond.

CHAPTER FIVE

The weave scarring on Henry's cheek looked black and deep in the firelight. He regarded me with obvious malicious contempt, then grunted in derision. 'Not so beautiful now, bitch, eh?' he said.

Then he strode over and dealt me a stunning blow to the side of my face, sending me flying to the ground.

The fall knocked the breath out of me, and it took me a long, painful time before I could get any more air in. I was crying, struggling for breath, my mouth full of dirt and my face smeared with it, and the impact on the ground had sent agony flaring through my back and hips and down my legs.

A back tooth had loosened, and I probed it out of its socket with my tongue and then spat it out.

'We need her alive for a while yet,' Madog snapped, and he came over and hauled me back to my feet.

Out of the corner of my eye I saw two men drag Ghent from the other cart, dumping him on the ground. He moved, but only a little and only sluggishly, and I thought he must be barely alive.

Madog took a knife from his belt and I flinched as he raised it. Both Henry and Madog chuckled, but Madog only used it to cut the rope bindings at my wrist.

'Do not think to run into the night,' Madog said. 'These hills are not called the Bearscathe Mountains for nothing. Bears roam here, and they are just emerging from their winter dens, fierce with starvation.'

As if to underscore his words I heard a long, low moan echoing about the hillside.

For an instant everyone within the encampment stilled, listening, before they resumed talking and moving about.

Madog gestured to one of his men, who brought over a skin of ale, handing it to me.

I was parched, and lifted it to my mouth with trembling hands, the metal mouth of the skin clattering against my teeth as I drank.

'We will need to move out soon,' said Madog, and Henry nodded. 'It will not be long before news of the lady's seizure spreads, and doubtless d'Avranches will undertake some foolish rescue.'

Oh please, I begged silently, please, *please* let d'Avranches find me.

I thought of my knight again, he who had sworn to always come to my aid if I needed him, and begged him to come save me.

Nothing happened, and I hated him.

Madog sat me before one of the fires, two of his Teulu standing guard over me, while he and Henry moved about, ordering men to break camp. As well as the Teulu there were perhaps a dozen English soldiers, and I thought they must be Henry's men. My cheek and jaw throbbed horribly from where Henry had struck me and where the tooth had fallen out. I cannot have been there long, but, even despite my pain, my exhaustion sent me into a fitful doze and I jumped in surprise when someone suddenly kicked dirt into the fire to douse it.

'Come,' said a voice, and one of the warriors pulled me to my feet.

I looked about, and saw with some surprise that while I had been dozing, the contents of my chests had been flung about the clearing — my kirtles, my chemises, my ribbons and baubles, as well as those of my women. The entire contents of the carts had been completely ransacked.

'Can you ride?' said Madog, walking over.

I looked at him, then back at the cart. Why couldn't I —

'No cart will go where we are going,' said Madog. 'Can you ride?'

'No,' I said.

'That was not the right answer,' Madog said, dragging me by the wrist toward a horse. It was a big, rangy animal, and it rolled its eyes alarmingly as Madog lifted me bodily into the saddle.

Again, pain shot through my back and hips.

Madog shouted to a horseman close by, and he rode over. Madog handed him the reins of my horse, then tied a length of rope about the horse's neck.

'Hang on to that,' Madog said, and then he was off to his own horse, mounting up and shouting to his Teulu to ride out.

My horse lunged forward, almost unseating me, and I struggled to find the stirrups with my feet. I clung grimly to the rope, but even once I had my feet firmly in the stirrups I found it painful and very difficult to keep my balance on the thin-backed horse, who not only shied at every shadow with regular monotony, but stumbled his way to his knees on numerous occasions on the steep track up which Madog led us. Twice a Teulu riding close by had to push me back into the saddle as I leaned so precariously I would otherwise have fallen.

I could not believe the agony now coursing through my body. Everything hurt — my face from Henry's blow, my back and legs, my belly, my hands which were still swollen and numb from being tightly bound for so long.

At one point Madog reined his horse to the side of the track and waited until I came level with him. He looked me over, his eyes narrowed.

'We will make camp soon,' he said. 'We have come far enough. No one can reach us without being spotted miles away, or without riding through a trap I have set lower down the mountain for them.'

'What do you want with me?' I said. 'For God's mercy, Madog, let me go. What have I done to you?'

'Mevanou,' he said. 'My son. As a wife and son was stolen from me, so now I steal a wife and a son.'

Then he kicked his horse forward, pushing past me back to the head of the column.

Despair overcame me. He blamed me for Mevanou's death? And that of his son? And why not! God alone knew what lies Henry had been feeding him.

Was I to be blamed for every death in England?

I wondered at the unlikely pairing of Madog and Henry. What were they about?

I wept in hopelessness and pain, hanging on grimly to the clumsy bastard of a horse I rode, trying to swallow my sobs so that the Teulu riding close by did not realise how lost in anguish I was.

Madog was going to kill me. If I had not known it before, I knew it now.

We rode until well after dawn when, finally true to his word, Madog commanded us to halt and make camp. We were in a clearing on a heavily wooded hillside, a little down from its ridge. My Teulu companion pulled me down from the horse — I literally fell into his arms, so exhausted and in so much pain I could do little else — then dragged me to sit by a camp fire being built and lit by another Teulu.

I could not have escaped had I wished to. I could barely move. I doubted I could even stand on my own. Madog could not invent any torture that would hurt me more than I hurt now. I sat by the fire, my hands shaking with weariness and distress, every breath almost too agonising to bear, when there came the sound of a horse behind me, and then the thump of a body beside me.

Gilbert Ghent! Sweet Christ Jesu, I had forgot him all this time. He must have been tied over the horse, for he was in no state to have ridden this distance. I shuffled over, touching his bruised and scabbed face, calling his name.

His eyes flickered open once, then closed almost immediately. I rested my hand on his forehead, feeling how cold and clammy it was, and prayed now that he *was* indeed lost in another world, for this one would be too horrifying and painful for him.

I wondered why Madog kept him alive.

A sharp pain knifed through my back, and I hoped I was not going into labour here and now. I would have no help or aid. Not from these men.

Madog and Henry ambled over, each carrying food and a skin of ale. They sat down at the fire, Madog offering me food, which I refused, and the ale, which I took.

'We have been hearing fabulous rumours about you, Maeb,' said Henry, his mouth half full of food.

I didn't say anything. I was past caring.

'It has been said,' Henry continued, pausing to take a healthy swig of ale, 'that you know the whereabouts of a fabled crown, gleaming with jewels more marvellous than any found in fairyland, and which even the Devil lusts after so intensely he is prepared to tear this world apart to get it. Is that so?'

I wondered who among those at Edmond's privy meeting had been spreading tales.

'No,' I said. I remembered how I'd seen all the contents of the carts searched. 'You looked through my belongings.'

'All that fancy flummery,' said Madog. 'Its expense would have fed a thousand of my people for a year.'

'And yet you want this diadem,' I said. 'For what? To melt down into coin to feed your thousands?'

Henry made a menacing gesture toward me, and I flinched.

He laughed and I hated him.

'What are you doing together?' I said. 'What dark cause can have united you?'

Madog gave a small shrug. 'Power, land, a castle or two that we have our eyes on. The earldom of Pengraic — at least that's what Henry wants, I doubt I'd get my hands on it. A chance to settle old scores; you can see Henry's burned into his cheek, and you know mine. I do not take the death of my wife lightly, Maeb.'

'She hated you. She said you had mistresses and bastard sons a-plenty to care overmuch about her.'

'Mevanou was my wife,' Madog snapped. 'She was stolen from me, cloistered in a damp dungeon and our son was left to die from neglect before Mevanou was driven to her death. You think I do not care about that? That I do not care about the dishonour? There was always going to be a price to pay for that humiliation, and you are it.'

'If you want someone to blame for Mevanou's death,' I said, 'then look no further than Henry. I am astounded to find you sharing a camp fire so companionably. Someone let Mevanou out of her chamber and chased her to, and then off, the roof of the Conqueror's Tower in order to smear my name. No one wanted — wants — that more than Henry.'

Madog looked sideways at Henry, and I realised that their alliance was as thin and insubstantial as moonlight.

'Henry's cheek bears the proof that God took my part over his,' I said.

'And God has abandoned you now,' said Madog, 'if your stained, piss-stinking appearance offers any sign.'

I winced, and said nothing as Henry chuckled. I dropped my eyes to Ghent instead and laid my hand on his cheek.

He still breathed.

'Tell us where this diadem is,' said Henry, 'and we'll save his life along with yours.'

'I do not know where it is,' I said.

'In Pengraic Castle?' said Henry. 'If we hauled your battered body before d'Avranches, do you think he'd open the gates so we could have a look?'

'*I don't know where it is! I know nothing of it!*'

Henry sprang to his feet, moving about the fire. He seized my hair, pulling my head back until I cried out with pain.

'Why have you run from London? Eh? What have you hidden along the path?'

'*Nothing!*' I screamed.

'Why have you run from London?'

'Because I loathe my husband!'

Madog grunted. 'She's said something sensible at last.'

Henry let my hair go and I bent forward, my face in my hands, sobbing.

'We do want this diadem,' Madog said, his soft voice infinitely more frightening than Henry's. 'We think whoever owns this diadem could control … who knows how great a territory? England, at the very least. Perhaps Christendom. Imagine the power.'

I raised my face, trying to speak through my sobs. 'Do you think that if I actually had this diadem I would not have smote you with its power by now?' I ran a shaking hand over my body. 'Do you think I would have allowed myself to sink to this state of disgrace if I controlled such power?'

'She makes a good point,' said Madog.

'She is a cunning witch,' said Henry, 'as my cheek attests.'

'Then we shall test her resolve,' said Madog, rising and kicking dirt into the fire to extinguish it. 'She cares for poor Ghent there. Let us see if she will save him from death.'

Henry smiled, and drew his sword.

'No, no,' said Madog, 'I have a much better plan.' He signalled one of the Teulu, and talked quietly to him in their own language for several moments. The Teulu nodded and walked away, calling to several of his comrades.

Madog came and sat back down, saying nothing for a while until two of the Teulu walked into camp dragging a stout tree trunk. As they struck away its thin branches, and as two others started digging a deep hole in the ground, Madog spoke to me in that soft, chilling voice of his.

'See that pole. They will set it securely into the ground soon enough. Meanwhile, others of my Teulu have set meat about the camp — just scraps of it, just enough to attract the bears. Now, you tell us where that diadem is and we will allow your knight here to live. If you do not tell us, then we will tie him to that stake, strip him of his clothing and leave him for the bears. Have you ever heard the scream of a man as he is being eaten by bears? I have. It is not pleasant. Now. Where is this diadem?'

'I don't know! *I don't know!*'

Madog shrugged. Again he signalled to his Teulu, and two came over, dragging poor Ghent toward the pole now being securely secured in the hole.

'I don't know!' I screamed. 'Please God do not kill Ghent ... I do not know!'

Madog gave me a considering look, then nodded at his men.

The men stripped Ghent of his clothing, then tied him roughly but securely to the stake.

'Stop!' I cried.

Madog raised his eyebrows at me, one hand raised to his men, who paused and looked over.

'Where?' he said.

'Please, please,' I begged. 'Don't kill Ghent. Please don't ... please ... for what *purpose*? I do not know where this diadem is!'

Madog shrugged and dropped his hand.

The men resumed securing Ghent to the stake.

Ghent was rousing. He moaned, blinking his eyes.

Oh sweet merciful Jesu Christ, don't let Gilbert die like this ... don't let him die like this.

'Lay the trail,' said Madog, 'then mount up.'

'By God,' Henry muttered, 'I shall remember this delicacy for when I am king.'

I closed my eyes, praying that Henry would never be king. The thought of any man being punished in this brutal, savage way sickened me.

Madog seized me and lifted me roughly atop my horse. The creature shied at the sudden weight; I slipped, grabbing for the rope, and Madog swore as he pushed me back into place.

'Fall off at your peril,' he said. 'The bears are starved enough for two.'

Gilbert, I thought, my mind numbed with shock. I looked over at him, and saw to my horror that his eyes were open and gazing right at me.

'Gilbert,' I said, and maybe he heard, because he gave a small smile and a nod.

Pain knifed through my back and hips, this time migrating into my belly as well, and I moaned, leaning forward over the horse.

A moment later, the horse lurched as a Teulu pulled sharply at the reins.

I turned once more to look at Gilbert. He was still watching me, and again he gave me a nod.

I wept, not only for him, but for me, and for my sheer exhaustion of life. If Madog was going to kill me, I wanted it to be quick, and not in the same torturous, cruel method he had devised for Gilbert.

We rode for some time, although I do not think we covered much distance. The track was narrow, and difficult for the horses, and we progressed only at a slow walk.

Shortly after we left the clearing where Gilbert was staked, we heard the first moans and grunts of the bears.

I did not want to listen. If I had been able to sit the damned horse without the need to grasp the rope I would have covered my ears with my hands.

We kept riding until we came to yet another small clearing in the forest.

There Madog halted us.

To listen.

Shortly after we arrived I heard the first scream. I cried out, covering my ears now that we were not moving, but even the thickness of my hands could not dull the terror and agony of those screams. They came, one after the other, barely leaving time for Gilbert to have drawn breath until I, too, screamed and screamed and screamed in company with Gilbert's terrible dying.

Henry rode over to me, tearing a hand from an ear. 'Where is the diadem?' he shouted at me, and all I could do was shriek back, 'I don't know, I don't know, I don't know!'

He still had me by the wrist and, in anger and frustration, he shoved it back at me, so unsettling my balance that I fell from the horse, hitting my head hard on the ground.

I blacked out.

When I finally blinked my eyes, and when the fog finally lifted from my mind, it was to realise three things.

One, that Gilbert had finally, gratefully, stopped screaming.

Second, that pain now regularly banded my belly like a hot iron girdle and only every few breaths. My time must finally be here, in this godforsaken wintry mountainous forest, surrounded by bears and men who hated me.

Third, Madog and Henry were engaged in a vicious argument, not fifteen feet from where I lay. They looked as if they had been arguing for some time, for they were now in full-flighted dispute.

The two men were standing face to face, spitting at each other with their words.

'If she knew where this mythical diadem was,' Madog was shouting, 'she would have told us by now! I am sick unto death of chasing around after your rumours.'

'All I need are a score of your men,' Henry said, 'and I can ride down to Pengraic Castle and —'

'You think I want to send my men on a mission that will see them killed? D'Avranches will fill the lot of you with arrows from atop the castle parapets!

'I am done with you, Henry. All I wanted was this woman to take my revenge for the slight done to me when Mevanou was stolen and she and my son murdered. I am within one knife strike of achieving that now. In regards to Pengraic Castle, I am going to use the cover of night to toss the body of the countess and Pengraic's cold, unborn heir as close to its front gates as I can get them. I will not —'

'You treacherous Welsh cunt,' said Henry. 'You will do as I want or I will hound you into Wales' pitiful soil!'

I thought Henry particularly brave, or stunningly foolhardy, to so address Madog.

'We had an agreement,' Henry continued. 'An *alliance*. You said you would help —'

Madog, in a lightning-fast move, wrapped his left arm about Henry's neck, squeezing it tight, while at the same time he reached down with his right and grabbed Henry's cock and balls. Then he wrenched backward with his left arm and lifted with his right, and Henry toppled over backward, a shriek coming from his mouth as Madog continued to hold onto Henry's cock and balls as he fell.

Henry instinctively curled about his injured genitals as he hit the ground, and Madog simply knelt down, drawing his dagger at the same moment, wrenched back Henry's head and cut his throat.

Madog stood, not even breathing deeply, his face impassive as he gazed at Henry choking his life out in gouts of blood at Madog's feet.

'I send a message to England's cursed king as well,' Madog said, 'that my lands are poison to his kind!' Then he looked about at Henry's twelve or so men. 'I have no argument with you. Leave now, and go back the way you have come.'

After hesitating briefly, the soldiers glanced at each other, then at the heavily armed Teulu about them, and then quietly mounted their horses and were gone.

Madog spoke to his Teulu, obviously giving them the order to mount up, for they all turned for their horses. Then Madog came over to me.

'You pitiful wretch,' Madog said softly as he knelt down by my shoulder. 'This is a sad place for you to die, but remember that so also did Mevanou die sadly. Your husband loves you and cherishes you and will mourn you, no doubt, even if you loathe him, as you say. I hope your death sends a message to this land's cursed Norman overlords … I will do to them as they do to me. Say a prayer, Maeb, for you have only moments to death.'

He lifted his knife, still wet with Henry's blood, grabbed my hair with his free hand, and pulled my head back to expose my throat.

I was rigid with terror, but also somehow peaceful.

It would soon be done.

Madog hefted the knife and, just before he brought it across my throat, I saw and heard the whistling flash of the sword that took off the Welsh prince's head.

Madog's head flew across my body, rolling away into the undergrowth, then his corpse toppled across my chest.

My mind could make no sense of what had happened, but I was repulsed by the blood spurting from Madog's neck and soaking into my clothes. I lifted my hands, using them to bat ineffectually at his body to try and get it off mine.

There was a knight beside me, holding a bloodied sword. Some part of my mind, still somewhat rational, realised it must have been this knight who took off Madog's head. He stood over me, clad in gleaming maille and a rich damson-coloured surcoat and with what was possibly a golden crown about his helmet.

I assumed he would now kill me.

But instead the knight took a quick look about — I was vaguely aware there was fighting about the clearing — then sheathed his sword, wrested off his helmet and sank to his knees beside me.

'Merciful *God*, Maeb!' Edmond said as he pulled Madog's corpse from my body. 'What has become of you?'

CHAPTER SIX

—◂•◂《✦》•▸•—

M y mind simply would not accept that this was Edmond. Edmond was sixty or more miles north along bad roads in Hereford. He could not possibly be here, even had he heard I'd been stolen.

I turned my head slightly to look around the clearing.

Scores of knights and soldiers, all mailled, helmeted and weaponed, had either killed or driven away the Teulu.

There were silver-backed wolves sniffing about the dead bodies.

This company — knights, soldiers, horses, wolves, Edmond — could not possibly have charged *en masse* into this clearing along a track on which horses could barely manage a stumble in a single line.

This was impossible. It was a dream. I was already dead.

Another vicious band of searing heat encircled my belly, radiating into my back and hips, and I cried out.

'Maeb!' Edmond's mailled hand gripped my shoulder. 'Maeb, for sweet Jesu's sakes, is it your time?'

I managed a nod, then cried out once more, clutching at Edmond's hand.

He muttered a curse, then tried to rise.

I gripped his hand with both mine, my despair and fright giving me abnormal strength, and would not allow him to stand.

'Jesu, Maeb,' Edmond muttered, then managed to turn enough to shout to one of the knights. 'Odo! The women! Bring the damned women!'

Oh, he had brought women with him, too. This dream thought of everything.

I screwed my eyes shut with the next contraction and wished desperately for a tight, closeted warm chamber with a thick bed smothered in coverlets. Surely this dream Edmond could provide that as well?

There was a scurrying of feet and then I heard Isouda, Ella and Gytha crying at my side: 'My lady! My lady! My lady!'

They would be dead also, and thus sharing my dream.

'I will leave you with your —' Edmond began, and I gripped his hand even harder, the links of his maille gauntlet pressing deep into the flesh of my fingers.

'Don't leave me,' I said. 'Don't go … *don't go.*' I thought that if I let his hand go everything about me would vanish and I would be cast adrift in the blackness of death with this terrible, terrible pain.

'My lord,' said Isouda, 'where is she wounded? This blood … there is so much of it …'

I could hear the horror in her voice.

'It is not her blood,' said Edmond, nodding to the dreadful corpse to one side, 'but Madog's.'

Now I gave a loud cry as the pain got immeasurably worse. I felt an unbearable urge to push, and knew the baby was only moments away.

'We need clean cloth,' said Gytha, who had very suddenly become quite voluble. 'Water, if you can manage it. A clean knife. Blankets. But we *must* have clean cloth.'

Edmond just stared at her.

'Arrange it!' snapped Gytha and, amid all my pain, dislocation, and disbelief that any of this was actually happening, I thought that a woman who could command a king in this manner was a woman worth keeping by my side.

Edmond once again turned his head and bellowed for the hapless Odo.

I don't know from where, but Odo did manage to find clean cloths, a single blanket and a clean knife. There was no water save for what some of the knights carried in their drinking skins, but Gytha and the other two women coped with what they had.

I gripped tight onto Edmond's hand and, with the king by my side, the corpse of a Welsh prince by my shoulder, and half of the royal court's knights standing about, gave birth to a son in that blood-soaked clearing.

When Isouda lifted him, wrapped in a woollen cloth, and laid him in my arms, I marvelled that both he and I had survived these past few days.

'My lord king,' I said to Edmond, who, now that his hand was free, had stripped off his gauntlets and was rubbing his hand which was red with welts from my terrible grip. 'My lord king, how is it that you are here? And my women … I thought you dead and yet here you be, too.'

Edmond glanced at my women, who left it to him to answer.

'If truth be told, Maeb,' Edmond said, 'I think none of us here truly know. I think it is a tale that will be told about fires for many years to come. And we will tell it to you, but not here, not now.'

Edmond had his men construct a litter for me and the baby, as well as one for Henry's body, and we slowly made our way back through the mountains. The wolves had long gone and I thought I must have imagined them. The company who had ridden with Edmond into that clearing where Madog had been about to kill me numbered among them many nobles that I knew from court, and who had travelled with Edmond on his funeral procession from Elesberie to Hereford. Robert de Lacy, Lord of Bouland and Alianor's husband, was here, as was Gilbert de Clare, Earl of Pembroke. Saint-Valery had come, too, and fought with the best of them.

They took turns riding by my litter, exchanging conversation, telling me how Adelaide's funeral went, and, in Saint-Valery's case, reciting great lengths of poetry, all of which was meant to entertain me and keep my mind from the uncomfortable jolting of the litter. They did not press me for details of what had happened to me, or to Prince Henry, and did not mind if, as often happened, I slipped into sleep.

I wanted to sleep.

Eventually, we came on the clearing where Gilbert had been tied to the stake.

The stake was still there, and the ground about soaked with blood, but his body was gone.

I thought the bears must have dragged it away to eat.

Edmond asked who had been tied here, and I told him.

'Ghent? Are you sure?' he said.

Was I *sure*?

'It was Ghent!' I said, a trifle tersely. 'Who else?'

Edmond exchanged a look with de Lacy and Pembroke, riding close by, then just nodded to me. He sent soldiers to scour the nearby forests for any evidence of Ghent's body, but they found nothing, and in time we moved on.

It took a day to reach the area where Madog had abandoned the carts. We stopped here for a night's rest, Isouda, Ella and Gytha collecting what could be salvaged of our clothing and belongings. I was overjoyed to see the carts, thinking that, if nothing else, I could at least travel more comfortably with my new son from now on.

My women bedded me and the baby in the cart in which I had travelled earlier, and I luxuriated in the cushions and coverlets. Here, also, we had access to a good stream, and Isouda and Gytha heated water and washed me completely, even my hair, removing from me the sweat of fear, Madog's blood, and that of the birthing.

Our company did not have much food with them, but from what little we did have (mostly taken from the Teulu's supplies), Edmond made sure that I had a good meal.

As I was settling down after the meal, Isouda, who was making sure the baby and I were comfortable, looked up and suddenly grinned. 'My lady, look what my lord king has found!'

I raised myself on an elbow and looked over the side of the cart.

Edmond was walking over to us, leading Dulcette.

I couldn't believe it. The last I had seen of her she had been tied to one of the carts as Ghent led our company toward Bergeveny. Then we had been attacked, and I was bound and blindfolded into the cart under thick covers.

Dulcette must have travelled all this way with us and then wandered off when the Teulu abandoned the carts. I was astounded. Dulcette was a costly horse, and that no one, not even the Teulu, had made off with her was astonishing.

'One of the soldiers found her wandering nearby,' Edmond said. 'He brought her in, and I remembered you riding her from the day of the hunt in the forest beyond the Tower.'

I burst into tears. Of all the things that had happened in the past day or so, the relief of seeing Dulcette safe was one of the most memorable.

Edmond tied her once more to the cart, then signalled Isouda to leave us. Once she had gone, Edmond climbed into the cart and sat by me.

'How is the child?' he said, making an effort to be interested.

'He is well,' I said, folding the cloth back from the boy's face so Edmond could see.

'And you?'

'And I, too. I am tired and sore and bruised, and I have lost a tooth from being struck in the jaw, but from all of these I should recover. My lord, please tell me, how did you and this company come to find me? And my women? I do not understand.'

Edmond breathed in deeply, looked for a moment at the campsite, and then began to speak. What he said I later had confirmed from my women, as many others among the company.

It was a most remarkable tale.

'We had buried Adelaide, as she had wanted,' Edmond began, 'in the cathedral at Hereford. We thought to tarry there a week, then return toward London, or however close the plague allowed us to come to that city.

'One night there came a clamour at the gates of the priory where we stayed. There was a knight outside, riding a most remarkable white horse, and he demanded to speak with me. One of my valets woke me, and I stumbled outside, cursing whoever it was.

'Maeb ... I know I spoke with this knight, but I cannot remember any of the conversation. All I can recall was that somehow the knight convinced me that there was a terrible battle to be fought and that I must rouse my court, my knights, my soldiers, and ride with him as fast as I might.

'I did not doubt him, not for a moment.'

Edmond paused, his face introspective. 'How can that be possible, Maeb? A strange knight arrives, he convinces me within moments to command all the knights and soldiers of my company forth, and I do just that.'

'I have met this knight, too,' I said. 'I can understand. Go on, if you please, my lord.'

'We rode out as soon as we could. No one complained. Everyone, as I had, simply rose, arrayed themselves in fighting manner, and mounted their horses.

'We followed the knight. We rode through territory I had not seen before and our horses never wearied. At times packs of silver and black wolves rode with us, beside us, among us, weaving in and out of the trees. It was always night, and always full moonlight even though the moon is dark now. Daylight never came.

'We rode on. Suddenly we came on a place were there had been a battle. Bodies littered the ground, the track was churned as if something large had laid across it, and had then been dragged away. We stopped and buried the bodies, thinking we would come back and retrieve them for Christian burial later. While we were there, three women came from out of the trees.

'They told us an extraordinary tale. They were Isouda, Ella and Gytha, your attending women. They told us of the attack on your company. They told us how you had been stolen away. They told us how twelve or more of the attackers had dragged them into the forest, there to defile them and later kill them.

'But no sooner were they deep in the woods, and the men, laughing and jesting, had turned to the women, than great wolves burst out of the trees and devoured the men.

'Yet the wolves did not touch the women, nor threaten them in any way. The wolves sat with the women until our company happened along, and then they melted back into the forest as strangely as they had arrived.

'Your women's horses were discovered, and, thus mounted, we once more followed after the knight, who brought us through Bergeveny. We travelled through that town, again at night, and what a strange silent ride that was, through streets whose inhabitants seemed so deeply asleep they never noticed our passing — and then into these hills and mountains.

'Here the knight said he would leave us, for he was tired, but that another would lead us the final distance.'

Edmond again paused, studying me thoughtfully. 'Maeb, this final knight was Gilbert Ghent. I would have known him in an instant: it was his horse, his blue surcoat, his devices, his voice. I know him well, damn it, and *this was Ghent.*'

I had tears in my eyes. No wonder Edmond had not believed me when I'd said it was Ghent who died at that stake. 'I do not doubt it, my lord. And I will tell you why shortly, but finish now, please.'

He sighed. 'Ghent kept urging us forward, saying that you were in danger. We burst into that clearing on all sides, Maeb. I know not how, for we had approached it in a single column, but so we did, and I found myself unhorsed and standing behind Madog as he made to cut your throat.'

Now my tears flowed freely. 'For the rest of my life,' I said, 'however much God grants to me, I shall never forget that moment when you dropped to your knees before me, having smote Madog's head from his shoulders. My lord … nothing I can ever say can thank you enough, or communicate to you my gratitude. I was dead and you resurrected me.'

I think emotion overcame Edmond for a moment, for he took some time to reply, only grasping my hand as I lifted it to him.

'Maeb,' he said, finally, 'we burst into that clearing in time to save your life, yet not my son's. Ghent did not lead us there in time to save Henry.'

'My lord, I grieve with you that you have lost a son, and that your firstborn.'

'What was Henry doing there, Maeb? Was he also a captive of Madog?'

'No.' I briefly told Edmond of Henry's part in the days leading up to his death and of the final argument with Madog.

'They were in an alliance, my lord,' I finished, 'and it dissolved about them.'

'Who did this to your face, Maeb?' Edmond said, touching my face gently with his hand.

I did not answer.

'Ah,' Edmond murmured. Again he sighed. 'He was a foolish boy, Maeb, and greatly unsuited, perhaps, to the role in which fate placed him. I am glad Adelaide did not live to know of his death, for it would have grieved her terribly.'

'I am sorry, my lord,' I said, and Edmond nodded.

'Tell me about Ghent, and this knight,' he said, and so I did. I spoke of the meeting between the knight and Ghent and how, so now I believed, the knight had told Ghent of his forthcoming death and, possibly, of what would come after.

'Ghent told me there was blood ahead, and that I must not grieve,' I said. I hesitated. 'But this was not the first time I have seen this knight.'

I told Edmond of the time the knight had led me through the forest on the day of the hunt, but not of the knight's role in my ordeal.

'I think you travelled the same path the knight led me onto,' I said, 'one of the ancient falloways of the Old People. What else can explain how swiftly you and your company made the journey from Hereford to this point?'

'Who is this knight, do you think, Maeb?'

'I do not know.' But here I lied, for by now I was almost certain of his identity.

CHAPTER SEVEN

—◆◆◆⟨◈⟩◆◆◆—

The next day we travelled to Pengraic Castle. It was a long day's journey, but Edmond was anxious to reach there both for my sake and for the sake of his hungry company. He had the foresight to send riders ahead to forewarn d'Avranches, who, by the time of our arrival in the evening, had the gates open and hot food ready from both keep and garrison kitchens.

Owain was waiting at the gate and was at the side of my litter immediately I came through.

'My lady!' he said, his face a wreath of worry lines.

'Oh, Owain,' I said, so glad to see him I could not express it.

I reached out a hand to him and he pressed it.

'I will come see you in the morning, eh?' he said, and I was stunned to see tears in his eyes. 'Give you time to rest.'

I gripped his hand, then let it go.

I was home, and safe.

Owain came to see me the next day as soon as he thought it polite. I was ensconced back in the privy chamber off the solar, although I had offered it to Edmond. He'd refused, saying he would find a mattress in the men's dormitory.

'My lady,' Owain said as he sat on the bed, taking my hand and patting it. 'Maeb.'

He smiled, and I embarrassed myself by beginning to weep.

'This is why I joined the church,' he said. 'I do nothing for the ladies but make them weep.'

I tried to laugh and ended up only weeping the harder. I waved my women out of the chamber, gesturing them to leave the door open, and then just lay there, tears falling down my cheeks, holding Owain's hand in both mine.

Once I managed to dry my eyes, we talked. I told Owain about how I'd been seized and how Edmond had saved me. How he'd sat there as I grasped his hand and watched as I gave birth to my son. This tale led to the falloways, and from there to the strange knight and what had become of Gilbert Ghent.

As with Edmond, I did not tell Owain about how the knight had aided me in the ordeal.

'What is this diadem Henry and Madog spoke of?' said Owain.

Thus, breaking the promise of the privy council meeting, I told Owain about the diadem and the Devil's efforts to get it back.

'The plague,' I said, 'it is the Devil's hound pack, sent to sniff it out.'

Owain made a sign against evil spirits, which was less a sign of the cross than it was a local gesture handed down from generations past.

'And the Templars suspect *you* of harbouring the diadem?' Owain said. 'They think your father stole it and gave it to you?'

I nodded. 'I am so weary, Owain, of saying that I do not have this diadem in my possession, nor do I know anything about it or where it might be. I don't think my father had it. He certainly did not give it to me. I do not deserve this mystery or the constant suspicious eyes.'

'My lady,' Owain said, 'I do not understand why my lord Pengraic allowed you to come all this way home to Pengraic Castle when you were so near your confinement. Particularly when knowledge of this diadem, and of your possible connection to it, has been noised about the realm. Sweet Lord Jesu, my lady, how many other brigands are there on the roads seeking to claim it from you?'

I did not immediately answer. I looked to the door, and saw that no one in the solar was close to it. I licked my lips, stalling for time, thinking.

'My lady?'

'Listen, Owain, what I tell you now you must treat as a confession. You must not tell anyone else. No one. Promise.'

His eyes narrowed in concern. 'As a confession, then. I promise not to gossip this about.'

'On your *life*, Owain. Tell no one!'

'On my life, Maeb. Sweet God, what is happening?'

I took a deep breath, closed my eyes briefly, and told Owain about the imps that I had seen at Edmond's Oxeneford palace and at our house in Cornhill.

Now Owain crossed himself in the manner of the Church, muttering a prayer under his breath.

'Maeb, you *must* mention this to a higher ecclesiastic. He will be able to —'

'Owain, *listen.*'

Haltingly, and in a very quiet voice lest I be overheard from the solar, I told him about the night I'd found my husband with the imp and what he had told me afterward.

'That is why I hurried back here, Owain,' I finished. 'I could not stay with my husband. I could not.'

Owain was shocked to the core, as I had been. He sat on the bed, still holding one of my hands, his face pale, rocking slightly back and forth, back and forth, as if to comfort himself.

Eventually he gave his head a little shake, perhaps to clear it of his fugue.

'I find this so hard,' he said, 'so hard.'

'I speak the truth, Owain!'

'I do not doubt it, my lady. I do not. But that my lord, who I have loved and respected all my life, should truly be this foul creature. I find it hard, Maeb.'

I was crying again. 'And you think I do *not*, Owain?'

Owain still struggled with what I had told him. 'All my life I thought there was something different about Pengraic,' he said. 'I had thought it a touch of the fairy, but instead it was the taint of hell? Oh, sweet God, Maeb. Sweet, sweet God.'

'What am I to do?' I whispered. 'What, Owain?'

'Who do you trust absolutely at court, my lady?'

I thought. Alianor de Lacy? Almost, but not enough, and I do not think she would be of any help even if I did trust her completely.

Who?

'Edmond,' I whispered.

'Aye,' Owain said, 'I had wondered. He was picked to save you from

Madog, and he was taken along the fallows in order to do so. That would not have happened unless he was of true and good spirit.'

'More of your tales of the Old People, Owain?' I said, trying to smile.

Owain tipped his head, acknowledging his love of folklore. 'You should tell Edmond,' he said, 'if for no other reason than this is his realm that the Devil tramples over, and he should know. But also because I think he will help you, and perhaps show you the way free.'

Oh, fateful words. But I nodded, and thought on it.

Later that morning, Sewenna came to see me. I had missed her cheerful, uncomplicated disposition, and I handed her the baby.

'Are you still feeding, Sewenna?' I asked.

She nodded, cooing over my son.

'Then can you take this child, as well? I do not wish to nurse him.'

Again she nodded and, folding back her chemise, put my son to the breast.

He suckled immediately, and I leaned back on my pillows, relieved.

I felt entirely disconnected from this child. I had longed for him and carried him cheerfully, but from the moment I knew what had fathered him ...

I wished him no harm, but neither did I want to nurse him. Sewenna could mother him. I didn't think I could manage it.

After Sewenna had gone I asked my women to help me wash and dress. I would sit out. I'd had enough of bed. A servant brought my meal just after midday, setting it on a small table before me and I was surprised at its size.

Did the kitchen think I should eat for a company?

But as I was enquiring, Edmond appeared, and said he would eat with me.

The servant brought a chair, and we sat, sharing the simple meal.

I felt a coldness from him and wondered at it. We talked, but only in somewhat awkward fragments and I grew increasingly uncomfortable, wondering why Edmond's mood was so reserved.

'You are looking much better, my lady,' he said, finally sitting back and wiping his mouth with a napkin.

'I am feeling so, my lord, thank you.'

425

'The child?'

'He is well also, my lord.'

'He should be baptised before I leave,' Edmond said. 'I will stand as sponsor.'

'That is a great honour. I thank you, my lord king.'

He gave a terse nod, acknowledging the thanks. 'Much of my company shall be leaving in the morning,' he said. 'Many of them have long distances to travel to reach their homes.'

There was an implied criticism there, and it left me fumbling for the right words.

'My lord, I am sorry I have been such a trouble to you and your company.'

If I had been waiting for him to wave the apology aside, then I was to be disappointed.

'Many, if not all,' Edmond said, 'will talk of your strange rescue, and of the extraordinary way we were led to your side. And that in time to save *you*, and not Henry.'

Sweet Jesu. When Edmond and I had last spoken of this he had not been so cold, nor had his voice this accusatory tone. Had he now begun to wonder if witchery was involved in my rescue and the concurrent death of his eldest son? *My witchery?*

'My lord, I —'

'Maeb, many will remember Henry's accusation of witchcraft against you. Many will wonder if witchery was involved in your rescue.'

I felt cold; Edmond's words had confirmed my fears. What had people been saying about their ride along the falloway? Was Edmond regretting now that he'd listened to the knight? Had he grown doubtful? Did he feel vulnerable? Did he think my very existence might now threaten him?

Suddenly I saw a yawning chasm before me, and it held all the perils of hell. Coupled with Edmond's coldness, it made me suddenly horribly aware of how alone I was in this world. My husband had always been there to protect me, if no one else could, and he had been a powerful protector.

But now ... no, my husband was no longer my saviour.

And Edmond. Edmond, too, had always supported me, but today I could feel and hear him distancing himself and I was terror-struck.

Without either my husband's or Edmond's support and protection, I was helpless against any who might move against me.

Who might accuse me of witchcraft.

Sweet Jesu, how had it come to this?

Edmond sighed, refilling his cup of wine and drinking of it deeply.

'You trail intrigue and mystery and trouble behind you like some women trail scent, Maeb,' he said. 'You *are* a trouble.'

Tears filled my eyes, and I could not reply. I hung my head, hoping he would not see the tears, and stared at my hands clasped in my lap. Gone was the man who had spoken so sweetly to me in Saint John's chapel.

'What is wrong between you and Pengraic, Maeb?'

I thought of what Owain had said to me, that Edmond might help me, and that this was Edmond's realm that the Devil trod over so vilely.

I thought of all the people dying of the plague and wondered if it was my fault they suffered.

But how could I tell Edmond? Would not the king's suspicions of witchcraft be completely vindicated?

'Maeb!'

'Oh, my lord, I am so sorry.' I let slip a sob, my hands over my face.

I wanted Edmond to move about the table and comfort me, I wanted that so badly, and yet he did not move.

He just sat, watching me, unmoved by my womanly weakness.

'Maeb, *tell me.*'

Owain had known there was something terribly wrong.

I could not hide it from Edmond, nor could I think of any lies that might plaster over the truth.

So I told him. Everything. The imps, and what my husband had told me — that he was the Devil's man, come to find the diadem.

Everything, save that single thing, that the knight had aided me through the ordeal. The only thing saving me now was that people believed that God had spoken in the great hall that day I'd undergone the ordeal, and not the knight's trickery.

I finished.

I could not look at Edmond.

There was complete silence.

Finally, unable to bear it any longer, I looked up.

Edmond was staring at me and I could not tell if he was shocked or thinking deeply.

Both, perhaps.

Suddenly he was on his feet, cursing foully. His chair had fallen and Edmond picked it up and threw it across the chamber so that it shattered against a wall.

I cringed, and Isouda and one of Edmond's knights rushed in from the solar.

'Get out!' Edmond shouted at them, striding over to slam the door shut.

Then he whipped about. 'By all the saints, Maeb, you were going to keep this from me? How long have you known, eh?'

'Only after you'd left for Elesberie, my lord. I am sorry.' Strangely, I was easier now that he was angry than sitting across from me, silent.

Anger would pass.

'I did not know what to do, sir,' I said, as clearly and honestly as I could. 'All I could think was to run home to Pengraic.'

'Jesu,' Edmond muttered, walking away, one hand rubbing at his forehead. He turned about again.

'You did not know at the Privy Council?'

'No, my lord, I did not.'

'But you knew of the imps, yes?'

I nodded.

'And yet you said nothing.'

'My lord, my husband had asked me not to. I loved and trusted him, and I had no reason then not to do so.'

'And yet you did not trust me enough to mention that imps crawled through my palace as well as your home.'

I wondered if this was the issue, that I had left it this long before deciding to trust Edmond.

'I was frightened, sir. And I trusted my husband completely.'

'You owed him loyalty before me?'

'Yes, my lord.'

He sighed, moving over to sit on the bed, which was the only place left for him to sit now he had destroyed his chair. 'I wonder if that is how it should be, that a wife should offer her loyalty to her husband before she offers it to the king.'

'It was how it was with me.'

'And now I am the first person you have told this.'

'No, my lord. I told Owain, my priest, this morning, as confession.'

Edmond muttered an obscenity. 'And what did he say?'

'That I should tell you.'

Edmond threw up his hands. 'Well, praise be to God for Brother Owain, for otherwise I should never have learned! Sweet mother of Christ, Maeb, I thought that you and I ... I thought ...'

I dropped my eyes. This was not just between a king and his subject, then, but between a man and a woman, too.

'So,' Edmond said, his voice profoundly weary, 'plague ravages my realm because the Devil thinks that his precious diadem is hidden here and the plague shall sniff it out. The Templars accuse you of harbouring the diadem, something you deny. But, lo, now I learn your husband is the Devil's own man sent to snatch the diadem from its hiding place and return it to his hellish master. Meanwhile, some deep witchery was used so that you might be rescued from death ... but not my son. Have I missed any salient facts, Maeb?'

I shook my head.

'You claim innocence in all this?'

Now I raised my face back to his. 'Yes, my lord.'

'And yet,' Edmond said, his voice now dangerously quiet, 'how remarkable a coincidence it is that sweet, pretty, innocent Mistress Maeb should first find herself in the Devil's lieutenant's household, and then, amazingly, find herself his wife. How astounding that, coupled with this, it appears that your father may have stolen this diadem and entrusted it to you —'

'I do not have it, my lord! I do not know where it is! I know *nothing* about this cursed diadem!'

'Then explain to me why this remarkably unadventurous plague travels only in your footsteps. Back and forth, back and forth.'

'Has it followed me back to Pengraic, my lord? Has it?'

He chewed the inside of his cheek. 'I do not know. I have no intelligence as yet. But my gut instinct tells me that you are not so innocent as you claim. Why did Pengraic marry you if not to get his hands on the diadem? And why do I think that the best way I can rid my realm of this disaster is to send your husband back to hell with a well-placed sword stroke and cast you into the seas, that the plague may follow you into its depths?'

I could actually feel myself go pale with shock.

Edmond gave a slow nod, acknowledging my reaction. 'Why should I not do that, Maeb?'

Again, I wept. I was somewhat astounded I had any tears left. 'I do not know, my lord.'

'And yet how God favours you,' Edmond said. 'I would think Pengraic had aided you through that ordeal save he was so panicked at the thought of you undertaking it.'

'The ordeal was carried out under the word of God. Raife could not have intervened even had he wished to do so.'

'In that I am inclined to believe you. And this strange knight, and Ghent ... I felt only good from them, not evil. So for the moment, Maeb, I am prepared to trust you — but not as I once did. Who knows what else you keep from me? Always the kernel of doubt will be there, and I will watch you more carefully.'

That stung. Badly.

'What will we do, my lord? What can I do, to win back your regard?'

He studied me thoughtfully. 'Whatever happens, Maeb, you shall be at the heart of it. This is war now, and you are a soldier in it. Your days of innocence — whether claimed or real — are over.'

CHAPTER EIGHT

Perhaps that day spent out of bed had wearied me, or maybe the seeds of the sepsis were already there, but later that evening I fell in to a fiery ague. I do not recall much about that night, nor the following week and more of days and nights, save that the fever sapped away at my strength and that I was consumed by pain and aches.

I dreamed during this time, much as I had dreamed when I was dying of the plague and hemlock. Again I saw the forbidden falloway and I could sense the knight sitting his courser waiting to turn me back if I stepped foot along that falloway. Unlike that earlier period of dying, however, this time I did not venture toward him. I stood at the entrance of the falloway and looked down its length longingly, but I did not attempt to walk it.

Isouda later told me I had been overtaken by childbed fever, and that Owain had worried it would carry me away. I became so sick, and so sensitive to any sound at all, that Edmond ordered that the castle come to a stillness when I was at my worst, so that the noise of the inner bailey and great keep might not torture me.

Edmond kept a vigil in the solar. Maybe he dreaded losing his soldier in the war ahead, maybe he dreaded losing me, I don't know. Maybe both. But for the ten days that I lay critically ill Edmond kept vigil, and it gladdened my heart when I later heard of it.

During this time, also, Owain baptised my son. Edmond and Isouda stood as sponsors, and Edmond named him Geoffrey, which was a fine name. Sewenna continued to feed him and he gained weight with every day. When, after two weeks, they brought Geoffrey to see me again I was astounded at his size and heaviness. For his part, Geoffrey seemed to have forgot his mother, for he fretted and cried when he was put into my arms and did not stop until he was again with Sewenna.

I felt a twinge of unhappiness that he did not recognise me, but it did not last long. I could not love this child, nor did I try overmuch to do so. My maternal instincts were utterly overwhelmed and defeated by the horror of his father.

Once I had emerged from death's shadow Edmond left me to recover and embarked on a tour of the Welsh Marches, visiting as far north as Scersberie. He arrived back at Pengraic Castle after five weeks with an impressive number of soldiers (most of the company which had originally accompanied him on my rescue, had left within days of their initial arrival at Pengraic). After a few days rest at Pengraic, Edmond then led these knights and soldiers on a foray deep into the Usk Valley, taking advantage of the disarray of the Welsh forces after the death of Madog ap Gruffydd and, in the process, recapturing Brecon Castle, which the Welsh had held for a number of years.

I grew stronger as the weeks passed. While Edmond was fighting his way up the Usk Valley, I spent my time within the castle, in Owain's garden, and praying over, and receiving comfort from, Stephen's grave. I also took Dulcette out for increasingly longer rides, always escorted by a goodly number of soldiers, and often d'Avranches himself.

D'Avranches, I think, came less to protect me than to pass the time of day with Isouda, who also rode out with me.

I envied them their smiles.

Eventually, some ten or twelve weeks after I had given birth to Geoffrey, Edmond returned to Pengraic Castle, and we had our first lengthy conversation since that day I'd told him of my husband's true identity. We had seen each other many times before now, of course, but Edmond had never lingered nor talked more than asking how either myself or Geoffrey was doing.

Now, fresh from his journey about the Marches and his impressive victory at Brecon Castle, Edmond had decided I was well enough to venture back to London.

We sat in the solar, eyeing each other.

'D'Avranches tells me another message arrived from Pengraic last night,' Edmond said.

'Aye. He commands me again to return to London.' My husband had been sending messengers thick and fast since he learned of my arrival at Pengraic Castle and the birth of his son. At first Raife had tried asking me to return to London, always appealing to me to trust him, then when that accomplished nothing, he ordered me to return. Raife had also sent numerous messages to Edmond, giving full account of the state of London, and requesting that when Edmond returned, to bring me with him.

I had sent little in reply, save that both I and Geoffrey were doing well and that his son thrived. I would return, I told the various messengers, if Edmond thought I should.

'I also received word that the plague continues to die out in London,' Edmond said. 'It raged furious for a full five weeks, but now ... there have been no new infections reported for the past ten days.'

But in the meantime many thousands had died. On top of the ice tragedy and the fire, it would take generations for the city to recover.

'And the plague has not spread from London?' I asked.

'No.' Edmond paused. 'It did not follow your return route to Pengraic via Sancti Albans, Elesberie and Wodestoch.'

'Well, if it did not follow me, then I do not have the diadem!'

Edmond gave an indifferent shrug of his shoulders. 'Or you left it in London. The plague has not moved from there because it has no need. It has done the same thing as happened at Pengraic Castle when you were here previously. It stopped. Maybe because it had found the location of the diadem then, too.'

'I —'

'Let me finish. That, plus the fact that Pengraic seems increasingly desperate to have you back in London, seems to me to indicate that the diadem rests somewhere in London and that you have the key to its location. Thus, it is time that we returned, too. I want this done with, Maeb. My realm is being torn apart by disaster after disaster, and they always follow in your footsteps. Now we go back to London and we finish this.'

'You are not afraid to face my husband?'

Edmond looked at me oddly. 'Afraid? No, why should I be? He is not after my realm, only the cursed diadem. I fear Archbishop du Bec more than Pengraic. And my dear, it is you who will need to face him, you who have the diadem, or the knowledge of its location.'

I could not argue any more that I did not have the damned thing. I could see no reason why I should go back to London, and no reason to see Raife again. I should stay here, and raise my son, the future Earl of Pengraic.

I want to stay here. But I could not say that. Edmond was as determined to get me back to London as my husband was to have me there.

Once more I prepared to take to the road between London and Pengraic. We would travel in a well-guarded company, for Edmond did not trust some other lord to not take it into his head that by seizing me he might have access to the diadem. We would also travel fast. Although there were carts in which I could travel if I needed, I would ride Dulcette whenever possible.

Edmond wanted London.

I did not take Geoffrey with me. He was vulnerable, particularly considering toward what we travelled. He would stay with Sewenna, and Isouda also would stay at Pengraic to oversee his care.

Isouda raised no objections — both her and d'Avranches' families had opened marriage negotiations.

Our journey was accomplished in the main with few troubles, save that of the towns we passed through that had endured not one but two successive waves of plague. Although we rode through these towns, and Edmond always stopped to confer with their men of rank to see what aid he could organise for them, we did not stay there. Instead Edmond led us from royal manor to royal manor so that we ate from his own purse, instead of from those towns and houses who were crippled by plague and needed their coin for their own purposes.

Edmond and I spoke only occasionally, and then only on the briefest of matters. I could feel his suspicion in every look, every gesture. He, as with so many others, now appeared certain that I had the diadem and there was nothing I could say to disabuse him of that notion.

I dreaded returning to London and to Raife.

After two weeks' travel we approached Oxeneford. It was still early in the morning, not yet midday, and I thought we would eat and then have an early night. I was glad, for I was tired and sore from the constant riding.

But perhaps an hour's ride from Oxeneford, Edmond waved on the majority of the column, including Gytha and Ella, and told me he and I were to ride to the Benedictine abbey of Godstou with only some fifteen soldiers and knights as company.

'Godstou Abbey?' I asked, Dulcette easily keeping pace with Edmond's big bay courser as we turned down a narrow roadway. 'Why?'

'There is a woman there I wish you to meet,' he said. 'One of the nuns. I knew her when I was a youth, and respected her mightily. She has recently joined the nunnery, deciding to spend her remaining years in service to God.'

He wanted me to meet a woman he knew as a youth?

'My lord?' I said.

'Her name is Uda,' Edmond said. 'She has powerful judgment.'

I felt extremely uneasy. 'Why do we need to meet with her, my lord?'

Edmond chewed his cheek in that manner he had when he was debating within himself how to answer a question. 'Uda is a powerful sage,' he said. 'She can see how matters rest within people.'

'I am to be *tested*?'

'Maeb, I am sorry for this, but I need to know one way or the other. I no longer know what to think of you, if you are to be trusted or not. I *want* to trust you, but should I? If we were but man and woman ...'

He shrugged. 'But we are not. Many tens of thousands have died because of this plague. I do not want tens of thousands more to so die. I will leave no stone unturned in order to do what is best for the people of this realm, not what is best for you. And if that means testing you until I am satisfied that you tell me the truth, then so be it.'

'It is a shame you did not bring the burning gauntlet with you,' I muttered, and Edmond surprised me by bursting into genuine laughter and he was still chuckling when we turned into the grounds of Godstou Abbey.

We were met by the abbess, a woman who surprised me by her youth. I thought she might fuss over the king, and perhaps force us to some chat over a cup of wine, but she showed us directly into a large chamber, warmed by a bright fire in its large hearth and then excused herself.

An old woman waited there. She sat by the fire like any good wife, rubbing her hands up and down her knees as if to calm their ache, or perhaps warm her hands. As soon as we stepped into the chamber she stood up, clapping her hands once, and crying out, 'Edmond!'

He strode over to her. She did not look directly at him and for a moment I was puzzled, until I realised the nun was blind.

'My boy,' she kept saying, patting his hand as he took one of hers. 'My boy!'

I had to smile. I had never thought anyone, not even Edmond's mother had she still lived, could have stood there and patted his hand and called the king 'My boy!' with the same love and verve and enthusiasm as Uda did. Even though she was old, she was still very lovely and I thought that she must have been a great beauty in her time. Her hair was pure white, and dressed simply in a long plait down her back, her figure slender although stiff, but it was her face, wreathed in such happiness at meeting Edmond again, that was her best feature.

Edmond too was smiling as I had never seen him — that this was a woman he loved as well as respected was abundantly clear.

Eventually, Uda calmed down and sat herself, gesturing to Edmond to pull over one of the stools. 'Who have you for me?' she asked.

'What makes you think I "have someone for you"?' Edmond said.

'Because I heard her enter at the same time as you,' said Uda. 'Have you brought one of your mistresses to meet me?'

Now I was privileged to witness my king blushing like a girl. He flicked a glance at me and flushed the deeper as he saw my smile.

Even Uda chuckled, patting Edmond's hand yet once more. 'Bring her over,' she said, 'and I shall see.'

Edmond gestured me over, standing back from the stool and indicating I should sit there. 'This is Maeb, Countess of Pengraic,' he said. 'We have travelled a long, long way to see you, Uda.'

'As if I was your only reason for travel,' Uda said, chuckling. 'Come, girl, give me your hand, and we shall see what is what.'

I extended my hand, more than a little nervous about what might happen, and took the one that Uda held out.

As soon as she felt my hand touch hers, she took firm grasp, then clicked the fingers of her other hand impatiently. 'Both hands, girl, if you please.'

I shifted the stool a little closer so she could easily hold both hands, and waited.

Uda closed her eyes, her head nodding a little as if she were listening to an unheard melody.

Then, very suddenly, her eyes flew open.

Previously her blue eyes had been unfocused, a little bleary with age.

Now they were bright, very clear, and completely focused on me — I shivered, for her eyes met mine directly, and they felt as if they saw down into the very depths of my being.

'Where did you find this girl, Edmond?'

'She fell at my feet one day,' Edmond said laconically.

'Is she yours?'

'No.'

'But you wish it,' Uda said. Her hand gripped mine tightly, relaxed, then gripped again.

'Your husband, girl. Do you know who he is? What he is?'

'Yes,' I said, and Uda unexpectedly chuckled again.

'Uda,' Edmond said, 'I need to know if she is true.'

'True?' Uda said. 'Who to? You?'

'I need to know if I can trust her,' said Edmond.

Uda's hands had relaxed about mine again, for which I was truly thankful, although she still held them firmly.

'She has a good heart and a shining soul, my boy. You can trust her as much as you can trust anyone. There is no darkness about her, no deceit.'

Edmond let out a long breath. 'Thank you, Uda. That is all I needed to know.'

'Maybe you,' said Uda, 'but I must speak to this girl. Go fetch the abbess, boy, and tell her we need some refreshment. And the good wine, not that stuff she keeps for the bishop when he attends us.'

My mouth twitched at the imperious way Uda ordered the king of England, but I kept the smile from blossoming until Edmond, like the good boy he was, went to fetch the abbess.

'Girl,' said Uda, 'we won't have much time. Listen to me. *You must trust your husband.*'

'But —'

'You know what he is?'

'Yes. But I cannot —'

'No "buts". I can feel that you are now distanced from him. That is not good. You must trust him.'

'I cannot,' I said.

Uda let go my hands and sat back in her chair. 'You are of the Old People, Maeb. Their blood runs strong in you. You have walked their falloways. Strange things have happened to you and you have taken them in your stride. Now, I dare not speak openly, but I can say only this to you. *Trust your husband.*'

I sat back, feeling cold at what she asked of me. She knew what my husband was. And yet she asked me to trust him?

Perhaps age *had* addled her wits.

Or was she, too, a servant of the Devil?

'And trust Edmond,' Uda said. 'He will be good to you.'

Then she sat back and age overcame her face again. Her eyes lost their focus, and became once more blurred.

When Edmond and the abbess returned, it was to find Uda and myself prattling on about the best ways of healing footrot in sheep.

Edmond helped me mount Dulcette, then he stood by her shoulder, one hand resting on the crest of her neck.

'You know I had to test you, Maeb,' he said. 'Both king and man needed it.'

'I know,' I said. Then I risked a smile. 'But are you not the fine one to toss accusations of witchcraft at me when you use Uda as your trusted aide.'

He grunted, and one corner of his mouth turned up, just a little.

'Witenie is close by,' he said. 'Two days' detour.'

My home, where I spent my entire life save for this past year or so. How far away it seemed now.

'My lord,' I said, 'I cannot think what might be found there. Have not the Templars been through my father's old estate with their fine comb of obsession? What could you and I find?'

'You would have the eye of familiarity,' Edmond said. 'Did your house have any secret chambers? Hiding places?'

'If so, my lord, they were also secret from me. My lord, the Templars *have* been there, as has the plague — and it moved on.'

Edmond sighed and nodded. 'To London, then.'

'What do we do when we get there? What do *I* do?'

'We find this diadem, Maeb, and we loose this realm of its plague. It must be in London.'

And you must have the key to the diadem's finding was the unspoken word between us.

I thought of returning to London, and of returning to Raife. I had a sick, hollow feeling inside of me, a bleakness I could not shake.

Raife ...

No matter what the witch-woman Uda had said, I determined not to trust him. How could she have wanted me to trust the Devil's right-hand man?

PART SEVEN

———•◦∞◦•———

THE DEVIL'S DIADEM

THE DEVIL'S GARDEN

CHAPTER ONE

———••◦◦◦•◦••———

We rode into London five days later. The last I had seen London it was barely recovering from fire and river tragedies. Then I had thought it a sad and wretched city — now words cannot even begin to describe the bleak horror of the place after the plague had scoured its streets.

We were to enter via Cripplegate, a fitting entry if ever there was one. But before we entered London we came across the ghastly evidence of the horror the pestilence had wrought on London — huge plague pits dug in the fields beyond its walls, some not yet filled in with soil. These were the worst, for the stink of their rotting, smouldering bodies was appalling, and everyone in the company, king and myself included, retched as we rode through the pall of stinking smoke. It was filthy; I could taste particles of flesh on the smoke, and it left a moist, grey residue on my mantle. Even the horses coughed from time to time.

The only creatures that seemed content amid the horror were the rooks feeding from the corpses.

There was a party to meet us at Cripplegate, a deputation of two aldermen (the only aldermen surviving, we later discovered) and a nobleman called Ralph de Warenne, brother of the Earl of Sudrie, who was now working in my husband's household.

'Greetings, my lord king,' de Warenne said. 'My lord of Pengraic awaits you and his wife in the Tower.'

Edmond nodded, looking down Wodestrate which led down to the markets about Saint Paul's. This street had been untouched by the fire that had spread from the bridge, but now … now it was lined with burned-out buildings, sometimes three or four in a row, and many others that were badly fire-damaged. There was almost no one about, a few people walking this way and that, their shoulders hunched, but no sign of the thriving wood market that usually lined this street. A few dogs wandered, barking now and again, but their movement and noise only served to further accentuate the desolation of the street.

There was stink here, too, partly of the burned buildings and partly, I assumed, from some of the bodies left inside them.

Further into the city I could see trails of languid smoke rising through the still, foetid air into the sky.

I felt ill.

Hell had visited this place.

'My God,' Edmond muttered, 'how is it that any have survived?'

'Only by the miraculous intervention of the saints, my lord,' said one of the aldermen. 'The plague showed us no mercy.'

'How many are dead?' Edmond said.

'Thirty-four thousand two hundred and fifty,' the other aldermen said.

Thirty-four thousand two hundred and fifty. My mind could barely encompass the number.

'And many more fled,' said the first alderman. 'London is home to dogs and rooks now, my lord, and little else.'

Tears ran down my face. Was I responsible for this? Could I have somehow prevented it?

'Are there any new infections?' Edmond asked, and the alderman shook his head.

'We have had no new reports of infection for nigh on two weeks now, my lord.' He paused. 'My lord king, we are glad you are home.'

Edmond nodded, and I saw tears glinting in his eyes, too.

And he would have been home earlier, if not for me.

And perhaps then dead of the plague, too, if not for me.

'Is there plague elsewhere?' de Warenne asked.

'I have not had reports of it,' said Edmond. 'It appears to have died down.'

'At least until the heat of summer,' de Warenne muttered, 'when it will doubtless re-emerge in its full anger.'

'Not if I can help it,' said Edmond, glancing at me, and leaving the other three looking puzzled.

We rode through the city, turning down West Cheap from Wodestrate.

Here was similar devastation, if not worse. Many tenement buildings and houses had gone, as had even some churches. There were buildings badly damaged and leaning but still standing — there was no one to tear them down. As we rode by one of them its roof timbers collapsed, sending our horses skittering and shying across the street.

'What is Pengraic doing to help?' said Edmond as we tightened our reins and pulled our horses back under control.

'Everything possible,' de Warenne said. 'He has every available man out aiding those who still survive, organising shelter, food, comfort. But our forces were hit hard, too, my lord. The Tower ... you will find the Tower almost deserted, and pits dug beyond its walls for your servants. It shall be easier to list those who survived rather than those who died.'

'Sweet Jesu,' Edmond muttered.

We were approaching the turn into Cornhill now.

'I will go home to my house in Cornhill,' I said, somewhat suddenly. 'Not to the Tower. With my lord's permission.'

Edmond looked at me. 'My lady, you shall be far safer in the Tower.'

I raised an eyebrow at that. 'I want to go home, my lord.'

'You won't avoid him there,' he said, low.

'I know, my lord.'

Edmond sighed. 'de Warenne, we will detour via Cornhill. If my lady's house is safe then I shall leave her there. But I need to see it is safe, first.'

'Thank you,' I said.

Our Cornhill house had largely escaped destruction, mainly because of the open areas about it. Nonetheless, it had been used as a hospital in the early days of the plague and two of the outbuildings had burned, and the roof of the main house was scorched.

To my utter relief fitzErfast met us in the courtyard. If he had survived, then the house might be in order.

He helped me down from Dulcette, a pale, thin version of the man I remembered.

'FitzErfast!' I said. 'I am right glad to see you live!'

'Not many others from the household do, my lady. There is only myself, a cook, three house servants and a man-at-arms remaining.'

I saw that he had my old eating knife at his belt, and I was absurdly pleased to see he had treasured it enough to use for his daily meat.

Edmond had also dismounted and came over. 'Are you troubled by any ruffians, fitzErfast?' he said. 'Beggars? Unworthy itinerants? The homeless?'

FitzErfast gave a wan smile. 'There are rich enough pickings and empty houses aplenty lying open for anyone who wishes in London, my lord king,' he said. 'We are left alone because there are still people here unafraid to wield a sword. But in any case, beggars and itinerants are few and far between. Either they died in the plague, or they are still too frightened to come near the city. It is safe enough here for my lady.'

'Nonetheless, I shall leave ten soldiers here to guard her,' said Edmond, and I breathed a sigh of relief that I was to be allowed to stay. 'What food stores do you have?'

'Enough for both my lady, her women, your men plus those already here,' fitzErfast said. 'Of recent times there has not been much call for food.'

'The house is habitable?'

'Yes, my lord. One upper chamber is water-damaged from a leak caused by a fire … but that leak is now fixed and the chamber only requires replastering to make it pretty. Meanwhile, it is still habitable.'

Edmond gave fitzErfast a nod and turned to me. 'Any of my soldiers can reach me at any hour,' he said, 'if you need help.'

'Thank you, my lord,' I said.

We looked at each other for a moment — an awkwardness that hung heavy in the air between us — then he nodded at me as he had just nodded at fitzErfast and turned back to his horse.

I was left standing in the courtyard with Ella and Gytha, a cart of our belongings, and the ten men Edmond had detailed for my care.

I felt very alone, adrift both in this ruined city and in my life.

Although it was a warm day, unusually so even for this time of year, the house was cold. The signs that the house had been used as a hospital during the worst of the plague were still here: cot beds, now stacked in an ungainly pile at the end of the hall; scorch marks in a score of places on the hall floor and on one wall; stacks of dishes; stacks of linens (I made a note to direct fitzErfast to burn them). There were no fires lit in any of the chambers, and the shutters closed in both the solar and my privy chamber.

'I will direct the cook to prepare a meal for nones,' fitzErfast said as we stood in the solar, Ella and Gytha moving to open the shutters and allow light to stream in.

I nodded.

'And I will send a man to bring wood, and set the fires,' he continued.

I nodded again. I was almost in tears at the loneliness in this house, and about us in the deserted streets.

'What will become of this place?' I said.

'Of this house, or of London?' fitzErfast said.

'Both.'

He gave a little shrug. 'They will both rise again, my lady. What appears a barren field today shall bloom tomorrow.'

'I had never realised you such the optimistic poet, fitzErfast,' I said.

He smiled, bowed, and left.

Ella, Gytha and I unpacked what we needed, made the beds, swept and did what we could to make the solar and privy chamber comfortable and homely. The cook brought us a meal at nones, and we ate, and then all three of us mutually decided to have a nap.

We were exhausted, and more than a little heartsick at this our first day back in London.

Ella and Gytha shared a bed in the solar — they would move back into their dormitory chamber once it had been cleaned and warmed, and I lay down on the bed in the privy chamber. I fell asleep immediately.

When I woke, several hours later, as dusk was falling, it was to see Raife standing in the doorway, leaning against the timber supports, a cylindrical leather document holder held loosely in one hand. Watching me.

CHAPTER TWO

I sat up, slowly.

I was shocked by the surge of emotion at seeing him. It wasn't hatred. It wasn't fear. It was, unbelievably, gladness.

I hadn't expected that.

'You do not need to be frightened of me,' he said, softly.

'I am not.'

He stood straight, propped the document holder against the wall, then walked over slowly and sat on the side of the bed.

He looked very tired, impossibly wearied.

'Edmond tells me the child is well,' he said.

'He is.'

'And you?'

'I am well.'

'You almost died,' he said, 'twice. First by Madog's hand, and then from childbed fever. By God, Maeb, I —'

'I am alive now, as you see, thanks to Edmond.'

'You should never have left the Tower,' he snapped. 'To travel so near your confinement, and then to be stolen by Madog and Henry!'

'If I was stolen then that was not *my* fault!'

He glared at me, then very suddenly he relaxed and gave a soft laugh. 'Look at me. I admonished myself over and over on the ride to this house that I must not snap at you, and yet it is the first thing I do.'

'You were worried.'

'Yes.'

'Because if I died then you might not find your precious diadem?'

'Because I love you.'

I dropped my eyes. I did not know what to think, or what to say.

'You have not been able to find the diadem,' I said, after a lengthy pause. 'No.'

'No doubt you searched this house inside and out while I was gone.' 'I did.'

'And yet still no diadem. Raife ... I do not have it. I never have.'

'The plague came here and stopped,' Raife said. 'The imps tell me it is here, somewhere. My master grows angry and fretful. He wants his diadem back.'

Oh, how easy those words now slipped into his speech. His master. The imps.

'If I have that diadem,' Raife continued, 'then all this is finished. The death. The terror. I can end it all.'

'Have you no soul to speak so easily of the death, the horror that has been visited on so many, among them your own wife and children? How can you still ride through this city, which has suffered so terribly, and still bear your head high? How can you —'

'Maeb, I will ask you again. Please, trust me. Damn it! I wish Adelie had found the time to teach you your letters! *Trust me.*'

He took my hand as he said that, and I pulled it away immediately. Why in the name of all the saints was he carrying on about whether or not I could read?

'I can't trust you,' I said.

'And yet,' he said, bitterness ringing every word, 'whenever you have asked me for trust I have given it to you. At the ordeal ... trust me, you said, and I did.'

'I am blameless in this, and you are not. I will not trust you.'

He looked away, the muscle in his jaw clenching and unclenching.

'Who were you,' I said, 'before you went down to hell?'

'A man,' he said.

'And what sin did you commit to be sent to hell?'

Raife's eyes narrowed and I wondered what lies he was conjuring for me. Then he gave a chuckle, which surprised me. 'I lusted after beauty,' he said, 'nothing but a bauble. It seems such a waste, now.'

'That was all?'

'It was enough.'

'You did not murder?'

'No, I did not murder.'

'What was your name?'

Sadness filled his eyes. 'I cannot remember.'

'How long ago did you live in your first life, when you were a man?'

'A long, long time,' Raife said. 'Countless generations. I had to spend a great deal of time in hell, you know, to work my way up to being the Devil's right-hand man. You just don't do that overnight.'

There was definite humour in his eyes now.

'Don't jest of it,' I said.

'Would you have me weep, as I wept when I thought you lost on the way to Pengraic? When Edmond sent word that you lay at death's door from childbed fever? When I thought constantly on the fact that it was Edmond with you at Pengraic and not I? Did you bed him, wife? Did you think to make a better alliance for yourself than that you made with me?'

'I did not bed him,' I whispered.

He reached out, touched my cheek briefly, then dropped his hand. 'I wish I could believe that.'

Trust me, I almost said.

'I did not,' I said.

Raife sighed, and looked away. 'I have heard rumours of how Edmond reached you on that mountain.'

'He used a falloway,' I said. 'The same knight who appeared to me in the forest east of London also appeared to Edmond, and led him to me.'

'You have powerful protectors,' Raife said. 'Who is it, I wonder, this knight?'

The way he said it made me think that he knew who it was.

'I believe it to be Stephen,' I said.

'Aye,' Raife said, 'it is Stephen, lost to the Old People, now. And Ghent too, from what Edmond said. Maeb, I am sorry for Ghent. He was good to you and loyal to me. I liked and respected him. He did not deserve that death.'

I was almost in tears at both his easy acceptance that the knight who protected me was Stephen, and at his sorrow for Ghent. That was genuine, I think. I could discern no dissembling beneath his words.

'I wish ...' I said.

'Aye,' Raife said, 'and I have spent these past months wishing, too.'

Then he rose, walked over to the door to close it, and came back to me.

'Tomorrow,' he said, 'the diadem. But not tonight. Not tonight.'

He stood me upright from the bed, unclothed me, and disrobed himself.

We went to bed.

We lay there side by side for a time, staring at the ceiling.

Then Raife sighed and rolled over to me. He kissed me, and caressed my body.

I would have thought myself sickened to have him touch me, but I was not. I might have been afraid, knowing what he was, but I was not. I *was* very sad, for everything that had been, and might have been. I think it was for that reason that I allowed him to make love to me, and perhaps even sadness that allowed me to respond to his touch.

I don't know what else it might have been.

For thirty years, I have convinced myself that it was sadness that made me accept him that night.

I did not once think that it may have been love, for that admission, literally and figuratively, would have led me to hell.

CHAPTER THREE

⟨∞⟩

I woke just after dawn the next morning. I lay there, listening to Raife breathe, knowing he, too, was awake.

The moment felt awkward for both of us, I think.

He rose after some minutes, opening the shutters of the window to let in the soft morning light. He stood there, the light illuming his body, gazing toward the Conqueror's Tower.

I wondered if he was thinking of Edmond.

Then Raife turned and bent down, lifting from the floor the document holder he'd brought with him the previous night. He came back to the bed and sat on its edge, close by me.

I sat up, looking at the document holder. 'What is it?' I said. As I did not know my letters I could not imagine what kind of document he might wish to show me.

Raife's mouth quirked in a wry smile. 'These months you were gone,' he said, 'I spent both half angry with you and half desperate to wonder how I could achieve your trust. The angry part of me did not want to bother. It said to me that if you did not wish to trust me, then so be it. We would both need to live and die with that.

'But the part of me which loves you begged me to find a way, *any* way, to try and make you understand ...' he paused, as if seeking his words carefully, 'my motives in what I do, and where I have been, and with whom I consort. That part of me drove me to construct this.'

He hefted the document holder in his hand.

'Raife?'

He sighed, then opened the document holder and slid out a large sheaf of tightly rolled loose vellum pages.

I expected him to unroll them, still unsure of why he wanted me to study written words I could not possibly understand, but Raife continued to sit, looking at the rolled sheafs of vellum, the fingers of one hand lightly tapping them.

'I sat many nights over these, Maeb,' he said. 'Imagine, the lord of Pengraic, a man of such immense wealth and power and nobility, sitting at his table late into the night sketching these poor drawings for you.'

'Drawings?'

He lifted a hand and pressed a finger against my lips. 'Just look at them, Maeb. Do not speak. Do *not* speak. Just look and, I pray to God, *understand*.'

Then, achingly slowly, Raife unrolled the first of the vellum sheets and showed it to me.

It was full of drawings, of peoples and forests, and of crowns and imps.

I looked back to Raife. 'Raife? What —'

'Just *look*, Maeb, I beg you, and *understand*!'

I looked back to the vellum sheet. Raife's finger pointed at the first set of figures and I saw a group of people much like the Old People depicted on the walls of Pengraic chapel. They were grouped about a man wearing a crown.

Raife's fingers tapped that figure wearing the crown and he lifted his finger, as if to point elsewhere, but at that moment a terrible stench filled the chamber and an imp appeared behind Raife.

'What is this, then, master? Is this what we have watched you poring over, night after night?'

I shrieked, shuffling away from Raife and the imp to the other side of the bed.

At the same time, the imp leaned over Raife's shoulder and made as if to grab the handful of pages.

Raife pushed the imp to one side and the vile creature toppled over onto the bed, one of his arms flailing out so that its hand hit my cheek.

Its touch was cold, moist, and nauseating, and I screamed once, then again.

The imp struggled to rise, as also did I, and for one moment we were both a tangle of limbs as we tried to escape the bed.

Raife had moved to the other side of the bed, reaching out a hand to try and pull me away, but I hit out at him in my panic and fear and all my resurrected loathing. 'Get away from me!' I shrieked.

Then, horrifyingly, the imp rolled right over the top of me — I felt its repulsive hand slide across my breasts! — and made an unsuccessful grab at the pages still in Raife's hand.

Servants were at the door now, concerned by the commotion, but Raife shouted at them to wait outside.

The imp had taken advantage of Raife's momentary distraction, lunging again for the pages. Raife stepped back, but the imp was quick. It had rediscovered both its balance and its senses and it managed to get its clawed hands about the pages. Raife and the imp struggled, back and forth, then Raife tore the pages from the imp and tossed them onto the coals of the fire, where they flared into flames.

'Damn you!' he cried, and I thought for one strange moment his voice was breaking. 'Damn you to hell!'

'Get out!' I screamed at both of them. '*Get out!*'

The imp hissed in frustration as it saw the pages curl into ash, then it vanished, but Raife reached for me.

'Maeb, please, you must let me —'

'Get out!' I shouted, angry and repulsed by his nearness, and wishing I had not allowed him to make love to me the night previous. 'Get out! I do not care if I never see you again!'

I paused, breathing heavily. '*Get out!*'

He stepped back, his face impassive.

'As you wish, wife.'

Then he collected his clothes, and left.

The moment the door closed I retched, struggling to the window to breathe in some air not yet befouled by either the imp or my husband.

I was so shocked, so terrified, I did not think again on what it was he'd been trying to show me.

CHAPTER FOUR

I was still out of sorts when I was summoned to the Tower just before midday. I wondered what had happened, why either Edmond or Raife could want me, but I called for Dulcette to be saddled, then I rode with a small escort as the sun was at its zenith.

The fields between the city buildings and the Tower, once used for jousting and games, were now humped over with recently dug plague pits.

I shuddered, and tried not to look.

It was a subdued world inside the gates of the inner bailey. I remembered the day I had ridden in here, jangling with nerves about my first day at court. Then it had been a bustling, crowded space.

Now there was one groom, two soldiers standing guard, a single horse tied to an iron ring in a wall, and no one else.

I imagined that Edmond must already have sent for more men-at-arms, for currently both city and Tower were horribly vulnerable.

The groom helped me dismount and I walked the stairs to the first-level entrance unescorted. The lesser hall was almost deserted. I saw Saint-Valery by one fire, and gave him a nod, gladdened to see him alive, and there were maybe fifteen others about, but that was it.

In the upper gallery de Warenne stood guard by the entrance into the great hall. He nodded as I came up. 'They are waiting for you inside, my lady,' he said.

I walked into the great hall. There was a table pushed close to the western wall's central fireplace and around it sat Edmond and Raife. There were documents spread over the table.

They both stood as I walked over. I sat down and they resumed their seats.

Edmond pushed a ewer and cup toward me and I poured myself some small beer, sipping it as I looked warily at Raife, and then almost as carefully at Edmond.

Why was I here?

Raife seemed to be wondering the same thing as he looked at Edmond enquiringly.

'It is time to end this,' Edmond said softly, and I quailed internally.

He was going to tell Raife that he knew who he was, and Raife would know I'd told Edmond.

For all that my husband was, I still dreaded him knowing I had betrayed his trust.

Raife raised an eyebrow at Edmond. 'End this?'

'This madness,' said Edmond, looking directly at Raife. 'The diadem.'

Raife flicked a glance my way.

'It is time to send you and your master's diadem back to hell,' said Edmond. 'I have had enough. This realm, this people, have had enough.'

Now Raife looked at me fully, and I saw the hurt at my betrayal clear on his face.

'Yes,' Edmond said, 'she told me. For pity's sake, Raife, you expected her to keep this silent? To put to one side that she had unwittingly wed a servant of hell?'

Raife was still staring at me, and now Edmond banged his hand on the table, making Raife jerk his eyes back to the king.

'By God, sir,' Edmond said, 'you have betrayed *everyone*! I have trusted you all my life, and for what? Adelie, her children — did they know? Of course not, eh? Have you spent the past almost forty years using this realm for your master's black ends, eh? Have you —'

'I have not betrayed either you, nor this realm,' Raife said. 'My only purpose as my master's servant in this mortal realm was to find for him the diadem. No other. The petty concerns of this realm were of no interest to him.'

Whatever resentment and questions Edmond had bottled up these past weeks now spilled out.

'For sweet Christ's sake, Raife,' Edmond said, 'why sit here these past thirty-six years? Why not just take the form of some anonymous ploughman and take the diadem as you needed? Why take the form of a great noble, lest you meant to use that power against me at some point? And why here in England? Were you so sure that the diadem rested in England? Are there other of your master's servants waiting in other realms? Can I expect them all to congregate here, in London, hoping to be the ones to lay their hands on this diadem? Can —'

Raife held up a hand.

'Edmond,' he said, 'I am sorry for the deception. I have been a true friend to you all my life, and remain so now. You will probably choose not to believe me, nor to trust me — my wife prefers to think me utterly malicious and beyond redemption — but I will try to answer your questions as honestly as I may.

'Why did I choose to take the form of a great noble? Edmond, do you honestly think I would have preferred to have been a ploughman living from day to day on the fruits of my toils in the mud? Besides, my nobility gives me access to most of the information that you have and access to all parts of the realm. A ploughman would have none of these. High nobility was needed.

'Why for thirty-six years? I had to be born, Edmond. I could not suddenly take flesh, nor position within society. I had to come to it naturally.

'Why here in England?' Raife shrugged. 'That was something of pure luck. My master knew where the starting point was — Ghaznavid, which was where the monk had re-emerged from hell — and we thought that he would have fled back toward Europe, as that was his home. Had I needed to I would have travelled. But, as luck had it ... the diadem is currently somewhere within England, within *London*, and if I am to believe the rattling of the Templars, then it is somewhere with Maeb.

'And, no, there are no other servants of hell sitting about Europe. I am the only one.'

'Somewhere in there you are lying,' Edmond said. 'I can smell it. But where? Where?'

'I tell only the truth,' Raife said.

Edmond grunted.

'I have a question,' I said, suddenly, and both men looked at me in surprise, as if they had forgot my presence. 'What is hell like, Raife?'

He looked at me a long time before answering. 'I cannot speak of it,' he said eventually. 'It is too terrible.'

'And yet you would drag me there,' I said, softly. 'Trust me, you say.'

'And I say it again, Maeb. Trust me, if you love me.'

'Enough,' said Edmond. 'All I wish is to see you gone, and I wager that Maeb wants much the same. I cannot attempt to rebuild this realm until I know it will not be devastated over and over again. It is in all of our interests, Raife, to see you gone and this damned diadem with you.'

'Maeb.' Edmond turned to me. 'You are connected with this diadem, somehow, I have no doubt. It must be through your father.'

I repressed a sigh.

'Let us suppose,' Edmond said, 'that your father brought the diadem home with him from Jerusalem. You say you have no knowledge of it, and I do not disbelieve you. Yet, somehow, you *do* seem to have the diadem or at least brought it in some manner to London.'

'I have *never* seen it,' I said, wearily.

'Be that as it may,' Edmond said, 'who else on your father's estate might your father have confided in besides you? Did he have a valet who travelled with him and back? A servant? A groom? Is there a priest on your estate who may have taken confession?'

I thought. 'My father travelled with a groom-cum-valet,' I said. 'His name was Eadgard. A man from the estate. But he did not come home with my father. When I asked, my father said that he had died on the way to the Holy Lands. My father brought no one else home with him.'

'A priest?' Edmond said.

'My father trusted and befriended the old priest,' I said, 'who was incumbent when my father left on his pilgrimage. But he died shortly thereafter, and a new, much younger man came to the church as priest. My father tolerated him, but did not overly like him. I cannot imagine that he would have confided in this priest.'

'Confessed to him?' Edmond asked.

'Perhaps,' I said, somewhat reluctantly.

'Anyone else on the estate your father was close to?'

'There is but one person. Our steward, Osbeorn. He was an intolerably lazy steward, but retained the post because my father liked him. They used to spend countless hours together in the evenings dipping their beards into cups of rough wine.'

'He is still alive?' Edmond asked.

I nodded. 'Unless he was carried away when the plague passed through Witenie.'

Edmond rose and shouted for de Warenne, who entered the great hall.

'de Warenne,' Edmond said, 'I need you to travel to Witenie, there to make enquiries about a man named Osbeorn. You will not travel as a lord in your fine tunic and mantle, but as something less … visible. I want no rumour of this spreading about the land. If you find this Osbeorn, bring him back here as speedily as you may.'

De Warenne nodded. 'He may not trust me, my lord. Is there some token I can take with me that he would trust?'

Edmond made as if to draw off a ring, but I shook my head. 'He would not know that ring, my lord king, and would suspect that he was being bribed by a wealthy lord into some black action. My Lord de Warenne, if you would accompany me back to my Cornhill house then I will give you something that Osbeorn will recognise as mine. That he will trust.'

I looked to Edmond. 'If I have my lord's permission?'

Edmond gave it with a nod.

'I will also —' Raife said, rising.

'I would appreciate it if you stayed here,' said Edmond. 'While we are waiting for Osbeorn's presence you may assist me in planning for the recovery of this realm when —' he glanced at de Warenne and moderated his words, '— when all danger is passed. Maeb, stay within the house, if you may, until I call for you again.'

I stood, dipped in courtesy to the king, and followed de Warenne from the great hall.

I gave de Warenne an item that I knew Osbeorn would recognise, then I sent him on his way.

I waited five days. In those five days I did not see Raife, nor Edmond. Presumably Edmond kept Raife close by him, whether in the Tower or when they were in London. Gytha told me that both had ridden about London on several occasions, inspecting damage, encouraging those who remained.

I was glad I did not have to see Raife, and was still so chilled by the memory of the imp in my own bed that I slept with Gytha in her chamber.

I did see much activity in the streets about Cornhill; there were more people about, mostly men, and also men-at-arms, and I thought that Edmond was bringing the men in to strengthen defences, or to help with rebuilding — or destruction, rather, as mostly, Gytha reported, these men laboured at pulling down dangerous buildings.

I spent these five days going through every single one of my possessions, and then through every chest, pannier, basket, storage vat and pot in the building. I turned everything upside down.

There was nothing. Not a single bead let alone a diadem of immense value.

Once I had done that, I spent my time in the solar, thinking.

I thought of Raife, and our marriage. I thought of the past year or so of my life. Just over a year, and in that time I had moved from the lowest rank of the nobility to the very highest. I had been seized and almost murdered; I had borne a child; I had become intimately involved in a battle with the master of hell himself.

I did not know how this was going to end, nor did I want to think about how it might end. My mind kept playing tricks on me, one moment trying to devise a possibility where Raife was not who he said he was, and where we might continue to live our lives as husband and wife, and the next moment rejecting that as an impossibility in the face of everything Raife had said to me.

I don't think I wanted to accept that. My mind kept going back to worry over everything Raife had said, trying to find that one reason that would give me hope.

But there was nothing. I could see nothing but bleakness ahead.

I could not sleep. I rejected the food fitzErfast sent to me, and which Ella and Gytha encouraged me to eat.

Everything was coming to a head, I knew it, and knew that somehow Osbeorn, if he still lived, would bring with him the seeds of my destruction.

Perhaps the destruction of my life; certainly of my happiness.

In my most honest moments, I could admit to myself that I didn't *want* the diadem to be found, that I wanted Raife and myself to continue as we had before all this horror had surfaced.

But that way, only a continuance of the plague and of death and horror.

This had to end, one way or the other.

Either way, I knew, would tear me apart.

On the sixth day after de Warenne had left, a soldier came from the Tower, and told me that Edmond requested my presence.

I closed my eyes momentarily, fighting to control the terrible churning in my belly. Then I opened them, and smiled, and rose.

CHAPTER FIVE

A gain, there was just Raife and Edmond waiting in the great hall. It was close to evening now, and servants had placed torches on the walls. They threw shadows about the immense chamber, and I felt that danger lurked in every dark, shrouded place.

Raife rose as I came in and came to meet me. He made as if to lean forward and kiss me, but I drew back.

'Please trust me,' he whispered. 'When I ask it of you, *trust me.*'

His tone stung my heart. If I could have, I would have trusted him, but the thought of that imp rolling over me, grabbing at my flesh, was still too fresh in my mind.

We walked over to the table and sat down. Edmond nodded at me, but did not otherwise speak to me.

Instead, he called for de Warenne to enter.

The man came in through the archway leading to the king's privy chambers. With him came Osbeorn.

I choked up with tears the instant I saw Osbeorn. He had always been a part of my childhood, a part of that life before now, when all had been innocent. He had been my father's friend.

He looked older, ravaged by the years and the time of horror when plague had raged through Witenie. His hair, what remained of it, was white, his face lined and pouchy. He walked with a shambling gait that spoke of his age and increasing infirmity.

'My lady,' he said when he saw me, and bowed. 'I am happy to see you. You have done well.'

'And I am happy to see you, Osbeorn,' I said, rising and kissing him on the cheek. 'Osbeorn, this is your king, Edmond, and here my husband, the Earl of Pengraic.'

I thought Osbeorn might have been unnerved at an introduction to Edmond, but he did not appear perturbed, and bowed to both Edmond and Raife, greeting them both with polite phrases.

'Thank you, de Warenne,' Edmond said, dismissing the man. 'Will you make sure that all entrances to the Tower are well guarded? Use all the available men. Then return and wait outside in the gallery.'

De Warenne bowed and left.

'Do you think the armies of hell are about to invade?' Raife said.

'I take no chances,' Edmond replied, then looked to Osbeorn. 'Osbeorn, you were steward to Sir Godfrey Langtofte, yes?'

'Indeed, my lord king.'

'And you were close friends?'

'Good friends, aye, sir.'

'You spent many evenings dipping your beards into cups of rough wine.'

Osbeorn chuckled. 'Yes, sir.'

'And this closeness continued after Sir Godfrey returned from the Holy Lands?'

'Indeed, sir.'

'Osbeorn, good man, do you know of any jewels or valuables Sir Godfrey brought home with him from the Holy Land?'

'There were nothing, sir king. My master, he came home with his life and a few clothes. Naught else.'

Raife rubbed his eyes with a hand, as if he were suddenly very, very tired.

'Nothing at all, Osbeorn?' Edmond asked. '*Nothing?*'

'His life, and his clothes, sir. Oh, and that old dusty piece of embroidery that he begged me give to the Lady Maeb here.'

'That embroidery came from the Holy Land, Osbeorn?' I asked.

'Yes, indeed, my lady. My master, your father, he loved it dear. Dusty rag that it was. He wanted you to have it badly.'

Both Raife and Edmond were looking at Osbeorn intently. 'An embroidery?' Edmond asked. 'An embroidery of *what?*'

'Of the Last Supper,' Raife said. 'Maeb showed it to me. It has no significance. I would have felt it otherwise, I am certain.'

463

'Where is it now?' Edmond said.

'It is in the Cornhill house,' Raife said.

'No,' I said, 'it is not. Not any more. I gave it to de Warenne as a token. So that Osbeorn here would know that he came on my behalf.'

We were all looking at Osbeorn who had no idea why the tension in the chamber had suddenly grown to deeply uncomfortable proportions.

'*This* cloth?' he said, and from the pocket of his mantle he drew the old embroidered cloth. 'I brought it to return to you, madam.'

Both Raife and Edmond moved, but it was I who took it from Osbeorn.

'Thank you, Osbeorn,' I said, then I handed it to Raife.

He unfolded it, showing the embroidered scene of the Last Supper to Edmond.

'It is nothing,' Raife said. '*Nothing*. Not even good embroidery. It has nothing to do with the diadem. I have no idea why Godfrey would have treasured it so much, or wanted Maeb to have it so badly.'

'Good sir,' said Osbeorn, 'Sir Godfrey did not like the embroidery as such, but he said that the depiction of sweet Lord Christ shows Jesu using an eating knife almost identical to the one that my Lady Maeb had as a child, so that the cloth always served to remind him of her.'

'An eating knife?' Edmond said, and glanced at the one that hung from my girdle.

The knife that Alianor had given me.

'What eating knife?' Raife said to me.

'The one I'd had since childhood,' I said. 'It cannot have any significance. It is not something my father gave me, and certainly not anything that came back from the Holy Land.'

Raife looked at the one on my girdle. 'That's not it. I remember you using a plainer one.'

'I did, yes,' I said. 'Alianor gave me this knife when first I arrived in London.'

'And your old one?' Edmond said. 'Your childhood one?'

'I presented it to fitzErfast, the steward at the Cornhill house, as a token of my esteem for him.'

'Jesu,' Edmond muttered. 'So the plague followed you around until you handed the knife to this fitzErfast. *That* is why the plague did not follow you back to Pengraic Castle? By God, Maeb, why did you not connect this sooner?'

'Because I thought it had no significance, my lord king! It was not my father's, he did not give it to me, and most certainly not after arriving back from the Holy Lands! I do not even know *who* gave it to me — it was, I believe, a baptismal gift from an unremembered well-wisher.'

'Could this knife have significance?' Edmond asked Raife.

'I won't know until I handle it,' Raife said. 'Does fitzErfast still have it, Maeb?'

'Yes,' I said. 'When I returned to London I remember seeing it at his belt, and was pleased he still wore it.'

'de Warenne!' Edmond shouted, then he looked at Osbeorn. 'You may go, good man. My servants will bed and feed you, and give you means to return to Witenie in the morning. But be sure never to mention a word of what you have heard in this chamber, for fear of your life.'

An hour. It took an hour for de Warenne to ride to the Cornhill house and return with the knife, and Edmond, Raife and I spent that entire time in uncomfortable silence.

De Warenne came in, handed the knife to me, then left without a word.

I held it in my hands and looked at it. It was as familiar to me as my own face, for I had used it since I was four or five until that moment some months ago when I gave it to fitzErfast. It was of good although unremarkable craftsmanship, having a twisted handle of silver and a steel blade. I could not see what possible connection it had to the diadem.

I lifted it to the table, then slid it toward my husband.

Raife hesitated, just very slightly, then picked it up, turning it gently in his fingers. 'You were given this as a baptismal gift, Maeb?'

'Yes. I think so. It *may* have belonged to my mother. I truly can't remember. I just know I have had it all my life.'

'The blade is of recent craftsmanship,' Raife said. 'Made within the past twenty or thirty years. Perhaps just before it was gifted to you, Maeb. But the handle, now … that is of ancient craftsmanship. Very ancient. It belongs to the time of the Old People. Maeb, who was your mother?'

'A woman of poor family,' I said. 'My father loved her, though, and made a match with her. Her name was Leorsythe.'

Raife looked at me sharply. 'That is a name of the Old People. It is from her, not your father, that you have your blood, Maeb.'

Uda, I thought. *Uda told me that I had the blood of the Old People. Uda herself must be one of the Old People.*

And yet I never took that thought through to its logical conclusion, or combined it with what she had told me. Not for thirty years.

'You seem to have made a study of these Old People,' Edmond said to Raife.

Raife gave an indifferent shrug. 'I listen to the myths, for they are strong about Pengraic. But, this knife — wherever it came from anciently — it has recently had work.'

'The new steel blade,' I said.

'Even more recent than that,' Raife said. He held up the knife, and tapped at the knobbed end of the handle with a finger. 'This end knob has recently been taken off and fixed back on again within the last year or two,' Raife said. 'I can take a good guess and say sometime after your father returned from the Holy Lands, eh, Maeb.'

I went cold. 'I lost it for a time,' I said. 'Some weeks. I was so happy when I discovered it in my chamber. I could not think how I could have overlooked it in previous searches.'

Raife gave a nod. 'Your father took it,' he said, 'and hid the diadem within it.'

'No!' I said.

'Yes,' Raife said.

'How?' Edmond said. '*How?* A diadem could not possibly fit in that handle.'

'We speak not of any diadem,' said Raife, 'but of the Devil's diadem and that is very subtle trickster. It can be persuaded to do almost anything you ask of it. Sir Godfrey would have needed no magic to hide it. He would simply have requested it of the diadem, persuaded it somehow. Maeb, your father left the embroidered cloth to you as a clue, as a pointer to the true hiding place of the diadem. God knows where he got the cloth … whether he had it made up himself, or if the cloth gave him the idea of where to hide the diadem. But it is here, in this small knife. Maeb, forgive me what I do now.'

Before either Edmond or I could speak, Raife struck the knife a hard blow on the edge of the table.

The knobbed end of the handle flew off, rattling several paces away on the floor.

Then Raife upended the knife over the table, and gave it a gentle shake.

What happened next is barely credible, but I swear I saw it with my own eyes. There was a glimmer of gold as something *poured* out of the hollow knife handle, and then, in the next moment, a small flash as it landed on the top of the table.

We had all risen to our feet at the flash, and now we stood, staring.

Resting on the table lay the Devil's diadem, a full-sized crown of gold and gems.

The diadem was beyond beautiful. I cannot find words adequate enough for it. I had thought the Devil's diadem would be a thing of darkness, of loathsomeness.

But this … yes, this I would have fought for, too.

It was a full circlet twisted by extraordinary workmanship into sweeps and arcs that supported the heavens — sun and stars and moon, all made from gems far brighter, indescribably more fiery and more glorious than diamonds. It spoke to me of unrestrained gaiety, of elegance, of grace, of wisdom beyond knowing, of power beyond comprehension.

Raife picked it up. He stood there with this wondrous thing in his hands, and then his hands moved, and for one astonishing moment I thought he was going to put the diadem on his own head.

But before he could do that — if, indeed, that was his intention — hell came to visit the Conqueror's Tower.

CHAPTER SIX

––––•••‹❀›•••––––

'Jesu!' Edmond exclaimed, and I turned to look at the south wall of the chamber, where he stared.

The stones in the wall seemed disfigured, as if shapes writhed beneath them. Then I gasped in horror, for I realised that those shapes were imps, struggling to emerge from the stone.

Is this how they travelled from hell to this mortal realm?

I had no further time for thought, for Raife snatched me by the wrist and strode toward the door leading to the gallery.

I cried out, but I could not resist him. Raife dragged me through the door, my wrist in one hand, the diadem in the other, and pulled me toward the stairs. I thought he would drag me down them, but to my surprise he pulled me upward, toward the roof and parapets.

Edmond was just behind us, and I heard him unsheathe his sword.

'Raife!' I cried, but he only pulled me harder, and he dragged me up those steps rather than that I climbed them.

'Let her go, Raife!' Edmond called as we emerged onto the roof. There was a narrow walkway from the parapets that bridged between the old Roman walls and the Tower, and Raife pulled me at a run along the top of the walls until we reached the southern wall abutting the Thames.

Just before we got there I managed to pull my wrist free. Instantly, Edmond grabbed me about the waist, pulling me to a halt tight against him some three or four paces from where Raife stood against the southern parapet.

'Edmond,' Raife said, 'let her go. Please.'

'Be damned if you wish,' Edmond said, 'but don't take her with you.'

'Maeb ...' Raife said, and there was such plea in his voice and face that I began to weep.

Edmond's arm tightened about me until I could scarce breathe.

'Maeb,' Raife said one last time, '*trust me.*'

He climbed onto the parapet, and looked behind him briefly at the terrible drop.

'Trust me,' he said again. 'I love you, and will do you no harm. I would *never* do anything to harm you. Trust me.'

He wanted me to trust him?

Uda had pleaded with me to trust him, and in that moment I wavered, but then I remembered that imp appearing in our chamber; how the revolting thing had crawled over my body, its vile flesh dragging across my flesh, and how, if Raife wanted me to trust him, I would spend an eternity with those foul creatures as my playmates.

I couldn't. I couldn't.

As if to confirm my decision, a malignant stink surrounded us, and I knew that the imps had emerged from the Tower and were now on the top of the walls with us.

Raife held out his hand. 'Maeb, come with me, please.'

He wanted me to jump from the parapets? All I could think of was Mevanou, her body twisting through the air as it fell from the parapets, her body splattered on the ground beneath the Tower.

'I can't!' I cried, 'Oh God, Raife, I can't.'

'I will *never* harm you,' Raife said. 'Please ...' Then his eyes focused on something behind Edmond and myself, and I knew it to be the imps.

'Christ save us,' Edmond muttered, and I could feel him move to look behind him.

'I can't,' I whispered. 'I'm sorry, Raife, I can't ... I can't ... Please don't jump, please don't —'

'Maeb,' Raife said, and his voice was full of such sorrow and regret and pain that I could not bear it, 'I love you.'

Then he put the diadem on his head and in a smooth, graceful movement, turned and leapt from the parapet.

I cried out, my voice hoarse with shock and horror, and then both Edmond and I were slammed against the parapets as five imps seethed past us and, without a single hesitation, leapt after Raife.

Edmond and I rushed to the parapet and looked down. It was a moonlit night and we could see the water clearly.

There were circles of ripples where Raife and the imps had gone in.

And for one, perhaps imagined, moment, I thought I could see the flash of gems deep beneath the water.

'Stay here,' Edmond said. '*Stay* here.'

I nodded numbly.

'Will you be all right?'

I nodded again. I could not tear my eyes from the water.

He hesitated, then he was running down a wooden staircase into the inner bailey, shouting.

I stared at the water. Behind me the inner bailey and the Tower came alive with men running and shouting, but all that existed for me was that patch of water, now rapidly calming.

Raife was gone.

Gone back to hell.

I sobbed, and wished now that I had gone with him. I clung to the stonework, looking down, wondering if it were too late for me to throw myself over.

Would he catch me, somewhere deep under the water?

Or would I merely die in agony as my crushed body sank down, down, down?

I saw a boat push out into the river, then two, and guardsmen started to probe the waters with their pikes.

I was too late.

Too late.

Sobs tore through me, and I sank to the stone flooring, shaking in horror and grief.

De Warenne emerged out of the Tower, and moved toward me. 'My lady!' He reached down, then flinched back as I struck him.

'Get away! Get away!'

He stood back several paces, helpless.

'Enough, de Warenne, go.'

It was Edmond. He waited until de Warenne had gone, then he walked over and lifted me to my feet, before holding me tight.

'Thank God you are safe,' he said. 'Thank God.'

CHAPTER SEVEN

We went to the Tower and down the stairwell. I thought Edmond would take me back to his privy apartments, but he took me to the first level and then down the outer stairs to the inner bailey. There were horses saddled and waiting there, including Dulcette.

'You can't stay here,' Edmond said, and I was glad, because more than anything I needed to get away from both Tower and river.

I was still crying and shaking. Edmond looked at Dulcette, then told one of his soldiers to lead her. He hoisted me onto his big courser, and mounted behind me, holding me tight as he kicked the horse into a canter, six or seven soldiers following us.

We rode hard through the streets of London. I thought initially Edmond was taking me back to the Cornhill house, but we rode west instead of north and before I knew it we were out of Lud Gate and riding through the country, at first west and then turning south along the curve of the river.

Here Edmond pushed his horse into a gallop, and he held on tight to me as we raced through the night. Eventually we drew close to, then passed, an impressive abbey and I knew we must be at Westminster.

Edmond finally slowed our pace and we rode into the courtyard, surrounded on all sides by substantial stone buildings.

He jumped off the horse, then lifted me down.

'Can you walk?' he said, and I nodded.

He led me through a massive doorway. We were met inside by a man I later knew as Nigel fitzRolf, the palace chamberlain. He carried a torch, and wore a deeply worried expression.

'My lord king!' he said. 'We were not expecting you … I had no idea … no word of warning …'

'Then I offer my apologies, fitzRolf,' said Edmond. 'Our arrival is somewhat unexpected, I grant you.'

'There is nothing ready, no chambers warmed —'

'Then light fires and set linens to bed and order something warm from the kitchen — *they* must have a fire going, for God's sake. Is the way to my chambers lit?'

Apparently not, for fitzRolf led the way himself, muttering as he occasionally darted to the side of a chamber to light a torch with the one he carried.

I paid no attention to what or where we were going. Edmond kept a light arm about my waist, occasionally glancing at me as we went.

FitzRolf led us finally to a large privy chamber. Servants scurried from behind our backs to set and light a fire in the fireplace, and to put linens and coverlets on the bed pushed against one wall.

'Send for wine and food,' Edmond said, and fitzRolf bustled away on his new mission, still muttering away to himself.

As soon as the servants had lit the fire, Edmond pulled over a chair close to it and sat me down, squatting beside the chair and taking one of my hands.

'Maeb,' he said, 'it is over, now. It is done.'

There was nothing to say to that, so I said nothing.

'You are safe here,' Edmond said.

I did not reply. I could think of nothing to say. Nothing in my head made sense.

'We will search the waters,' Edmond said, and I gave a nod. I did not think they would find anything.

'I need to make sure he is gone,' Edmond added, and at that silent tears rolled down my cheeks again.

Edmond murmured a curse. I felt sorry for him … he obviously was not sure how to deal with me.

A servant came in with wine and some bread and cheese and dried fruits. He set them down near us, and Edmond waved him away.

Edmond poured out a cup of wine, took a gulp himself, then brought it over to me. 'Drink,' he said, and I surprised myself by doing so.

473

I emptied the cup in several swallows, and Edmond refilled it, and brought it back, lifting my hands to it so that I held it.

I took another mouthful while Edmond poured his own cup and emptied it in one draught.

'God's truth,' he said. 'Were those imps from hell?'

'Yes,' I said.

'Jesu … they crawled from the wall!'

'Yes.'

Edmond poured himself another cup, then brought over the ewer and refilled my cup.

This was strong wine, and I thought we would both be drunk very soon.

'They stank,' Edmond said, and I nodded.

He pulled over a chair to mine and sat down, putting the ewer of wine on the floor beside him.

We both ignored the food.

'What am I going to do?' I said.

'You need not worry.'

No. I supposed not. I drank my wine and held out my cup for Edmond to pour me some more.

'I will send for your women in the morning,' he said. 'And your belongings.'

I drank the wine. My head was swimming now, and I knew I should stop. 'I want to sleep,' I said, and Edmond nodded, set aside his cup, and held out his hand.

I rose, and let him lead me toward the bed.

'Turn about,' he said, and he unlaced my kirtle then held it as I stepped out of it.

I pulled my chemise over my head, handing it to him.

His eyes were very dark.

Then, naked, I crawled into bed, pulling the covers close.

Edmond leaned over and kissed my cheek. 'I will watch over you,' he said.

I would have replied, save I fell straight to sleep.

I woke some time later. It was still deep night, not yet close to dawn. My mouth had a sour taste in it from the wine, and my head ached a little.

I opened my eyes.

Edmond was asleep in one of the chairs, his feet resting on the other one.

I lay there a while, then I rose, as quietly as I could, wrapping a woollen coverlet about me. I opened the door, and asked the guard standing there where the privy was.

When I returned, Edmond was awake, sitting in the chair, rubbing his face as if very tired.

There was a pitcher of small beer set on a table, together with cups. My mouth still tasted horrible, and I poured myself a cup, swilling the beer about my mouth, getting rid of the taste. I raised my eyebrows at Edmond, and he nodded, so I poured him a cup and carried it to him.

He drank it, and I took his cup and set it aside, then slid my hand into his.

'Come to bed,' I said.

I suppose it is easy to criticise and say, *You only just lost the man you loved, why now take another to your bed?*

I had my reasons.

I badly needed comfort, and Edmond would provide that.

I was a woman alone and in a dangerous world, and Edmond would protect me. There had been only Edmond and myself on the parapets when Raife jumped, and I was sure that soon rumours would start about whether or not he had jumped or if he had been pushed. Perhaps Edmond was above the rumours, but I knew that fingers would point my way. I'd had too much scandal attached to me already; this could tip me over the edge. I needed Edmond's protection, very, very badly, and I needed to ensure I had it.

I needed protection for my and Raife's infant son, too. He was only a few months old, with vast estates and wealth — I needed Edmond so that Geoffrey could hold on to his inheritance. I knew that aristocratic vultures would be circling the earldom of Pengraic by morning.

And, finally, I suspected strongly that I was now carrying another child of Raife's. I cannot say how, for it was only days since Raife and I had bedded, but somehow I knew it. I wanted Edmond to think this was his child, and thus also afford it his protection.

Edmond was my hold on life, my single protector, and I needed to consummate that protection as soon as I could.

Besides, I would be a liar to say that I was not already well on the path to loving him. I loved Raife with a passion, Edmond with a quiet, solid regard.

Edmond was no fool, and knew precisely my reasons behind my leading him to the bed. He may not have suspected that I was breeding again (although he might have done, for he was aware that Raife and I had spent a night together), but he certainly understood all the other reasons.

He loved me, I knew, and lusted for me, but he apprehended also that when he bedded me he solidified his control of the vast wealth of the earldom of Pengraic. My son Geoffrey would become his ward, and until Geoffrey reached his majority Edmond would control all the Pengraic wealth and estates. It would help Edmond enormously if the boy's mother was compliant and willing and not a force pulling Geoffrey the other way. Edmond as king was already a powerful man. With the wealth (and the subsequent military resources) of Pengraic behind him, he was virtually untouchable, personally controlling a third of the land in England as well as almost half of the Welsh Marches.

Bedding a scandal-ridden widowed countess was a small price to pay to ensure such power. Keeping me from another noble's bed was an absolute necessity, because if he didn't then his hold over Geoffrey's wealth might be compromised.

But … as much as a king and countess took to the bed that night, it was also man and woman, and a man and a woman who had been moving toward each other for some time. Our love-making was sweet and simple; comforting, warm, full of aching promise and hope and, perhaps, even a little redemption.

When we were done I lay in his arms and cried for everything I had lost, and he held me and comforted me, and did not mind my tears. One of the things I came to love about Edmond was that he did not resent Raife, nor was he jealous of him. I could, and did, weep for Raife often in the coming months and years, but Edmond allowed me that, and did not complain.

From that night, Edmond became the centre of my existence.

Of my new life.

PART EIGHT

THE FALLOWAY MAN

CHAPTER ONE

As I had known it would, terrible scandal erupted the day after Raife's death. The only witnesses to his death had been Edmond and myself (and five imps, but neither Edmond nor myself deluded ourselves that they would spring to our defence!). There was not even a body. Some refused to believe Raife was dead at all — the rumours that the Earl of Pengraic had been seen here, there, over that mountain or beyond the seas in Normandy or other realms within Europe continued for many years. He was even spotted in the Holy Lands, and beyond, in those exotic empires far to the east.

It was the rumours that either myself or Edmond had pushed him to his death that were the most damaging, however. We both stood to profit from Raife's death: Edmond gained control of Raife's vast wealth and power; I gained the king. Edmond had never hidden his interest in me, and the fact — noised about within the day by servants from the palace of Westminster — that I had gone straight from the tragedy of my husband's death to the king's bed did neither myself nor Edmond any favours.

It was a tense six months. The country had been devastated by plague and, subsequently, there was still unrest in many parts, while Raife's untimely death prompted a power struggle within the aristocracy and a small, but no less unnerving, power struggle against the king. I saw little of Edmond for many months as he rode about the country at the head of what amounted to a medium-sized army, gleaned from his own lands as well as those of the earldom of Pengraic.

The Church and the Templars, now a powerful force within English and European society, aided Edmond, backing him against claims he had murdered Raife. They did not back me. I think both Church and Templars would have happily thrown me over the parapets of the Conqueror's Tower after Raife if they thought they could manage it.

But they backed Edmond. Edmond, from both his position as King of England and his control of the Pengraic wealth and estates, was now a supremely powerful man, and one from whom the Church thought it could profit.

The Templars wanted more land and wealth in England.

Edmond could manage that for them.

The Church wanted total freedom from secular control, taxes and influence, as well as land and patronage enough to establish half a dozen new monasteries.

Edmond could give it that.

It was a heavy price for Edmond to pay, but he paid it.

He could have abandoned me — he could still have exerted control over the Pengraic wealth without me through his wardship of Geoffrey — but he did not. He brazened out some of the rumours, he led his army into the thickest of the rest of them, and he did what he had to in order to ensure the support of the Church and the Templars.

At least there was a Pengraic son and heir for whose paternity there could be no doubt. I thanked God for that, day and night, for otherwise I think the earldom of Pengraic would have been broken up. If Edmond did not have wardship over an undoubted legitimate Pengraic heir, then Edmond could not have held onto the lands and wealth for Geoffrey's majority.

I stayed at Westminster for some of this time, but under Edmond's orders and a heavy escort removed myself from Westminster to the royal manor at Elesberie for many months until the fuss died down.

Eventually, given Edmond's efforts and the fickle nature of rumours, the scandal lost its force. Edmond returned to Westminster for a few weeks, then came north to Elesberie to see me.

I was waiting in the courtyard of the manor house, nervous and excited in equal amounts. I was concerned that the time apart, and the efforts Edmond had been forced to go to on my behalf, might have dimmed his passion for me, but I need not have worried. He jumped down from his horse, a wide grin on his face, his eyes alight with joy, and seized me in a bear hug from which I could not escape for long minutes.

Eventually he put me down, breathless from his embrace and kisses.

'You are well, my lady?'

'I am, my lord.'

He held me out at arm's length and looked me up and down. 'You *look* well. You have grown some roundness. It suits you.'

I blushed. The roundness he referred to was all in my belly.

Edmond smiled at my discomfort, and then, arms linked, we went inside.

That night we made love for the first time in many months. I was deeply relieved that he still felt passion for me, and that his eyes still warmed whenever they looked my way. I did not deceive myself that he would remain true to me, or that I would remain forever by his side, but I was grateful for whatever time he gave me and knew that he would not cast me away without support. I had the four manors Raife had given me on our betrothal, but I did not doubt that Edmond would eventually add to those.

We lay side by side, still slightly sweaty from our love-making. Edmond gave a small sigh, and ran his hand over the mound of my belly.

'It would be best,' he said, 'if you named Pengraic as the father of this child.'

Raife *was* the father of the child, but it suited me if Edmond thought he himself might be.

'Of course,' I said.

Edmond's hand continued to rub, back and forth, back and forth. It was enormously soothing.

'The King of France has approached me,' he said. 'He has offered me the hand of his youngest daughter in marriage.'

I froze, all the pleasure of our reunion vanishing in an instant.

'Maeb, no matter how much I wish it, you know I cannot marry you.'

'I know,' I said, unable to stop the tears from running down my cheeks.

'The scandal … no one would accept you as queen.'

'I know,' I said, dashing the tears away with the back of a hand and wishing they did not flow. And I *did* know that Edmond could never wed me, but even knowing it did not stop the pain.

'Shush,' he whispered, kissing away the marks of the tears. 'Negotiations can take years. We will bicker this way, and then that way, back and forward.' He kissed me again, and smiled a little. 'Possibly even sally forth on a small war or two to make our points.' Another kiss. 'And besides, the girl is but eight. I could not bed her for years.'

'I know.'

'And yet still you cry for me. Ah, Maeb, you shall not lose me. Believe me, any wife I take to queen will weep ten times the tears over my adoration of the Lady Maeb and her hold over my heart than you will ever weep over me.'

I smiled a little now. He was teasing, I knew it, but I loved him for making the effort.

'Oh, Maeb, surely you know I loved you from that moment you fell at my feet? You were, *are*, so lovely, so transparent, so honest. Raife adored you. This king adores you. I have half a mind to lock you in a dark, dark dungeon so that the Pope shall never see you for he, too, would forgo all his vows to have you at his side.

'But, all jesting aside, my lovely woman, do not think that I will ever let you go, nor let go the hold you have over my heart.'

I thought he was being kind. At that time I did not truly believe him. I thought that eventually his fascination with me would fade, his passion ebb, and I would be put aside, albeit with a gentle kindness.

I did not know then that Edmond would keep every promise he made to me for the rest of his life.

In the middle of a cold, frosty winter, six weeks after Christmastide, I gave birth to my second son, Hugh. It was an easy, gentle birth which hardly pained me at all, and, compared to his brother's, accomplished in comfort and safety.

I delighted in this baby from the moment of his birth. I could not wait to hold him — I think I snatched him from the midwife's hands — and I put him to the breast immediately. Edmond, who, while not present at the actual birth, had been pacing about in the hall of Elesberie manor and was in the birthing chamber the moment the midwife allowed it.

If I had ever doubted the strength of Edmond's love, I did not at that moment.

He had tears in his eyes, whether of relief or happiness (or both) I do not know. He reached out a tentative finger and touched the baby's head.

'Look at his hair,' Edmond said. 'It is as black as yours.'

I have to admit some relief that Hugh then, as later, always took after me in face and form and did not in any manner resemble Raife.

My son thrived. Edmond loved him as his own.

We spent until early summer at Elesberie, then Edmond made the decision to bring me back to Westminster for his summer court.

It was risky. Neither of us knew if there remained any widespread ill-will against me, or if indeed, there might be any risk to my life.

But my major enemy, the Templars, were now negated. They had more land, more wealth. Their murmurings about my sins and possible connection to witchcraft had vanished. I do not know what Edmond told them about the diadem, but to my knowledge they never mentioned it again.

I think that possibly they had decided that if they could not control it, then it were better that no one could.

Nobles had also been to and fro at Elesberie where Edmond had continued to hold court, albeit a smaller court than he had held at the Tower, or did at Westminster.

None of these men, their wives or their sons, showed me any resentment.

Edmond's own sons, Richard and John, stayed long months at Elesberie and they treated me respectfully, if a little coolly.

I do not think they welcomed Hugh, who they believed was their illegitimate brother. Illegitimate or not, he posed a threat to them.

So I returned to Westminster with Edmond and with our son (for so he was treated), Hugh. It had been a year since I had been south to London and Westminster, and I was astounded at the change.

The plague had indeed vanished with Raife's death, and now the realm and its peoples breathed easier. Hope had replaced fear, rebuilding had replaced devastation. London, so shattered by fire and plague, was still a place of empty spaces where once had been buildings, but these spaces were now clear of burned timbers and harboured gentle carpets of flowers and small shrubs. In other places new buildings had sprung up, some completed, others still to be finished.

The streets were alive with people once more. Edmond later told me London had witnessed an influx of some fifteen thousand new souls in the past year alone as people flocked to the city from this realm, and others, to take advantage of the burgeoning trade and market in rebuilding, and of the need for crafts and people to ply them.

We stopped briefly at the city, then rode south down the banks of the Thames to Thorney Island. Even though I had stayed there some weeks after Raife had died, I had mainly kept indoors. When I had left, it had been at night, and I had been heavily hooded against both the dark and the rumours.

So now, when we clattered over the wooden bridge to Thorney Island, it was as if I was seeing Westminster for the first time. The abbey and its monastery — the smaller but no less grand newly built church of Saint Margaret's — the great hall, the palace, the village. It was summer now, and everything shone under the sun.

People from the village and servants from both abbey and palace lined the street for the final approach to the palace, and they cheered and waved ribbons attached to sticks. They called out Edmond's name, over and over and, to my utter astonishment, mine.

I wondered how much coin Edmond had caused to be spread among the crowd for them to shout my name so.

We rode to the entrance of the great hall, the household members among our company continuing on to the living quarters of the palace to fit it for our return. Hugh and his nurse, Blanche, were among them. I hated being parted from him, even for half a day, but even I could see the sense in keeping him quiet and safe in our privy chambers in the palace rather than in what I could already see was the hubbub of the great hall.

Someone had organised a grand reception. I suspected it to be Edmond, for he did not appear surprised at the welcome — although perhaps that was merely the experience of his kingship.

No. He *had* known, for he had made sure I was dressed in my finest, including the jewelled girdle and coronet that Raife had given me.

A groom helped me down from Dulcette (the only friend who remained with me since I had arrived at Rosseley Manor two years before), and Edmond came over. I had so often thought of him as ordinary, but today he was handsome, strong, powerful, every inch the king. His wiry dark hair had been cut fresh close to his scalp, he was smooth chinned and cheeked and dressed in the most sumptuous of robes and jewels.

He smiled, and kissed me, softly, lingeringly, in front of everyone who was standing outside the entrance to the great hall.

'Edmond,' I said softly, 'my nerves are screaming.'

'Then they do so quietly,' he said, 'for you look as calm as a still lake.'

'My lord,' I said more formally as the palace chamberlain approached, 'I —'

'Ah, fitzRolf,' Edmond said, turning to the man.

FitzRolf carried in his hands a pillow, with whatever it contained covered in a dainty cloth. Edmond lifted the cloth aside, and there was a crown — not as beautiful as the Devil's diadem, but a crown nonetheless set with magnificent gems. Edmond lifted it, looked at it, then set it on his head.

He held out his arm for me.

I hesitated, thinking that I should not take it. That it would be an impertinence before the court and nobles and so soon after the scandal of Raife's death.

'To hide in the shadows,' Edmond said softly, 'will be to admit to everything whispered. You may not wear a crown, but you rule my heart, and I want this clearly understood by everyone in this court.'

I took a breath, then his arm, and together we walked up the steps into the great hall at Westminster, the princes Richard and John following behind.

CHAPTER TWO

I was not queen, and not given the benefit of that rank, but I stood beside Edmond in place of a queen, and thus commanded respect. In many cases it may have been a false respect — smiles and courtliness to my face, dark words behind it — but never again did anyone challenge or accuse me.

They may have tried in the months following Raife's death, but that time also witnessed the rise of Edmond's power base. King, ward of the infant Earl of Pengraic and thus controller of the vast Pengraic fortunes and land, and with the power of the Church (themselves the second largest landholder in England behind the king) solidly behind him. He was unassailable. Some at the court might not like me, but Edmond loved me, and that is what mattered.

It may have been unwise for Edmond to marry me, but it was equally unwise for any to attack me.

I became an accepted part of court, and of Edmond's life.

What surprised me as the years passed was that Edmond did not tire of me. I had assumed he would, as he had of all his lovers. But, no. He continued to shower me with love and dedication. I have no doubt that there were many at court who would have wasted no time in whispering to me rumours of any dalliance that Edmond had embarked upon. But there were no whispers.

There were no lovers.

There were no rumours.

I saw women at court flatter him and preen before him, and even when

Edmond did not realise he was being watched, his expression always was one of disinterest. Women more beautiful than I sought his bed and were rejected with utter indifference.

The marriage negotiations with the King of France's daughter came to naught having dragged on for almost six years. Then Edmond's ambassadors considered a German princess, then one from one of the Iberian states. There was a daughter of Scotland paraded before him.

But always, there were problems with the negotiations. They would start with enthusiasm, and then founder amid myriad difficulties.

It became obvious that Edmond would not marry again. His son John married and fathered a son, and then another, and after that there was little purpose in Edmond trying to father more male heirs. His sons would do it for him.

Edmond relaxed.

I relaxed.

Edmond showered me with far more than love and dedication. As the years passed he granted me lands and estates until I became wealthy and a powerful landholder in my own right — all these lands will go to my son Hugh on my death as Edmond has provided for the three daughters I gave him over time.

I loved Edmond. Not with the same passion as Raife, but with such steadfastness and respect and friendship that he became the pivot of my life.

The passion I'd once given Raife I now gave to his son, Hugh.

It is strange that the child I conceived with Raife during the early, good times of our marriage became a stranger to me, and the child who was conceived amid such doubt became the adored child. Even the three daughters I eventually bore Edmond — Heloise, Ellice and Adète — while loved and cherished, were nonetheless always second to Hugh in my heart. I tried not to show it, but they all knew.

Geoffrey stayed at Pengraic for the first six years of his life. In all that time I did not see him. He was raised by Isouda and d'Avranches; they were his effective parents, not I.

When Geoffrey was approaching the sixth anniversary of his birth, Isouda and d'Avranches brought him to court.

Edmond and I laid on a great welcome for him, but it so intimidated Geoffrey he refused to leave d'Avranches' side for the first day (even then he was too much the man to hide behind Isouda's skirts). He gave me a sullen bow, and Edmond an even sketchier one.

He refused to talk with us, only answering in the barest of monosyllables when d'Avranches exhorted him to speak.

He looked like Raife.

That is what I found hardest to bear. He looked so much like Raife (and thus also like Stephen), and yet I think he hated me. Even then, even at six. It became more obvious as he grew.

I knew I had failed him, but what else could I have done? When he was an infant I could not have taken him back to London when the plague was in the land and the issue of the Devil's diadem yet to be resolved. In the year afterward it was deemed too dangerous, and my position too uncertain. After that, well, I moved about with Edmond a great deal, and I did not want to risk a small child on the move from Pengraic to eastern England.

Of course, I carried Hugh about with me everywhere during this time. I would have been aghast at the idea of leaving him behind.

Geoffrey continued as a stranger to me all his life. He treated me with a cold tolerance, I think, only because I was so closely tied to Edmond, and Edmond was untouchable ... the king was needed as a contented ally.

But Geoffrey had heard the rumours surrounding his father's death, and he always blamed me for it. We talked of it just once, when he was nineteen and taking the full responsibilities (and lands and powers) of the earldom on his shoulders. 'Talk' doesn't quite describe it. I had broached the subject, somewhat tentatively, and in reply Geoffrey actually spat at my feet and then walked away.

It devastated me then and still does. How could I have allowed that child to slip away?

But I did, and I did it because of Hugh.

Everyone assumed that Hugh was Edmond's son, even Edmond, I think. Hugh certainly always thought that Edmond was his father and addressed him as a son did a father. Hugh is treated by all as a prince in everything but name. Edmond was not the bad parent I was, and never favoured him over his older sons Richard and John, nor even over Geoffrey, but even so Hugh somehow stood out from all of them.

In any grouping of Hugh, Richard, John and Geoffrey, it is always to Hugh that people turn first, always at Hugh that people smile first. He is so favoured, in beauty and talent and courage and sheer, blinding magnetism, that he is a natural leader.

Unsurprisingly, Richard, John and Geoffrey resent him for this.

Richard and John also fear Hugh. Because of his wealth and popularity, and supposed parentage by Edmond, Hugh represents a shadowy, but very real, threat to the throne of England.

All three also resent that Edmond endowed Hugh with much land and wealth so that by the time Hugh was twenty he was almost his older brothers' equal in lordships and lands. Combined with what I will leave him on my death ... Hugh can never be anything but a powerful nobleman.

Hugh has inherited my propensity to acquire enemies just as he has inherited my looks.

There is another, quite extraordinary thing about Hugh.

He is almost entirely of the blood of the Old People.

He is a Falloway Man.

CHAPTER THREE

————◆◆◆◆————

Uda told me when I was heavily pregnant with Hugh that he was of the blood of the Old People. Edmond had brought her to Elesberie for Christmastide court. I avoided her whenever possible, because I had not trusted Raife when she'd pleaded with me to do so and I thought she would remonstrate with me. But Uda never mentioned Raife to me, or the issue of trust. All she was interested in was the child I carried.

'He will be a Falloway Man,' she said. 'Mark my words.'

I didn't mark them. I pushed them to the back of my mind. At that time of my life, in the year after I'd lost Raife, all I wanted was to huddle behind Edmond and simply forget everything that had happened the night Raife died, and the events which led up to it.

By the time Hugh was a toddling boy I had completely forgot Uda's words. Uda had died shortly after Hugh's birth and she'd never seen the boy. And all I wanted to do was to enjoy my son and cherish him.

But when Hugh was six, I lost him.

Hugh's sixth year was the last in which I would have him to coddle. After his seventh birthday he would venture ever more into the world of men, learning the art and craft of weaponry, battle, the courtly skills of the knight and the subtleties of the nobleman. But I had this last year to hold him close.

That summer I was pregnant with Ellice, the second of the daughters I bore Edmond. Edmond was in the north of England, and I had decided that I would take Hugh and Heloise into the meadows beyond Thorney Island to play for the afternoon. We had an escort, and Gytha (to whom I was becoming ever closer) and the children's nurse, Blanche, came — as well as several servants — all in a company which rode either in cart or on horse out to the meadows to chase butterflies and picnic.

I played a while with the children, and then we ate. It was a warm day and by then I was tired — I was only two months away from giving birth. I asked Gytha and Blanche (and the servants and men-at-arms, too) to watch the children, and I sat in the shade of one of the carts to doze.

I fell heavily asleep.

When I woke, it was as if I had been caught in a dream. I was aware of Gytha and Blanche playing with Heloise, and of the servants and men-at-arms standing about, but I could barely hear their chatter. Everything was hazy in the heat.

I could not see Hugh and became anxious about him. I rose, a little unsteadily, and looked about.

He was nowhere.

I tried to call to Gytha and Blanche, but my voice was muted, and they did not hear me.

I walked around the cart, looking everywhere. The land here was flat and almost treeless — he could not be hiding, and if he was not hiding, then he was lost, for Hugh was nowhere to be seen.

I walked further from our little picnic spot, calling Hugh's name. I still could not see well, either the heavy sleep or the heat haze made sight difficult.

Now I was becoming frantic. I called Hugh's name over and over, stumbling through the meadow. He had been stolen, I knew it. Another Madog had appeared and was even now pinning a terrified Hugh to the ground, razoring the blade across his throat. Some of my unknown enemies at court had taken him, factions allied with Richard and John, perhaps, keen to see the illegitimate prince removed.

I turned, and suddenly there he was, standing fifty or so paces away, his back to me. I had looked there a moment ago, and he had not been there, but I did not care what mysteries lay behind his sudden appearance. It was enough that he *was* here.

'Hugh!' I cried, walking toward him as fast as I could.

Then I stopped, staring. A moment ago there had been but Hugh standing there. Now a knight on a horse was beside him, and a woman with long, shining golden braids bending down to Hugh her hand on his shoulder.

They would snatch him! The woman was about to lift him to the knight, who would run away with him!

I opened my mouth to scream but then Hugh turned to look at me and the woman also.

Hugh smiled, as did the woman, and somehow the panic in my breast calmed.

I was much closer to them now and the woman's face seemed familiar.

Then I realised that the knight, so bright in the sun, was sitting a white courser whose diamond-entangled mane dragged along the ground.

It was the strange knight.

Stephen?

Now I was terrified that any sudden move or word on my part might scare him away. I moved slowly toward the three, smiling and holding out my hand for Hugh. When I came close he took it.

'This is the sun-drenched knight,' Hugh said, and turned back to the knight.

I looked up and the knight lifted away his helmet, and, yes, it was Stephen, smiling at me with such gentle love that tears filmed my eyes.

Then I looked at the woman and realised it was Uda. Uda as a beautiful young woman.

My hand tightened about Hugh's. 'Don't take my son,' I said.

'We will not,' said Uda, 'do not fear. We are merely making ourselves known to him.'

'Why?' I said, perhaps a little defensively.

'Because he is the Falloway Man,' said Stephen, and then suddenly I was alone in the meadow with my son and Stephen and Uda had vanished.

I stared about, but Stephen and Uda were nowhere to be seen. I crouched down by Hugh, taking him by the shoulders. 'Hugh? Are you well?'

He smiled at me, so beautiful. 'Of course, mama. Why should I not be well?'

Then he walked away from me, back toward the horses and cart, his sister and her guardians, and I had to hurry to keep up with him.

Whenever I tried to speak with Hugh about this day, and the meeting with Stephen and Uda, he always smiled at me and said he had totally forgot, and what day did I mean? After a few months I supposed he had totally forgot it, and thus I did, too.

I did not ever see my strange knight again, or Uda. Nor did I ever step onto a falloway again for the rest of my life.

It has not been until now, close to my death, that I realise that Hugh had never forgot that day and that the falloways had never forgot him.

CHAPTER FOUR

M y world went to nothing when Edmond died. Some days it felt to me as if there was naught remaining of any worth or comfort. Edmond had been my lover, my confidant, my protector for almost thirty years. Even though many weeks, sometimes months, might pass when I did not see him and he was busy on his progress about the country, still I knew he was there, and messengers shuttled back and forth between us regularly. It was enough that I knew he lived, and thought of me, and our reunions were always sweet.

But now he was dead. Nothing filled the gap he left. My world now became one of complete emptiness. Always the passing of Stephen and Raife had hung about me like shadows, but Edmond had been there to lighten my days, and push the shadows away, and make me laugh.

Now I had lost three loves, those three brilliant men who had stood framed in the sun on the steps of the Oxeneford palace chapel so many years ago.

They were gone, and the shadows became heavy, horrid, menacing.

I felt utterly alone, and inconsolable in that loneliness. People surrounded me — my lady companions, the stewards and servants of my estates, minstrels and jugglers, priests and sundry visitors, even Owain who now writes these words — but none of them could console me, nor fill the terrible void that Edmond's death created.

Gytha, still with me and my closest friend, could not even begin to fill that empty space.

My children tried. My son Geoffrey made the suggestion (from duty, nothing else) that I remove myself to Pengraic and was doubtless immensely relieved when I declined. I could not face Pengraic and all its memories yet, nor the cold regard of Geoffrey. My daughters offered their homes for their mother, but they also (as their husbands) appeared relieved at my decision to refuse their kindness.

Hugh abandoned his own wife and young family to return to me, but after some weeks I told him to go home. I loved Hugh with all my heart, but even he reminded me of loss, both of Raife's and of Edmond's. At thirty he was in the full bloom of his beauty and power, one of the distinguished nobles of England, and I admit that I was jealous of his youth and the future before him.

During my time by Edmond's side we had lived either at Elesberie or at Westminster, with the occasional foray back to the Oxeneford palace where I'd seen the first imp, or to one of Edmond's other royal manors. But now, with Richard on the throne, I was welcomed at none of these places and so I moved to my manor of Remany near Glowecestre.

Remany was an estate that Edmond had given me. It was large, had a big stone manor house, and was in a beautiful and peaceful part of the country. It was far from court — neither the new King Richard nor his younger brother John wanted me anywhere near the new court — and yet close to the Welsh Marches. I felt somehow connected to Pengraic, yet distant enough from it that its memories did not haunt me too intensely.

Here I thought I would rebuild my life in peace. Find something other than a husband or lover to focus on.

Try not to think of the past.

Gytha and I went for long walks, often accompanied by Gytha's daughter, Guietta. (Guietta had been an unexpected addition to my household some fifteen years earlier, when Gytha's swelling belly had announced that she was breeding. I did not know who Guietta's father was, nor did I ever ask.) I was long past riding now, and in fact had largely given up when my lovely Dulcette had died years before.

I spent months with my steward, learning the rhythms of the seasons that I had known as a girl and largely forgotten during my adult life at court.

I began, slowly, to take pleasure in life once more.

And then ... then ...

* * *

A half year after Edmond died, close to Christmastide of my fifty-first year, I grew ill. It was a slow, insidious malaise, creeping up on me so silently that it took me weeks to become fully aware of it.

My fatigue increased with each day so that after some weeks my mind was so fogged with exhaustion I could not string two thoughts together. I could not sleep, even though I longed desperately for it, and my temper grew so short that now my ladies actively sought reason to avoid me (all save Gytha, who endured my ill temper with stoic goodwill). Increasingly, I could not keep any food down, save the sloppiest of gruels, such as you might feed a baby, and more often than not they, too, returned straight into the light of day. My limbs grew skeletal, but my belly grew large and uncomfortable, as if it was drawing into itself my remaining life force. I looked as though I was with child, although I knew I could not possibly be so.

All through winter, herbalists and physicians came and went. They bled me, they medicated me, and nothing helped. Even Owain's ministrations did little other than allow me to snatch a few hours sleep at night.

By early spring I knew I was dying. I knew it, everyone knew it. No one mentioned it. False cheer swirled about me like the lies you feed an idiot child, while all the time Death's fingers clawed deeper into me.

Then, twelve days ago, Hugh returned to see me. He breezed into my solar where I lay on a couch, and he bent down to me as if he could not see that I was wasted and dying and kissed my mouth.

'Lady mama!' he said, using his childish expression which I always loved, then sat down in the chair, smiling slowly at me.

Despite my general despondency and pain I smiled back. I was glad to see him, if only to say goodbye. 'What do you here, Hugh?' I said.

'What do I here? Ah, madam, what a question to ask of the son who adores you. I had heard you sickened, and thus I am here.'

His expression sobered. 'I came. I had to. And now I will stay with you until we part.'

My eyes filled with tears. How had I managed to birth such a wonderful child?

As quickly as his expression had sobered, now Hugh's face once more lit up with humour. 'And I have brought you a gift! Am I not the dutiful child?'

He snapped his fingers, and a servant hurried forth from the doorway. In his arms, the servant carried a large, rolled up, linen covered bundle.

'Roll it out on the table under the window,' Hugh said, and the man complied, carefully unknotting the ties holding the bundle, removing the linen, then rolling out what lay beneath.

It was a tapestry, very large. I struggled up on one elbow, thinking to rise and walk over to view it. Hugh assisted me to sit, but then he gestured me to stay where I was for the moment. He waved the servant out of the chamber, asking that he close the door.

There was just Hugh and myself in the chamber now.

'I commissioned this tapestry two years ago,' Hugh said, 'when I knew your time was close.'

Two years ago? But then both Edmond and I were in full health. Who could have known that within two years one of us would be dead and the other dying?

'It tells an amazing story,' he said. 'The story of my father.'

Of Edmond? I smiled at him, thinking him the precious man to do this for me.

Hugh leaned closer, and his green eyes became vivid, bright, compelling. 'But before you view it I beg you to remember something my father told you many, many years ago. Speak not the word, for remember that the wind shall carry your word to all the corners of the earth, as also to the ears of God and of the Devil both.'

I went very still, utterly shocked. Raife had said that to me, *not* Edmond. Hugh knew that Raife was his father?

Hugh's eyes were still fixed on mine. 'I have always known, my lady,' he said, softly. 'I have known everything. *Remember what my father told you.*'

I could scarcely breathe. Hugh had known?

'Mother,' he ground out, '*will you remember it?*'

I managed a nod. 'Speak not the word,' I said. 'Yes, I will remember it.' I said it, and I promised I would remember it, but I had no idea why he told me this.

And then my brain came out of its shock enough to piece together what Hugh had said. This tapestry told the story of *Raife*?

Speak not the word, Hugh mouthed at me, and again I gave a nod.

Then he assisted me to rise, and took my arm, and led me over to the table by the window on which rested the tapestry.

I studied it for a long time, and then suddenly I understood what it meant, and I understood what Raife, the poor doomed man, had been attempting to do that day he tried to show me the drawings on the vellum pages that the imp had tried to snatch.

I had refused to trust him, when I *should* have trusted him, when I had *promised* to trust him, and in the refusing, I had committed such an act of betrayal that I could not now bear it. It was all too much, and the events of thirty years ago rushed forward and enveloped me, and I gave a loud cry, and fainted.

I came round after a short while.

Hugh had carried me back to my couch, and was holding my hand, chafing its cold flesh between his two warm hands.

'What have I done?' I whispered. 'Sweet Jesu, Hugh. Sweet Jesu …'

'Remember,' he said, and I nodded. *Speak not the word.*

Hugh gave a lovely, soft, gentle smile. 'It would have been so much better had you learned your letters,' he said.

Oh, yes, because then Hugh's father could have written it for me, because to speak it was to alert the Devil to what was really happening, and that Raife could not do. But because I did not know my letters, Raife could not *write* the truth. Instead he, like Hugh now had, had drawn it for me, but I'd not had the time to understand before the imp tried to snatch the pages and Raife had destroyed them to save himself. If the Devil had seen what was on those pages … oh, sweet God, Raife would have been utterly undone.

All Raife could do, then, was to implore me to trust him.

To simply trust him.

And I hadn't. He had tried so hard, but I would not trust him, nor even try for a single moment to understand what he really was.

Then Hugh leaned forward and kissed me on the mouth — a lover's kiss.

I stared at him.

'That was from my father,' he said, 'who thinks you are nothing but a dear, sweet trouble, and who wants you to know that he loves you very much.'

And now, twelve days after that day, I am going to ask Owain to write a little in the voice of his pen, because I *cannot speak the words.*

CHAPTER FIVE

OWAIN'S TESTIMONY

My lady, the countess that was, wishes me to relate now the tale worked into the tapestry. Because I have sat here these past days and writ down each word of her testimony, and given my own knowledge of the myths of the Old People, I could easily understand the tapestry when she showed it to me yesterday.

It depicts a story from the Old Times, the pagan times when the Old People lived upon this land, before the Celts came, and before the Anglo-Saxons came, and before the Viking raiders or their cousins, the Normans, lived here. It depicts those peoples I was long familiar with, both from the legends of my youth in Crickhoel and from the strange figures depicted on the walls of the chapel in Pengraic Castle.

It depicts the Old People, to whom I owe even more loyalty and honour than I owe to our sweet Lord Christ.

The tapestry initially tells the story of a mighty prince of the Old People, resplendent in his citadel in the ancient mountains. On his head he wore a magnificent and enchanted diadem, fitting symbol of his rank and power, a diadem worked by the ancient forest magic of fairy hands. About its crown danced the sun and the moon and the stars of the heavens drawn in jewels that, as the countess that was, once said, were more glorious than diamonds.

Then one night, while the ancient prince slept, a long-fingered imp, a malevolent sprite from hell, came to the prince's chamber and stole away the diadem.

The imp took the diadem to the Devil, trading it for favours from the satanic prince. Above, in the realm of the Old People, the prince awoke to find his diadem gone. He could smell the lingering odour of the imp, and knew to what dark master the thief would have ferried the diadem.

The prince could think of only one way to recover his diadem. He took himself down to hell, and, over the centuries, worked his way through the ranks surrounding the Devil until he became the Devil's trusted confidant.

It was not something I could do overnight, the earl had said to his lady.

Yet still the prince did not know where the Devil had hid the diadem.

Then one day, horribly, the Devil cried that his diadem had been stolen, gone! Taken to the mortal world! The Devil hatched a scheme where the hounds of hell would scent out the diadem and, of the deepest irony, sent his favourite captain — the prince of the Old People in his disguise — into the mortal realm that he might be the one to carry the diadem back to hell.

But the prince, masquerading as the Earl of Pengraic and by now wed to a fair lady he loved beyond life, meant to trick the Devil. He endured the horror that the Devil unleashed on this mortal realm and followed the trail the horror laid down until he came to the diadem's resting place. He retrieved the diadem, his lady present at his side, and it remained only for him to retreat into the ancient world of the Old People with his lady for his task to be complete.

But his lady refused to go with the prince. He begged and pleaded, but she refused, for she believed him only an angel of the Devil, and could not understand his true nature.

And he could not *tell* her, for the words would carry straight to the Devil, and neither would be safe until they were within the realm of the Old People.

I can write this, but my lord of Pengraic could never *say* it to his lady, for that would have jeopardised both of them.

And my Lady Maeb could not read.

My lady wept when she showed me this tapestry. I think the knowledge of what the earl had truly been almost destroyed her.

She wept until I thought she would do herself harm, but after a time she wiped her eyes. She laid trembling fingers on the final panel of the tapestry.

It depicted the castle of Pengraic, and again it showed the prince of the Old People and his beloved lady … but exactly what it showed I will not say.

Not yet.

CHAPTER SIX

Thus, finally, I come to the end of my testimony. I have been the most stupid of women. The blindest.

But what would have happened if I *had* gone with Raife that night? If I *had* trusted him?

My son Hugh would have been born into a very different life, true, but one that now I think he has not missed out on entirely. What he has hinted to me over the past days has been extraordinary.

I would have foregone thirty years with Edmond, and I regret not one moment of those thirty years. I loved him and he me, and together we had three beautiful daughters who have made good marriages and have given us grandchildren more than we could have hoped.

No, I do not regret not going with Raife that night.

But I do regret not trusting him.

Tomorrow I will make preparation to return to Pengraic Castle. The journey there may likely half kill me with fatigue, but that no longer matters. I am dying and I need to return to Pengraic. My son Hugh will come with me.

Thus ends my life, thus ends my testimony.

Owain may write the final words if he wishes.

May God forgive me for what I am about to do, and may my soul find rest. Owain, I wish you a blessed life, and peace, and I thank you with all my heart for writing down these, my words.

Do with them what you will.

May the gods of the land and the seasons have mercy on my soul, and may sweet Jesu forgive me that my soul shall not be his.

THE TESTIMONY OF
HUGH DE MORTAIGNE, EARL OF WESSEX,
KNOWN AS HUGH THE WOLF

———◆◆◇◆◆———

This my testimony, writ the week after my beloved mother's death. I have abandoned Pengraic Castle and am currently resident in Glowecestre. I have left my brother Geoffrey's fool wife Erheld to wonder where my mother's body is. She will not bother to wonder long. She will just be glad the old woman is dead, finally.

All I wanted to do was to get out of Pengraic Castle on that dawn following my lady mother's passing. I'd had enough — of Erheld, of the damned castle, of the emptiness of my life. I had only wanted to stay long enough to secure this my mother's testimony, order my horse saddled, and then leave.

Can you imagine if Geoffrey had read this? Sweet saints, he would have burned it and then spent the rest of his life trying to cleanse the sin out of Pengraic and the stain out of his own soul.

Of course, that might have been quite amusing to watch, and would have provided me with no end of humorous ways to needle him.

But it is far better he never know the entirety of his parents' lives.

My mother wanted Owain to write this epilogue to her testimony. But Owain is dead, and it is up to me to recall my mother, and speak as witness to her passing.

What will I do with this testimony then? Pass it to my favoured child, I suppose. I can entrust Guietta with this.

My mother, Mistress Maeb Langtofte, Countess of Pengraic, mistress of King Edmond, mother to five children. I loved her. Deeply. My lady mother spoke of her love for me in her testimony, but little of what I felt for her. I have never loved another woman like I loved my mother. I have never loved another *person* like I loved my mother, although my love and esteem for Edmond came close. I was fortunate to have been raised under Edmond's parentage. I don't think either I or my real father would have lasted more than a year without one of us killing the other if we'd been forced to inhabit under the same roof.

You may wonder how much of my mother's testimony has been Owain's voice, how much of him filtered through his pen into my mother's words. Not much, I have to say. This document was my mother through and through, from her extraordinary inability to understand how lovely she was (and what power that could give her) to how sweetly foolish she was to not understand those about her, from my father to me.

How she ever thought that I really believed Edmond was my true father I do not know. I kept up the pretence, but I thought that she would surely have *realised* that pretence. She kept her innocence, and her innocence of vision, until the day she died. I also cannot believe that I fooled her completely into thinking I had forgot that day when I was six, and I met Stephen and Uda for the first time on the falloway. How can any mature woman be so misled by a child? *My* mother, saints bless her!

Oh, how I loved her. I twisted her around my little finger all the days of my life and she never knew it. But I never caused her harm nor hurt. Not her. Not Edmond. They were the two I never hurt. Everyone else has been game for the hunt.

My mother I watched over until the moment of her death. I was her salvation, bred by my father partly for that purpose.

But more of that later.

I am grateful Geoffrey was not at Pengraic Castle when we arrived. We had enough trouble with his wife Erheld. The thought of what may have happened had Geoffrey been there appals me.

Few people like or respect Geoffrey. They might respect his power and station in life, but they do not respect the man. Not my lady mother Maeb. Not Edmond, not Geoffrey's own somewhat pathetic wife, not even King Richard, sitting pretty on his new and much-anticipated throne. People only tolerate Geoffrey for his wealth and his rank. Otherwise Geoffrey is a boorish, self-absorbed, self-important, talentless cunt, existing only on the strength of his father's name and his mother's notoriety. Jesu Christ forgive me such language in this the epilogue of my mother's life. God knows how either my mother or my father bred him. I have always held the suspicion one of the imps had a bit of a hand in the making of Geoffrey. It can be the only thing that explains him.

I will not tolerate him. I piss on him. I actually did it once, too, when I was eight, and got beaten for my trouble. Not by my lady mother, mind, nor Edmond, nor even by Geoffrey himself, but by some groom Geoffrey paid to do it. That's the kind of man Geoffrey is, even when a boy.

As for my sisters. Well, they are just women, and of little importance. They made good marriages. They claim to be happy. They have modest lives. None have died in childbirth yet. I see them rarely.

My mother, as Uda had spoken the words to her, called me the Falloway Man. I doubt she really knew what that meant — another thing my mother ignored in all her sweet innocent blindness was the fact that she, like me, was full blood of the Old People. It didn't matter that her father didn't have a drop of the old blood in him. The only thing Sir Godfrey did well was to make off with the Devil's diadem from under the noses of the Templars (I chuckle whenever I think of it — Godfrey bumbled his way through life until he did the one sensible thing of his existence by pinching something the Templars wanted very, very badly). It was Maeb's mother who counted, the forgotten Leorsythe, the parent who bequeathed Maeb her bloodline. I note in my mother's testimony that she said several times the only thing her father left her were rags and a bloodline.

Nay, sweet mother, he left you rags only. It was your mother Leorsythe who left you the bloodline that counted.

I, of course, had the old blood handed to me by both my mother and my father, and my father a prince of that line, too. I have considerable power in the mortal realm, partly because everyone assumes me Edmond's son, partly because of the lands and titles I hold, partly because of my own beauty and what my mother called my magnetism (I have used that beauty and magnetism well; by the time I was five and twenty I had seduced half the court, men and women, to my ends), and partly because I command the falloways.

I could walk this realm at night from border to border if I wished and no one would know. I could seduce who I wished, murder who I wanted, and yet be hundreds of miles away by dawn and no one the wiser. It is a fabulous power, but I try not to misuse it. I respect the falloways and all they lead to.

Stephen, my older brother, taught me the ways of the Old People. I first met him when I was six, as my mother related, and from then until I came into my majority as a man I travelled with Stephen on the falloways once or twice a week. He was all of the old blood, too, and probably meant to be the falloway man of his age, but the plague put an end to that. Instead, after his death, he watched over my mother from the falloways and protected her as much as he could.

He was the reason she did not die from plague and hemlock. It was his horse that pushed her back, his wolves that snapped and snarled her way back into life.

I noted my mother prayed over Stephen's grave in the chapel at Pengraic Castle. She never realised that his body was not there, although Owain knew. My father gave Stephen's corpse back to the falloways, as I did my mother's. Gilbert Ghent's body was never found (he was another man of the old blood, although he was not permitted into that first falloway down which he lost my mother). Ghent's body, too, had been given back to the falloways — probably by the bears, as there was no one else there to do it.

I travel the falloways, sometimes with the wolves, sometimes with the bears. They are both my friends.

Once, someone found me rubbing the cheeks of a wild wolf while on a hunt. Now they call me Hugh the Wolf. It amuses me — it also adds to my aura and thus my power. But I need to be careful. As my mother truly stated, I have inherited her propensity to make enemies, and in John and Geoffrey, perhaps even Richard, I have very dangerous enemies indeed.

Ah, I have digressed when all I intended to do was write the ending of my mother's life and of what happened then. But I will add one last thing to my mother's testimony, make one further observation.

My mother Maeb tried desperately to protect my father through her testimony. Having discovered the reason why my father could never *tell* her who he really was — the words would reach the ears of the Devil, and thus ruin my father's chances of stealing back his own diadem — my mother then tried very hard throughout her testimony not to alert the Devil herself.

She failed, of course (I smile as I write this, for it is but another example of how my mother's innocence lasted to her very end). I am sure that if the Devil had been listening to her somewhat extended testimony then he would have understood quite well what Maeb tried so hard not to say.

But the Devil, of course, would have known who my father was the instant my father put that diadem to his head. From that moment he was beyond the Devil's reach.

Since that night, my father has wanted nothing else but to have my mother back at his side. If people, including myself (I learned the true tale very early from the mouth of Stephen, who one day took me to a dark place far beyond the fallows to tell me), have kept our mouths shut then it was to protect Maeb herself. We wanted her to be reunited with my father, but were not sure if the Devil was still interested in her, or interested in revenging himself on her, so we were careful — thus, my rather tortured effort with the tapestry I had caused to be stitched. Someone had to let her know the truth, somehow.

Ah, if only she had known her letters, how much easier it would have been. A scribbled line or two from my father and all would have been sorted!

Would she have jumped with my father that night if she had truly understood?

I don't know. As my mother said herself, she has never regretted those thirty years with Edmond. She loved both men.

None of it matters now.

I will finish in a moment by relating the tale of my mother's passing. Then I will return to my mother's estate of Remany, collect my daughter Guietta (yes, even Gytha was one of my youthful conquests) and take her to one of my estates … perhaps *not* Rosseley at which I have installed my wife and legitimate brood of children.

I will give Guietta the testimony to keep; for her children, perhaps.

Guietta is of the old blood, too, like her mother, and like Owain. None of my other children bear the blood.

So, to the tale of my mother's passing. Forgive me if I mix tears with the ink on this page.

Gytha, Owain and I took my lady mother back to Pengraic. It was a relatively short journey, but Maeb was already so ill it almost killed her. We arrived late one night, I desperate to get my mother inside and at some rest, only to be met by Geoffrey's wife, Erheld.

She did not appreciate the fact we had not asked her husband's permission — Geoffrey currently being at court, thank the saints, or else we may have been left out in the cold.

Our party waited just outside the wicket gate, she stood just inside it, whining.

I didn't have time for Erheld.

I dismounted, pushed past her, and shouted to the guards to open the gates. They obeyed me instantly, further darkening Erheld's temper. The moment we got my mother's litter inside I picked her up (sweet Jesu, she was as light as a child) and carried her into the great keep, shouting ahead to the servants to make ready the privy chamber for her.

Erheld would have to sleep elsewhere.

Mother Maeb was not long for this world. Once she was comfortable I stood with Owain and Gytha in the solar.

'It will be tonight,' I said, soft, lest Erheld sitting in her chair by the fire overheard.

Both Owain and Gytha nodded.

'How will we …?' Gytha said, looking pointedly at Erheld, and then at the servants standing about.

'All will be well,' I said, and again both Gytha and Owain nodded. Then they glanced at each other.

'My lord,' said Owain, 'Gytha and I have talked. We wonder if … if it is possible that …'

'You want to go with her?' I said.

Gytha's eyes filled with tears. 'Yes, my lord. We will not leave her.'

I studied them a moment. 'You know what this means?'

510

'Yes, my lord. We trust you with the task,' Gytha said. Then, 'Guietta will need her father now, my lord.'

'I will take care of her, Gytha. But, Owain, Gytha, I must ask this one last time. If I do as you ask then you will turn your back for all time on God and his saints. Is that what you wish? Owain, even you?'

'I have loved God and his Son and saints,' said Owain, 'but not so much as I have loved the Old People. I have always had a foot in both worlds, my lord. You know that. Now I would step fully into that world where my blood lies. And where my loyalty lies — to your mother and father.'

I nodded at him, then looked to Gytha, raising my eyebrows.

'I love your mother as much as you,' said Gytha. 'My life, and my eternity, will be empty without her. Even the blessing of sweet Christ Jesu cannot fill that void. I will follow Lady Maeb. Please, my lord, allow me this.'

I gave her a nod, too, and a small smile. 'Owain, Gytha, thank you. You have been better family to my mother than,' I tipped my head toward Erheld, the gesture also taking in the absent Geoffrey, 'her own family. My brother and sisters well knew how ill my lady mother was, and yet you two are the ones standing here, not they. Be ready then, for those hours before dawn.'

I did not sleep. I sat by my mother's side, watching her grey face, hearing her labour for her breath and waited for the castle to quieten. Owain and Gytha also sat in the chamber on the other side of the bed.

Deep into the night I rose, looking at Owain and Gytha. 'You are certain?' I asked one more time.

'Yes, my lord,' they said.

I reached for my sword belt and buckled it on.

'My lord,' Owain said, 'you knew that over the past two weeks your mother has been giving me her testimony?'

I nodded. I knew it.

'My lord,' Owain said, 'I cannot finish it. Not now. It lies among my possessions, there.' He tipped his head toward a small bag to one side.'

'I know, Owain. I will take care of it.'

'Geoffrey must not —' Owain began.

'I *know*, Owain. I *will* take care of it. But for now we must move.'

Then I closed my eyes and reached for the realm of the Old People, opening the falloways.

'It is done,' I said, opening my eyes. 'We must go.'

Very gently I lifted my mother. She moaned a little, but otherwise made no sign that she was aware of any of our presences.

'She will need a warm wrap,' Gytha said, reaching behind her.

'It does not matter now,' I said, and Gytha straightened again.

We left the privy chamber.

Everyone was asleep and appeared hazy, as if they were insubstantial.

We were in the falloway — I had opened it so that it stretched inside the castle. No one would disturb us.

We walked down the stairwell and then out into the courtyard of the great keep. I found myself wondering how many times my mother had walked this route. She had lived so little of her life at Pengraic Castle, and yet she always considered it her home. Despite the horror she'd endured here during the plague, she still loved it.

No wonder.

Pengraic Castle is the most hallowed of the few portals remaining that lead into the realm of the Old People.

We continued through the inner bailey, under the northern keep and then through the outer bailey.

When we got to the northern gates it was to find them standing open and the world beyond shining.

This night, this special night, all the falloways of the land opened onto the northern gate of Pengraic Castle.

My mother's breathing was now harsh and irregular. She did not have long.

I stepped through the gate, Owain and Gytha right behind me.

The ridge leading up to the mountain of Pen Cerrig-calch behind Pengraic was alive with torchlight. The mountaintops, all the hills about, were lined with light. Tens of thousands of people lined the ridges and hilltops, each holding a torch.

The Old People, come to welcome their lady home.

Silent tears slid down my cheeks. I did not want to let my mother go. I knew that she had life beyond this death, life reborn into the fold of the Old People, but even so I mourned her. I could not contemplate my life here in this realm of England without her presence. I have loved her so deeply, so completely …

'My lord,' Owain murmured behind me, and I gave a nod. I walked forward, Owain and Gytha still close behind me, and from among the torches of the Old People three riders came. Their horses were magnificent: one chestnut, one white and one a bright bay, their manes dragging to the ground, tangled about with diamonds.

Ghent, my brother Stephen, and my father, whose name as a prince of the Old People cannot be written here.

My mother drew in a rattling breath, shivered a little, and passed.

I could not hold back a choking sob. I hugged her to me, so reluctant to let her go.

'You must,' said my father. He had ridden a little ahead of the other two now. His face had lost its care, all the lines and weariness that my mother so often described in her testimony, and now gloried in youth and vitality, in strength and splendour.

Atop his head glimmered the diadem, for which he had risked so much.

I was shaking, but I made the effort to collect myself, for what I now needed to do could not be accomplished without steady hands.

Very gently I laid my mother's body on the ground and knelt to kiss her goodbye.

Goodbye, Maeb, this realm will be the vastly poorer for your absence.

Then I stood and in one fluid movement, one stroke, drew my sword from its scabbard and took off Owain's and Gytha's heads.

Oh, sweet Jesu, I wanted to take off my own head then. My grief was so profound that I could not bear it. I knelt, resting the point of the sword on the ground, my forehead on its pommel, and wept, my entire body shaking with the force.

'Hugh.'

It was my mother's voice.

I rose, shakily, and turned about.

There Maeb stood, not two paces from me, looking as beautiful as I remembered her from when I was a young boy.

Her body, as those of Owain and Gytha, had vanished.

She held out her arms, smiling as I remembered, and I stepped forward and hugged her to me.

She was warm and solid in my arms, and she held me as tightly as I held her.

'Hugh,' she whispered. 'Hugh, I have to go.'

'I want —'

'No. You must remain here. The world needs the Falloway Man for a while yet.'

She leaned back. Her green eyes brimmed with tears. 'Thank you, Hugh,' she said, kissing my cheek. And then without waiting for an answer or a smile from me, she turned.

She walked first to Stephen. He leaned down from his horse and they gripped hands. They spoke, kissed briefly, and then my mother gave his hand a tight squeeze before letting go and turning ...

Suddenly my father was there, his big bay horse filling the path. He held down his arm for my mother, lifting her atop the horse behind his saddle. She slid her arms about his waist and rested her cheek on his back.

Her face glowed with contentment.

Then something coming from behind bumped me to one side. Sweet Jesu! It was my mother's grey mare, Dulcette, dead these twenty years! I did not believe it possible — but then, had not Dulcette *always* found her way home to my mother? Dulcette wandered past my father and mother, pausing a moment so my mother could pat her, then walked further up the falloway, no doubt looking for a stable for the night.

I looked back to my father.

For an instant my father's gaze held mine. It was full of respect and love and some sorrow, and yet joy also, for finally he had Maeb back with him, as he had always wanted.

'Be well, Hugh,' he said. 'When you want it, when you think it time, this diadem is yours.' Then he turned the horse and moved back.

I could see, just for one moment, Owain and Gytha standing with Stephen and Ghent, and then, too suddenly, too horrifically, everything was gone. The tens of thousands of Old People, the torches, Ghent and Stephen, Owain and Gytha, my father.

My mother.

The falloways.

All gone, leaving me to weep in the cold night air, the wind whistling past me as I stood on the ridge leading to Pen Cerrig-calch.

GLOSSARY

Adelaide, Queen: wife of the king, Edmond.

Advent: a period of preparation before Christmas. In medieval times it was often marked from Martinmas, 11th November, through to 24th December, the Vigil of the Nativity of Christ.

Aldermen: see City of London governance.

All Souls Day: 2nd November.

Amble: horses which could amble were prized animals in medieval Europe. Ambling was a very fast but extremely smooth walking gait that was faster than a trot and could cover much ground at little expense of energy to the horse. Few horses now can amble as the gait lost fashion after the medieval period and horses were no longer bred for the trait. But for an idea of what they could do, search for Peruvian Paso horses on YouTube; Peruvian Pasos are a breed of horse that can trace their descent from the medieval ambler, and their gait is very similar.

Anatolia: modern-day Turkey.

Assizes: English criminal courts. The word comes from the Old French.

d'Avranches, Ralph: garrison commander at Pengraic Castle.

d'Ecouis, Fulkes: a Templar Knight, recently arrived from the continent.

Bailleul, Mistress Yvette: a senior attending woman to Lady Adelie de Mortaigne.

Baynard Castle: a Norman castle in London, situated in its extreme south-west corner, close by the current location of Blackfriars station. Its castellan (or keeper) is Geoffrey de Mandeville, Earl of Exsessa.

Bears: brown bears were once widespread over Britain. They were hunted to extinction just before or during the Norman era. Nevertheless, the British travel advisory still recommends you avoid the cracks in the pavement.

Beaumont, Roger de: Earl of Warwick.

Bec, Tedbald du: Archbishop of Cantuaberie.

Bethune, Robert de: Bishop of Hereford.

Blanche: a nurse.

Blois, Gervase de: abbot of Westminster.

Blois, Henry of: Bishop of Wincestre, and one of the highest Norman noblemen (grandson of William the Conqueror) in England.

Braes: underdrawers worn by men, usually made of linen.

Bretagne, Alan de: Earl of Richemont and Constable of the Tower.

Chemise: an under tunic of linen, or perhaps of wool, worn beneath the kirtle, or over tunic.

Cinque Ports, The: the term is a Norman French import, meaning 'five ports'. These were the five most important south-eastern ports in England: Hastings, New Romney, Hythe, Dovre, and Sandwich. In medieval and early modern times they were the key to England, and were kept secured at all costs.

City of London governance: little is known about how the City of London was governed in the earlier twelfth century. It had twenty-four wards, or administrative areas, each having an alderman (possibly more than one). The portreeve was the king's top official in the city and was responsible for collecting revenues. Also of importance were the Constable of the Tower, and whichever nobleman was castellan of Baynard Castle in the south-west of the city. There was no mayor until the later twelfth century.

Clare, Gilbert de: Earl of Pembroke. His wife is Isabel.

Conqueror's Tower, The: the Norman Keep (known as the White Tower when it was whitewashed in the later twelfth century) of the Tower of London complex.

Courser: a horse often used for hunting by noblemen when they may not have wished to risk their expensive destriers.

Craon, Robert de: Grand Master of the Templars.

Destrier: a nobleman's war horse.

Douai, Roger de: a knight favoured by the king.

Dulcette: Maeb Langtofte's horse.

Eadgard: a servant of Sir Godfrey Langtofte.

Edmond: King of England.

Elesberie, Royal Manor: the royal manor at Elesberie was very large, possibly containing as much as 2,000 acres of land.

Erheld: a Norman noblewoman, wife of Geoffrey de Mortaigne.

Falloways: the long forgotten paths of the Old People.

fitzErfast, Robert: steward at the Earl of Pengraic's London house.

fitzRolf, Nigel: chamberlain of the king's palace at Westminster.

Gernon, Maude: wife of Ranulf de Gernon. Countess of Chestre.

Gernon, Ranulf de: Earl of Chestre. Kinsman of Ralph d'Avranches.

Ghent, Gilbert: a knight in the Earl of Pengraic's household.

Ghaznavid: an empire centred in modern-day Afghanistan.

Gilda: a midwife.

Godric of Mappestone: castellan of Godric Castle on the Wye.

Guietta: Gytha's daughter.

Gytha: a London serving girl, known for her abilities with the dressing of hair.

Hallow's Eve: 31st October, the day before Hallowmas, now known as Halloween.

Hallowmas: the celebration of All Saints Day on 1st November.

Hauberk: a long 'shirt' of maille, reaching generally to mid-thigh. In Norman times it also came with a hood, or coif, and its sleeves reached to the elbow, sometimes lower.

Henry, Prince: eldest son of King Edmond and Queen Adelaide.

Herepath: an army road or route.

Holloways: almost literally, a hollow way. Holloways were narrow thoroughfares, often sunken, through the back country of England. Many of them have been used for thousands of years.

Horse-riding for women: generally only noblewomen would have ridden horses at this period. If they wanted to actually ride (i.e. control) the horse then they most likely would ride astride. Women could also ride 'aside', that is, sitting sideways on the horse on a saddle that was more chair than saddle — it did not resemble riding 'side-saddle' at all (side-saddle riding did not exist at this point). If a woman rode aside then she had no hope of controlling the horse and someone would need to lead the horse for her.

Hose: stockings, generally made of wool, they would be knee high and held up by garters, or thigh high and tied with laces to the waistband of the braes.

Holbournestrate: Holborn, just west of twelfth-century London.

Hours of the day: clock time, where the hours of the day were evenly divided into twenty-four periods, was virtually unknown in the twelfth century. Most people within hearing of church or monastic bells orientated themselves within the day by the canonical hours. The Church divided the day into seven, according to the seven hours of prayer:

- The day began with *Matins*, usually an hour or two before dawn.
- The second of the hours was *Prime* - daybreak.
- The third hour was *Terce*, set at about 9 a.m.
- The fourth hour was *Sext* (originally midday).
- The fifth hour was *Nones*, set at about 3 in the afternoon (it was not moved to midday until sometime during the thirteenth century).
- The sixth hour was *Vespers*, normally early evening.
- The seventh hour was *Compline*, bedtime.

These hours were irregular both within the day and within the year; the hours orientated themselves around the rising and setting of the sun, and thus the hours contracted and expanded according to the season.

Hugh of Argentine: Master of the Temple in England. The Templar

518

church in the earlier twelfth century was located on High
Holbournestrate just to the west of London.

Innocent II: Pope of the Church.

Jocea: a midwife.
John, Prince: third and youngest son of King Edmond and Queen Adelaide.

Kendal, Mistress Evelyn: an attending lady to Adelie, the Countess of
Pengraic.
Kirtle: a closely fitted tunic worn by women over their chemise. Laced up
the back, generally it had flowing bell-shaped sleeves, a full skirt, and a
tightly fitted body. It could be made of wool, linen or, for the very rich,
silk.

Lacy, Gilbert de: Lord of Longtown, Weobley and Ludlow, member of
the Knights Templar.
Lacy, Alianor de: wife of Lord Robert de Lacy.
Lacy, Lady Isouda de: widowed member of the powerful Norman family
of de Lacy.
Lacy, Robert de: Lord of Bouland and of Blachburnscire. A powerful
Norman noble.
Langtofte, Godfrey: nobleman, former pilgrim and sergeant within the
Order of the Knights Templar. Father of Maeb.
Langtofte, Leorsythe: Maeb's mother.
Langtofte, Mistress Maeb: attending woman to Lady Adelie de
Mortaigne, Countess of Pengraic.
London: twelfth-century London was a place of many open spaces,
fields, orchards and market gardens. Most buildings were of wattle and
daub or timber, although more stone houses were being built. Its
population would have been about sixty thousand.
London Bridge: London Bridge in the twelfth century was a wooden
structure, as it would remain until the famous medieval stone bridge
was built from 1176. The early medieval wooden bridges were
constantly being destroyed: by storms, by fire, or by rogue Vikings
tying a rope to the bridge from their ship and then pulling it down as

they rowed away (the children's rhyme 'London Bridge is Falling Down' is based on a Viking song commemorating the event).

Ludo: Master of the Horse to Raife de Mortaigne, Earl of Pengraic.

Madog ap Gruffydd: a Welsh prince or rebel, depending on which side of the border lie your loyalties. 'Ap' means 'son of', so the name means 'Madog son of Gruffydd'.

Maille: the Norman term for chain mail. (The term chain mail was not used until the seventeenth century.)

Mandeville, Geoffrey de: Earl of Exsessa and castellan of Baynard Castle in London.

Marcher Lords: the Marcher Lords administered the Welsh Marches, a frontier zone between two peoples, two languages, two cultures. They had extraordinary liberties, ruling their lands almost as kings, and were highly independent of the English king. They had the liberty to run courts, establish laws, collect taxes, build castles, run prisons, markets, fairs — essentially they had complete jurisdiction over their subjects. They were very powerful men in Norman England. See also Welsh Marches.

Martinmas: festival of Saint Martin, 11th November.

Mevanou: wife of Madog ap Gruffydd.

Montgomerie, Gilbert de: Earl of Scersberie, and one of the powerful Marcher Lords.

Mortaigne, Adelie de: Countess of Pengraic, wife of Raife de Mortaigne.

Mortaigne, Alice de: daughter of Raife de Mortaigne, Earl of Pengraic.

Mortaigne, Ancel and Robert de: twin sons of Raife de Mortaigne, Earl of Pengraic.

Mortaigne, Emmette de: daughter of Raife de Mortaigne, Earl of Pengraic.

Mortaigne, Geoffrey de: son of Raife de Mortaigne, Earl of Pengraic.

Mortaigne, Joanna de: daughter of Raife de Mortaigne, Earl of Pengraic.

Mortaigne, John de: son of Raife de Mortaigne, Earl of Pengraic.

Mortaigne, Raife de: Earl of Pengraic. The most powerful of the Marcher Lords, and one of the most important of the Norman aristocracy.

Mortaigne, Rosamund de: daughter of Raife de Mortaigne, Earl of Pengraic.

Mortaigne, Stephen de: eldest son of Raife de Mortaigne, Earl of Pengraic.

Old People: the ancient peoples of Britain before the arrival of the Celts and Celtic culture in the millennium before the Common Era. Genetic testing shows that a small percentage of British people (and of British descent) still carry some DNA from the Old People.

Osbeorn: steward to Sir Godfrey Langtofte.

Owain, Brother: priest at the chapel in Pengraic Castle.

Palfrey: a highly prized riding horse, usually one which could amble (see Amble).

Pen Cerrig-calch: the mountain that backs Pengraic.

Peverel, Ella: a Norman woman of good family.

Plough Monday: the first Monday after Twelfth Day of Christmastide celebrations. It traditionally marked the return to agricultural work after the Christmastide celebrations.

Portreeve: see City of London governance.

Privy chamber: a private chamber meant for the use of a lord and his family.

Roche, Walter de: Earl of Summersete. His main base in central England is Walengefort Castle, just south of Oxeneford.

Richard, Prince: second son of King Edmond and Queen Adelaide.

Saint-Valery, Ranulph: a knight from Lincolescire, attached to King Edmond's court. Saint-Valery is a renowned poet.

Sewenna: a wet nurse in Pengraic Castle.

Small beer: weak beer, generally less than 1% alcohol. Most people drank small beer in preference to water.

Solar: a solar was a private day chamber found in many great houses. It was somewhere the lord and more particularly his lady could retreat and be alone (be *sole*) from the bustle and lack of privacy of the typical medieval household.